THE AFFAIR

Also by Val Hopkirk

Relative Strangers

THE AFFAIR

Val Hopkirk

HEADLINE

First published in 2001
by HEADLINE BOOK PUBLISHING

10 9 8 7 6 5 4 3 2 1

All characters in this publication are fictitious and any resemblance to real persons, living or dead, is purely coincidental.

British Library Cataloguing in Publication Data

Hopkirk, Val
The affair
1. Domestic fiction
I. Title
823.9'14 [F]

ISBN 0 7472 7397 9

Typeset by
CBS, Martlesham Heath, Ipswich, Suffolk

Printed and bound in Great Britain by
Clays Ltd, St Ives plc

HEADLINE BOOK PUBLISHING
A division of Hodder Headline
338 Euston Road
London NW1 3BH
www.headline.co.uk
www.hodderheadline.com

To M and R, for support and encouragement
beyond the call of duty.

Acknowledgements

Thanks to the Royal Geographical Society for opening its doors to us and in particular their expeditions organiser Shane Winser, who gave unstintingly of her time, talents and experience; Emma Jolly for invaluable help on the intricacies of feeding the multitudes and who generously allowed us to use the name of her successful catering company; Dr Raj Bhamra who raised eyebrows amongst his colleagues when consulting them about how to poison people but not unto death; Chris Caldicott, intrepid explorer/photographer and owner of the World Food Café in Covent Garden, who, amongst other things, guided us through the minefield of local dialects, habits and supply problems to base camp; Diana Goodman who read the manuscript at an early stage and made invaluable suggestions and encouraging noises; professional musician and singing teacher Graham Wiley who set himself the task of helping us perform 'The Flower Song' by Delibes and almost succeeded . . . Other guinea pig readers include May Vane-Percy, Geraldine Dennen and Brenda Porter, while June and Keith Hutcheson fed and watered us at their home in Cape Town during the creative process. As ever, grateful thanks to a wonderful editor Marion Donaldson as well as agent extraordinaire Carole Blake.

Chapter One

Carol Mitchell's day started in exactly the same way as had a thousand others. But before it ended her marriage would never be the same again.

For now, humming to herself, feeling life was not too bad, all things considered, she started her daily lists, which her husband described as a cross between good organisation and self-flagellation. First, the old perennial, supper: 'Pork chops out of freezer BEFORE leaving, dozy; buy spaghetti, short kind.' The kids hated the long stuff. 'Wash E's leotards; remind B about tickets; grey suit (& navy blue?) to cleaners; DON'T forget cash for Mrs H.'

She glanced at the kitchen clock. Hurry, hurry, ten minutes before she had to be out of the house. On dank days like these it was a wrench to leave the warm, cosy kitchen and drive through sleeting rain to her part-time job but she forced herself. The money was useful but what drew her out was the adult conversation when she got there; otherwise, she joked, all she'd talk to were children and house plants.

Carol finished stacking the dishwasher with most of the breakfast things before scribbling, 'Dental appointment for K; phone electrician AGAIN.' She would bribe him with her body if necessary. 'Organise school run.' She groaned; it always took too much time and people chopped and changed at the slightest whim. 'Pick up Katie from Brownies.' Only once had she forgotten and according to the youngest, waiting on her own until everyone had gone had practically blighted her childhood.

She nibbled the end of the pen. Each day was crammed with too many things to fit into too few hours but because she was 'career-free', as she described it, and had come comparatively late to marriage, that was the way Carol liked it. OK, she had several loads of washing to sort out before leaving the house, a terrorist attack would have left the place looking neater and they hadn't done more than give the kitchen a lick of paint since she'd decorated it seven years ago but she was four days late.

Four whole days.

She found a space at the top of the page to insert and underline: 'Chemist, pregnancy testing kit!!' grinning to herself. Lists were her life and when the time came she'd probably instruct herself to 'push baby out, must'.

Mechanically she began grading clothes into little piles while humming to the Dionne Warwick song playing on the radio which urged her to 'say a little prayer'. Appropriate words for someone who'd been trying for a baby for two years. Carol sank back on her heels in front of the gaping washing machine and speculated on how Ben would react if she really were pregnant. Soon after they married, when she'd brought up the subject, he asked her to wait a while. His three children were quite demanding and in view of the circumstances she acknowledged it was a wise decision. After five years, realising how keen she still was to have their own baby, Ben had been frank about his lack of enthusiasm. He accepted it was selfish but now the children were finally settled, a new baby might bring with it jealousy and perhaps feelings of rejection. When, uncharacteristically, she persisted, they came to an agreement; they would do nothing to stop her becoming pregnant. At once she had given up the birth control pills. When a year had gone by and she had not conceived, Ben said he would still prefer to leave it to fate rather than medical intervention. Fully understanding how much he'd hate going to some clinic and having to masturbate into a bottle, she went on waiting. Nothing had happened, until now.

This evening she would break the news that she was late and do the test in the morning when he was around. If it was positive, would Ben be pleased? Probably not. He would still be worried about the effect on the three kids and, like many men, he hated the changes a new arrival would bring. Would he show this reluctance? No. But she was not too concerned. When the baby arrived she was quite sure he and the kids would love it.

Carol was busy programming the washing machine, about to sling on a warm coat, when she became aware that under the noise of the radio the telephone was ringing. With one movement she closed the door of the machine, at the same time silencing the radio with her other hand before she snatched the receiver off its cradle.

'Hello?'

For a second or two she listened to stillness although it was possible to hear sounds similar to distant wind.

'Anybody there?'

No one answered. The phone was on a downward trajectory, midway between her ear and its cradle, when she heard a whine followed by a piercing whistle coming down the line so the receiver went back up against her ear. Again she listened, wondering whether it was someone phoning from abroad and struggling with a bad connection. Once more she asked if anyone was there. When the words came they were from a high-pitched voice but distorted by some device which made it impossible to distinguish whether the caller was a man or a woman.

'Carol Mitchell, your husband's fooling you.'

Her head jerked back as if she had been slapped. She made an attempt to interrupt and ask who was speaking but the voice did not pause. Carol's hand tightened around the receiver as she heard the strange robotic tone echoing down the line, telling her things she did not want to hear, revealing a secret she had never suspected.

The call lasted for only seconds and afterwards she could remember every nuance of it, how she'd had to concentrate to understand what was being said, how her heart began a drumbeat so loud she thought it might drown the sound, how she'd asked, in vain, who was speaking. And how she did not even have the satisfaction of slamming down the receiver. The caller had beaten her to it.

Shoulders rigid, her hand still resting on the phone, she stepped back as if the instrument was noxious. It seemed unreal that only a few minutes earlier her mind had been taken up with mundane domestic details like pork chops and dry cleaners. Sinking down on to a chair she began to take deep breaths, trying to control her racing pulse. Why would a person say these repugnant things? To punish him, to hurt her? Why? It must be someone they knew, somebody in their circle, or why take the trouble to disguise the voice? It was a hideous thought that a friend would try and disrupt their marriage in this way.

She had to control her whirling brain, calm it down. She was a grown woman, able to deal with a crisis quickly and efficiently, and she would handle this one. Action. She needed to do something. Carol picked up the phone again, pressed 1471 to get the caller's number and listened to the operator intone that the person had withheld the information. Well, she couldn't have imagined it would be that easy.

For a long time she stood in the silence of the hushed house and looked out at the rain pattering on the windows. Her eye settled on the photograph of Fay, on top of the dresser. She'd have liked to move it upstairs years ago but thought it best to leave it there, to prove the children's mother had existed, had once been a part of their lives. Mrs Perfect. Smiling into the camera, confident, attractive. Well-loved. But that did not square up with what the caller had said – that her husband had been responsible for his first wife's death, as if he had murdered her himself. 'He was having an affair for two years and when she found out she killed herself,' the voice resonated. 'Ask him.'

But Fay's death had been a tragic accident. The coroner's official verdict called it 'accidental death'. His official report was kept in Ben's filing cabinet and she had read it.

There had been a pause and Carol thought the connection had been broken but then the voice spoke again and this time the words were far more poisonous.

'He's always been a man who couldn't keep his zipper up,' the person hissed, 'and don't think he's changed. He's still screwing around.'

But if the caller had lied about Fay, this wasn't true either. Was it?

Although it was a continuing source of wonder that she was his wife, it had never before crossed Carol's mind that her darling Ben could be unfaithful. There were no signs of it and surely some instinct would have told her if he found their relationship lacking in some way? Although he was an attractive, high-profile journalist and broadcaster, working in an environment surrounded by clever, good-looking women, he never gave the impression of being someone who needed to make conquests to boost his ego. Carol firmly believed a man would not roam if he was happy in his marriage and Ben gave every appearance of being content, though she had to admit, it was a long time since she had dissected their relationship. There had been no reason for it.

She recognised she was the one who loved the most but wasn't that the case in most partnerships? It was true their lives revolved mainly around the family. The three children formed the major part of the couple's plans and conversation but she had always thought this was a welcome refuge from the intense pressure of Ben's role as a major opinion-former. And yet had she been right to be complacent?

Her head was beginning to ache. Soon, she was certain, Ben would deliver a perfectly logical explanation. That thought reassured her, but only for a little while. However sternly she told herself not to jump to conclusions, to wait until she heard what her husband had to say, she could not rid herself of an uneasy feeling. And could not prevent a disloyal question surfacing: was there any truth, even a grain, in what the caller had spewed out? Whatever Ben said, would she ever be able to dismiss those hurtful accusations from her mind? The phone call had succeeded in achieving that much anyway.

She would not, could not, wait until evening when he came home from the office to talk it through; that would be another nine hours and the children would be around. However much she tried to reassure herself that the caller was simply a crank, her heart began to thud as she pressed number one on the memory button. Phoning Ben at the newspaper was a fairly rare event as he hardly ever had time to chat. Editing the political section of the broadsheet Sunday took up much of his energy. Like the rest of his harassed executives, he was over-worked, under-staffed and spent his life with his ear glued to the phone, 'beating the bushes', as he called it, to garner tips that might lead to exclusives. Tuesday, the first day back in the office after the weekend, was usually the lightest of the week and since he was a senior editor and did not have to account for his movements she was certain he'd come home when told what had happened. Keep calm, she instructed herself, just give him the facts.

After two rings Ben answered and as soon as he recognised her voice, cut in, 'I know why you're phoning and I haven't forgotten.' He chuckled. 'How many points do I get? The tickets are booked.'

His eldest daughter had been dropping hints she would like to take a few friends to the Rising Yellow concert for her fifteenth birthday and Carol had not been able to get through to the box office since it opened. Despite her best intentions to remain composed, when she thanked him she could not keep a quiver from her voice.

'You sound upset, what's up?'

'Yes, I am upset. I've just had an anonymous call.'

'Good God. What about?'

'Someone saying awful things about you.'

There was the shortest of pauses. 'Like what?'

She hesitated, wishing she could discuss it face to face. She would hate him to think she had believed the caller but still she needed him to come home and reassure her. And he wouldn't do that unless he realised how the call had affected her.

'They said you caused Fay's death.'

'What crap.' When she did not reply there was a smothered expletive. 'You don't believe that, do you? You can't.'

'No. Of course I don't.'

She must have hesitated a fraction too long before replying for she heard his intake of breath. 'Everyone knows it was a car accident. Fay swerved off the road.'

'The caller said it was really suicide.'

'But she was alone in the car. So how could they possibly know that?'

Carol was penitent. 'Yes, but—'

'Sweetheart, don't let this shake you up. It's complete balls.' And when she said nothing, Ben sounded impatient. 'Carol, anyone who doesn't give their name doesn't deserve to be believed.'

'There was something else. They said you were having an affair for two years before Fay died.'

The line went silent.

She took a deep breath. 'And that you're having an affair now.'

The moment the words were out she regretted them. She couldn't believe this was true; in any case it would have sounded softer had she said it to his face instead of blurting it over the phone.

'I think I'd better come home.'

It was then that she became frightened.

Chapter Two

Ben Mitchell forced his way into the traffic snarl running across the High Street away from Canary Wharf oblivious to the cacophony of horns from frustrated drivers awaiting their turn. Who the fuck would make an anonymous phone call to his wife? Their home number was ex-directory and given only to close friends. Of course a professional journalist could access the number or a friend might have passed it on, but what was the motive for saying those things to Carol?

His first thought was that it could be somebody at the office who wanted his job. Maybe they were trying to destabilise him, the theory being that by making mischief between him and his wife it would cause him to take his eye off the ball. But he could count on one hand the number who knew about the affair. And it had been years ago, why bring it up now?

As he drummed his fingers impatiently against the steering wheel Ben thought back to the agonising days following Fay's death. He had not been able to go back to the office for weeks after the accident and his colleagues put that down to his understandable grief. But it was not grief alone; it was full-blooded, five-star, middle-of-the-night guilt, something he couldn't bring himself to discuss with anyone.

Like today, the events eight years ago had been triggered by a phone call, though he knew who had dialled the number that time. Fay had immediately contacted Ben at the office to tell him she knew of the affair in Technicolor detail. It had propelled her out of the house and into the car, probably to drive to his office and tackle him about it. Thank God she had left the baby with the daily. Ben had been on his way home when Fay had been found, steering wheel embedded in her chest, her car wrapped around a tree. But he would put money on it that her death was not suicide. Not Fay. It had been an accident caused by her emotional state, thinking tortured thoughts instead of concentrating on driving. And for that he never ceased to blame himself.

His contrition and remorse had to be submerged because he was also having to handle the grief of three motherless children. He was going through the worst time of his life, unable to sleep, spending hours staring out of the window begging her forgiveness and worrying about what he should do about the children. Five-year-old Emmy seemed to have regressed to babyhood and was wetting her bed most nights and once demanded a dummy. The eldest, Becky, had turned unnaturally quiet and it was not until long afterwards that he'd found out how much she had been holding in her misery to spare his feelings. Although Katie was barely a year old then, the atmosphere in the house had its effect on her and she often cried for no apparent reason.

When he'd first met Carol he could not bring himself to be frank about the state of his first marriage. In truth Ben had always fought shy of baring his emotions, especially about his late wife, and though Carol had heard much of the circumstances surrounding her death, he had not talked to her about his feelings for Fay. Somehow Carol had from the start gained the impression that he and his late wife had been sublimely happy. To the outside world he and Fay had striven to give that impression but once or twice he had braced himself to tell Carol the truth, or at least try and debunk the image of the faultless paragon. Yet each time he stopped himself. Because of the children, he felt he had to be loyal to their mother's memory.

The truth was that Fay was tiresome. She had inherited a fair amount of money from her father and it made her too independent, an independence that bordered on arrogance. She was restless, never satisfied, always looking on the dark side of life. However much he tried to cheer her up, it was never any use. Once he bought a second-hand convertible for her birthday and when a friend, admiring the car, told Fay, 'Your husband must really love you,' she replied almost sneeringly, he thought, 'So he says.'

It was the sort of sour remark that slowly, insidiously killed his love for her. He was ripe for an affair when a political reporter on his newspaper, Caitlin Thomas, came along and pursued him. Full-lipped, flirtatious and married, which made her safer, he had to admit he had enjoyed their two-year liaison. Great sex followed by the best office gossip and no complications.

After the inquest Ben had angrily accused Caitlin's husband of making the call which had indirectly caused Fay's death. The man had not denied it. 'Don't blame me,' he had retorted. 'It wasn't the messenger that killed your wife but the message.' After Fay's funeral, Ben made it clear to Caitlin there was no future for them and she had abruptly departed to Washington, surprisingly taking her husband with her.

Listening to the eulogies at Fay's graveside Ben had wept bitter tears, distraught at the idea of three young children having to grow up without a mother. He vowed to devote himself to the children's upbringing and try as well as he could to ease their pain.

Yet in the still of yet another sleepless dawn he had the guilty thought, which he'd never confess to a living soul, that without Fay, life was more tranquil. Her volatile nature had more than once caused the older girls to be wary of her, one moment hugging and kissing them, the next screaming as though they had committed an atrocious crime rather than leaving socks on the bedroom floor. When he suggested, as tactfully as he could, that she might need counselling to control her mood swings, it provoked a temper tantrum which developed into a sulk lasting a week. Because of their three children, Ben would never have left her, though for him the marriage began to go wrong after the birth of Emmy. Fay lost all interest in sex and they had constant fights about it. Nevertheless Fay remained a head-turner and he enjoyed the envy of colleagues when she turned up to functions on his arm. She was skilled at flattery and pretended to be absorbed in conversations with his associates, which later she said were boring. And Ben noticed she spent virtually no time with women though that did not stop her from disparaging them afterwards. On the rare occasions he could persuade her to give a dinner party for colleagues, she demanded a rundown of their backgrounds. The richer they were, the more trouble she took; but she was less concerned with whether or not the guests had a good time than whether her flower arrangements were admired or the butter was perfectly iced.

He had almost curled up with embarrassment when she invited the high-powered women from his office to accompany her upstairs and leave the men to their port and cigars. When he'd castigated her later she replied that that was the way Mummy and Daddy had done things in Hong Kong. He should have been forewarned, having been introduced to Fay's mother, and wished he'd remembered the Russian proverb, 'If you seek a wife, look first at the mother.' Julia Campbell was a social climber who had imbued her daughter with all the characteristics of a snob. After that Ben did almost all of his entertaining in restaurants.

When he had first met Carol he had been through a series of pointless sexual couplings while coping with a succession of unsatisfactory live-in nannies and was tired of the responsibility of being both mother and father. He resisted having another live-in nanny and had managed reasonably well though he was dog-tired juggling the demands of a punishing job and three needy children. And his mother-in-law had not made life easier with her threats about court action amid demands that she wanted to see more of her grandchildren.

Subconsciously he had been searching for a woman who was loving, kind and uncomplicated, the exact opposite of Fay. And, above all, she wouldn't be overly ambitious. He needed a home-maker, not the kind of female usually found in a national newspaper office. But Carol was clearly not suited for the cut and thrust of journalism and seemed to be drifting while she waited to discover her niche in life. He had started as her mentor but as their friendship developed he found himself more and more wondering how she would get on with his girls. He had come to appreciate her lack of artifice. She had a sweetness of temperament which appealed to him and was so unlike his first wife.

Since Carol had entered their lives Ben and the children had been existing in calmer waters. She was much less formal, and though she liked things neat, she wasn't an obsessive like Fay. Happily he had pulled down the shutters on his previous life and hadn't had cause to think about it for many years.

Not until today.

Carol brewed herself a cup of freshly-ground coffee and tried to shake off the feeling of gloom. Usually Ben's journey home took forty minutes but in this kind of weather London traffic usually came to a standstill. She calculated he could not arrive before eleven then remembered with dismay that she should have been at work long ago. As she dialled the office she wondered briefly if she should pretend she was unwell but Lisa Jolly, who owned the company, would ask too many questions. Better to be vague and say something had cropped up which she needed to deal with at once.

It had taken Carol three years of working part-time at Jolly Good Food, a small but busy catering company, to forge a firm friendship with the boss and the rest of the gang. After finding out that she would not be coming in that morning, Lisa did not wait for a fuller explanation. 'What a bloody nuisance.' She sounded tense. 'Andrea's not in yet either. So I'm two short. You will be here tomorrow, won't you?' Carol assured her she would not let her down again.

Carefully she stepped over the pile of washing still waiting to go into the machine and made space for her cup amongst the breakfast things still cluttering the table. She ought not to pre-judge Ben, to take the word of an anonymous caller before she heard his side of things. Ben certainly had the opportunity to play around for she never asked him to account for his movements and as the political editor he often worked the same long hours as the House of Commons. He could be involved with someone at Westminster or at the office and she tried to conjure up names of his female colleagues but couldn't recall him mentioning anyone in particular. The way he told it, he operated in a nearly all-male world. But was that just a cover?

Perhaps he was looking elsewhere because she had become less interesting to him. Whereas before she could contribute conversation from her own activities, now she had to live vicariously through his experiences of attending great ceremonies like the state opening of Parliament, appearing as a political pundit on television or interviewing the famous and powerful. She had enjoyed looking after the children but it hadn't exactly stretched her; certainly she didn't think she was as stimulating as when they first met. Ben did appear to be interested in what went on in her life but, she thought with a pang, was this because it mostly involved his children?

Their weekends were structured differently from other people's because Ben had to work on a Saturday and therefore took Monday off instead. Once he'd roused himself from bed, Sunday was devoted to the children. On Mondays after the kids had gone to school, they had been in the habit of going back to bed though Carol realised with a start that a series of domestic chores – visits to the dentist or the DIY store – had intervened lately to prevent this.

Was Ben happy with their sex life? She had no way of knowing. Their lovemaking was gentle, always had been ever since they had met. He seemed fairly undemanding and their routine varied only occasionally. Sometimes she faked an orgasm but rationalised this by thinking it was good for his ego. He had never asked for oral sex and as she had always been too inhibited to suggest it or perform the act without asking, she was relieved.

An image of Ben's naked body stretched out on the counterpane after they had last made love came into her mind. At the time he had seemed sated by their exertions but she had to admit sex was not the most important part of their relationship, at least for her. She loved the sensuousness of being stroked and caressed but the pity of it was that she had never been able to bring herself to tell him what she most liked and after seven years she felt she'd missed the opportunity. Why couldn't she tell him? Probably because she wanted to maintain his confidence that he was a lover who satisfied her in every way. Perhaps she was being complacent and the uneasy thought occurred that if the caller was right, it would be because he needed a less inhibited partner.

Long ago Carol had lost the courage to question him on how their lovemaking compared with that of his first marriage. But she had never been able to rid herself of the feeling that Ben must surely find her a contrast to Fay who undoubtedly was better looking and apparently had been an ebullient character who loved partying. Carol had submerged the idea that Ben had deliberately chosen someone who was Fay's exact opposite so he would not be tempted to compare them, either physically or temperamentally. She had overcome those early feelings of jealousy by convincing herself it was illogical to be envious of someone who was beautiful, accomplished and dead.

Several times during their early courtship they had discussed how exaggerated the role of sex had become in today's world. Of course they enjoyed it but she, and until now, she thought, he, had wanted something more from marriage than physical passion – companionship, sharing, the feeling that he cared what happened to her. Ben made her feel secure.

Until today.

She estimated there was still half an hour before he would be home. What was the best way to tackle him? He was a fairly difficult person to confront for he had a great facility with words. When she was agitated, what she wanted to say didn't seem to come out right. A day or two later she would find herself thinking of a perfectly-reasoned argument and wonder why the hell she hadn't been able to verbalise it at the time.

This lack of confidence was the prime reason she had quit journalism. At first she had been proud to be picked by her regional newspaper group to work for its national daily in London but that did not last. Soon she came to hate the jobs she was ordered to do. Having to contact kiss-and-tell merchants was not why she had become a journalist. Once she had to spend two days at a hotel near London Airport 'baby-minding' a prostitute signed up by her newspaper to dish the dirt on celebrities who had been her clients. It was grisly, pretending to be solicitous to that loathsome woman, and Carol had been at her lowest ebb. The woman had been trying to increase her fee and Carol was supposed to keep her sweet so she would stick to the contract. It was a horrible job as the news editor readily agreed, 'But someone has to do it, kid,' he said, 'and that someone is you.' He had ordered her back to the hotel to wait with the subject until the actual interviews, conducted by her more world-weary colleagues, had been published.

The only good thing that had come out of the new post was meeting Ben.

At the end of that miserable stint Carol had retreated into the office canteen and, oblivious to her surroundings, sank her head in her hands and permitted shame to engulf her. She had fought for a place at the college of journalism, picturing herself as part of a team discussing a large-scale investigation or the contents of the leader page. And what had she ended up doing? The dross that more experienced reporters went out of their way to avoid. Only last week she'd had the phone slammed down on her by a vicar who refused to answer questions about his alleged affair with the male verger. When she'd asked the news editor for a transfer to the features department, he dismissed her brusquely and said she'd have to earn her passage to what he considered was easy street.

Sitting dolefully in the canteen, she promised herself she would re-think her career. She wasn't cut out to be a reporter, she wasn't tough enough. Maybe she could get herself a place on a woman's magazine. After all, she had a reasonable degree and a year's experience after university with a Bristol news agency.

Watching nearby, Ben told her later she looked so miserable he was desperately willing her not to cry. He wouldn't have known how to cope with a woman weeping in the middle of the canteen. But he had enough compassion to move to her table where she soon found herself pouring out her woes into his sympathetic ear.

Over the weeks he became her mentor and because of this interest from a senior journalist on the paper her colleagues seemed to treat her with more respect. Carol decided to delay plans to look for another job, flattered to receive attention from one of the best-looking men in the office. He was also an object of great sympathy among the female staff because he'd been tragically widowed and left to bring up three young children on his own. Most important of all there did not appear to be a hint of a woman in his life. Nor, during the following weeks, did he make any romantic overtures to Carol who persuaded herself he had not noticed her increasing fascination with him.

When she found herself daydreaming about him in every spare moment, she had to confront the fact that she had fallen in love. She accepted it was unrequited but then what could she expect? Why would such an impressive man, someone who could have any woman he chose, consider such an unworldly person? The following week, without any hint there was a change in their relationship, to her delight he invited her to dinner. She agonised over whether this was a proper date or whether there would be other people present and he simply needed an escort. Or maybe he was going to give her more career advice, although she dismissed this fairly quickly, thinking that he could do this equally well in the office.

In the event she was guided to a table for two in an expensive and discreet restaurant, and over a delicious oyster pie, which she could only toy with, he told her how his wife had died and how his children had been suffering. This was the first of many outings though their dates appeared to be spur of the moment events and after each she would never be certain he would ask her out again. On the fourth occasion, after a candlelit dinner in a Thames-side hotel overlooking the London Eye, he suggested they go to his home for coffee. First, they tiptoed into the children's rooms and Carol gazed down on the sleeping faces, rosy and warm. She felt Ben's muscular arms wrap around her waist as he stood behind her, his head resting on the top of hers. This was how it could always be, she could not stop herself thinking. If only . . . But the dream was too far removed from her orbit, he was too far removed.

When they came downstairs Ben suggested substituting the coffee for a late-night drink and for a time they sat in silence, sipping brandy from balloon glasses. Oh God, she thought, she must be boring him and was about to talk brightly about a story she was writing when, almost casually, he leaned forward and, taking her chin in his hand, tilted her face. The kiss started gently, stopped, started again then grew in intensity. His lips were firm and warm, his probing tongue gentle. She leaned forward, lost in the moment, savouring the feel of his strong fingers as he stroked her throat, then her collar bone, and when his hand started unbuttoning her blouse, her skin broke out in goose bumps. His eyes were half closed as he pushed the material off her shoulders before impatiently unhooking her bra. They slid back onto the sofa; now his long fingers were fondling her breasts but he never stopped kissing her. Her nipples hardened under his touch and she slipped her hands underneath his shirt to caress his naked back, clinging to him thinking she never again wanted to be a separate person.

They stretched out on the sofa and his fingers stroked her body lightly, his hands delicately exploring while she, eyes shut, hoped that her sexual inexperience would not disappoint him. Neither of them had said a word but their bodies seemed to adjust to one another, fitting together like a simple jigsaw puzzle. When she sensed that he was about to enter her body, she was aroused and waiting—

And then the door opened. A tousled-haired little girl stood in the doorway, rubbing her eyes and peering into the dark room.

'Daddy?' she wailed. 'Where are you? I can't see you.'

Ben raised his head above the top of the sofa and gave a little cough while Carol lay motionless beneath him.

'I'm just having a little lie-down, darling,' he panted. 'What is it?'

'I'm thirsty.'

He slid a rueful glance in Carol's direction and said, 'OK, go back to bed and I'll bring you some water.'

They disentangled themselves and he hissed, 'Passion killer.' But after they had dressed hurriedly he stroked her cheek. 'That's one thing you have to learn about kids, no sense of timing. Sorry.'

And when he took her home he said, 'Next time, we'll go to your place.'

Dreamily she let herself into her one-bedroom flat. There was going to be a next time.

She could not help comparing this lovemaking, interrupted as it had been, with the technique of a previous boyfriend. Within seconds he would begin the quickening motions of uncontrollable urgency which led towards his release. Then he would shudder, withdraw and lie back gasping, not realising – probably not caring – that she had barely started to be aroused. She'd nicknamed him 'Ferry Sex' – roll on, roll off – and had chucked him.

Making love with Ben, when it finally happened a few nights later, was as wonderful as she'd hoped, gentle, loving and best of all with no sense of urgency, no domination. His body seemed to be reacting to her needs and he spent time searching hers for triggers which would give her pleasure. Even when his hands and mouth brought her to a crescendo he had held back, waiting. Then while she was still shuddering as the intensity of her need erupted, he reached his own climax.

It took some time for their breathing to quieten down. She hoped he would say something significant for she was desperate to know what he wanted from the relationship. An affair? Less? More? The most important question she could not ask. If he had evaded it or, worse, tried to qualify his answer she would have been mortified, bringing to mind the words Prince Charles had said on his engagement day, a quote no woman in the world would ever forget, 'Yes, whatever love means.'

She lay with her head in the crook of his arm while Ben lazily traced a finger around the base of her neck. 'I love . . .' he said and she held her breath. '. . . being with you.'

Two weeks later he introduced her to his family. She had no experience with young children, and these three were just emerging from the trauma of the shocking suddenness of their mother's death. She did not quite know what was expected of her and so she played a role. This Carol became unreal, an actress who overdid things. Most weekends Ben asked her to come on picnics or trips to the museums which he seemed to think important for them. And for these children she used mountains of energy and never became cross, never said 'no you can't' or 'not now' or 'I'm tired, go away'; never lost her temper. She was never anything other than interested in them and what they were doing. Of course it could not last but by the time reality intruded she was married and a full-time wife and mother.

His proposal came when she least expected it and only three months after their first proper date. They had been walking along the banks of the Thames at night. It was their favourite spot, on Battersea Bridge, looking in the direction of the Houses of Parliament where he spent much of his working life. They stood in silence for a while and he placed an arm casually around her shoulders, asking when she planned to leave the newspaper. She was still searching for a career which interested her, and she said she hadn't a clue, adding, 'My problem is that I don't know what I want.'

He had no such difficulty, he told her. He knew precisely what he wanted. He wanted her to marry him and stay with him and the children for ever. She caught her breath and thought, This is the one perfect moment in my life.

Not giving her time to speak, he said he had naturally discussed his plans with his older daughters and they had sent him out with a message for her.

'Now I have to get it right,' he said. 'They said: "Please, please, please, please say yes".'

As he folded her in his arms and kissed her tenderly he seemed sure there would be the right answer from her when she was finally allowed to breathe, as there was. The following day she joyfully gave in her notice at the newspaper and four weeks afterwards found herself walking into Chelsea Register Office with three flower girls and a handful of family and friends, to become Ben's wife and, simultaneously, stepmother to his children.

Until Ben arrived home, Carol decided she didn't want to think, that she had to keep herself occupied. She went upstairs, opened a door and gazed at the chaos in Emmy's bedroom. How many times had she tried to drum into that child that Tuesday was wash day and she had to strip the bed? Irritated, she ripped off the duvet cover with unaccustomed vehemence. Then she perched on the edge of the bed. This was nothing to do with the twelve-year-old.

She ran her fingers over the cane chair she had lovingly re-sprayed and one part of her brain thought she should find time to do the other one. As she began to dust the bedside table she caught sight of the little pottery mug Fay had made for Emmy's christening. Eight and a half years after the tragedy it would be wrong to say the older children did not remember their mother but she rarely cropped up in conversation. Carol thought that was natural, given they were so young when she died. In the early days, she was careful to try and talk about their mother as naturally as possible and a few mementoes of Fay's life were still around the house. Becky treasured the decorated photo album Fay had compiled for her fifth birthday and Katie's prize possession was the silver locket Fay had bequeathed her from her jewellery collection.

Hanging on the wall in Emmy's bedroom was a photograph taken nearly eight years previously, a few weeks after Katie had been born. Smiley faces, heads tilted around the central characters, the mother and her new baby. A beaming Ben sat next to them, secure, seemingly content within his happy family. But the picture was skewed. When they had posed for it, that smiling, proud father had been 'screwing around', according to the anonymous caller, had been having an affair for two long years, had been cheating on that family.

Could he be doing the same to her?

Chapter Three

Lisa Jolly counted out the number of canapés to be coated in prawn sauce and thanked her lucky stars she'd been able to persuade Connie to come round right away to help with the rush job. Living nearby, she was a stalwart who never seemed to mind being called in at the last minute. Lisa cast a despairing glance at the trays waiting to go into the ovens.

'Where the hell's Andrea? She should've been here an hour ago. Can you all work late?' she asked the two other kitchen helpers. 'We're up the creek if we can't deliver these by five.'

The unaccustomed silence in the spacious Fulham basement was broken only by the sound of carrots being grated against the mandolin.

When Lisa had been bequeathed the Fulham house on the death of her mother she had joyfully given up her job in the City and exploited her hobby and her surname to found Jolly Good Food. Most of her work came from regular contracts with local firms needing impressive lunches for potential clients, supplemented by weddings, anniversaries and Bar Mitzvahs. Luckily, since she started four years ago Lisa's marketing skills had never been called into play since word-of-mouth recommendations proved to be the best advertisement of all.

Carefully Lisa spooned small samples of each of the sauces into what the industry called Freddie's Pots. These would be kept in one of the fridges for a couple of days until any danger of possible food poisoning would be over. Why 'Freddie'? The identity of the man who had donated his name was lost in the mist of time and she hoped it did not commemorate someone who'd died from salmonella. All she did know was that she would never fail to keep these samples for she was more fearful of the health inspectors than she was of the Inland Revenue.

As she worked Lisa reflected that it was unlike Carol to let her down at the last minute. She would phone later to find out what had happened. In three years Carol had rarely been absent, she had never even been late, a testament to the health of those kids.

She and Carol had met when Lisa had advertised for part-time staff. Carol applied, saying she needed some outside stimulation for a few hours when the children were at school and Jolly Good Food provided the answer. Hours were flexible, pay was OK and it soon became clear she thrived in the congenial kitchen working with three or four lively women, most of whom were also mothers of young children.

It was surprising that she and Carol had become friends. Lisa was an extrovert, always trying fresh experiences, whereas Carol was more hesitant, less sure of herself. But their friendship developed when Carol, a gentle, patient listener, supported Lisa through the break-up of her long affair with that two-timing bastard Tim. Since he had left the scene six months ago she hadn't met anybody who'd turned her on. But as she now readily admitted to Carol, she and Tim had run out of steam and what she missed most about him was a warm body in bed next to her. She was looking for someone like Ben, attractive in a kind of rugby player way, intelligent, socially presentable, a twinkle in his eye, and, her highest praise, clean fingernails. Privately Lisa suspected Ben might've been naughty in his day but that was in the past. He seemed devoted to Carol. And Carol patently adored him.

As Ben worked long hours and Lisa was unattached, a state she hoped was temporary, they were able to spend time together. Lisa had become a familiar face around the Mitchell household and like Carol enjoyed the company of children. They in turn responded to a grown-up who treated them almost like adults and as Ben's only sister had removed herself to New Zealand, Lisa had become their unofficial auntie.

When the children were occupied elsewhere, Lisa suggested some diversions to take them away from domesticity and cooking and Lisa's verve had inspired Carol to branch out into new avenues. Salsa dancing did not last long because both women had trouble co-ordinating their limbs. Pottery was tried but discarded as being too static. The Pilates exercise class survived a whole term before it was given up in favour of professional singing lessons. That had stayed the course. It was a bonus that their teacher, a professional singer, was a young, attractive musician. He had the disconcerting habit of placing his hands on his pupil's diaphragms to test whether or not they were breathing properly. Carol just about coped with it but Lisa would ham it up and behind his back feign a faint. It was a sad day for her when he announced his engagement.

They decided to play a trick on Ben and the children at Christmas. It had worked exactly as they had planned. Just before the pudding Lisa ostensibly begged Carol to join her in a song and reluctantly Carol had agreed. Then, while Lisa pressed the button on the CD player she just happened to bring with her, the two of them went into their much-rehearsed 'Flower Song' by Delibes, which they had been practising for many weeks. True, the British Airways theme song would never sound the same to them again but it had been one of the most satisfying moments of Carol's life to observe Ben's jaw dropping in the direction of the floor while they warbled this difficult duet. It took some doing to impress the children at the same time but Carol achieved this ambition as well. Lisa still swelled with pride at the memory of her friend's pleasure all these months later.

She was bending over the Aga to check on the last batch of canapés when there was a sound of clumping down the basement stairs. Startled, she looked up to see her regular cook, Andrea Wilmot, clinging to the banister, a plastered leg swinging awkwardly sideways as she descended clumsily into the room.

The Australian twang boomed round the room. 'Isn't it a bugger. I've broken my soddin' ankle.' Andrea made slow, painful progress towards the nearest chair and sat down with a sigh of relief. 'You can't believe how heavy this bloody thing is,' she wailed, giving the plaster an irritated thump with her hand. 'I can't drive, I can hardly walk. I can hardly wipe my bum.'

'Thanks for sharing,' said Connie with a straight face. 'But you don't need legs to chop onions.'

Andrea disregarded this. 'The killer is I've got to back out of the Brunei trip until the plaster is off.'

Expressions of sympathy came from everyone though Lisa tried not to let her relief show. Andrea was the best cook she had ever employed. The girl was working her way round the world but already she had been working here for nearly eight months and Lisa hoped she would never move from London. Her cooking credentials were excellent and though she was often crude she was a cheery presence in what could be high-tension situations.

'I hate to let them down,' Andrea was struggling to get off her coat, 'but how can I manage like this in a rainforest? You can just see me hopping through the jungle, dodging those snakes with my crutch.'

For weeks the women had been regaled by Andrea's machinations to get onto a field trip to a rainforest in south-east Asia. She was to have been gone for a year and Lisa was dreading trying to find a replacement as competent and with such a sunny temperament.

'Pass me the onions,' said Andrea. 'It looks like you're stuck with me. They say it'll be twelve weeks before they can cut off this bloody cast.'

Chapter Four

Ben drove swiftly up the drive into the front garden which had been turned into a parking space. For once he was able to manoeuvre into the tiny drive because today nobody had parked haphazardly across the entrance.

He turned off the ignition and closed his eyes. Why should Carol take any notice of someone who accused him of having an affair? He had never given her any reason to doubt his fidelity. But he couldn't be a hypocrite. Sure, he'd been attracted to other women since he had married Carol but he had never allowed anything to develop from it. Well, maybe a mild flirtation that had meant nothing on either side. He had learned his lesson. Sexual ecstasy was wonderful at the time but for him there had been a heavy price to pay. He appreciated Carol's loving nature and if he did not feel overwhelming lust for her, wasn't that a good thing? Passion had not served him well in the past.

After seven years he would describe their sex life as adequate, though she was somewhat inhibited. But they'd got to the stage where it would be difficult to change, they should've done that years ago. Lately he'd been working such long hours he didn't think he could manage it more than once a week. In fact, he remembered guiltily, they'd missed out on lovemaking on several Mondays.

Nevertheless she made him happy and as Ben turned his key in the lock and looked around the hall he once again enjoyed a moment of pleasure. Carol had redecorated the entire house, enthusiastically helped by the children – God, she was good with them – who were under the impression they had chosen their own colour schemes. She had softened the over-dramatic décor and it looked more like a woodland glade than the imitation country house style favoured by Fay.

From the start of their marriage he had been desperate to avoid any further changes in the children's routine and not for the first time told

himself how lucky he was that Carol had readily agreed to stay in the marital home. When he persuaded Fay that they should buy the imposing three-storey villa built for prosperous City merchants in the late 1890s, she had had reservations. It would be a long time, she complained, before the property in Tollbridge Road would be gentrified like many of the other streets in Battersea as it was still flanked by a series of low-rise council-owned flats. And she'd been right. The road was still rather shabby but the house was spacious, it suited them fine and Carol had transformed it into the home he had always known it could be.

Ben dropped his briefcase on the floor under the hall table as Carol appeared at the top of the landing. He smiled at her as she made her way down the staircase but her face did not light up as it normally did when she saw him. He noticed how rigid her body was and how strained her face. He could have saved her from this if he'd been candid at the outset, then the call would not have had such an impact.

He folded her stiff body into his arms. 'Darling, I'm sorry you've had such a shock. Let's sit down and I'll answer any questions you like.'

She did not reply, instead walking ahead of him to the living room to perch on the edge of the sofa. The room was in half-light, rain beating against the windows. She shivered as he sat down next to her and he took hold of one of her hands. It was icy.

'Don't let this call upset you. That's exactly what they want.'

She gave a tremulous smile. 'Just tell me it's a pack of lies. That's all I need to hear.'

Ben lifted up her chin and held her gaze. 'I am not,' he said with emphasis, 'having an affair and I hope you can believe that.' He met her eyes fearlessly and she nodded, appearing to accept his word.

'Then what was all that stuff about you not being able to keep your zipper up?'

'That's more junk.'

'Is it?'

'Why are you believing a nobody on the phone instead of me?'

Her face was reddening. 'Maybe that "nobody" is telling the truth.' Ben was genuinely stunned and she reacted.

'Why not? I sit here day after day never knowing where you are.'

'But I phone you, every single day.'

'That's my point, you could be anywhere. How do I know you're not with another woman?'

'Because I'm bloody well not. I haven't laid a finger on anyone else since we met.'

'I bet you've had offers.'

'Yes, I have,' he shouted, stung. 'And I turn them all down. But since you believe I'm screwing around anyway, I might as well have gone ahead.' Her face crumpled and instantly he realised he had gone too far.

'Look, I didn't mean that. I wouldn't be unfaithful to you. Please, Carol, you need to believe that.' She stayed silent. 'Have I given you any reason not to trust me?' She stared at him, still, it seemed to him, unconvinced. 'Haven't we been happy together?' he demanded. 'Why would I need anyone else?'

Her voice began to quiver. 'You were happy with Fay yet they said you had someone else.'

'I wasn't happy with her,' he said quietly. 'Long before her death our marriage had become a nightmare.'

'That's not the impression you gave me.'

'I didn't want to colour your opinion of Fay, for the children's sake.' Ben tried to keep his voice level. He had never actually lied to her about the state of his first marriage but nor had he attempted to correct the notion it had been happy. He had castigated himself for not telling her the truth about his first marriage. He should've done it right at the beginning, but why admit he'd committed adultery to someone who had put him on a pedestal? He decided against mentioning this; instead he told her the reason was that he didn't want to prejudice her opinion of the children's mother. 'I thought if you believed the marriage was stable you'd be better able to reinforce their good memories.'

This seemed to inflame her. 'You honestly thought that I would've let it affect the children? It doesn't show much confidence in me.'

'I'm sorry. I thought I was doing the right thing.'

She was silent for a moment. 'Why did you let me think Fay was the perfect wife, the love of your life, someone I had to measure up to? The things I did to try and make you feel I was worthy enough to fill her shoes . . .' she faltered.

'Worthy? Carol, don't underestimate yourself. Please, don't allow this crank to poison everything we've built up.' He squeezed her hand but she withdrew it.

'No, Ben, I need to sort this out. If the caller was right about one thing, you can't blame me for thinking they're right about the other.'

He gave an exclamation of irritation. 'You're so naïve sometimes. I can only think . . .'

'Naïve?' Carol interrupted hotly. 'That's fucking unfair. All I did was pick up the phone and listen to the poison and now suddenly I'm to blame.'

Ben was astounded. Carol never used that kind of language.

'Can't you see?' he asked. 'Someone is obviously trying to cause trouble between us. There are dozens of rivals out there who'd like to unsettle me and the easiest way to do it is through you.'

'Why did they accuse you of being responsible for Fay's death?'

'I have no idea. It's downright malicious. That's what makes me think I know who made the call.'

She leaned towards him. 'Who?'

'Fay learned about the affair from the woman's husband. It's possible he's still nursing a grudge.'

'After all this time? Why wait until now? It doesn't make sense.'

'That's what I intend to find out.'

'How will you do that?'

His eyes crinkled. 'I don't think you realise what an influential man you're married to. I used to be a shit-hot political reporter and I still have my contacts. They'll let me have a look at phone records and we know the exact time of the call, which should narrow it down.'

'I'd really like to know who it was.'

'I promise I'll do my best to find out.' He paused to examine her face anxiously. Was there a slight thaw in the atmosphere? 'I'm really sorry it's happened. Oh, sweetheart, don't let it get you down. They'll have won then.'

She relaxed against the sofa and ran her fingers through her hair. 'All this has made me nervous about picking up the phone. God, what a terrible morning.'

'Darling, you do believe me, don't you? I'll say it again. I've never been unfaithful and I don't intend to.'

She gave the start of a smile and he seized the moment.

'Come on, let's have a cup of tea.'

Carol seemed less tense as they made their way to the kitchen but he was by no means certain the matter had been laid to rest. He was genuinely sorry the trust his wife had placed in him might have been dented by the caller's allegations. It was the old newspaper trick, one bit of truth in a

web of lies. It meant the subject couldn't deny everything but had to resort to the 'it was taken out of context' defence. He wished he could get his hands on the person who made the call.

As she watched him filling the kettle, his broad back bent over the sink, Carol was filled with uncertainty. She wanted to believe him. No hint of guilt clouded his features and his manner indicated he was keen to let the subject drop. But she was not ready for that. Carol took a sip of the hot tea and nerved herself to risk his irritation. If they didn't talk about it now, when would be a better time?

'Ben, about Fay . . .'

Abruptly he put down his cup with what she thought was annoyance but she ploughed on. 'Surely you must've realised I had a sense of inferiority about Fay? She seemed perfect for you, beautiful, talented, super-confident. If I'd known you weren't happy with her, can't you see it would've made my life easier?'

He gave an impish grin. 'You mean you wouldn't have tried so hard.'

Carol smacked him smartly on the hand. 'Don't wriggle out of it like that.'

'Why rake up the past? It never does any good.'

'You're wrong. If we don't thrash it out it'll keep on worrying me and that won't help either of us.'

Ben was grudging. 'If you must. I don't like talking about it because I was unhappy for most of the time. Fay was a discontented woman. I could do nothing right. I used to get in, have supper with the kids and once they were in bed I'd disappear to the pub simply to get away from the rows.'

'What did you row about?'

'Everything. Money, the kids, the house – it wasn't good enough for her. Nor was my job. I was a reporter at the time and she didn't think it was worth bragging about.' He raked his fingers through his hair. 'She was always worrying about what other people had and how they lived. It spoilt things. Look at the children's names. So pretentious. It caused an almighty row when they became known by their pet names.'

Carol had been told it was Becky, egged on by her father, who had insisted on being known by her second name, Rebecca, instead of Siobhan. And it was Becky who had abbreviated the names of her sisters, Emmeline to Emmy or Em and Katerina to Katie.

Ben was staring into the middle distance. 'But what I hated most was the way she behaved with the children, playing a kind of Russian roulette with them, one minute all hugs and kisses, the next screaming at them for the smallest thing. That's why I couldn't walk out. I was their ballast, the constant in their lives.'

'Do you think you were responsible for her death?'

He looked pained. 'It's true she was in an emotional state when she went into that car. So to an extent I was. I used to justify my behaviour on the grounds that if we'd been happy I wouldn't have needed anyone else and Fay might still be alive. It took many years of soul-searching to be able to admit that I took the cowardly way out. I should've made more effort to repair the marriage.'

'Sometimes that's not possible.'

'I think we should've been divorced because although we tried to keep our differences from the kids they were beginning to be affected. We all were and eventually I looked for sympathy and affection and found it with someone else.'

'But if the affair lasted two whole years, why didn't you marry the woman after Fay's death?'

At first Carol didn't think he was going to answer, then he said softly, 'It wasn't that kind of relationship.'

'What kind of relationship was it?'

He hesitated. 'Exciting, forbidden fruit, not real life. Besides, she was already married and I was wracked with guilt about Fay's death and that finished it off.'

'Were you in love with her?'

'I couldn't have been. I let her go.'

Carol was beginning to regret her insistence that they talk about the past. Was he trying to spare her feelings? It was obvious he had cared deeply for the woman because an affair of such duration could not be solely based on sex. She hoped to God he wasn't still carrying a torch and that the decision to marry her was not a compromise.

'Do you regret that?'

He lifted her to her feet and smiled. 'How can you ask that? I met you.'

This time she allowed her body to relax into his and heard him say, 'Are we OK now?'

He had tackled each accusation the caller had made, as far as she could deduce, with frankness and she should have been reassured. But the fact remained he would never have volunteered any of this had he not been forced. Did that matter? Yes, there were things in his past that affected their present. But she had always trusted him and hated the idea of probing further.

Slowly she nodded. 'We're OK.'

'In that case,' he smiled, 'let's go upstairs. I don't have to be back in the office just yet . . .'

Lying curled up in each other's arms afterwards Ben assured her that she was the only woman in his life and that their marriage was for keeps. It wasn't something she could remember him ever saying and it had the effect of making her suspicious. Try as she might, she could not banish from her mind the nasty, hissing voice saying, 'Don't think he's changed. He's still at it.'

Perhaps that was what made her hold back from telling him about being four days late. And she was relieved that she had stayed quiet because an hour after he had showered and left, she went into the bathroom to discover she was not pregnant after all. She had allowed herself to hope and the disappointment was acute. She sat on the edge of the bath for many minutes without moving, trying to suppress tears and wondering whether she would ever have a baby. She decided not to mention this false alarm to Ben. What was the point?

During the rest of the week she started nervously whenever the phone rang, only relaxing when she could identify the caller at the other end of the line. As if by arrangement she and Ben did not refer again to the anonymous caller but the allegations had unsettled her more than she would admit. Carol could not put out of her mind Ben's reply when asked if he had been in love with his mistress. She'd wanted a vehement denial, not the unsatisfactory reply he gave: he couldn't have been because he let her go – not because their passion had died but because of the intense guilt he was experiencing over his wife's death. The thought tormented Carol that, if circumstances had been different, would he now be married to that woman?

Chapter Five

On the following Saturday morning when Ben could only just have arrived at the office Carol was already exhausted with the effort of getting three children up and out of the house, looking like little models. Granny's lips would purse at the sight of jeans, trainers or tracksuits and it was better for Carol's peace of mind if they met Fay's mother in their Sunday best. Driving towards the Richmond water park Carol marvelled at her ability to combine the duties of arch nag, dresser, cook and chauffeur. She disliked having to hand the children over to Julia Campbell who still treated her like some sort of hired help.

She would never forget the first time she'd made the trip over to Julia's house a few weeks before she and Ben were married. Julia had insisted on hosting Christmas that year and Ben had reluctantly agreed. 'Let's get it over with, darling,' he'd said, 'then we don't have to go there for years and years.'

How diffident and insecure Carol had been and, as if aware of her mood, Julia had taken pride in underlining the wonderful Christmases they'd had in the past. With Fay. She pointed to the wooden fairy on the top of the tree which Fay had carved herself. Everyone but Carol knew that under the tree they always put the baby Jesus in the crib which Emmy had spotted in a shop window on an outing with her mother when she was barely four. The ragged paper chains around the room, which the children had made on the Christmas Eve before their mother's death, were past their best but no one considered throwing them out.

Carol had felt excluded, out of tune with their Christmas rituals, realising that the biggest problem about inheriting other people's children was not having a history to share. Carol was the outsider trying to create a new family unit which had come together through tragic circumstances. These children were expected to live with a virtual stranger and as they sang carols after Christmas Eve tea, another family tradition, she silently prayed that her life with them would work out.

In the beginning it had been very difficult. Ben was expected back at the newspaper after a one-day honeymoon, leaving Carol to care for a thirteen-month-old baby, a fractious five-year-old and her mistrustful sister who was two years older. It was true the older two girls had wanted their father to marry her but naturally they had no concept of the life shift it entailed for her. She did not mind that her beloved sports car was sacrificed for the much-ridiculed Volvo estate; what she missed most was the loss of her privacy. In those days she was never alone, never herself and never completely at ease with them. She had long given up her weekly sessions at a smart Mayfair salon but having to confront the possibility that she could be infested with lice when one of the girls picked up nits at school made her feel, for a while, out of control. The entire family had to shampoo their heads with a vile-smelling substance every day.

The biggest transformation, however, was not being in charge of her time. The children had the upper hand and she always seemed to do what they wanted, at least when she was still inexperienced in dealing with them. When Ben came home he was usually tired and she wanted to appear as if she was managing extremely well, being the perfect consort. Naturally he asked how everything was, concerned about how she was getting on but his work, as always, was his priority for, as he said, without the money he earned how would they manage?

Carol bought dozens of books on step-parenting, each more confusing than the last. One or two seemed to suggest she would feel instant love for all of her stepchildren, others were more realistic, pointing out that older children especially could resent her coming between them and their father. As it was with Becky. She was the oldest and had the strongest memories of life with her own mother, and Carol's patience was sorely tried by her continuing rudeness and resistance to all attempts at friendship. Ben appeared to be sanguine about the behaviour of his eldest, saying she would come round in time. And he was right but only after two years of hard graft.

Although it was never spelt out, Carol felt enormous moral pressure not to hurt the children because of the pain they had experienced already.

For the first year she felt as though she was living on a stage, with an audience comprising Ben's friends and Fay's mother watching every move. Several well-meaning friends suggested that the children should be very grateful to her as she had 'rescued' them. But Carol was wise enough to discount this. The kids had no idea of the sacrifices she was making and she didn't want them to be grateful. Though Ben's friends welcomed her into their circle, casting her in the role of heroine, there was one exception; Fay's widowed mother, Julia Campbell. Carol suspected she was jealous of her influence on her beloved grandchildren and Carol tried to be understanding about this.

But there were great chunks of her new life that Carol thoroughly enjoyed. She loved being the hub of a family unit. Her parents had both died when she was in her teens and her only brother was making a living as a systems analyst in Canada so it was a novelty to be needed and for her absence to be noted. But because everything was new to her, from shopping to dealing with a sudden accident at school (Emmy dropped a piece of gym equipment on her foot and needed to be taken to casualty), Carol felt tired most of the time.

What suffered most in those early days was her sex life. More often than not she would be fast asleep by the time Ben came home, exhausted by the sheer physical effort of maintaining the organisation needed to run all their lives. Ben was very understanding. He had been scarred by the trauma of Fay's death too and he didn't know how to talk to the children about their mother. That job, too, was left to Carol and whenever appropriate she had encouraged them to relive their memories. As the years passed, real life began to assert itself until the bed-wetting ceased, the crying at night was over and even Becky would smile and ask her opinion about things.

Today the children were complaining volubly about having to put on posh clothes to go to a swimming pool. As usual Carol ignored their protests, knowing that Julia would have booked somewhere smart for lunch. Hamburgers would not do for Julia Campbell's grandchildren.

The children's grandmother was forever criticising the way they were being brought up, the way they behaved, the way they were dressed. She complained constantly about not being able to have them to stay over. The truth was the children had adamantly refused but Carol thought it kinder not to pass this on. In any case, her conversations with Julia were limited to the briefest of exchanges. Despite Carol's best efforts, the woman made it clear she regarded her son's second wife as little more than a nanny. Understanding how she must have suffered over the untimely death of her daughter, Carol tried not to be hurt by her attitude. Indeed, she made great efforts to treat her sensitively but if Julia ever noticed this she showed no signs of it.

Early in their relationship Ben had said that once a month was about enough attention from their grandmother, otherwise her sense of values might rub off on them. 'The woman's a snob. You should see the way she talks to that housekeeper of hers. I don't want them to get infected by that kind of attitude.'

In all things concerning the children Carol rarely questioned her husband and in any case from what she had seen of Julia she agreed with him. It had fallen to Carol to maintain the link with Julia, sometimes taking them to the imposing home she shared with her housekeeper in Wimbledon. The older woman usually resisted making visits to the children at their home, saying the memories were too painful.

A tap on the shoulder from Becky drew her attention to the turn-off for the water park. The form on these occasions was to hand over the children with as much speed as courtesy would allow. Although Julia had grudgingly admitted to Ben recently that Carol was 'quite good' with the children, there was still a distance between the two women. But today, as Carol was about to say goodbye, the immaculately-coiffed Mrs Campbell asked if she could spare time to have a coffee while the children were changing into their swimsuits.

At once the three of them began to clamour that she could then watch them plunging down the snake-like slides and Carol overcame her reluctance and smiled her acceptance. She followed Julia into the glass enclosure which overlooked the palm-filled swimming area. Nervously Carol cleared her throat, wondering what it was Julia wanted to discuss. This was the first time they had been completely alone. Always before, she had dropped off the children so quickly that no real conversation was necessary and on the few social occasions they had met up, Ben was around to take the brunt of Julia's constant complaint that she did not see enough of the children.

Carol need not have worried. Julia simply wanted to make sure the birthday present she planned to buy for Rebecca would not be duplicated. As it was a computer costing several hundred pounds, Carol assured her there was no danger of that. They were interrupted by excited screams so piercing they penetrated the glass panels. Katie wanted to demonstrate her bravery in following her sisters up the slide they had nicknamed Mount Everest. Carol was secretly pleased they did not expect her to join them. She had a fear of heights.

After a few moments of chit-chat Carol was about to take her leave when she was disconcerted to see Julia take out a delicate handkerchief to dab her cheeks. A pair of moist blue eyes stared into hers. 'I wonder if you could help me,' she sniffed. 'I don't think Ben realises that these children are my life. With Fay gone they're all I've got.'

Carol felt an unexpected wave of sympathy. This woman might be lonely but she had never seen her other than in full command of every situation.

'If things had been different the children would've been with me all the time in my home.'

What an extraordinary thing to say. Had she been fantasising about Ben being killed as well, leaving the children orphaned?

Carol's brow furrowed and Julia added, 'Didn't you know? After Fay died I offered the children a home so Ben would be able to get on with his work. But he refused.'

Allow the children to live with her? That was the last thing Ben would have wanted. Carol opened her mouth then closed it again. This was a minefield. Whatever she said could be misconstrued.

'At that time the children were in a terrible state. Each month it seemed they had a new person looking after them.' Julia gave an expression of disgust. 'I use the words "looking after" in the broadest sense. You should have seen what the children looked like. Ragamuffins. Once I had to give Katerina a bath, she was so grubby. And their clothes! Buttons hanging off, hems down, in a dreadful condition.'

Apparently the last straw came with a new nanny who was a university graduate. Ben had actually allowed her to see the girl's CV.

'Trying to impress me, I suppose.' Julia pursed her lips. 'I happened to be with all of them when Katerina said one of her first words. It was "Homer". I was thrilled because I deduced that the nanny's classical education was having some effect and I said as much. Well, I believe in praising staff when they do good work. But it appeared that "Homer" was some character in a cartoon series.' Julia's expression was glacial. 'Ben laughed with the rest but it was clear to me that the nanny used to plonk the children in front of the television whenever it suited her. I could not allow my beloved grandchildren to be brought up in this way by an irresponsible father. That, my dear, is why I was considering taking them away to live with me.'

Ben had never mentioned this. Luckily Julia was the kind of woman used to talking at people rather than with them and appeared not to notice Carol's lack of response.

'Of course their father would've been able to see them whenever he wished.' Julia was unstoppable. 'I had no intention of keeping them from him at such a terrible time but he had no one to look after them. What would any concerned grandmother have done? I felt I had no choice. He was working the same stupid hours he always does and he had a succession of child-minders from who knows where. I, on the other hand, had all the facilities these children needed and a full-time carer around. We were all set to go to court and then, out of the blue, he came along and said he was getting married.'

Carol kept her expression neutral, though inwardly she felt as if someone had twisted her insides. Julia was telling her that Ben had been in a hurry to find someone to mind his children.

'As soon as Ben told us he was going to get married again my solicitor said it was no use going on with the custody battle. I'd just be throwing my money away. I've tried every which way I can to have more time with my grandchildren. My pleas have fallen on deaf ears as far as Ben is concerned so I thought I'd ask you to intercede, woman to woman.'

Ben had proposed to her to block a custody battle with his mother-in-law?

Carol's attention was diverted momentarily by a forest of hands frantically waving as the three children linked bodies to catapult down the slide. Julia gave them a cheery smile and instinctively Carol decided that whatever her thoughts about Ben it would be unwise to ask questions. She would not give this woman ammunition to use against him. Where the children's welfare was concerned they had to present a united front. If there was something in this custody thing she would prefer to have it out with her husband when they were alone.

She bent over to gather up her handbag. 'I'm sorry, Julia, but as their father, Ben has the final say about what they can do. I can't help you.'

Julia put the handkerchief away. 'You mean you won't. You know,' she continued conversationally, 'it was the last straw when Fay found out about that Caitlin woman. She phoned to tell me. The poor darling was quite demented but I had no idea she was going out in the car. In the state she was in she couldn't have concentrated on driving. But if Fay had lived she planned to leave him so you see, Ben would've lost custody of the children anyway.'

Carol stood up. 'Sorry, I have to go. I'll pick the children up at five.' Without a backward glance she sought the refuge of her car, where she sat frozen, trying to come to terms with what she had just heard.

Thank God Ben wouldn't be home until the early hours when his Sunday newspaper was put to bed. She couldn't face him until she'd thought things through more carefully. She was inclined to think Julia was exaggerating but why should she be trying to stir up trouble now? Ben had made no secret that the children were part of the package when he proposed, so why should she be troubled by the idea that Julia's possible threat had catapulted him into a decision? The children were and remained a major part of his life but he could have had anyone he liked to look after them. He had chosen her because he loved her, hadn't he?

Even through her delight at his proposal she had queried the suddenness of it and she could still remember his answer: 'The children were my first concern and I had to be sure that they liked you as much as I do.' Liked! In the excitement of the moment she had not dwelt on the exact words. But now it came to her clearly. He had not said 'loved' but she had never had reason to dwell upon the phrase until now.

An unpleasant thought reared its head. If she had turned him down, how long would it have taken him to find a replacement? But no, she remembered his expression when he was asking her to share his life. He couldn't be such a great actor, could he? She didn't think he was capable of such deception. Still, it wasn't a good feeling to learn that Ben might have another secret. Over the years he should have found some way of telling her about the custody threat.

Did he or did he not love her? She was having the turbulent thoughts of a teenager. These were questions that used to plague her in her early days of romancing, long before she'd met Ben. And here she was, a mature woman, married for seven years, asking herself the same questions. It was pathetic.

Steady on, she thought. Even if his proposal had been precipitated by the threat of the court action, surely they had shared too much by now for their marriage to be a sham. He wasn't overly demonstrative but every so often he would look across at her, always at unexpected moments, like when they were in the middle of working in their small garden, and say, 'What a lucky day it was when I met you.'

Carol pulled up at a red light to find she had been driving on automatic pilot. Instead of taking the turning to home she found herself only a quarter of a mile away from Lisa's house. This was a day when she would be putting her feet up, having a cup of tea. Jolly Good Food was strictly a Monday to Friday operation. The business made enough money to keep the weekend sacrosanct so Lisa could have some semblance of private life, although what private life was a moot point since the departure of her lover six months ago.

Carol had been in the habit of listening to Lisa's woes more than talking about her own, which mostly concerned the children. This was the first time she'd faced a serious problem between herself and Ben and she wasn't sure how much she wanted to confide. But only seconds after Lisa had led her into the hallway she felt the tears prickle behind her lids and was about to launch into the whole story when to her dismay she heard the strident tones of Andrea from the living room.

'What's up, mate? You look like a wet weekend in Wagga Wagga.' Andrea was sitting in the biggest armchair, legs slung over the side, one encased in plaster.

Carol hung back. She didn't feel strong enough to put on an act and turned back towards the door. But Lisa restrained her and whispered that Andrea would not be staying long.

Andrea dominated the conversation, moaning about the bloody accident which had ruined her life. Apparently the Brunei expedition organiser had been devastated to learn she had lost her key member, the team's cook, and had begged Andrea to try and help them find a replacement until she was well enough to travel to base camp. She tried to persuade Lisa to let her have the freelance staff list so that she could ring round and see who might like a jungle adventure but Lisa gave her short shrift.

'It's taken me years to train that lot. I'm not having them enticed away.'

Andrea guffawed. 'What about you, Carol?'

'What a good idea.' Carol smiled for the first time that afternoon. 'I can ditch my husband, three children, my job, the house, the residents' association, the PTA. Easy. I don't think anybody would notice I was gone.'

'It's not for a year, it's just for a few weeks, until I can get back on my feet. What about it?'

'I can't bear humidity.'

'Not a problem under those trees.'

'I don't like creepy crawlies.'

'They run from you.'

'I have sensitive skin.'

'They give you cream for that.'

Carol grinned. 'Andrea, give up.'

The Australian struggled to her feet. 'You'll never get a chance like this again.'

'Thank God,' said Lisa and Carol in unison.

Once they had seen Andrea safely through the door, Lisa took her friend's arm and walked her back to the sitting room. 'Are you going to tell me what's happened?'

Carol stood up and walked to the window to stare out over the cul-de-sac. She watched an old lady try to curb her exuberant terrier and a young mother, two children dancing round her heels, obviously dressed up for a party, climb into their station wagon. From far way she heard her own voice.

'I don't know if I'm making too much of this but I've just found out that Julia and Ben had a fight over the custody of the children. She only backed down when we got married.' She looked round at Lisa's uncomprehending face. 'Don't you see? That's why he married me in such a hurry. He needed a nanny.'

'That's just dramatic nonsense,' Lisa exploded. 'He's never made any secret that it was important for the kids to have a mother. He was looking for one and he chose you. But he would never have married you if he didn't love you.' She crossed to a side table bearing an assortment of drinks and began to pour two large glasses of red wine. 'D'you fancy a joint?'

Carol shook her head. 'You know I don't touch the stuff.'

'OK, I just thought you could use one.' Lisa took a deep gulp at her glass. 'Ben probably didn't tell you about the Julia thing because he never took it seriously. The old bag wouldn't have stood a chance of taking the children away from their father. It's not as if he was mental or a drunk or something. She's trying to make trouble between you two. Don't let her succeed.'

Carol was about to wave away the glass when Lisa insisted. 'You need this,' she said and handed her the wine. 'You amaze me. You've been married to Ben for what, seven years? And you're still twitching about his reasons for marrying you.'

'Maybe, but after what's gone on this week I don't think I know him.'

'What do you mean?'

'This isn't the only thing he's kept from me.'

Lisa's eyes grew wider as she heard about the anonymous phone caller and the allegations about Ben. 'He let me believe he had a happy marriage,' said Carol, 'when for two years he was having an affair with this woman Caitlin. But what's really getting to me is that the caller was positive the leopard hadn't changed his spots and that Ben was still screwing around.'

'I don't believe it,' said Lisa stoutly. 'Ben is very much a family man and after what happened to Fay I can't see him jeopardising his second marriage.'

Carol took little comfort from this and stared moodily at her reflection in the window. 'The caller's achieved this much. I won't be able to take anything for granted now. I might've been able to handle what Julia told me if my faith in Ben hadn't already been shaken.' She turned round, her face beginning to crumple. 'What you probably don't realise is that I've never felt completely confident about Ben, even now. He meets such interesting people and I feel dull by comparison and whenever I'm out with him I imagine people are wondering what he sees in me.'

'What rubbish,' Lisa snorted. 'You've a great body, amazing hair, you're a striking-looking woman.'

'Funny-looking, you mean.'

'Don't run yourself down,' said Lisa who had always thought that Carol had the kind of features that a seventeenth-century Italian painter would have found attractive, though it was true she had a stronger jaw line than was acceptable in these days of bland baby-faced female news readers. And though she moaned constantly about her straight, heavy hair, everyone in the kitchen would gladly swap.

'You're good for him and he's smart enough to know that.'

'Yes, I'm good enough to look after his children and his home but what else? According to Julia, not much more.'

'Steady on, Carol. You're going down a very dangerous path.' Lisa's tone was gentle. 'Look, you can let this maggot eat into you and destroy what you and Ben have or you can judge him by his actions. He needs you as a haven to come home to.'

Carol surprised herself. 'There must be more to a marriage than that.'

Chapter Six

Sunday brunch was the best meal of the week according to the children because eggs, bacon and all the trimmings were their favourite food in all the world. Carol thought it might be because they also had their father's undivided attention.

She prided herself on serving the full English grilled fest, plus extras like organic sausages, wild mushrooms and hot croissants. Becky, miserly with compliments where her family was concerned, had been overheard to say that 'Carol serves the best brunch ever.' And she took some trouble with the look of the table, giving each child in turn the task of choosing the colour for the linen and arranging the centrepiece of seasonal flowers.

It had been easy to avoid mentioning her conversation with Julia. When Ben finally came to bed in the early hours after putting the political section to press, he touched her shoulder but she feigned sleep and soon heard the soft sonorous sound of his breathing. She stared at the ceiling and it occurred to her that much of what they talked about was who would pick up the wine, when he would be back for supper or what time they had to be somewhere. Perhaps she had always been fooling herself that they were well suited.

It was in this mood that she served the brunch. Ben usually slept until almost noon on Sundays and was woken up unceremoniously by three lively youngsters jumping on his slumbering body. Sometimes they did not give him time to dress but this morning he'd managed a quick shower and arrived in the kitchen freshly shaved and wearing jeans with the linen shirt Carol had picked out on their last holiday in North Wales. It had been a surprising find in a gloomy shop where they'd sheltered during a particularly heavy downpour. Ben asked each child in turn what she'd been up to and Carol's heart ached as she watched him bend his head towards Katie telling him of her triumph at playing the piano for school assembly. She caught him looking at her quizzically once or twice and she made a great effort to appear cheerful.

'Who wants to hear a joke?' asked Ben.

'Me, me,' shouted Katie and Emmy together and though Becky made a poor pretence of looking skywards, like the others she craned forward.

'You'll laugh at this one,' Ben began, as he always did.

'No we won't,' grinned Emmy. Ben's so-called funny stories were usually atrocious.

'A woman gives birth to twins and her husband's supposed to go and register their names but he asks her brother to do it instead. And when she finds out she says, "Oh no, my brother's an idiot. What name did he give my baby girl?" "Denise," says the husband. The woman is very impressed. "That's a really nice name. What did he name the boy?" "De-nephew."'

Emmy put her face in her hands, Becky threw a napkin at her father and Katie groaned. Thoroughly satisfied at their response, Ben appealed to his wife. 'You liked that one, didn't you?' And she smiled and said it was quite up to standard.

He stood up. 'Let's clear this stuff away quickly and get to the park. Darling, go and have a sit-down with the papers, I'll sort out these little monsters.'

Battersea Park, serving a wide cross-section of the community, from eggheads to jocks, made an effort to cater for everyone. Football, baseball, basketball and tennis leagues were in evidence at weekends and the well-attended concert complex usually had performances for all tastes, some geared to children. Being a fine spring day they opted for a game of rounders, which attracted a few other players, and by the time the Mitchell children went home they were rosy-cheeked from their exertions in the fresh air.

For once there was no protracted bedtime as the two younger children were worn out by their exertions, and Becky went to listen to music with a friend. Quiet descended on the house.

'Well, Mrs Mitchell, what shall we do tonight? Dancing at the Savoy? Hit the casino? Or would you prefer a night in front of the box?' This was a familiar verbal routine and it always amused her. As he sat down next to her on the sofa, instinctively she reached out for his hand. He was sitting back, seemingly quite relaxed, looking at the screen, an amiable expression on his face, but for the first time she became aware there was no answering response. His hand lay comfortably enough in hers but it was passive. His eyes and attention remained focused on the television and she realised with a start that this was how it usually was. Too often she was the one who initiated any tactile contact between them.

As she gazed blankly at the screen, snapshots formed in her mind of their life together. Ben praised her constantly for her cooking skills, for the way she handled the children. Occasionally he complimented her on her appearance, but try as she might she could not remember when he had last given her a bear hug or one of those long, slow, wet kisses. She used to think that well-married couples didn't do that after the first flush of courtship. And had it worried her? Not particularly. Ben's lovemaking, though perfunctory these days, was satisfying enough. He always ensured she had an orgasm, which was more than most men did, according to her friends.

She had long accepted that he was not as physically demonstrative as she was and until now it had not bothered her. Life was too crammed with organising the day-to-day activities of three young children and a fairly big house to allow time for navel-gazing. Once again she looked at their hands, her fingers intertwined in his, not the other way round. That summed up their marriage really; she was like an eager puppy, the supplicant, she supposed, while Ben lay back and received the affection happily.

She had convinced herself that if she tried to please him, looked after the children well, fed him well and kept herself trim she would have a happy marriage. And she had. Until the phone call and Julia's unwelcome news about the custody threat. Had she been inveigled into playing the happy housewife and mother? Why really had Ben, handsomest man in the office, respected political commentator, chosen her? Maybe now was the time to find out.

On impulse she leaned over, took the remote control from his hand and switched off the television. Ben gave an exclamation of annoyance. 'I was watching that.'

She ignored this, and without preamble told him about her conversation with Julia, nervousness making her sound aggressive.

Ben stared at her with an expression of bewilderment. 'I didn't tell you about the custody because I didn't take it seriously. It wasn't relevant to us.' His voice was matter-of-fact.

'Wasn't it? At the very time you were battling with Julia over the kids you asked me to marry you. I'd say that was relevant.'

He frowned. 'Julia doesn't like me. She'll always put the wrong connotation on anything to do with me.' His eyes never left her face and although she scrutinised him carefully she could detect no sign of guilt.

'Look, in the time we'd been seeing each other you'd never mentioned marriage,' she said, conscious she was hurrying her words. 'Then I discover that your proposal came at the very time Julia was threatening to take you to court. What am I to believe?'

'I asked you to marry me because I wanted to. Of course the children were involved. I made no secret of that. I needed to know they approved.'

'But Julia said—'

'After seven years with me you'd rather listen to that woman?' he interrupted wearily. 'I find that depressing.'

Carol's throat began to close up and she willed herself to sound steady. That was one of her biggest problems. She had never been able to argue coherently without the threat of breaking down. Ben, on the other hand, used to the cut and thrust of office politics, did not suffer from the same drawback. How had he managed so promptly to get her on the defensive? All she wanted was for him to say he married her because he loved her and so far he had not done that.

'I'm sorry about that, but just for once try and think of it from my point of view. After that phone call, Julia's revelation is the last straw.'

His voice rose. 'You're not still thinking about that, are you? You said you believed me.'

'I did. I do. But how do you expect me to react when you keep so much from me? You could have a secret life with a mistress. I wouldn't know.'

He gave a deep sigh and took her hand, gripping it tightly. 'Carol, all the things you're complaining about were in my past. I wanted a new start with you and the kids. That's why I avoided talking about anything to do with Fay.'

'If you'd been more open with me then maybe I wouldn't have been so insecure, always feeling that I was in her shadow, that you would've been happier with her than with me.' Why the hell couldn't he say now that he loved her, that he couldn't live without her, they would be together for ever, corny things which she needed to hear right then?

'You know the truth now, doesn't it make you feel better?'

It didn't but what good would it do to say so? Tentatively, she nodded and he drew her towards him. 'I don't want us to fight. I'm happy with you. Aren't you happy with me?'

'Yes, but since the phone call I've started to question things.' As soon as the words had left her mouth she regretted them for he gave a tut of exasperation and the benign mood between them evaporated.

Ben went to the drinks cabinet and poured himself a large Scotch. Carol had gone to bed and it had taken all his self-control not to let his displeasure show. Initially he had been sympathetic towards her, understanding how she would feel listening to that stream of poisonous allegations from an anonymous caller. He had hoped that by now he would have had information about the call so he could track down the perpetrator but his contacts had urged patience, saying it was an incredibly difficult task to isolate one call from the thousands made in the south London area. He hoped he would not have to wait too long. But it irritated him that she was prepared to take the word of anybody who bad-mouthed him rather than believe him.

The whisky tasted bitter and he added a dash of water, swirling the mixture round in his glass. God, that phone call had been bad luck. Carol had given every appearance of being happy until that pack of lies had stirred her up. He paused. Well, most of it was a pack of lies. His zipper had been well and truly shut since he'd met Carol although he had to admit that last week he had been tempted. Any man would have been. His dinner companion had been looking exceptionally sexy but he had been strong-willed. Made his excuses and left, as they say.

Julia's spiteful disclosure too, contained an element of truth. He had not taken her silly threat of trying for custody seriously but it had prompted him to sort out his life. Carol was eminently suitable and the children liked her. To that extent Julia was right. He had put the needs of his children above his own. After the chaos of the temporary nannies, what Carol provided was the kind of well-ordered home background he needed. She suited him damn well. The two of them had jogged along pretty happily and if his pulse didn't race when he was due to see her then what the hell. After seven years of marriage, who could still expect fireworks?

He had always known Carol loved him more than he loved her. But didn't there always have to be one in the marriage who was in control? He had tried not to take advantage of that, although Carol and the girls made it clear he was the focal point of their lives. If he had a regret it was that he found it difficult to be as spontaneously demonstrative with his wife as he was with his children. Adversity had forged an intense bond with his kids, something Carol, however sensitive, couldn't fully share.

He toyed with the idea of having a second drink but decided against it. Tomorrow he would try and make amends. Once they'd packed off the children maybe he could take her out of London and have lunch in a country pub.

In the event, Ben's good intentions came to nothing. He was woken early by a summons from his editor with the news of a surprise resignation from the government. Ben had the coveted home number of the beleaguered politician and was expected to pull out the stops for an exclusive interview for the daily paper in the group.

Chapter Seven

By the time Carol arrived at Jolly Good Food she felt as if she'd already done a day's work but being amongst a group of light-hearted, gossiping women was such a contrast she did not regard it as a regular job.

It had taken her many months at Jolly Good Food to become accustomed to the intimate way the women in the company talked about things. They seemed to have no inhibitions, discussing their lives from every angle, emotional, aspirational and gynaecological. She grinned remembering Andrea's first comment when she heard that Carol was trying to have a baby. 'Aw,' Carol had noticed that Australians always seemed to start their sentences with this peculiar sound, 'my ma says there's nothing to it. Get him to shove it in and afterwards you stick your legs into the air and stay like that.' When Carol laughingly protested it wouldn't present a pretty picture, Andrea retorted, 'What do you want, mate, glamour or a kid?'

Today, however, when she arrived at work the atmosphere in the kitchen was tense and there was none of the usual banter. Lisa had received a last-minute summons from an important client. Unexpected visitors from Munich were coming to inspect the company for a possible friendly take-over. For Lisa's small business it would mean a longer and more lucrative contract, the difference between jogging along and making a decent profit. She was determined to impress with an imaginative and delicious lunch for what they had been warned were hearty German appetites. And that was in addition to fulfilling the other orders.

When she wasn't helping with the massive amount of chopping needed for the giant casseroles or filling pastry cases for a sixtieth anniversary party, Carol stood in front of the cooker keeping an eye on a wayward sauce, which was threatening to curdle. With no time for breaks, Carol and the other helpers produced more servings from that kitchen than ever before. Afterwards, looking at their drained faces, Lisa said quietly,

'Thanks. That was a good team effort and you'll see your reward in this month's pay packet. Now go home and put your feet up, there's another busy day ahead tomorrow.'

Put her feet up? Chance would be a fine thing, thought Carol as she trundled the loaded trolley down the supermarket aisle so rapidly that sparks almost flew from the wheels. The weekly order of groceries for the Mitchell household seemed to last a shorter time these days. To make matters worse the car urgently needed petrol and the local petrol station would have to choose this time of day to have its forecourt dug up, wouldn't it? She waited impatiently in the line of cars waiting to fill up and when finally she arrived at the school gates to pick up the two youngest children, she was harassed and late.

'We've been waiting aaaages,' wailed Katie.

'Shut up,' snapped Emmy, 'don't be such a baby.'

'Don't talk to your sister like that,' said Carol automatically and snapped the safety belt shut around Katie's plump tummy. 'I'm sorry I was a little late,' she added before shifting gears and moving away. 'Did you have a good day at school?'

'I won a gold star for reading,' shouted Katie.

'I had a horrible day.'

'Good work, Katie. Why was it so horrible, Emmy?'

'Louise isn't talking to me.'

'Oh well, best friends never stay cross for long.'

'Louise's mother says you shouldn't have taken so many of us in the car at my party. It was dangerous. She said it was a wonder we weren't all killed.'

Carol gave a startled glance at Emmy through the rear-view mirror. For the child's twelfth birthday last month she'd dreamed up an idea she thought would amuse her daughter. Instead of throwing the usual kind of kid's party she had borrowed a friend's car and had what they'd afterwards named the squashed mini outing. Six, or was it seven, guests were piled inside the car sitting on top of one another, with her in the driving seat. They'd all been given a birthday box comprising items such as a toy horn, a balloon and a party hat. It had been a hilarious occasion with the children giggling, pressed tightly together, tooting their horns and trying though failing to blow up balloons with mouths creased with laughter. And just to make things more exciting Carol had driven them around the block. Once. At five miles per hour. Then they'd cut the cake inside the car and when they'd washed it down with lemonade, they played a succession of sitting down entertainment and a few card games. Emmy's birthday celebrations had been a tremendous success, described endlessly in the playground afterwards and apparently exciting the envy of many who were not there.

'Maybe if I'd driven in traffic it wouldn't have been safe,' said Carol, 'but the road was empty. And you loved that party, you told me so.'

'I didn't know it was dangerous,' Emmy muttered. 'I wish we hadn't had it now. Louise says she's not going to be allowed to play with me again.'

Carol shifted into second gear and indicated left as she steered the car around the corner and then into their narrow drive. 'That's just silly talk.'

'It's not silly. It's all your fault.'

'It's not Mummy's fault,' shouted Katie.

'Yes it is.'

''Snot.'

'Stop it, you two, and help bring in the shopping.'

The day continued to deteriorate. Becky returned from gym club without her new, expensive pair of trainers. She 'thought' she could've left them in her friend's mum's car. Or at school, or at the club. Carol tried to track them down. The trainers were not at the school, nor at the gym, and while waiting for Becky's friend's mother to arrive home, she tried to assure Emmy that her best friend would make up their quarrel the following day. Nothing would placate Emmy but for her to phone Louise's mother. After hearing what actually happened at the party, the woman apologised. She had been given a different sequence of events in which the children had been 'driven miles, very fast.'

When she tried to reach Becky's friend, the number had been changed, all of which she would not have minded had Becky shown the slightest interest in the proceedings.

The eldest girl was becoming bolshy towards her, usually when her father wasn't around. Hormones, everyone told her, but the problem was she was influencing the two younger ones who until then had given little trouble. Perhaps, Carol mused, she reined in her irritation too much so that when she let rip she sounded worse than she felt. Bottling everything up was making her feel resentful towards the kid. She wondered how a birth mother would react in these circumstances. Not having been one yet she didn't know, though friends with teenage children told her to grit her teeth and sit it out for four or five years. A great help.

The teenager's indifference, coming on top of the problems with Emmy, made her see red. 'It'll serve you right if we can't get them back. You're becoming a spoiled young miss. You don't know how lucky you are.'

'Yes I'm very lucky, when my real mother was killed in a car crash,' shouted Becky and rushed upstairs and slammed her bedroom door.

Carol sat down, her head in her hands. This was the first time for years that Fay's name had been mentioned. She gave a hefty sigh. Who'd be a stepmother? However supportive Ben was of her decisions she never really felt she had the last word in the discipline department. Once or twice she had caught Becky pleading with her father to countermand her wishes. To his credit Ben always took his wife's part, even when he told her later he thought she might have acted differently.

Although it had been over a week since the anonymous call, whenever the phone rang, as it did just then, Carol's heart would still beat uncomfortably. Her hand hovered over the receiver while she chided herself for her timidity. It was Alison Taylor, wife of the features editor on the newspaper and one of Ben's closest colleagues.

'Hello, stranger.'

With a pang Carol remembered she had not fixed up the promised return supper party and began to make her apologies but these were brushed aside as Alison asked if she and Ben were free that night. And yes, she did realise it was last minute, but this was a top screenwriter from Los Angeles whom she and Ben would enjoy meeting. He was witty, charming and indiscreet, with access to the best Hollywood gossip. Unfortunately tonight was the only time he was free. 'Let the guys make an effort for us,' was Alison's rallying call. 'It'd make a great change, wouldn't it?'

Carol said she would ring back once she had contacted Ben. He had mentioned something about not being home for supper but as they had been stiff with each other she had not asked questions.

'Don't let him put you off because of that damn paper,' said Alison. 'It's time we winkled them out of the office.' This was a constant refrain between them and Carol had found her a useful ally in the past.

It had been ages since she and Ben had been out together as a grown-up couple rather than as parents, and the evening sounded as though it could be fun. A dinner party in which she listened to stimulating company would help her relax and maybe help build bridges between them.

Ben's direct line was answered by his long-standing secretary, who volunteered to look in his diary but came back with the news that Ben had a dinner already booked in at Fontana's.

Mindful of Alison's instructions, she asked, 'Is it anything he can cancel?' She was keen enough on the dinner to plough on. 'I'd really like him to get out of it if at all possible. How important is it?'

The secretary told her that this was a meeting with the boss of a lobby company and she wasn't sure if they could switch nights. 'But if you like, I could ring Caitlin's office and find out.'

Caitlin. It was the second time she had heard the name in a few days. It was such an unusual name, it couldn't be a coincidence, could it? A chill began to creep over her body.

She couldn't trust herself to say anything but her silence was rewarded by the secretary volunteering that Ben's dinner engagement was with clients of Caitlin Thomas Communications. She had given him the tip-off for a couple of terrific exclusives in the last six months. 'They're old mates,' the secretary went on cheerily. 'I believe they worked on the same paper years ago. Carol? Carol, are you still there?'

In a daze Carol said please not to bother, it wasn't important, then made her goodbyes and put down the phone.

It was the same woman. It must be. That was why the caller phoned. Ben was still having an affair with her.

Chapter Eight

Caitlin Thomas snapped on the light and looked around her empty flat. She had tried everything in her armoury to get Ben here. At dinner last week she had even gone as far as brushing her breasts against his arm, to no avail. So far.

She was certain he had been aroused by her but not enough, it seemed, to accept her offer of a nightcap. Pity. If just once she could take him to her bed and re-create the memorable sex they'd once enjoyed, he would be hers. She'd had several affairs since Ben but no other man had the capacity to overwhelm her, make her forget about everything. Nor, since him, had she experienced such intense orgasms.

It had been a two-year affair which, as far as she was concerned, had grown into something much more. True, Ben had never declared himself, his loyalty would not allow that, but no man could make love to her the way he did out of pure lust. Not only were their bodies attuned; Caitlin knew how he thought and they had spent hours plotting his progress up the ladder. It was no coincidence he had been head-hunted by the Sunday newspaper for which he now worked.

She had been hoping he would leave his wife when the bloody woman went and got herself killed. Though they hardly ever discussed his marriage, someone like him would never stray if he were happy at home. Once Ben found out it was Caitlin's husband who'd blown the whistle on their affair to Fay, his guilt put an end to any hopes Caitlin might have entertained about a future together. 'Every time I looked at you I'd be reminded that Fay would still be here if only . . .' he'd said at their last meeting. 'It's not your fault, it's mine, but last night . . .' He'd looked away but not before she'd seen he was close to tears. 'Last night Becky was crying so hard I had to sit comforting her for hours.'

She had never pleaded with a man before but that night she made a fool of herself, trying to persuade him that time was all they needed, that he would see things differently when everything settled down. She could see he was slipping away from her and despite her entreaties he had been firm.

'I'm sorry, Caitlin, I have to think of the kids now.'

She could fight another woman, but she was powerless against three small children.

She wandered into the bedroom, pleased she had employed a professional decorator to help her with the colour schemes. The flat was tiny, part of a converted stable block, but its chief merit was that it was in the centre of Covent Garden, around the corner from the Royal Opera House. She had persuaded her accountant that her newly-prosperous company needed a base in town to put up visiting American clients. But more often than not it was she who was the main beneficiary. The accountant had given her a sly look which implied he well understood what her motives were but like all good financial advisers, what was not talked about was not official and had not happened.

The move to Washington had been traumatic. Her husband insisted on going with her. After breaking up the affair between her and Ben he pleaded for their marriage to be given another chance, assuring her that once they were in a new environment things would be better between them. 'I'll look after you, like I always have. We were happy once. We can be again.' In her low state she had allowed herself to be persuaded. But how could it have stood any chance when Ben still occupied her every thought? Within a year they were divorced.

Now she had returned to London, wealthy, successful, and after eight years was curious to know whether her feelings for Ben were still as intense. Over the years she had been preoccupied in building her international lobbying company and thoughts of Ben still surfaced now and then. When she heard about his re-marriage she had retired to bed nursing a bottle of brandy, all hopes of ever building a life with him dashed.

And when her partner suggested it would be a smart move to establish a London office to service their American clients she had volunteered to set it up, not, she told herself, because of Ben but because there was nothing to keep her in America.

Employing the 'can do' skills she had honed in America she discovered from the maître d' of Shepherd's, the restaurant frequented by Westminster politicos and their groupies, when Mr Mitchell would next be dining there. Then she arranged 'by accident' to be seated at the next table.

Caitlin had been thrilled at his reaction to seeing her again. He'd been surprised, yes, but there was delight as well. After their respective guests had left, it was inevitable the two of them would join up for coffee and brandy and they spent a happy half hour exchanging news on what had happened in the intervening years. She was not a skilful interviewer for nothing and hurriedly skipped over his rise through the ranks to political editor to focus on more personal matters.

It was what he didn't say about his wife and their marriage that set her thinking that all was not lost. A man who was in love did not describe the woman in his life as 'really great with the kids', 'a genuinely nice person', and, God help her, 'peaceful to live with'. Caitlin would've expected him to enthuse about his wife's warmth, talents, her capacity to enliven his life, but there was none of that. Where was the passion, the admiration for her appearance, the appreciation of the vital spark which ignited their marriage? Great with the kids? He made her sound like a child-minder.

It wasn't good enough. And when a marriage was based on qualities other than love and lust it must flounder, sooner rather than later. She was about to turn forty and what she wanted more than anything in the world was to be Ben's wife, living in the country, with their family. Tonight would be their fourth meeting and she had never felt so alive. The spark between them was as strong as ever. Surely he was as aware of it as she was?

As she began to stroke cleansing lotion across her jaw line Caitlin studied her face dispassionately. She was forever grateful for inheriting something which drew men to her side, call it charisma, sex appeal, whatever. To her the face was not particularly beautiful. Her nose was a shade too long, the jaw a little too strong. Undoubtedly the best thing about her face were her eyes. Large and rounded, they blazed with violet light. Now, as she aged, not quite so burning bright, she thought, carefully wiping a tissue in the circular movements so favoured by top New York beauticians. Her ex-husband had been very supportive after the facial nips and tucks and if truth be told she missed having him as 'the wife'. He had been unable to find suitable employment in Washington and had opted to take on the management of their smart penthouse flat and organise the extensive networking dinner parties essential in that city.

She missed his skills and did not begrudge the alimony she was paying. He had done well in the divorce settlement and, on her money, preferred life over there, even without her.

Foolishly, Caitlin had told him the baby she was carrying was his. Only a DNA test taken during the dying days of the marriage, when the child was less than a year old, showing a ninety-nine per cent probability that he was not the father, convinced him.

It was Ben's child, of course.

Chapter Nine

Carol sat down, her hand still on the phone, the name echoing in her brain.

Caitlin.

All those protestations of innocence, Ben's brown eyes staring with such sincerity into hers, fooling her completely. Could she know so little about her own husband? It didn't tie in with the Ben she thought she was married to but the doubts persisted. Every time she tackled him with something, he would tell her just enough to calm her down, but never the entire story. He'd had plenty of opportunity, after the phone call, after their discussions about Julia, to mention Caitlin. If their association was innocent, why wouldn't he?

She rang Alison to say the newspaper had beaten her and Ben wouldn't be free for supper. Feeling forlorn she began to get ready to go to work. Even in this frame of mind she did not feel she could cry off today, knowing how much Lisa depended on her. As she banged the front door she reflected how her life had been built on putting herself last.

Carol thought her face must be reflecting her gloom for as she walked in the door Lisa suggested they have a coffee in her tiny office, tucked into a disused corridor. But she was mistaken. Lisa, an ardent user of dating agencies, wanted to regale her with the frightening story of her previous night's encounter.

Apparently the evening had started well enough, with Lisa thinking that for once she was meeting an equal. He had picked an upmarket wine bar frequented by people in the City. Lisa was familiar with the area as it had been her place of employment for some years. Trying to recognise the blind date was always somewhat awkward but not in this case. He had described himself quite well (unusually, since most added several inches to their height or subtracted years from their age) and she gained a favourable impression. Educated, presentable, with a well-paid job, he was attentive, laughing at her jokes in the right places. She began settling in to enjoy herself. But after only two, albeit large, glasses of wine his conversation began to be interspersed with risqué remarks bordering on the obscene. He didn't seem to notice that these did not amuse her. Then he moved his chair so they sat next to one another instead of opposite and ran his forefinger down her bare arm telling her she looked 'hot' and why didn't they forget dinner and go to a little hotel he knew around the corner.

'I got up to leave and, would you believe it, this made him furious. He started shouting, ranting on about how I was leading him on, calling me a prick teaser. In front of everyone. It was horrible. Thank God I was able to get to the car in time otherwise who knows what would've happened.' She leaned back on her chair and gave a heavy sigh. 'I've got to stop doing this.'

'I'm not sure dating agencies are the answer.'

Lisa's eyes flashed with anger. 'God, you married people irritate me. You're so smug.' Carol started to apologise but Lisa cut her off. 'Forget it, it's not your fault I'm being prickly. What's good about these agencies is that they bring together people who want to cut the dating crap because they're ready for a relationship. That's when it works. The bad thing is that at the back of one's mind there's always the question, "why does he have to do this?" And he's probably thinking the same.' She gave Carol an almost impish glance. 'But I have to take a chance. Who knows, I might meet someone like your Ben.'

Carol gave her a somewhat jaundiced gaze. 'I'm not so sure you would. I found out another secret my husband hasn't bothered telling me about.'

But Carol's story that she feared Ben was still involved with his former mistress did not have the reaction she'd expected. She'd anticipated her friend would be furious on her behalf. Instead, while agreeing it looked bad, Lisa cautiously suggested she wait to hear Ben's version of events before immediately leaping to conclusions. 'What proof do you have? If he were having an affair with this woman, would he be dumb enough to write her name in his office diary? Would he take her to – what was the restaurant?'

'Fontana's.'

'One of the places where he's pretty damn sure to bump into somebody he knows? Even I know the head chef there.'

Her words did not provide any comfort. 'Lisa, why didn't he tell me about her after that call? He admitted they had an affair so why couldn't he say he'd met her again? Why not, if it was purely business?'

Lisa snorted. 'Are you kidding? What man in his right mind would tell his wife he was meeting an old flame? Especially the one who was around when his wife died.'

Still Carol was not convinced. 'I have the feeling he's not being straight with me. How can we go on like that?'

'You're sure it's the same Caitlin?' asked Lisa.

Carol nodded emphatically.

Lisa pondered briefly. 'You know what would convince you there was nothing going on? If you could see them together, then you'd know.'

'That's impossible. In any case, Ben seems to be good at putting on an act.'

Lisa clicked her fingers. 'Why don't we gatecrash their dinner?'

Carol was aghast. 'I couldn't. I'd hate that more than anything.'

'Not if they didn't know we were there.'

Carol was sitting with her shoulders hunched. 'It wouldn't work.'

'Yes, it could. Don't look like that. I told you I know the chef. Why don't I ask him if there's a discreet place where we could tuck ourselves away? See them without them spotting us? Before you say anything, let me see if it's possible and then you can make up your mind.'

When Carol protested she could not possibly spy on her husband, she would prefer to have it out with him at home, Lisa pointed out that Ben could wrap her round his little finger. She would never be sure whether or not he was holding back the truth. Carol was inclined to agree.

To Carol's dismay the chef proved perfectly amiable, agreeing instantly that the two women could spend some of that evening watching how Fontana's operated. Why wouldn't he? Showing the ropes to trainee restaurateurs was part of his obligation to the business and Lisa had sent him several clients over the years. Having discovered that the ever amiable Mrs Porter from next door would be free to baby-sit, Carol went along with Lisa's plan. Rather than tackle Ben about it first, she hoped Lisa's theory that he would hardly conduct an affair with such bravado in public would turn out to be correct. But even if it were purely a business dinner, surely he was taking a chance meeting up with an old flame? It was eight years ago but he could hardly look at her and forget they had made love, could he? Despite her misgivings, Carol could not resist the chance to see for herself what was going on between her husband and this woman.

Nevertheless it was with a distinct feeling of being disloyal that she met the chef and, pulse racing, watched as Lisa asked idly if she could check the bookings for that evening, 'just to get an idea of numbers and groupings.' Because she was such a close friend the chef assured Lisa that would be no problem.

They leaned over the book together. Caitlin Thomas's name jumped off the crowded page, together with the bracketed addition 'plus one'. A table for two at eight o'clock. Where were the so-called clients Ben's assistant had mentioned? Another lie. And if Ben was taking the trouble to cover up with his office, it had to be for personal reasons, nothing to do with a story for the paper. There was no other construction to be put on it. He didn't want his secretary to know that the dinner was tête-à-tête.

They had to make a show of being fascinated by the preparations before the restaurant opened its doors. They were introduced to the head waiter with a flourish and while Lisa peppered him with thoughtful questions Carol couldn't help worrying about whether or not she was doing the right thing. Shouldn't she return home and have this out with Ben in privacy? Wasn't she sinking to his level by snooping on him? In the half hour before Ben and Caitlin were due to arrive Carol was in a ferment of indecision and had to be restrained by Lisa from leaving the restaurant several times.

Under the guise of checking the table layouts they soon discovered which table was earmarked for Miss Thomas and her guest. Lisa chose what she described as the perfect observation point, a corner table, flanked by a giant fern, where they could sit and watch and barely be seen.

'We'll be damn unlucky if he notices us over here,' she whispered, suggesting that Carol sit with her back to the room. 'And if he does, we'll just have to brazen it out and claim it's an amazing coincidence.'

She insisted they go through the menu, although eating was the last thing on Carol's mind. 'You must make an effort,' said Lisa kindly. 'I know how you're feeling but we must act the part. Actually I haven't eaten since last night and I'm starving.'

Carol caught herself looking at her watch every other minute. Her mouth dried up but she could hardly force herself to drink the bottled water, brought by a chatty young waiter who had presumably been ordered to be extra attentive. He tried to persuade them to try the Barolo 'on the house', as he exclaimed loudly, but Lisa turned down the offer with a smile, explaining that they were off wine for a day or two.

Lisa tucked into the French bread and tried to decide between the cassoulet and the stroganoff. Evidently the adrenaline provoked by snooping on the couple was not affecting her in the same way.

Carol was making a brave attempt to chew a piece of fegato alla salvia, pink, as it was cooked in Florence, when Lisa put her fork down. 'They've just walked in the door. Don't turn round until I tell you they're settled.'

As the minutes passed, Carol's agitation increased. It took every ounce of her willpower not to swivel round and stare. Lisa's eyes were fixed at a spot above Carol's shoulder, giving a running commentary. 'They've picked up the menus and the waiter's opening a bottle of wine,' she said softly.

'What's she like?' Carol couldn't help asking.

Lisa made a face. 'She's much older than I imagined. About Ben's age, I suppose. Laughs a lot. A real phoney, I'd say.'

'How's he looking at her?'

'Can't make out, they're discussing the food, I think. Yes, the waiter's taking their orders. She's drinking some wine, he isn't. Did he bring the car?'

'Probably. What's he doing now?'

'She's talking a lot, he's listening.'

Carol could wait no longer. She tapped Lisa on the ankle with her foot. 'Is it safe to turn round?'

'Yes, I don't think they'd notice.'

Carol's eyes went first to the woman, so sleekly groomed she might once have been a model, dark hair cropped and shiny. She wore a grey wool trouser suit, the jacket open to show a dark top cut low. She wasn't conventionally beautiful but she looked, Carol thought miserably, like a somebody. Sitting alongside Ben on the velvet banquette, running her fingers along the top of the wine glass, she said something which made Ben throw back his head and laugh uninhibitedly in a way Carol hadn't seen for years. The sight of her husband animated, obviously enjoying himself, hurt.

Caitlin was leaning in to him as she talked, so their shoulders were touching. Ben's eyes had flickered downwards, towards the swelling of her breasts. A business dinner? Too much cleavage for that, thought

Carol. Discussing ideas of mutual interest at dinner was a perfect alibi to meet but anyone watching those two would assume there was something personal going on. There was a flurry at the table as Ben grabbed Caitlin's hand. Caitlin had been reaching up to smooth a wayward lock of Ben's hair when he stopped her. Carol's heart began to hammer. Caitlin was pouting prettily but Carol noted that Ben had still not let go.

Carol turned back to Lisa and tried to steady her trembling hands, conscious that her friend was watching her with concern. 'I've seen enough,' she said. Lisa beckoned for the waiter and he discreetly escorted them through the swing doors leading to the kitchen. Carol supposed she must have said her goodbyes and made her thank yous to the restaurant manager and staff but she could remember nothing until they were in the taxi.

They sat in silence before Carol began to fume.

'Did you see her? Touching his hair? You don't do that unless you're very close. And he was definitely looking at her body. I don't blame him. It was all there on display.'

'You can't prove anything on what you've just seen.'

It was as if Lisa had not spoken.

'And if it was so innocent, why were they there alone? Why did he pretend to his secretary that that woman was parading him in front of clients?'

'Perhaps there was a change of plan.'

'He was having a great time, anyone could see that.'

'Yes, I'd say he enjoyed her company but Ben's sociable, he'd hardly sit there with a sour expression. And I didn't think there was any romantic stuff from him.'

'He held her hand.'

'Only to prevent her from mucking about with his hair.'

'But anyone could see there was a strong attraction between them . . . an electricity. Even across the room I could feel that.'

Lisa, she noticed, did not contradict her. All her friend did was urge patience. Before tackling her husband shouldn't Carol wait until she had more definite proof? Be more aware of Ben's schedule? Take note of how often he met Caitlin, that type of thing? 'You could be jumping to conclusions. After all, you only looked at them for five minutes. Less.'

Carol did not want to listen to any more. 'It's not about time, it's about instinct. Whatever they had, Lisa, it's not over, I'm sure of it. If they aren't having an affair, they soon will be. That woman's after my husband and he's not running away.'

She asked the driver to drop her off first.

'Don't confront him tonight,' cautioned Lisa, 'wait till you're calmer.'

It was good advice though Carol was unsure about whether she had the self-control to wait. She felt she was operating at third hand, looking at herself from the outside. She supposed she should feel angry but instead she was steeped in sadness.

The man she had almost worshipped since the moment they met had turned out to be no better than all those other husbands her friends told her about. What was the most hurtful was remembering how he would look at her sometimes, especially after they had made love. She had thought there was real tenderness in his eyes and although he was not as demonstrative as she would wish, he had made her feel cherished.

She hated this feeling of helplessness, drifting from fury to panic. He obviously had little regard for her, treating her like a supine, malleable housekeeper, grateful for crumbs from his table. Why had he never told her that he and Julia had fought over the children? Another secret. What else was there to discover about him? The answer was obvious. From what she had observed at the restaurant, he and Caitlin had resumed their affair. If it had ever stopped.

How to deal with this overwhelming bleakness? What she wanted to do right then was wallow in her misery and go upstairs to lie on the bed and cry. She thanked Mrs Porter for baby-sitting and thought about checking on the children who were all upstairs in bed. It was something she always did whenever she had been out – she enjoyed the sight of their peaceful faces snuggling against the pillows. Tonight she decided not to risk it. Becky, at nearly fifteen, was likely to be still stirring at this time and she wanted to avoid having to put on an act.

She went into the living room and poured herself a glass of wine. As she sat on the sofa staring at the blank TV screen, she began to have wild thoughts. She would leave him. She would go far away and hide and start a new life. When he couldn't find her he would worry, he would come looking in vain. That would serve him right. She finished her drink and began pacing the room, unable to settle. Here she was looking after his children, in his house, and she could not even allow herself the satisfaction of packing a suitcase and storming out. She could not bring herself to up sticks and abandon the children, not with their history.

They were innocent victims in all this. It was a pity Ben didn't consider their welfare before surrendering to his own selfish needs.

But this time she would not allow him to sweet-talk his way out of trouble. She had to calm down, and think about her choices. She passed a weary hand over her forehead. She still loved him, unfortunately. But how could she endure living with him, knowing he was making love to someone else?

As her anger subsided she began to blame herself. She had been so grateful to him for marrying her that she hadn't taken the precaution of hiding this from him. She had been pliant, adoring and transparent, characteristics she had fooled herself mattered to him. In the early days he had said that what attracted him to her was that she was different from the calculating and ambitious women he usually met. She'd been a fool for allowing herself to be treated as the undemanding stay-at-home wife. Seeing Ben at his ease with that pushy woman had shaken her faith in him. Could she share her life with a man she didn't trust? Surely when trust died, everything, the whole system, went down?

Despite Lisa's strictures she was determined to confront her husband when he came home. How could she lie in bed alongside him thinking he might have made love to someone else that night? Whatever it took she intended to force the truth out of him. However hurtful it might be, it was preferable to living a half-lie, trying to second-guess his thoughts, his feelings. How she would deal with it in practical terms she had not yet worked out. It would be intolerable to be under the same roof, knowing that he was involved with another woman. But she couldn't just storm out and leave the children. She didn't think she was tough enough to make them bereaved a second time. But, she reminded herself, if that had to happen, it wasn't her fault. If Ben had been able to keep his zipper up – the strange voice echoed in her head – none of this would be happening.

Carol tried to occupy herself by doing the quick crossword, something that normally took her only six or seven minutes. But she found her mind wandering back to the scene in the restaurant. Abruptly she switched on the television, but it was the kind of game show she hated. Indifferently, she switched channels until she came across a bouncy red-head doing a make-over on a girl who worked in a bike shop. The presenter was promising to work miracles with the girl's appearance. That's what I need, thought Carol bitterly, a make-over on my life.

It was nearly midnight by the time she heard Ben's key in the door. She had fallen asleep on the sofa and the television was showing an ancient black and white movie. Hastily she smoothed her hair and tried to focus. She had rehearsed her first words but now they had gone completely from her head.

Ben was all smiles, apparently pleased she had waited up for him, and for an instant she was disarmed. He appeared untroubled, not her idea of what a furtive adulterer would look like at all.

'What's kept you awake?' he grinned. 'Must be a great film. Don't let me interrupt.'

Abruptly she switched off the set. 'Where have you been?'

'I told you this morning, I had a business dinner.'

'Who with?'

He unloosened his tie. 'You don't usually quiz me. What's up?'

'Because I was in that restaurant. I saw you with that woman.'

His brow furrowed. 'You were at Fontana's? Tonight?'

'I was there with Lisa.'

He looked puzzled. 'Why didn't you come and say hello?'

'You didn't look as though you'd welcome an interruption from your wife.'

'What are you getting at?'

'Do you usually have business dinners alone with a woman?'

'Her clients' plane was delayed. They joined us later.'

'Really.'

Ben sat down. 'What's all this about, puss?'

'That's the woman you were fucking when Fay died.' She could see that her self-assured husband was taken aback. 'Julia told me her name. That's Caitlin.'

His face muscles stiffened. 'Yes.'

'Ben, why didn't you tell me about her?'

'Because I knew you'd misunderstand. It's nothing, just business, that's all.'

'Please have the guts to be honest with me for once.'

'I am being honest. It was all over between me and Caitlin when Fay died. We split up and she went to America. Now she's back and she's given me some great stories. There's nothing more to it.'

'If it's all so innocent, I'm asking you again why didn't you tell me about her after the anonymous call.'

'For the very reason you're angry now. I knew you'd put two and two together and make five.'

That did it. Carol rushed at him and punched as hard as she could, trying to land on his face. But he dodged aside and caught her arm.

'Don't be such an idiot. You'll wake the children.'

'The children!' she yelled, allowing all the hurt and hate to spill out in the sound. 'That's all you think about, all you've ever thought about.'

He rushed to close the door, pausing to listen, but there was no sound from upstairs. When he turned round his voice was cold. 'I'm not sure there's any point in carrying on this discussion until you've calmed down.'

'Oh no. You're not getting away with that. We're staying here until you come clean.'

'What's the point? You're obviously not in the mood to believe a word I say, and I don't believe you were in the restaurant by coincidence. You were there to spy on me and I resent that.'

Carol drew a deep breath. 'Look, I've just had someone telling me out of the blue what went on when Fay died and insinuating that you play around. What was it they said: "Can't keep your zipper up". Then I find out by accident that you're seeing an old flame, something you should have told me yourself. What do you expect me to think?'

'I'd expect you to take the word of a husband who has thought of little else but your happiness since you met him.'

Unexpectedly, this caused Carol to laugh. How pompous. For a heady moment her gloom was lifted and for a second she was filled with bravado, not caring what would happen.

'Ben, if you could hear yourself . . .'

His aura of self-confidence collapsed and he looked distressed. Instantly she softened, half thinking that this might be another act but unable to help herself. She still loved him, that was the problem.

'Carol, I don't think you have any idea how much you mean to me.' His voice was quiet and still Carol wondered why he couldn't bring himself to say that he loved her. The words that any woman would want to hear under these circumstances. Yes, she did have an idea what she meant to him. A mother substitute for his children, someone who ran the household, rarely bothering him with detail, and someone who never feigned a headache when he needed physical comfort. Oh God, what bitter thoughts about a man who until a week ago she had loved unquestioningly.

'I'm sorry if I've made you unhappy. That's the last thing in the world I want and I can understand why you're worried about me seeing her. But that's history. She and I never talk about the past. There's no spark between us. We discuss only business.'

No spark? An image of the two of them together flashed in front of her eyes. How could she believe that?

He explained that Caitlin had only been back in London a few months and it was incredible how many top-grade contacts she had garnered around her. Her last tip-off had led to a front-page splash and a story on the centre spread, something he didn't manage often. That was why he was bothering to stay in touch.

'I was too cowardly to tell you about Caitlin and for that I'm sorry. I suppose I was foolish to think you wouldn't find out but she's never come on to me so I never saw her as a problem. It's as dead for her as it is for me.'

Carol remembered the sight of his animated face as he and Caitlin laughed together but she said nothing.

'I'll never be alone with her again and that's a promise.'

It was the best outcome she could hope for, she supposed.

Chapter Ten

Lisa nodded in the direction of the office as Carol entered the kitchen the next morning. Waiting for them on the desk was a flask and a plate of biscuits still warm from the oven. It was just what Carol needed, hot coffee and words of comfort.

Lisa was more persuaded by Ben's explanation than Carol was. 'Didn't I say there was nothing between them? I was right.'

Carol gave her an old-fashioned look. Lisa did not know how hurt she had been to witness Ben's face, alive with interest and all directed at another woman. And she couldn't put out of her mind that sex with this woman had probably been more exciting than their lovemaking. She imagined stolen afternoons, in sunlit hotel rooms, with champagne on tap, and long leisurely baths together. She shook herself mentally. What did she know? She had never had an adulterous affair and to dwell on what might have happened would send her mad.

'How are you going to handle it?' asked Lisa.

Carol's knuckles tightened round the cup. 'I wish I could switch off and think about something else. The only hope for our marriage is if I don't go over and over what's happened. I have no real evidence, no proof, only my instinct, and right now Ben's word doesn't seem enough for me.' She stared absently out of the window, trying to find a way to express her state of mind.

'Maybe I put him too much on a pedestal and I didn't really know him. I thought he was different and it's taken seven years to find out that he cheated on his first wife so why am I surprised he's cheated on his second?' She stopped when she saw Lisa's shocked expression.

'What are you saying? Your marriage is wobbling because you saw your husband in a restaurant with another woman? We only saw them for a few minutes. I think you're making massive assumptions. Get a grip.' Lisa prodded her arm. 'But tell you what. I'll check out his story about her clients coming on later. The restaurant manager would probably remember if he had to set more places or move them to a larger table.'

They were interrupted by the sound of stomping along the corridor, followed by the door being pushed open with the end of an aluminium crutch.

'Sorry, guys, but the fishmonger was out of scallops so I ordered prawns. Is that OK? Otherwise we have to let him know right away.'

Lisa said it was fine and rose to go back into the kitchen. Taking her cue, Carol also stood up but her way was barred when Andrea put her crutch across the doorway.

'You're not leaving until I spill my guts out and you help me with my problem.' Carol sat back down again, glad of a diversion. Apparently Andrea had spent the last couple of days frantically phoning anyone she'd met since she landed in Britain, trying to find a replacement to go to Brunei for the three months she would be in plaster. She'd had some success. There had been a woman, a chef with the Planet of Food Café, who had gone to the British Geographical Association the previous night for an interview. But would you credit it, the expedition organiser had just phoned. Though anxious to find a substitute they'd had to veto the applicant on the grounds that her mild asthma might flare up and make her life intolerable in the rainforest.

Andrea leaned heavily against the doorway and shifted her weight onto her uninjured foot. 'They don't know what a lucky escape they had. In my opinion that girl was a complete dictator, a cross between Saddam Hussein and Milosevic,' she laughed. 'It's a bugger trying to find someone who'll fit in, work with the team, not make waves. Living in the camp can be fun, but only if everybody gells. I don't suppose you've got any ideas, have you? They're getting pretty desperate. They need the cook to fly out in ten days.' She wriggled her crutch into the top of the plaster. 'It's so itchy I could scream.'

Carol looked doubtful and Andrea added, 'It's not all sweat and bugs. This base camp is set in the most beautiful scenery, on a river, and when I was on a similar expedition we had great fun, parties, barbecues, swimming, so paint a decent picture when you're telling people.'

'I can't think of anyone who could leave just like that,' said Carol, but promised she would think about likely candidates, hoping that would shut Andrea up so that Lisa could telephone Fontana's.

They were busy in the kitchen and Carol did not want to nag her friend so it was more than an hour later that Lisa came up to her, wreathed in smiles.

'You've been worrying for nothing. Apparently two characters turned up just before closing and guess who had to move to a table for four? Your dear husband and his companion. So you see, he was telling the truth.'

After her stint in the kitchen Carol found herself buying an apology, the ingredients for honey-roasted duckling, one of Ben's favourite dishes. It was rare she cooked a special meal midweek but if she were to accept he was telling the truth and his liaison with Caitlin was on purely business terms she'd have to offer the olive branch.

When she let herself into the house, the answering machine was blinking. Ben had left a message to say he was still tied up on a story and would be a little later than planned, probably after the younger children's bedtime. 'Kiss them goodnight from me.' Carol pressed the erase button. It was always the children.

At nine o'clock she gave in to hunger pangs and polished off a portion of the duckling. It was delicious and as she spooned out the remainder into a container for the freezer she decided that by now Ben would certainly have had a snack at the office. He could make do with some bread and cheese. At nine thirty he rang again to apologise and said it was going to take him a bit longer. He sounded excited. The story was developing into a first-class scoop. A minister at the Treasury had been accused of misappropriating grant funds awarded to a company he had run before his Cabinet career.

'Did the story come from Caitlin?' The question was out before she could bite it back.

The line went quiet before he said, 'Yes.' When she said nothing he added briskly, 'That's why she's useful.' Carol could hear the sound of chatter in the background and she thought she could hear a woman laughing. On impulse she asked, 'Is that Caitlin I can hear?'

'No. There's a whole crowd of us here working on the story but I am in phone contact with her because the civil servant supplying the evidence won't talk to anyone else but her. I told you, that's all there is to it.' He promised to get home as soon as he could.

Carol's eyes wandered around the kitchen, the silence relieved only by the ticking clock. Night after night they sat here, eating an enjoyable meal together, before watching television. It was all Ben wanted to do after the exertions of the office. And if she was honest, until recently she had been perfectly content with her life, asking nothing more than to be the hub of the household.

But it was true that with every month that passed the children needed her less. Their time after school was filled with hobbies and friends. She didn't figure except as a taxi driver, but that was natural and she didn't resent their growing independence. But without the children and with Ben being so taken up with his career, what would be left for her? Was that a good enough reason to want her own baby? It could fill her days but eventually she would have to face the problem again, and she did not want Ben to regard her as fit only for motherhood. Until now she had not questioned her role, being content to be his lover and companion. But if he did not see her in that way, what was left? Was there something else out there, as fulfilling, as challenging, but something she could achieve under her own steam?

Why was she suddenly feeling discontented? It wasn't only the events of the past week although they had the effect of focusing her thoughts on what she was doing with her life. In the quiet reaches of her mind she had begun to feel a need to nurture a part of herself that had lain dormant. She used to harbour aspirations of doing something out of the domestic arena. In the early days of their marriage she had toyed with the idea of freelance work. Increasingly she found her contacts had moved, that her ideas took weeks to be acknowledged and when she was finally given an assignment she'd had to cancel as Katie had developed measles. She had decided that the life of a self-employed writer was peripatetic and not compatible with running a home and three children.

Her reverie was interrupted by the sound of Katie calling for a glass of water and when she eventually came downstairs to the emptiness of the sitting room she clicked on the television set, mainly for the comfort of background noise. It was the movie channel and her attention was drawn briefly to a shot of zebras stampeding across a plain. She looked it up in the film guide to find it was an old Stewart Granger movie called *King Solomon's Mines*. There he was pushing his way into a jungle clearing, looking amazingly unscathed by heat, insects or danger, followed by a luminous-looking woman. Carol checked the cast list to find that this was Deborah Kerr. As they hacked their way through the dense undergrowth Carol smiled, thinking how impossible it would be to worry about school runs and late-working husbands in a situation so far removed from domestic life.

Her thoughts were cut short by another phone call from Ben who said he was on his way home and precisely at that moment the door opened and there he was, the phone still stuck to his ear and a huge bunch of her favourite blue irises outstretched towards her. Immediately her mood lightened. He shepherded her into the kitchen. She never failed to be delighted at his arrival, he brought with him the energy of the outside world and after all these years she still loved to be with him. He seemed to be getting even better looking as he grew older, the brown eyes a little more crinkled but as animated as they ever were. He opened a bottle of burgundy, all the while telling her about the Treasury story. As his words tumbled out, Carol couldn't help wondering why he was going into more detail than usual. Maybe this was a cover-up to avoid talking about what he must know was on her mind. She had to get over this. She would never be able to rebuild confidence in Ben while she was analysing his every word and action.

She could not bring herself to mention Caitlin's name but waited for him to make some reference to her. If their liaison were as innocent as he claimed, surely she would crop up in the conversation, especially since she was pivotal to the story. But by the time they turned out the light and Ben kissed her goodnight, he still had not mentioned her name. Carol's unease increased. As she lay, trying to get to sleep, visions of the night's television film floated across her mind. Instead of the film stars, she conjured up the faces that she had watched with such trepidation in the restaurant the previous night – Ben off into the jungle carrying a limp Caitlin in his arms.

As Carol lay, apparently peacefully at his side, Ben's mind also refused to shut down. All the way home he had worked out how to handle any questions she might put to him about Caitlin and he was worried that she had made no reference to her. He'd been aware that the chat was one-sided, that he was being over-voluble.

It bothered him that Carol had been a silent watcher when he and Caitlin had been having dinner. Her clients had been delayed and did not join them until later in the evening. Although he had not bargained for a tête-à-tête, he had to admit he enjoyed the evening. Caitlin had always been a lively companion and she'd lost none of her quickness of mind.

When he had first seen her again a few months ago his reaction had been a mixture of pleasure and shock, but thankfully the intense physical attraction between them seemed to be missing. He reminded himself they had been friends as well as lovers. Their first meeting had been somewhat stilted as both of them were wary. That was only to be expected and when after their next encounter they had formed an amicable, mutually advantageous association, he had congratulated himself. Who said it wasn't possible for men and women to operate without sex complicating things? As far as he was concerned, the dinner had been a pleasant business meeting but still, if he had been aware of Carol across the room he doubted if he would have been quite so relaxed. He had to make himself amenable to any would-be contact, male or female, if they were to choose him rather than his rivals. It was standard newspaper practice. If only he could make Carol understand that. But he had to admit he was like any red-blooded male. As Caitlin had leaned forward to pour the wine he caught a glimpse of her rounded bosom, reminding him how attractive he had once found her body. From then on memories of their lovemaking kept intruding, though he thought he had taken care not to let any of this show. And until the arrival of the clients they had talked mainly about the Treasury story. Ben was grateful she'd brought it to him – for old times' sake, she'd said – and he hadn't questioned her motives. His newspaper, allegedly a supporter of the government, was undoubtedly the most suitable to carry a story that would embarrass them.

But it was still a pity Carol had found out she had come back into his life. When they parted, Caitlin had merely brushed her lips against his cheek. He had felt nothing and had not responded in any way, though he did wonder how she would have acted had not the clients been watching. But his behaviour convinced him that he had the self-discipline and stability through his marriage not to succumb to temptation. Not that Caitlin seemed to be offering herself, but he couldn't rid himself of the feeling that if he had made a move she would not have rebuffed him. Nevertheless he was conscious that an onlooker, especially a suspicious wife, might have gained a wrong impression seeing them so relaxed together. Any wife would be bound to worry about the reappearance of somebody who'd played such an important part in his past. He must try to convince Carol of the truth, that he had not had an affair since they met and despite any temptation she might imagine, he wanted to stay faithful.

Chapter Eleven

It was when they were driving away from the fracture clinic that Andrea burst into tears. Alarmed, Carol pulled into the side of the road. The Australian had been her usual boisterous self, joshing with the nurses, who had given her the bad news that her ankle would have to be re-set. That hadn't seemed to faze her. But now she was sobbing, saying she couldn't bear the idea of being in plaster for an extra three weeks. 'Why should they wait even longer for me?' she wailed. And when Carol tried to comfort her, added, 'You don't understand. This expedition was perfect for me.' Apparently she had applied to join several previous field trips and had been turned down before the organiser had chosen her for this one.

The base had been established six months ago, with financial sponsorship from the Sultan of Brunei, so it was well kitted out. They had ironed out most of the problems. It wasn't like making fire by rubbing two sticks together. The kitchen had a range, plenty of helpers and the huts even had flush loos, for God's sake. She'd heard the weather at this time of the year was damn near perfect, apart from a downpour at four o'clock every afternoon.

'I was hoping they could manage for a few weeks without me, but they'll never agree to wait longer.' And she began to sniffle into a tissue. 'That's why I've been looking for someone who only wanted to go out for a short time. Someone who wouldn't do the dirty on me by staying on.'

Carol patted Andrea's shoulder sympathetically before starting the car up again. Try as she might she could not think of anyone who fitted the bill and who could get away at such short notice.

Andrea turned a woebegone face towards her and Carol found herself saying, 'If there was any way I could help, you know I would.'

'I'm sure you would. But you have three kids.'

That evening over the tea table with the children Carol found herself exaggerating her role in Andrea's dilemma.

'Guess what, I've turned down a trip to a rainforest in Brunei so I can stay here and cook your fish fingers.'

For a second there was silence before the barrage began.

'We can cook our own fish fingers,' said Katie.

'Where's Brunei?' asked Emmy.

'A small country in Asia.'

'Why'd you turn it down? It'd be cool.' This was from Becky. She had seen a film about the rainforest and said it would give her cred at school if she had a step-mum who was going off to the jungle.

'We're studying rainforests at school,' said Katie. 'If they keep on cutting down the trees we won't be able to breathe.'

'That's rubbish,' said Emmy. 'We're in England.'

'No, she's right,' said Carol. 'It's all to do with the oxygen they make that helps the earth's atmosphere.'

'How long would you be gone?' asked Becky.

Carol relented and stuck closer to the truth. 'I wasn't really offered the job. How could I go off and leave you three for a whole school term?'

There was another outcry.

'Yes, you could,' said Becky. 'I'm fourteen, nearly fifteen. I could look after the others.'

Carol smiled at this. There was a running battle between them over Becky's habit of staying out well past the agreed time at weekends, and she could imagine how eager she would be to have her freedom for a while. Her father was more easily persuaded to agree to sleep-outs and visits to under-eighteen discos.

'I don't need looking after,' said Emmy.

'Daddy can do it,' piped up Katie.

'He can't, stupid,' said Emmy. 'He's at work.'

Carol dished up the baked beans. 'That's enough. I can't go and that's it.'

But the children would not leave the subject alone. For the rest of the evening they pored over maps and pestered her with questions about what she would be doing, who else would be there and what kind of things she would see in the jungle.

They were still at it when Ben came home from work. He hadn't taken off his coat before they rushed at him and told him how Carol had the chance to become an explorer in the rainforest.

Carol smiled at their enthusiasm. 'They've already shipped me out there,' she laughed. 'I know why they want to see the back of me. They'd be up to no good.'

Once the tea things were cleared away and the homework finished the children settled down to watch television in the sitting room before bedtime.

It was while they were having their supper that Ben asked where the idea of a trip to the rainforest had come from. Carol brought him up-to-date about Andrea's tribulations with the plaster and her desperate search to find a short-term replacement cook. Ben's reaction surprised her.

'I wish just for once you'd think about yourself. If you didn't have a family to consider, would you go?'

Carol hesitated. 'I'm not sure. I don't know how good I'd be. Andrea says it's the trip of a lifetime. But for someone like me it's impractical.'

'Why?'

'Come on, Ben.'

'I'm not saying it would be easy, but we could muck in.'

'Ah, so you want to get rid of me as well.' She was only half-joking.

Ben asked her to stop tidying the table and sit down. 'I want you to be selfish for a change. If you'd like to go on this trip I think you should seriously consider it. After all, it's not something that crops up every day.'

Carol was puzzled. 'How can I? Who would take Becky to gym classes, Katie to pottery and Emmy to piano? And that's only on one day.'

He took her hand. 'That's just it. You've been a slave to those kids and it's my fault. I've let you be. We can solve that. You're bad at asking for help. But I'm not. I've no doubt Julia would fly in on a broomstick at a minute's notice.' Carol grinned and he went on, 'Yes, we'd all hate it but we could put up with it for a short while.'

Carol poured him a cup of coffee, for an instant picturing herself free of all domestic ties, striding through the rainforest in the sort of clothes Deborah Kerr had been wearing. The vision faded as rapidly as it had come. She couldn't see herself in that role. It wasn't feasible and she found she had said it out loud.

'Yes it is,' he said firmly. Instead of making her feel warmly disposed towards him because he was encouraging her to accept an opportunity of a lifetime she felt immediate suspicion. With her out of the way, wouldn't it be far easier for him to continue his affair with Caitlin?

He seemed to read her mind.

'Darling, if you think I want you out of the way, you're quite mistaken, but don't you think it's about time you did something for yourself, something that would take you out of the domestic arena? You've spent years looking after all of us and it'd do you good to get out into the world.' When he saw her looking perplexed, he added, 'And I don't count working at Jolly Good Food, which as far as I'm concerned is more of the same. If you're intrigued by the idea of being in a rainforest, I say have a go.' He leaned across and kissed her lightly on the nose. 'I'm trying to be bloody unselfish for once. At least give me credit for that.'

She stroked his cheek. 'Thanks, it's nice to be appreciated but I'd worry too much about what was happening back home. Anyway, I probably wouldn't be any good. Come on, the news is about to start.'

It was strange, thought Carol, rolling out a piece of shortcrust pastry at work the following morning, how everyone was conspiring to get her out of the country. First the children, then her husband and, since Andrea had mentioned it, the girls in the kitchen. She thought they'd be on her side, agreeing she shouldn't go. On the contrary.

'You'd have such an adventure,' said Connie.

'And you'd get away from this miserable weather,' said Yvonne.

'No housework, no kids,' added Pauline.

Carol brushed aside their comments. 'That could equally apply to any of you,' she said. 'I don't see any of you volunteering.'

'We can't afford to. You can,' said Connie.

Only Lisa advised caution, saying it was not a good idea, but then she was probably more worried about having to replace her in the kitchen. But Carol had misjudged her. Over a mid-morning coffee Lisa told her that her doubts were not about her business but about leaving such an attractive husband alone at such a vulnerable time in their marriage.

'We had a heart-to-heart last night,' said Carol, 'and he's almost convinced me there's nothing doing with Caitlin.'

'Almost?'

Carol's brow creased. 'Maybe I read too much into it. Who knows?

Anyway, I wish we hadn't followed him.'

'Well, it brought things out into the open.' Lisa cocked her head. 'Do you really want to go into the middle of nowhere?'

'It hasn't been offered and it might never be. But if the circumstances were different I think it would do me good to stand on my own two feet.'

Since the anonymous call she had begun to think more about her own needs and to feel that she had been relying too much on Ben for her fulfilment. If she were honest she would like to be able to change, become someone who always knew what to say, the kind of woman people consulted, one of those people who stood up and spoke and others listened.

She leaned back in her chair. 'Imagine being in a rainforest. Nothing to worry about except what's going on there. No school runs. No bickering children.'

'No Ben,' interrupted Lisa. 'There are a lot of women preying around, you know. Women like Caitlin.'

'He's surrounded by gorgeous young things every day of his life. If I couldn't trust him to be on his own for three months, we wouldn't have much of a future, would we?'

'Maybe he does need to see what life would be like without you. I reckon he'd appreciate you more.' Lisa gave her a sideways glance as she topped up their cups. 'What about the plan to have a baby?'

'I suppose waiting another three months won't make much difference. I still have quite a lot of time.' She sighed. 'But I can't go. It's impractical. How could I let Julia take over? The girls really don't like her and Ben can't stand her.'

Lisa put down her cup and said, 'If you really want to go, I could help out.'

'That's sweet of you but you've enough on your plate.'

'I wouldn't offer if I didn't think I could cope and it would be an adventure for me as well,' said Lisa. 'Aren't I always going on about how I'd love to have kids and settle down? This might cure me.'

Carol shook her head. 'I couldn't ask you to do it.'

'Why not? I know them, they like me and as far as I know Ben can stand me.'

When Carol pointed out she had a business to run, Lisa brushed that objection aside. The children were at school between nine and three and after that she could just as easily work the phones and do paperwork on a computer from Carol's home as from her own. In any case, she would enjoy being the children's surrogate mother.

Carol stuck out a tongue. 'As long as you're not a surrogate wife.'

'Ben and me? Come on, we're mates.'

When Andrea turned up for her shift she was amazed to hear there might be a possibility of Carol being her replacement. Enthusiastically she emphasised that Carol would be the ideal person from her point of view as she had a family to return to and wouldn't be tempted to extend the contract. Despite her protestations, Carol found herself being driven into a corner, with Lisa relishing the idea of being a housewife and mother, albeit on a temporary basis, and Andrea spotting a chink in the hitherto invincible armour. To every problem Carol unearthed, the other two found a solution. Lisa would fetch the children from school while Andrea offered to stock the Mitchell freezer with ready-made meals. At the end of her shift Carol found herself at least agreeing to be interviewed by the expedition's organiser at the BGA headquarters, secretly thinking it would be a waste of time. Why would a professional organisation accept someone with no experience of working in tropical conditions?

Andrea fixed the appointment for the next afternoon, fearful that Carol might back out, and as she and Carol stepped through the impressive doorway of the association's building overlooking Kensington Park, the Australian was unaccustomedly reverent. In a hushed voice she pointed at the list of names of illustrious explorers, highlighted in gold leaf, who had passed through the same portals. The names invoked memories from Carol's geography lessons: Stanley, Livingstone, Edmund Hillary, John Hunt, Colonel Fawcett, Admiral Birkitt, Dr Richard Leakey, Peter Scott, Freya Stark.

Andrea introduced the head of the expeditions office, a slim, wiry woman in her early forties. Phoebe Tugendhaat offered to give them a lightning tour. First she took them to the famous Map Room housing the world's largest private collection then to the picture library where the grave faces of intrepid travellers, long dead, gazed down at them. She pointed out that this was the very room where in 1881 the bet was struck that Phineas Fogg would never be able to go round the world in eighty days. But it was the small suitcase belonging to Captain Titus Oates, abandoned when he left the tent to disappear into the snow, that really stirred Carol's emotions. For the first time she felt a real thrill of anticipation at the possibility of being even a small part of living history.

Phoebe, used to living and working surrounded by these historical artefacts, was more matter-of-fact, informing them that as she had to prepare for a seminar on expedition planning she would have to be brisk about the interview. In the absence of the leader of the Brunei trip, who had established the base camp six months previously, she had been entrusted with the task of hiring any back-up staff.

Andrea had already briefed Carol on the trip, which was to establish a biodiversity centre on the banks of the River Belalong deep in the rainforest. The field study centre needed not only scientists but 'civilians' for administrative and catering duties. It would be hard work but rewarding. The main purpose of the interview was to assess whether or not Carol's personality would gel with the rest of the team. According to Andrea that was far more important than her skill as a cook, which in any case Andrea had vouched for.

Phoebe closed the folder decisively. 'I can't see any problem. Subject to your medical, I think you'd be eminently suitable. You already work as part of a team in a busy kitchen and I think you'd be a welcome addition in base camp. I wonder if you could possibly be ready to leave in ten days? The butterfly expert over there needs some crystals rather urgently and we don't want to send them unaccompanied.'

Before Carol could open her mouth to say that would be impossible, Andrea butted in, 'No probs. She's dying to get out there, aren't you?'

To her surprise Carol found herself nodding, though rather feebly, but hoped she sounded convincing when she said she would do her best. In truth she was in a state of panic as Phoebe took her hand in a firm grip and asked whether she could come in the next day for a medical and, if she passed, some jabs, and of course a detailed briefing. Dry-mouthed she walked in a daze towards the tube station, listening with half an ear to Andrea chattering excitedly.

Until then Carol had regarded the whole thing as something of a fantasy, an event to be talked about in an abstract kind of way but something which wasn't really going to happen. Yet a few minutes ago she had pledged to turn her life upside down, leave husband, children, familiar surroundings, and in ten days' time venture into the unknown. She had just committed herself to three months in the middle of a rainforest, surrounded by people she didn't know, away from those she loved. The whole scheme was crazy. She could not leave the kids, it was impossible to be away for that length of time. Carol's steps slowed and came to a halt. She had to turn back right now and tell Phoebe there had been a terrible mistake, she could not possibly go.

But her way was barred. Andrea held out a crutch to prevent Carol from moving. 'You want to go back in there and say you can't go, don't you?' She did not wait for a reply. 'Well, it's your prerogative to do that. It's your life, mate. No one can make you do anything you don't want but just take a couple of minutes to think about it.'

Impatient shoppers brushed past them as Andrea leaned on her crutches and blocked the centre of the pavement. Neither woman gave the passers-by a glance.

'Think about it. Do you want to be the little woman at home all your life? Isn't there somewhere, deep down, a little voice that says there has to be more to life than looking after a family only? Don't you sometimes long for a change of routine?'

Carol wanted to say she was happy with her routine and then remembered her yearning for a life makeover.

'Well, it ain't never going to happen, not unless you make it happen. Why should your husband and kids want you to do any different? They like you being at home, at their beck and call, washing, ironing and seeing to things.' She tapped her crutch on the pavement for emphasis. Carol had never seen Andrea this serious. 'Don't you sometimes wonder if there's more to life than that? You have so much potential but unless your husband and kids see you in a different light, they're never going to alter. Why should they? When you're doing something completely different, in a strange environment, it starts a chain of events which changes everything. And it will change you. I know what I'm talking about.'

When Carol made no comment Andrea blurted, 'Don't make a decision you'll regret for the rest of your life. Ask yourself: when will you ever get the chance to have an adventure like this?'

Carol thought of what Lisa had said to her after the anonymous phone call: Ben needed her as a haven to come home to. That had been Lisa's opinion. And Carol clearly remembered what she had replied. That there had to be more to marriage than that.

She turned her head to look at the imposing façade of the BGA on her left. To the right were the steps leading towards the entrance to the District and Circle lines of the tube station.

Slowly she put her hand under Andrea's elbow and together they continued on their way, Carol helping her friend to navigate the steep descent which led to the underground.

Chapter Twelve

The Royal Brunei Airline jet taxied up the runway and with a stomach-thudding whoosh was airbound. Carol sat back in her window seat and imagined Ben and the children watching the sky as her plane disappeared from sight.

The last ten days had been chaotic, exacerbated by Ben's unhappiness at the prospect of having Lisa running affairs in the house. He'd been soothed by the children who were wholehearted in their praise of her; she was fun, they said, and didn't expect them to dress up like Grandma did. Becky clinched it by saying that Lisa treated her like a grown-up – 'not like some people.'

Carol had left lists and timetables in every room of the house and spent much time worrying that Lisa might find it difficult to dovetail the children's activities and ensure they all had lifts at the right time. 'I do know how to organise, you know,' said Lisa mildly when Carol decided to colour-code each child's schedule. But there were so many things for Lisa to take on board. Would she remember to leave on the night-light in Katie's bedroom? She hadn't written it down in case the other two read it. Katie didn't ever talk about her fear of the dark but of course her sisters were in on the secret. Then there was the weekly ordeal of doing the dreaded plaits for ballet lessons. She hadn't liked to go on about it but it sometimes seemed to Carol that the teacher was more strict about the look of the hair than the position of the feet.

Packing had been a tense business. Andrea had volunteered to take the children to the cinema so she and Ben could have some peace, but his concerns about having a stranger around the house resurfaced when Carol mentioned that Lisa would be staying overnight occasionally to help out in the mornings. Carol had asked the two younger girls if they would double up to make room. She had to persuade Ben of the wisdom of the idea, especially on Saturday nights when he worked late. It was either her or Julia, she reminded him. 'No contest,' he said when this was pointed out.

Julia had been furious when she'd heard about the arrangements. 'You have no right to allow a stranger to look after my grandchildren when I'm fit and willing to have them,' she said angrily. Becky had been the one to solve the problem, pointing out that she and her sisters would never consider leaving home during term time and that Julia would hate to live in their house. Julia could find no answer to that.

Because Carol hadn't been able to space out the injections for tetanus and cholera, her arms were swollen and tender and she longed for a cup of tea and an early night before her long flight. However Ben did not read the signals and long before she'd finished packing he suggested they could spend the time far more pleasantly. She could finish her packing when the children came back from the cinema.

She would be away from the marriage bed for twelve weeks and she didn't think this was the moment to plead tiredness, aching limbs or anything else. So she gave her husband a warm smile. When he saw her taking the diaphragm box out of the dressing table drawer she could feel his eyes on her but he made no comment as she went towards the bathroom.

Maybe it was because he felt more relaxed knowing she was taking precautions or perhaps because they could make as much noise as they liked, but their lovemaking was more satisfying than it had been for years. It was the first time they had climaxed together for months and Ben appeared inordinately pleased with himself. She smiled now, remembering how she had teased him. 'Perhaps I ought to leave more often.' And when she'd asked how he would manage to hold out for three months, he said he would take refuge in work. The fact that he hadn't asked how she would manage was par for the course.

The trip to the airport had been passed almost in silence, the children suddenly realising that their mum's great journey was starting at last and she wouldn't be at home for three months. Carol had turned round to survey the solemn faces. God, what am I doing? she thought. They need their mum. This is selfish of me. Good mothers wouldn't leave their kids. Her eyes began to fill with tears and Ben had been sympathetic.

'You know, it would help if you kept a diary. Write something for the paper afterwards. It'll be good copy.'

Carol agreed it was a great idea, appreciating his efforts to introduce a practical note into the emotionally-charged atmosphere.

'I'd read that,' said Becky.

Emmy perked up at the idea. 'I'll keep a diary as well, Mum. Then when you come back you can see what we've been up to and we can read yours.'

This seemed to cheer them up and they fought amiably about who should be allowed to push her trolley towards the freight department of Royal Brunei Airways where she was to check in the five packages she was taking out to base camp since they had proved too big to be classed as hand luggage.

But when her flight was called, Katie's lips began to tremble and again Carol was overcome with misgivings, wondering what would happen if she asked to be taken home instead of boarding the plane. But Ben began to cuddle Katie and reminded her that Mummy was going to have a wonderful time and would be home before she knew it. Carol would have liked a moment to hold Ben close before kissing him goodbye but because the children were crowding around, there was no opportunity.

She stretched out her legs and circled her ankles, exercises which were supposed to help circulation. Luckily the seat beside her was empty and she was able to use it for her belongings, including the BGA file. The association had given her a thorough briefing on what to expect at the camp under the leadership of Alex Woolescroft and what he would expect of her and she would use the long journey to plough through the thick wodge of notes.

During the briefing she had been told a great deal about hygiene both in the kitchen and at base camp, stressing how important it was to keep equipment and stores dry. She was advised on the clothes to take, especially a stout pair of walking boots and trainers, several pairs for everyday wear since they tended to rot in the high humidity. They had rushed her through a medical check-up and having pronounced her fit had arranged for a series of injections to protect against an alarming list of possible diseases. She had been given a couple of videos to take home, one called *Adventures in the Rainforest* which the BBC had shot a couple of years earlier. She had watched them with Ben and the kids who afterwards had expressed envy at her luck. Seeing the place through their eyes did have the effect of bolstering her courage and lessening her fears about facing nature in the raw.

Phoebe Tugendhaat's tone was bland on being asked whether there was a problem with venomous animals. 'Newcomers often have an exaggerated fear of snakes, scorpions and that sort of thing. But we've never heard of anybody being killed by one.' She laughed. 'I doubt you'll be the first.' Carol had tried not to show the alarm she felt at this ambivalent response. Phoebe went on to tell her that after six months some people would go 'stir crazy' and needed to be brought out but as Carol was going for only three months she was sure there was no danger of that happening to her.

Though scientists from all over the world would be in residency at base camp, Phoebe made a joke about the greatest need being for cooks. No women from Brunei would volunteer because of strict Muslim laws regarding women being alone with males. And their menfolk regarded that kind of work as menial. The kitchen staff was recruited from Malaysia or the Ibans, the forest people. There were two types of scientists at the camp, undergraduates working in their gap year and others gathering material for their PhD theses. They spent long hours trekking to find new specimens or peering down microscopes cataloguing their finds. Because of this, food assumed greater importance than it did at home. 'We always say that morale only goes down when the food is bad,' said Phoebe, who gave Carol a file of well-loved recipes involving pasta and baked beans. Andrea had warned her that the cook could become the pivotal figure in camp life. Most of the menus would be fairly basic because of the primitive cooking conditions and the fact that fresh supplies were only available once or twice a week, if they were lucky. But Andrea was certain that with Carol's imagination she would be able to spice up the meals and had written out a few suggestions.

The smiling stewardess brought some freshly-squeezed pineapple juice in a proper crystal glass, one of the benefits of travelling Club class, an upgrade sanctioned by the Sultan, the major sponsor of the trip. Carol drained the glass, appreciating the tangy freshness. The pilot announced that they were flying at thirty thousand feet and that their first stop would be Dubai. This was the first time she had gone off on her own since she married seven years ago and she had a sudden feeling of freedom. Unlike her last trip to Disneyland, there were no little hands tugging at her sleeve, peppering her with questions, no one constantly asking when they would arrive. No one making demands for water, saying they were bored or asking to be taken to the lavatory.

Something caught her eye as she closed the folder. It seemed the admin.

assistant who had filled in the papers had made a mistake with her name. The 'l' had been left off Carol. It was obviously a typographical error but when she flicked through the rest of the documents, including the arrival details and all her medical forms, she found it spelled the same throughout.

She was about to begin the task of replacing the missing letter when she paused.

Caro. Caro Mitchell.

That name had rather an exotic ring to it. She had always disliked being called Carol, blaming her parents for being unimaginative in giving a December-born baby such a seasonal name. But what a difference the loss of one letter made. She could imagine that a Caro would be far more assertive than a Carol. A person called Caro could be anything she liked, outspoken, not afraid to try things, meeting people as equals and welcoming new experiences. People would remember the name. It wouldn't just fade into the background.

She put her pen back into her handbag. It would be fun to see if a name could make a difference to her personality.

Ben had advised her to walk up and down the plane whenever she could but she felt too inhibited. That was her major problem, she was too self-conscious. Repeatedly she told herself that other people were far too preoccupied with their own activities to notice what she was doing but she had found herself frequently holding back. Part of the problem stemmed from childhood. Her father had been a domineering man and had little patience for what he dismissed as 'female chat'. Since her marriage to Ben she had blossomed but nevertheless at dinner parties with his friends, who rarely discussed anything other than political shenanigans, she tended to remain an interested listener rather than a participant. She read papers and magazines and Ben mostly told her what he had been up to and what was going on, but she was still on the sidelines. She supposed it would be impossible to match the knowledge of the people working in Brunei but she had diligently done her homework on the country, hoping to fill a few gaps.

She took a deep breath, levered herself out of her seat and stood in the aisle. Here goes, she thought. Caro wouldn't think twice about pulling that curtain aside and walking to the back of the plane. Economy class was full and she hesitated, for the aisle was blocked by stewardesses with trolleys. She circumvented them and arrived at the catering section, ignoring the curious stares. Asked whether she needed anything she thanked them but no, she was merely taking exercise. Carol was smiling as she regained her seat.

Buoyed up by this tiny triumph she told herself that she had a chance to reinvent herself when she landed in a strange country, meeting new people and with no history. If she wanted to be taken seriously she had to force herself to be more assertive. Someone called Caro would hardly take a back seat. She would force herself to contribute, instead of letting it all pass over her and losing momentum.

From now on she would be a Caro, with all that implied.

Caitlin Thomas had been ringing Ben's office phone for the past hour and could hardly hide her impatience when, on the ninth time of trying, he finally picked up the receiver.

'Where've you been? I've been ringing for the past hour.'

'Dropping the kids off at their grandmother's.'

She was bursting with the news. Her spy had interceded with the Home Secretary and had reported that Ben might be able to push him for a quote for tomorrow's paper. 'Here's the private number where you can find him now.'

She brushed aside his expression of thanks and suggested they meet for a drink after the first edition. 'I have a few ideas on how you can milk some more from the story.' Ben apologised and explained he had to be home early as he was in sole charge of the kids. His wife had flown out that morning for a three-month stint in some remote outpost in Brunei.

Caitlin was astonished at her luck. Three whole months on his own? After replacing the receiver she hurriedly took out the Reader's Digest atlas of the world and eventually located the tiny kingdom. Thousands of miles away, she thought gleefully, in East Asia, on the north coast of Borneo. As she fixed herself a gin and tonic she reflected on how nicely life was shaping up. Business couldn't be better, thanks in part to her brilliant contacts in the government.

Her only sadness was the decision to send young William to boarding school. She had done so with a heavy heart, but really, with her fourteen-hour days and the erratic nature of the young women she was able to hire to look after him, he was better off surrounded by his pals. Or so she told herself. His first exeat had been traumatic. It had taken her an hour to persuade him to leave the car and go back to school but the headmaster had told her later he had settled down at once and joined in a chess game. Children. They gave you grey hairs, and for what?

If anyone had told her how besotted she would become with this tousle-haired boy she would have laughed. She was in the habit of going to the school every Saturday afternoon in the hope of catching a glimpse of him playing in some team or other. He was far too preoccupied with the game to take much notice of her but occasionally she was able to snatch a hug when no one was looking. It was too early to say that he bore much resemblance to his father, his features being too child-like, but now and then he would turn towards her and she would suddenly get a glimpse of the Ben she had loved and her heart would melt.

Until recently she had had no intention of telling Ben of his son's existence but lately she could think of little else. She dreamed of the day she would introduce them and spent many happy hours speculating on how he would accept the news. She had prepared herself for any eventuality, for shock, disbelief, even denial. But always the dream ended with Ben's acceptance, his delight at the discovery of a son and his renewed fervour for what she could offer him. In all these dreams his wife had faded into the background. Hearing that Carol had disappeared from the scene for three months on some hare-brained excursion, leaving Ben and the children to fend for themselves, gave Caitlin the idea that she might profit from her absence.

Caitlin had now persuaded herself that Ben's marriage was in trouble. When the end came, which couldn't be long, she would be there to offer sympathy, support and love. She would embrace Ben's children as her own and it would be particularly good for William to have ready-made siblings. In those circumstances she would work from home and take William out of boarding school to concentrate on welding them all into one big happy family.

Reality hit home when she unwrapped the Marks and Spencer sushi prepared for one. It wasn't going to be easy to persuade Ben that life would be better for all of them without Carol. For years he had been unhappy with Fay but resisted any suggestions of leaving her because of his children. But the children were older now and Carol was not their real mother. In any case, how much could she care for them if she was willing to leave them for such a long time?

Since her return from Washington Caitlin had begun to make new friends and it was true that a number of men had shown an interest in her. But if they weren't married they were sad loners who had left it too late for a real partnership. She had taken some pleasure in a few casual flings in Washington but they hadn't brought her real happiness and she had no intention of going down that road again. Anyway, none of these flirtations interested her, not when her affections were engaged elsewhere.

Next time it had to be Ben.

Chapter Thirteen

Dawn was breaking over the South China Sea as the jet swept over the capital of Brunei. Carol's first glimpse of Bandar Seri Begawan was a circle of gold as the rising sun struck the roof of a large mosque. The captain announced that eighteen-carat gold had been used, by order of the Sultan. 'It's the most expensive place of worship in the world,' he said proudly.

As the passengers waited for the cabin doors to be opened, the stewardess shyly made her way to where Carol was gathering her belongings together. 'I notice you have a yellow scarf. That is the royal colour and no one here would wear it, out of respect for the Sultan and his family. I hope you don't mind me mentioning it.'

Carol thanked her, wondering how she had missed this important fact in the briefing notes. Everything else had been punctiliously itemised so it was bound to be her oversight. Hurriedly she removed the offending neckwear, folded it and placed it at the bottom of her tote bag.

The intensity of the humid air hit her as she descended the plane steps. It was as if someone high in the heavens had emptied a cauldron of boiling water and put a lid on the country so none of the steam could escape. Carol had taken to heart the instructions to cover every inch of flesh and had bought several pairs of lightweight cotton trousers to wear with her long-sleeved shirts. She had been told that the wearing of trousers by Western women was tolerated but local females were mostly confined to long, flowing robes topped by head-enveloping chadors. Shorts for BGA people were absolutely forbidden except out in the field.

Her face and neck prickled as she descended to the tarmac and climbed on board the bus to take her to the terminal. Thank goodness the bus was air-conditioned. Around her the ultra-modern airport looked much like any other except the workers going about their duties seemed not to hurry as they did in Western cities, their long, white pantaloons lending an Arabian Nights atmosphere to the scene.

Amidst the bustle of the marble-walled arrivals hall the figure of a tall, elegant blonde stood out. She was in her early thirties, pale hair scraped back in a ponytail, wearing the regulation khaki chinos and shirt. But Carol was reminded at once of a school friend who, although wearing the identical uniform to the rest of them, somehow managed to transform hers into a designer outfit. Even without the BGA placard held above her head Caro would have recognised her as the type of well-bred young woman she had seen around the Kensington headquarters. Without these enthusiasts, some of them volunteers, Phoebe had said, the hard-up but prestigious organisation would have found it difficult to maintain its international service.

Francesca Stone had been in Brunei for nearly two years as the liaison officer between London and base camp. She held out her hand. 'Welcome to Brunei, Caro.'

There it was. The mistake had followed her from London. She opened her mouth to correct the woman then found herself keeping quiet.

As the two of them walked towards the freight hall Francesca chattered brightly. She had been due to return six months earlier but explained she had extended her visit 'because she loved the country'. Apart from escorting new arrivals to the hotel where it was hoped they would have a good night's rest before setting off upriver, Francesca would collect supplies from customs, a task that needed both patience and diplomacy.

Papers were produced, brows furrowed and Francesca appeared to have hit a problem. 'Look at this carnet, five packages accounted for at Heathrow,' she was saying to the customs official. 'Now you're telling me there are only four. What's happened to the other one?'

The woman gave an almost imperceptible shrug of the shoulders. 'We cannot give you what is not here.'

Francesca turned to Caro. 'Did you count the packages yourself?'

Caro tried to control a feeling of panic, remembering the confusion at the freight desk and with Katie clamouring for her attention. 'No, I'm sorry, I didn't.'

'Ummm.' Francesca screwed up her face. 'So we don't know if the carnet was correct. That's a pity,' she said. 'If there's a problem we need to know at which end it happened.'

'If you don't check,' the customs officer butted in, 'the stuff disappears before it gets here. We cannot be held responsible.' She changed the number from five to four and asked Francesca to initial the alteration.

Swiftly Francesca took the papers and scanned the list of contents on the customs declaration form. 'Shit, shit, shit,' she said, under her breath.

The missing package was for the butterfly man, as Francesca called him. George Cruikshank was a senior scientist, a world-renowned expert, funded to come out for only a short period. He needed a rare kind of crystal to preserve his specimens and now he probably wouldn't be able to finish the project in his allotted time. She wasn't sure if he would be able to wait for fresh supplies.

'It would be the package they're desperate for,' she said eventually and gave a little shiver. 'Alex will go berserk.'

Carol was mortified. What a start to the trip. 'Nobody told me,' she began but Francesca ignored this.

'Too late for that.' She strode off pushing a trolley piled with the four remaining boxes. Carol followed in her wake, thoroughly despondent, and wondering what kind of leader this Alex was who could cause such trepidation in this self-possessed young woman.

Things did not improve. Carol was unpacking in her soulless but thankfully air-conditioned hotel room when Francesca appeared. She had sent an urgent email to London requesting replacement crystals, and the news was not good.

'London say it'll take at least ten days to re-order the stock,' she groaned. 'I'll have to give Alex the bad news on the short-wave radio tonight.' She suggested they have a quick snack before Caro's jet lag caught up with her.

They were the only women in the dining room and Francesca explained that it would be most unusual for a Muslim woman to eat in a Western hotel. In any case she would never be left alone with a man who wasn't her husband. That would be against strict Islamic law. Local gossip had it that a young couple had been denounced by the girl's mother for being alone in a house, watching television. The couple had been forbidden to see each other again.

'None of that will bother you out there,' smiled Francesca. 'You only have to worry about Alex.'

Francesca did not need much prompting to talk about the thirty-five year-old ex-Marine Alex Woollescroft, who had become a professional expedition leader after training in environmental sciences at university. Apparently he had been born in South Africa but had been adopted by an affluent British couple from Hampshire. According to the briefing notes Caro had read, he had once belonged to a UN peacekeeping force in Kosovo and had run jungle warfare training courses in Belize. 'He pretends to like women,' said Francesca with a trace of asperity, 'but he's typical army. Women are there to serve, at table or in bed.'

'He sounds frightening. I hope I won't have much to do with him.'

Francesca gave a short laugh. 'Don't kid yourself; you'll be under the scrutiny of those fierce brown eyes from the moment you set foot in base camp. He prides himself on knowing every damn detail of what's going on. He can be charming, very charming when he wants something, but if you dare query any of his instructions he reminds you that in the army he ran a whole squadron including the entire transport fleet of Land Rovers in Kosovo and had a two million quid budget.'

'Is everyone browbeaten by him?'

'I'm not.' Francesca sounded too strident and for a moment Carol wondered what her relationship was with this formidable man. Francesca added that in her opinion Alex was using this experience merely as a stepping stone to establishing his own expedition agency. She took a swig of juice. 'What I'd give for a gin and tonic,' she sighed. 'Never mind, you can have a beer when you get to camp.'

'Are the rules that strict?'

'Here, yes, but unlike Saudi no one's been flung into jail yet.'

They arranged to meet at six the next morning. That would give them time to see some of the wondrous sights of the capital before Caro caught the boat downriver to Belalong at ten o'clock.

Lying back on the bed in the four-star hotel's characterless bedroom, a wave of sadness engulfed Carol. This was the first time she'd been alone for years and she felt lost. She had left the family she loved to cope on their own. Ahead was life in strange surroundings, with a boss who by all accounts was going to give her hell. What had possessed her? What was she trying to prove by running to the far ends of the earth? She was unused to lying alone in a large double bed instead of cuddling up against Ben's warm body.

Suddenly she needed to hear his voice, to know she was still part of a family that loved her, that had not forgotten her. She started to smile. Dammit, she had been away one day, she wouldn't last a week at this rate. She had to stop having such melodramatic thoughts. In any case it would be about seven in the morning at home and she wouldn't be too popular if she woke them up at that hour on a Sunday just to tell them she had arrived safely. Instead she set her alarm for five thirty when it would be about lunchtime in Britain.

A previous occupant had left a Lonely Planet guidebook, which for some reason had not been removed, and she flicked open a page. 'This tiny oil-rich sultanate is known chiefly for the astounding wealth of its Sultan,' she read, 'its tax-free subsidised society and the fact that statistically at least, its 280,000 people enjoy one of the highest per capita incomes on earth.'

She wandered to the window and looked out towards the harbour from her second-floor room. People were unhurriedly shopping at the kiosks offering a huge array of local fruit and vegetables but on the outskirts there seemed to be little traffic and Carol realised the populace would probably be worshipping at the mosques. Returning to the guidebook she understood why. 'Brunei' she read on, 'is a little slice of Islamic heaven. Alcohol is virtually unobtainable, there is no nightlife to speak of and the political culture encourages quiet acquiescence to the edicts of the Sultan.' Just the place for Becky, she thought mischievously.

Despite being exhausted she had a fitful night and awoke feeling worn out. Her sleep had been plagued by dreams of disturbing images, caterpillars hatching on a tree trunk, one becoming a giant butterfly with a man's head, the features contorted with fury.

She tried not to let her low spirits affect her conversations with the children who as usual had commandeered the phone as soon as it had rung. They were happy to hear from her and Emmy again reminded her to keep a diary. But their excited chatter was mainly about their imminent visit to the local animal shelter. Lisa had come round last night and suggested they ask Dad whether they could go and choose a kitten.

Carol couldn't keep the sharpness out of her voice as she asked to speak to their father. Hadn't she and Ben vetoed getting another cat after Muffin was killed in the busy road outside their house? The children had been devastated and they agreed it would be unwise to put them through another possible trauma again.

When Ben came on the phone, instead of giving her prepared speech about how much she was missing them all, especially him, she found herself getting irritated about the kitten. He was justifying himself, saying he wanted to make up to them for her absence and she let him know how upset she was that he'd come to the decision without consulting her. He was sorry she was cross about it but after Lisa had put it into their heads he couldn't back down, the children were too excited.

When the call was over Carol regretted she had been sharp with him, she was sad at being excluded from a major moment in the children's lives. Becky had mentioned something else which had niggled her. They would be going to a pub for lunch afterwards. Carol couldn't remember the last time they had gone out to Sunday lunch as a family and couldn't douse the frisson of annoyance. As she packed her overnight case ready for the journey upriver she began to simmer down and chided herself for being petty about the kitten. She could understand Ben's need to treat the children.

Francesca arrived on the stroke of six to take her to the capital's most important attraction. Troughs of running water flanked the entrance of the Omar Ali Saifuddien Mosque and Carol saw hundreds of worshippers busily engaged washing their feet before walking barefoot into the interior. Close up, the marbled structure was even more dazzling than it had appeared from the plane and Carol wondered how much it had cost for the builders to fashion an entire dome of solid gold. Apart from a couple of American tourists, she and Francesca were the only females in sight. In spite of being briefed about this, it still seemed very eighteenth century in what was ostensibly a modern country. When she mentioned this, Francesca told her of a custom that had caused her some disquiet when she had first come across it. 'The women adopt a softer tone when addressing men. Any man has to be talked to in a lighter, more coquettish manner, whether it be a husband or a street sweeper. Some of the women are extremely well-educated and they talk normally to me. But as soon as a man appears their voices go all fluttery. It's second nature, they don't realise they're doing it.'

Across the river from Bandar, Francesca pointed to the horizon dominated by a collection of wooden houses built on stilts, Kampong Ayer, the largest water community in the world. 'Next time, make sure you go over to see it. Thirty thousand people live there and the houses are fantastic, some of them very "Homes and Gardens".' Francesca explained that the Sultan had offered the water people the chance to settle on land, in a purpose-built, beautifully-planned town. They had turned the proposal down flat, preferring the cool breeze of the waterway to the most palatial surroundings.

As they made their way to the pier in the BGA jeep, packed to the roof with supplies, Francesca pointed out the road leading to the Sultan's residence which had seventeen hundred rooms, five swimming pools and – what had impressed her most – two hundred and fifty-seven bathrooms. 'Never far from a loo, that would suit my youngest,' laughed Carol.

The humidity had risen to ninety degrees and Carol felt as though she had walked fully clothed through a shower. Francesca showed no signs of discomfort and watching Carol mop her brow assured her that eventually she, too, would become acclimatised to the heat. 'It'll only take a couple of months.' She smiled. 'If you don't go near air-conditioning.'

They arrived at the wooden jetty to board a newly-painted ferry, looking, Carol thought, more like a pleasure boat than a working vessel. Then followed the laborious business of loading the supplies of which the first to go aboard were the precious packages from London. Francesca supervised the loading of the packages from the landing quay onto the motorboat, counting them carefully.

'Do people at the camp know about the missing box?' It had been a worry running through Carol's mind all morning.

'Afraid so. I didn't speak to Alex personally, he was out on a field trip, but I left a message.' She gave Carol a reassuring smile. 'Look, he will explode, there's no point in pretending he won't, but I'll try and sort something out. All you can do is apologise. For God's sake don't try and duck the responsibility. That will send him ballistic. Better to say sorry and ride the storm. He doesn't bear grudges, that's one thing I will say for him.'

'When is he getting back?' asked Carol.

'These field trips sometimes take a day, sometimes a couple of weeks. Depends what they're looking for and how lucky they are.'

Carol was pleased to discover there would be a respite before she had to face her boss's wrath.

Francesca prepared to depart, satisfied everything was on board. 'My work is mainly co-ordinating with Alex,' she said, 'and as he's away there's not much point my accompanying you to the camp. Our rep Angus

Roberts will meet you with the jeep and take you to the longboats. You'll get to base camp about a couple of hours after that, well before dusk. I believe you're sharing a hut with Zoe. She's the expedition nurse and with Alex away she'll have time to show you the ropes.'

Carol greeted the news that she would be travelling to the rainforest on her own with a mixture of disappointment and nervousness. Until then she had assumed that, as she was totally inexperienced, somebody would be with her to guide her through the first days.

'I haven't had time to ask you about the routine at base camp,' she began but Francesca brushed this aside with the assurance of one who had experience in the field.

'You'll soon learn as you go, we all do. Don't worry.'

But ever since Carol had found out about the snakes in the forest she had been worrying and she attempted to find out whether there were many in the vicinity of base camp.

Francesca was brisk. 'Not that many.'

'That many'? How many was that? Fear of the answer kept her quiet. Francesca added with a hint of a smile, 'If you do come across one, keep still and let it slide across your shoes.'

Slide over her feet? Carol thought she must be kidding. At least she hoped she was.

'Just remember, if you go out at night, however bright the moon take a torch with you to sweep the ground in front of you with the beam and scare off any snakes.' With that, Francesca waved farewell and got back into the jeep.

As Carol watched her leave, she made a silent vow never to venture out at night.

As she walked up the gangway, following the muscled young boy carrying her holdall, she became aware that she was the object of a certain amount of curiosity. Gangs of labourers, wrestling with crates of vegetables, paused to watch as she settled herself under the canopy stretched across the bows and fastened her life jacket, an essential safety precaution. Carol gave a half smile and a dozen pair of eyes looked away at once.

With a surprising burst of speed the gangway was hauled up, the engines started and the ferry made its way into the centre of the muddy river. Although she was under the shade of the canopy, the heat was intense and Carol wished she could roll up her long-sleeved shirt and change into shorts.

They passed a sprinkling of flat-roofed houses which thinned as they made their way inland through the tidal channels. She was startled by the sudden revving of the engines as the boat veered sideways to avoid a relay of barges heavily laden with gravel on its way to the capital. The man in the wheelhouse waved an arm and shouted angrily as the line of barges scraped against the side of the ferry.

As their boat made its steady way into the mangrove forest Carol caught a glimpse of a colony of proboscis monkeys with their hugely extended noses. It was like being on a trip to the zoo without the cages. She wished Ben and the kids could share the experience and had a sudden image of what she would usually be doing on a Monday morning in Battersea. By now she would have just finished doing her third load of washing having battled through the rush hour traffic to drop the kids off at school. A quick coffee then she would have rushed to join Lisa and the gang at Jolly Good Food. Instead, here she was, the wind whistling through her hair as the boat cut through the water, creating a breeze, a welcome change from the heavy humidity in the capital.

A group of small children stood waving energetically on the bank and as she returned their greeting Carol experienced a surge of confidence. Lisa had said often enough she was a competent cook and Ben had always been grateful for how calmly she coped with the unexpected ups and downs of family life. Right at the beginning, when she had just moved in, and Ben was out of London, the baby had been taken ill. The doctor urged her to take her at once to the hospital. Having no idea where to go, Carol bundled Katie into a blanket and raced out with the other two children in tow to the corner of the road. There she flagged down the first woman driver she spotted. Luckily, it turned out well. The baby recovered and the Good Samaritan became a friend.

Recalling how easily she had overcome her fear when faced with that crisis, how bad could it be out here? She made a promise to herself that in this new job she would never allow her insecurities to show. She had gathered from Francesca that as her boss was a hard taskmaster, it was essential not to show weakness. Carol had too often taken the easy way out to avoid confrontations but Caro would not allow herself to be bullied. If Alex was going to give her a hard time over the loss of the package she would apologise, not shy away from blame, but, she lectured herself, in no way would she grovel. No one had told her about the problems of transporting packages. If she had been warned, she would have been far more assiduous instead of leaving it to airline freight departments. It was a problem of inexperience not carelessness, as she would point out.

As the pilot steered the boat deeper and deeper into the mangrove swamps, the light became shut out by the dense vegetation. Apart from the vibration of the engines, Carol was struck by the stillness around her. The forest was quiet and the river banks deserted. Although she had not slept well, she remained alert, absorbing what she could of the exotic greenery as it passed in a blur of speed. In the lowland tropical forest she glimpsed mist-shrouded trees and much greener vegetation than she'd seen in the English countryside.

After more than an hour the noise of the engines suddenly slackened and there, round a bend in the river, were a collection of small buildings. As they neared the landing stage, Carol could make out what looked like a store, with an iron sign tacked to its roof. Alongside were rows of makeshift canopies, shading the jetty. The pilot manoeuvred the boat alongside the bank and a crew member flung a length of rope to a waiting boy, who deftly knotted it round a wooden post. An outstretched arm, belonging to a thickset man in his middle forties, helped Carol down the steps. He wore the regulation khaki, his sturdy thighs bronzed beneath a pair of superbly-creased shorts. It could only be Angus Roberts.

'You must be Caro,' he said, extending his hand.

She nodded, loving the sound of the name.

The man excused himself after introductions, saying he needed to check out the packages and the list of supplies sent from Bandar. Just as Francesca had not once taken her eyes off the loaders, nor did Angus and Carol began to realise how meticulous the organisation had to be. She could see that her excuse, not knowing the checking had to be done, might be seen as a poor one when supplies had to come all these thousands of miles. Eventually Angus was finished and suggested as it would be another half hour before the longboats left, they could have a refreshing drink. Coca-Cola was safe, he informed her, if the seal was unbroken. 'There's a filtered water supply at base camp so you'll be OK to drink it there,' he said as they made their way towards the small tin-roofed bar. He suggested they sit indoors where it would be cooler.

The Indian owner brought over the ice-cold drinks, proudly

proclaiming this was thanks to his newly-acquired generator. Wincing at the bill, Angus commented that the price had doubled to two Brunei dollars, which explained how the owner could afford his new equipment.

Carol asked if it was possible to extricate her holdall from the boat as she wanted to change into shorts. Angus advised against it. 'Best to wait. Not many Western women around here.' She took some ice from her drink and held it against her cheek. 'No,' said Angus. 'The back of your neck is better. Lowers the temperature.'

Though keen to learn more about the routine of camp life, Carol could make no headway as Angus seemed keen to do the talking. He appeared to be fixated on his boss. According to him Alex Woollescroft was lucky to have the job. He was not as well qualified as some of the other applicants; the way he was sounding off, Carol suspected he had probably applied for the job himself.

However hard she tried to divert him towards general aspects of the camp, Angus returned to his dissection of the camp leader. 'He runs that place like a tinpot dictator,' he said dismissively. 'Not surprising bearing in mind his background. Trouble is, the chap has a huge chip on his shoulder. It's a culture thing, comes from being born in the colonies. He tries to be more British than the British.'

Carol hoped she wouldn't have much to do with this disagreeable man. He was the kind of ex-pat who gave the British a bad name. But if she thought her silence might deter Angus from babbling, she was wrong. Apparently he had few chances to talk to his compatriots, stuck as he had been in this outpost for two years, so he took the opportunity to talk about himself, why he preferred living out there and about his recent marriage to a Malay woman.

'I'm a real dinosaur. Couldn't be doing with one of your sort any more. It's great for men out here. I come home to find my drink and supper ready, my kaftan laid out on the bed and if I'm in the mood, my wife as well,' he chortled.

Carol repressed a shudder and couldn't resist saying, 'I can see why you married her. But why did she choose you?'

He didn't appear to take umbrage. 'Oh, she tells me all the time she's very happy. And why shouldn't she be? She has a house, status. I'll soon give her some kids. Mind, I'm twenty-five years older than her so I'd better get on with it.'

Carol hoped fervently that the other males in the camp wouldn't be so unlikeable.

When they hiked over to a smaller landing stage, a series of long canoes had been tied to the bank and their equipment and supplies were already loaded. The boats were long and shallow-beamed and Carol hoped they were sturdy enough for the journey. When she mentioned this, Angus broke into a laugh. 'They are much sturdier than they look. So are the oarsmen.' He explained these boats had to be light because when the river was low it was necessary to get out and push.

Carol thought he was exaggerating but changed her mind when he went on, 'The rapids are the worst. You have to push uphill. This river's quite dangerous when there's a flash flood.' When he saw her expression he added, 'Don't worry. After the spell of dry weather we've just had the water level is very shallow. You might be asked to get out and walk because of the weight of the stuff but the water won't come past your ankles.'

Walking in the water? OK, there were no crocodiles but what about those crustaceans which were said to burrow underneath the skin? Carol hoped she wouldn't disgrace herself by showing fear. Caro wouldn't do that and the thought steadied her.

Angus held out his hand in farewell and gingerly Carol manoeuvred herself down the steps of the jetty to perch in the middle of the boat, surrounded front and back by sacks and boxes. The two oarsmen smiled encouragingly as they pushed off from the river bank and she wondered whether they could speak English. If they overturned or got into difficulties she hoped they would understand the world 'help'.

As the longboat entered the rainforest through the winding tributary of the Belalong River she breathed in appreciatively. The air was fresher and clearer than in the capital, and the colours seemed to be enhanced. There was no sign of human life anywhere, no advertisements, no log cabins, no picnic sites. Angus had told her that she would see little other traffic as the base camp was the only port of call along the banks. Building was outlawed in this heavily-protected conservation area and since historic times there had been no local people holding rights to the land or waters in the forest reserve. Indeed the BGA had taken over a year to obtain permission to build a camp and only then because it would be a training venue for students from Brunei University.

She gazed upwards at the canopy of trees as high as skyscrapers, overwhelmed by their majestic beauty, feeling insignificant against their grandeur. It would be no hardship to spend three months in such surroundings and she vowed that one day she would bring Ben and the kids to see all this splendour.

The only sound breaking the stillness during the two-hour journey over brilliantly clear waters was the wash from the paddles. Occasionally the man in the prow called over his shoulder what she assumed was an instruction to his companion. She admired their skill as they negotiated the often blind bends in the river. After a short while they came across one of the first of a series of rapids. At one stage the water level dropped and the oarsmen motioned her to climb out of the boat so they could haul it over the fiercely-rushing rapid. She found the cool water lapping over her trainers refreshing. The river bed was not muddy, as she had expected, but lined with pebbles, easily visible, and she found her anxieties slipping away.

Then without warning the tranquillity was broken and, as if someone had turned on a tap from above, the heavens opened. The heavy downpour drenched them all within seconds but unlike British rain it was warm. Carol lifted up her face, luxuriating in this unexpected soaking, and as the torrent continued she understood why the cargo had been so carefully covered in tarpaulins. Then again, without any obvious signs of it lessening, the rain ceased as suddenly as it had started. But although her clothes were sodden she had no sensation of being cold and within minutes her shirt was steaming in the heat, drying rapidly. Throughout the rainstorm the paddles of the boatmen had not slackened, maintaining the quick movements, propelling the boat towards base camp.

Exhaustion was beginning to set in and Carol lay back in the boat, fighting a desire to close her eyes, when she was brought back to reality by a shout from one of the oarsmen. He was pointing vigorously upstream. As the boat slowed down to navigate a bend she was suddenly presented with the sight of a collection of wooden huts, presumably their destination. This isolated outpost was to be her home for three months and Carol's heart increased its pace as the boat rapidly approached the steps of the jetty. A wooden walkway led up to what appeared to be a very large log cabin resting on stilts. She assumed this must be the main building, the dining room and kitchen complex, built, Francesca had told her, to accommodate up to forty people. The rest of the huts were gathered in a cluster nearby.

There was no sign of life even when the crew began unloading and Carol picked up her luggage to follow the men up the walkway. As they deposited the packages on the open balcony, Carol stood uncertainly, waiting for someone to appear. She had not expected banners but this silence was unnerving. After what seemed an age there was a sound of running feet from behind the hut and a short, thickset figure burst into view.

'You must be the new cook.'

She smiled at the man.

'Good,' he went on, giving her no chance to speak. 'Just point out which package has the crystals. I'm desperate to get on.'

This was the worst introduction to the camp she could imagine. It was obviously the butterfly man. Carol coloured and was about to make an abject apology when she remembered the promise she had made to herself – no cringing, as befitted her new persona.

'There's no easy way to tell you this,' she said, trying to hide her nervousness. 'Your package was lost in transit and—'

'Lost? I can't believe it. How could you let that happen? Surely you didn't let it out of your sight.' She was reminded not of a world-renowned scientist but a frustrated child, venting his disappointment just as Emmy did when she was banned from going to a disco with her sister. She looked him straight in the eye, as she had learned to do over the years with the children.

'It was too big to fit into the overhead locker,' she said, trying to sound more authoritative than she felt, 'and they insisted on putting it into the hold.'

He sat down on an overhanging branch which had grown so low over the balcony it served as a bench and began to mop his brow.

'They always say that.' His tone reflected his exasperation. 'You should've ignored them.'

Carol stood her ground. 'I was given no choice and I have no way of knowing whether the parcel was lost at Heathrow or Bandar.'

For a second he paused before snorting, 'This is a bloody nuisance. I won't be able to finish the project.'

'I realise how inconvenient it is but I can't do much more than apologise.'

His anger seemed to evaporate. 'This is always happening,' he said. 'I shouldn't have jumped down your throat. I'm sorry.'

'Francesca's hoping your package will turn up but I believe she's already emailed London for replacements.'

He stood up. 'Thank goodness for that. Let's begin again. Welcome to our camp. I'm George Cruikshank.' He held out his hand. 'You must be Caro.'

'Yes,' she said with a surge of optimism, 'I am.'

He picked up her holdall and she followed more cheerfully up the wooden ramp. He offered to show her the way to her quarters which he said she would be sharing with the camp nurse, Zoe. He put her bag down and waved an arm airily in the direction of another large hut which had an air-conditioning box built into its side.

'That's the laboratory,' he said, 'the only place where you'll be cool. But we don't encourage live specimens to visit, only dead ones, I'm afraid.' His shoulders began to heave with laughter and she was reminded of Katie after she'd heard a particularly excruciating joke from Ben.

The camp appeared to be situated at the bottom of a valley, enveloped by the forest. The temperature must have been in the middle thirties and the humidity seemed quite high but she did not find it disagreeable, as she had in the centre of the city. George was gazing at the sky. Towers of dense cloud hovered overhead and he pointed upwards. 'That means rain. Any minute. It'll clear the air.' He had hardly finished when she heard the sound of heavy rain hitting the leaves. Her clothes had only just dried out and she rushed to the shelter of the large hut's verandah but George remained in the open, lifting his face to the rain. 'It's good for the complexion,' he shouted, with another heave of the shoulders. Within seconds his khaki shirt was soaked. He made his way towards her, water dripping off his nose, chin and elbows. 'Doesn't take long to dry out here. You'll find that out.'

'I already have,' she smiled. He looked incongruous standing in the middle of a forest with his longer-than-conventional shorts, well over his knees. He couldn't be married, she thought, noticing his ankle socks and sandals which would have been pensioned off long ago by a well-meaning wife. He picked up her bags and she followed him to a group of smaller huts.

'How do I tell my family I've arrived safely? Is there a phone I could use, or email?'

'We're pretty well kitted out for all of that,' he said. 'Only problem is Alex. He won't allow us to use the generator for personal messages. You can understand. We have to reserve the power for work and emergencies.'

'Then how do you get in touch with your family?'

'Not a worry for me,' he said cheerfully, 'haven't got one. But we have people going to Bandar regularly and if you give them the email address the lovely Francesca will send a message.'

The lovely Francesca? Maybe later she would pursue the subject. By then they had reached one of the huts and he said, 'These are your quarters and as far as camps go it's pretty good,' and added that he would see her later after work.

The hut was small, only five metres square, but remembering the warning about avoiding creepy crawlies on nocturnal outings, she was delighted to find it had its own flush lavatory inside an interior compartment, complete with washbasin and a shower. There were two small cupboards, both already crammed with clothes, though one had a small space to one side. Carol hesitated, wondering whether she could colonise it, when the door was flung open and a tall redhead stood on the deck.

'Caro Mitchell? Zoe Evans. Camp nurse. That's your bed over there. I like to shower early in the morning. Hope that's OK.' She did not wait for Carol to respond. 'Sorry about the wardrobe but as you're only here for a short time I thought you wouldn't need much space.' Throughout this her face remained unsmiling and to Carol's disquiet the dark eyes which stared at her seemed unfriendly.

For an instant Carol was tempted to mollify her roommate and assure her that she would fit her clothes around hers. But that was how Carol would react. Not Caro.

'I brought a few more things than will fit in here,' she said firmly. 'Can I help you move these?' Without waiting for a reply she unhooked an armful of clothes still on their hangers and laid them on Zoe's bed, amazed at her audacity.

'There's nowhere else to put them,' said the redhead.

Carol ignored this. 'I'm sure you'll be able to sort out something.'

Before the nurse could argue Carol forced her face into a tight smile. 'We're going to be sharing this place for months so I think it's sensible to try and get along, don't you?' She waited for the thaw.

Instead, Zoe made an angry grab at the clothes and said, 'Now I'll have to put these in the store,' and without another word marched out.

What was her problem? Having just arrived it couldn't be me, thought Carol. She began to unpack her bag, lifting out a framed picture of Ben and the kids, and reflected that whatever was bothering Zoe it had to be more than the lack of cupboard space.

It didn't take long to unpack and inspect the quarters. The shower was a rudimentary affair consisting of a tin rose attached to a rigid pipe but everything was spotless, from the narrow wooden bed to the floorboards. She positioned the picture on a shelf next to her bed, her toilet bag she hung on the washbasin tap and folded a cotton T-shirt under her pillow. At this point that was as much as she could do to settle in.

She poked her head outside. A slight figure, in the regulation shorts and T-shirt, emerged from the next hut and offered Carol a friendly smile. 'Welcome. Need any help?'

So they weren't all like Zoe. The woman walked briskly over and introduced herself as Diana Parsons. 'I'm known as the ant lady around here.' Carol was struck by a pair of intelligent grey eyes set in the worst pockmarked face she had ever seen. The woman had perfect teeth and lustrous dark hair, flecked with strands of silver, and apart from her complexion could have been a beauty. Carol made a great effort to keep her gaze fixed on the woman's eyes and remarked that this place must be paradise for her.

This polite remark opened the floodgates. For the next fifteen minutes Carol was subjected to the life history of the forest's ant colonies, especially the giant camponotus gigas, on which Diana was writing a thesis for her PhD. 'At first I was torn between studying the habits of the macaranga specimens,' Diana went on, 'because they are so closely associated with the genus crematogaster, but in the end I remained loyal to my gigas.' All of this went over Carol's head but she was charmed by the woman's enthusiasm.

The scientist blinked and took out a pair of spectacles whose arms were taped to the lens by Elastoplast. 'I'm forgetting my manners. You must need a drink or something. Let me take you to the dining room and introduce you around.'

'I have met a couple of people already,' Carol told her, 'the butterfly man and my roommate. I seem to have got on the wrong side of her.'

Diana appeared to study Carol intently for a moment. 'I'm not surprised. She doesn't like competition.' She smiled. 'Zoe is used to being queen of the camp around here. You shouldn't let it bother you.' The thought of spending the next three months with an antagonistic roommate filled Carol with foreboding but as the new girl she decided it was better not to press Diana. As they walked towards the main block, Diana added, 'Medical people can be a bit brusque, comes from playing God.' She gave a smile of such warmth that Carol believed she had found an ally.

Diana pushed her spectacles back onto her nose and offered to ask the kitchen staff to rustle up some food but Carol thought it would be a better move to introduce herself before eating.

The two women on duty in the kitchen, with their open expressions and wide smiles, gave her an unqualified welcome, one she came to realise was typical of the country. Carol had been told that she would share the duties of running the kitchen with one of the local staff who had been in charge since the camp had been established. She had limited knowledge of English palates but apparently was more than adept at dealing with the camp's Chinese supplier. Carol hoped that the selection of recipes she had brought with her would give her a measure of respect as it was doubtful the current workers would have tackled these menus before.

Diana passed her into the care of a tiny person, introduced as Anak the kitchen quartermaster. She was from Malayasia, over the border, and had been working at the camp for more than two years. Her heavy black hair was coiled tightly on top of her head and her skin was unwrinkled. Carol judged her to be in her middle thirties, but she could be much older. She was pleased to discover Anak's English was adequate enough to describe the daily routine. Breakfast preparations began at five, a simple lunch was served around noon and the main evening meal had to be on the tables by six thirty. Numbers did not vary unless there were visitors, when they might have to produce food for up to forty people. 'And when royal princes come, from our country and yours, we get special supplies from Bandar. But every day, all British people very hungry,' she smiled.

The kitchen had an outside oven fuelled by huge canisters of butane gas. It was a far cry from the ones at Jolly Good Food but Carol had been warned what to expect. There were only four rings on the hob but she was happy to see there was an additional source of heat from a smoking barbecue a few metres away from the dining hut.

Anak explained that although there was electricity at the camp it was reserved mainly for lighting and emergencies and Carol had been warned there was no spare capacity for aids like the mixers or graters they took for granted in Lisa's kitchen. Water, although rationed, was fairly plentiful and came from the camp's filtration system.

The kitchen walls were lined with wooden shelves, holding stacks of catering-sized cans of baked beans, tomatoes, sardines and packets of pasta. Everything was hung on beams 'to keep away from rats', according to Anak. 'They everywhere,' she sighed, but added with evident satisfaction that there were rat traps all over the floors and the support staff were paid money per rat body. Carol thought it best to keep quiet about her hatred of rodents. She supposed it would become evident soon enough.

Anak itemised some of the problems they faced. Porridge unless eaten within two days went mouldy and however much they tried they were unable to store the Britons' favourite cereal, corn flakes. Anak wrinkled her nose describing how damp they became however airtight the storage jars. On the brighter side, fresh meat and vegetables arrived twice a week from the capital but during the rainy season when the river was dangerous they couldn't rely on the longboats getting through. Luckily, April was the dry season and she and her helpers had already unpacked the longboats in which Carol had arrived.

In addition to breakfast and supper the cooks had to provide members going on field trips with rucksacks full of food and liquid. They had to produce special meals when visitors came to see the camp. Anak told her proudly that their visitors included people from their sponsors such as Shell and also Yamaha Motors who had donated the generator. 'Your Prince Andrew came last year. Great pleasure for us. Now I give you eggs and fresh fruit,' smiled Anak.

'And tomorrow,' said Carol, 'I'll start work.'

She sat alone in the cool of the dining hut, forking mouthfuls of lightly-cooked omelette. Never had eggs tasted so delicious and she realised it had been many hours since she had eaten. Anak had prepared a fruit platter of mangoes, guavas and papayas and the sight of them reminded her that mangoes were Emmy's favourite fruit. She glanced at her watch. It would be early morning at home and the children would be getting ready for school. She was hit with a wave of longing. It had seemed such an intriguing idea in Lisa's kitchen, with everyone, Andrea especially, egging her on. It was out of character to remove herself from all those familiar surroundings, simply to prove to Ben how much he would miss her. The push she had needed came from Ben and the kids encouraging her to be adventurous. And it had all appeared seamless with Lisa offering to step into her shoes.

But would she come to regret this impulse to get away? If Ben didn't have to worry about the children and his meals, maybe he wouldn't miss her. She gave herself a mental shake. That was defeatist thinking. Caro wouldn't take that line. It wouldn't occur to her that an absence of only three months could destroy the bonds forged within a family. Of course the children would love having Lisa around, especially as she'd probably indulge them, but that couldn't be a substitute for the nurturing she had given them over seven years. As for Ben, wouldn't he, like her, miss the warmth of their bodies cuddling up in bed? This was followed immediately by a disloyal thought. Would he cuddle up with someone else, as the caller had suggested? She chided herself for thinking like that. She had to trust him.

She had hoped that being in a new place with new challenges would enable her to forget all the old problems and it was true that since leaving England she had managed to push out of her mind the sight of Caitlin thrusting out her chest at her husband and his reaction to her flirting. But now the vision came back to torment her. Of course she had understood that by leaving the coast clear for twelve weeks she was testing Ben and his loyalty.

If her marriage couldn't survive this absence, better to discover it now, she thought, than much later on.

Chapter Fourteen

The chairman was poised before the microphone, waiting for the clamour to cease. At the *Sunday Chronicle* table Ben and his colleagues turned their chairs to face the podium. This was the moment when the major award of the evening was to be announced and the reason the Grosvenor House ballroom was packed to its fire regulations capacity. These awards were the most coveted in the newspaper village as candidates were judged by their peers.

To win the Newspaper of the Year title meant a circulation rise, an increase in advertising revenue and bonuses for the top editorial executives. Ben and his colleagues were quite relaxed; they had won the title last year and it was unlikely to be awarded to the same paper twice running. If a Sunday newspaper had been honoured one year, there was a tendency for a daily paper to be chosen the next time.

Finally the chairman achieved a hush. She began to open the envelope, handed to her by Fleet Street's oldest serving columnist. There was a roll of drums and she read: 'For the first time in our history a newspaper has achieved the almost impossible – unanimity amongst the judges. We were impressed by its vigilant news coverage of the flood rescue, the hard-hitting leaders and some major scoops in the political arena. I congratulate all who work on it and call upon,' she paused theatrically, 'the editor of the Newspaper of the Year . . .' the occupants of the room tensed for the big moment, 'the *Sunday Chronicle*.'

Ben, who had already sampled liberal amounts of his proprietor's hospitality, felt a hard slap on his back as his colleagues whooped and hollered in triumph. His editor almost ran to the platform and held aloft, in Wembley-like exultation, the handsome silver plaque, engraved with an illustrious list of previous winners since the award was established seventy years earlier. As number three on the paper Ben was showered with congratulations from all sides and as if already briefed, several waiters pushed their way through the cheering crowd bearing magnums of champagne, courtesy of a grateful proprietor. What a pity, thought Ben, Carol was not here to share the moment.

He was about to raise a glass, containing what he had noted appreciatively was a vintage Krug, when he felt a caress on the lobe of his ear. He recognised the touch at once. In the old days it had been a sure-fire signal of her intentions and he turned round sharply.

Caitlin was a magnificent sight. Her scarlet dress made her pale skin glow like alabaster and the way the dress was falling off her shoulders made it impossible to ignore the generous curves spilling out in front. He had noticed her earlier, of course, but had kept his distance. She had clients to entertain and he certainly didn't intend to provide gossip for his scandal-hungry colleagues, particularly as most of them knew Carol was thousands of miles away.

Caitlin was smiling down on him and before he could turn his head away she had bent over him, her breasts pressing against his shoulder, to kiss him on the lips, a fraction longer than was polite. Or necessary. With embarrassment he noted he was the object of a great deal of attention from his colleagues. And, God help him, again he found his traitorous body aroused.

'Congratulations.'

'No, I should thank you.'

'In that case I think I deserve a dance.'

He shook his head, too embarrassed to stand up. 'I'm hopeless at dancing. I have problems co-ordinating my feet.' But his deputy grabbed him by the arm and good-naturedly lifted him off his seat and propelled him towards the dance floor. Carefully Ben held Caitlin at arm's length. The band had lessened its tempo to a slow beat which drew many more couples onto the floor. It became so crowded it was impossible to do more than sway to the music.

She pressed her supple body against his and lifted her face to stare at him, eyes gleaming triumphantly, when she felt his response. At once he pushed her away.

'Why are you fighting this?'

He shook his head. 'I'm not going down that road again.'

'Pity.'

They carried on dancing, Ben careful to keep a decorous space between them, and Caitlin began to regale him with gossip she had heard that night about a rival being poached for a television station. He began to relax, feeling the danger had passed.

When the music stopped, Caitlin told him she had said goodnight to her guests and would he be an angel and escort her to the car park. 'It's probably stupid of me, but I feel in need of protection on a night like this.' And looking around at the florid faces of the inebriated journalists he had to agree with her.

As he waited for her to emerge from the cloakroom he hoped she would take him at his word. She remained as always a vibrant, entertaining woman who was also a valuable contact but he didn't want to get romantically involved again. Nor did he want to dent her pride.

As they stood in the lift, Ben careful to stand apart, Caitlin appeared preoccupied and Ben decided maybe her previous behaviour had been due to an excess of alcohol and excitement. He would see her to the car, they would part as friends and he would never refer to her remarks again.

In the car park Caitlin extricated the car keys from her bag and pressed the remote control button. There was a flash of lights from a silver Mercedes coupé parked a few yards away.

He raised an eyebrow. 'Should you be driving?'

'I stick to water on these sort of occasions.' So it hadn't been the alcohol.

He was about to open the driver's door when Caitlin stepped close to him, put her arms round his neck and drew his head towards her. 'I think I deserve a goodnight kiss,' she said softly.

Ben made an involuntary step backwards but she clung to him. Try as he might the combination of alcohol and the feeling of her warm body leaning against his overcame his resolve. He found himself burying his face in her hair, overwhelmed by the scent of her. With a groan he reached under her stole and cupped her near-naked breasts. He felt her nipples harden against his hand. Feverishly he sought her lips and at once her tongue explored his mouth in the way that had always driven him to a frenzy. All restraint gone, he pushed her fiercely down onto the car bonnet and heard her moan in pleasure. Right then nothing else existed but the two of them, panting, wanting, needing each other. This urgency, this passion, was how it used to be.

As she began to unbutton his shirt, her eyes glistening with desire, Ben became aware of the sound of exuberant singing. It brought him to his senses. With an immense effort of will he pulled Caitlin to her feet and, breathing heavily, watched the crowd of revellers making their way down the stairs. He began to refasten the buttons on his shirt, the combination of fright and guilt subduing his libido.

Wild-eyed, Caitlin stared up at him and in an acknowledgement that the moment had passed opened her car door, flung her handbag violently onto the passenger seat before climbing in behind the wheel. She pressed the button to wind down the window.

'Just don't blame it on the booze.'

Before he could reply she had gunned the motor and was speeding up the ramp towards the exit.

Chapter Fifteen

The last of the stragglers was leaving the dining hut after the breakfast shift. It was Carol's third day as part of the kitchen team and she had been too busy during the days to worry about what was happening at home, or indeed anything except keeping pace with the chopping and cooking needed to feed thirty ravenous scientists and ancillary staff. And at night, when her thoughts did turn to how Ben and the children would be managing, she fell into a dreamless sleep almost as soon as her head reached the pillow.

She collapsed onto a wooden stool, raising her eyes to the ceiling, a haven, she'd been told by Anak, for insects and, she suspected, bats as well. It had to be swept regularly but Carol constantly expected some survivor to fall down onto her bare arm.

She surveyed the pile of dirty dishes about to be tackled by two kitchen helpers.

'How on earth do people stay so slim when they eat so much?' she called out to Anak.

She was unaware of how her voice had carried and was faintly embarrassed when Diana called out, 'It's all we live for. What else is there to do but work and eat?'

Apart from Zoe, everybody had been welcoming though it was Diana who appeared to be keeping an eye on her, making sure she was included in the groups that gathered after supper to mull over the day's events. Carol was grateful to her because her roommate was keeping her distance, coming in just before lights out and barely exchanging more than a few words in the morning.

She soon noticed that though she asked the scientists about themselves or their work, never once did they show any curiosity about her background, seemingly content to know she was an efficient cook. Diana explained this was because people viewed living at base camp as being in limbo land. 'There's no past, no future, just the present,' a comment that went straight into Carol's diary.

It was true. Even in the short time she had been here she admired the dedication with which they approached their work. The post graduates among them seemed to have been chosen as much for their sober personalities as for their brains. They toiled until darkness and then after supper many of them returned to the lab. However late they worked they would still be queuing up for breakfast by six.

A pat on the shoulder made her start. George's ruddy face beamed at her.

'May I join you?' he asked, putting his cup of coffee down on the table. 'I haven't much to do now,' he said, wiping his forehead with a blue-spotted handkerchief, 'until the next consignment of crystals gets in.' Those bloody crystals. She was damned if she was going to apologise again. She had done enough penance already, worrying about them ever since she landed. As if reading her mind, George added, 'I'm sorry. That was unforgivable to bring it up again. Comes from being stuck behind a microscope all these years, talking to dead creatures. You forget your manners.'

Carol's face crinkled. 'If you practise on live creatures you'll find we don't bite.'

'All right, let's start by asking what brings you here?'

She explained about Andrea's accident and how the BGA had thought her a suitable replacement. She was able to describe her abilities matter-of-factly rather than down-playing them as usual, gratified that her new personality seemed to be taking charge without too much effort on her part. Of course this was easier when she was not immediately regarded as someone's wife or mother. She had taken off her wedding ring when Anak pointed out that it might be a hazard to hygiene but she decided there and then that however homesick she became she would not thrust details of her family life onto her new companions. For the past seven years she had been seen as Mrs Ben Mitchell and it would be a welcome change to be regarded as a person in her own right, a fellow professional.

In return George explained about life at base camp. According to him the atmosphere was serious during the day because all scientists had certain projects for which they were responsible. Off duty, he continued, the group liked to relax with a glass of beer or wine since alcohol was forbidden in town. She'd already found out that it rained promptly at four every afternoon but had she heard the six o'clock cicada? He was knowledgeable about the local flowers, plants and insects and she was fascinated to learn that in this part of the rainforest scientists were collating new species of flora and fauna every week and they estimated that seventy per cent of specimens in the insect world remained to be discovered.

As she and George talked, Carol heard a loud cracking sound, which seemed to go on for a long time but he seemed unperturbed. 'That's a couple of trees falling over. They do crash down suddenly because they're shallow-rooted. It starts a domino effect – when one goes, so do dozens more.'

He gave her a hard stare. 'That fine English skin will be like a magnet for mosquitoes and sand flies. I hope you're taking the larium.' When she assured him she was conscientious about taking the pills to keep malaria at bay he went on to talk about some of the other problems she would encounter, mainly about the humidity which reached eighty per cent every day. 'It can go up to a hundred degrees,' he said. 'It's like walking through treacle. Afternoons are the worst so see that you pace yourself.'

He explained that mealtimes were regarded by camp personnel as special, because they provided a welcome break from routine. If the standard fell, there would soon be complaints because good food was important for morale. 'See, that's why Alex is such a good leader,' he enthused. 'He understands we need meals at regular times. It provides the security of routine. Order. Necessary when you're far from home. Alex insists people change for meals, not wear muddy boots, that kind of thing. He's right, we Brits like structure and standards. This is the best camp I've been in because it's run on military lines.'

'If he's so good why did he leave the army?'

'Alex says he had to. The army's changing and, the way he put it, obviously not for the better.'

'Why doesn't a scientist run the camp instead of a former soldier?'

'I think the BGA find these camps are best run by army people, they've got the right experience and, judging by this camp, I'd say they were right,' replied George. 'He has his hands full keeping the project going and he's also responsible for the overall safety of everyone here as well as in the field. Then there's the tricky task of keeping diplomatic relations sweet with the Bruneians.'

Carol couldn't resist it. 'Can he also walk on water?'

George chuckled. 'Wouldn't be surprised.'

'With all he has to do, why is he away from his post now?'

'He's taken some moth men to Fish Eye Falls to install some traps. They're going up the north face, which is a fiendishly difficult climb, and he felt he should lead it. He should be back in a couple of days.'

Two days. She'd been so caught up in her tasks she'd almost forgotten the return of the Fuehrer.

George noticed her concerned expression. 'Alex is a strict taskmaster, no doubt about that. Won't tolerate sloppiness.' She was aware of his gentle eyes on her. 'He won't be pleased about those crystals, but he can't eat you.'

'Are you sure?'

She promised herself that though she might be dreading the forthcoming encounter, she was damned if she would let it show.

In his office in the heart of Canary Wharf, Ben was nursing a cup of black coffee, hoping the aspirin would still the throbbing of his temples. The newsroom was unusually subdued, with the rest of the living dead trying to make some semblance of being in charge of their actions. Luckily he had nothing important in his diary. He began a desultory trail through the morning papers. There was no mention of the awards ceremony except in their daily stable mate, and even they had given only a couple of paragraphs to it. In his world these were the equivalent of the Oscars but outside the business who cared? He was about to make himself a second cup of coffee when a knock at his door heralded the arrival of a courier who said he had a special delivery.

The envelope was unstamped and heavy, stationery of such quality, he assumed it was from 10 Downing Street. But the customary address was not on the back of the envelope. He ripped it open, his eyes skipping to the signature. Caitlin. He had managed to submerge all memory of the encounter in the car park. Now it was as if a curtain had been ripped apart and he could see in Technicolor the splash of scarlet over the silver coupé as she lay waiting, submissive. What the fuck could he have been thinking of? This thought was swiftly followed by 'Thank God Carol will never find out.'

Was Caitlin going to try again to resurrect the past? But a quick scan of the letter made him relax. Of all things it was an apology. Phrases leapt out at him. 'I never should've allowed it to happen . . . the evening was wonderful for both of us. Don't allow guilt to spoil what we have together. We're too good a team . . .' He read the letter once more and put it on his desk. He walked to the window, oblivious of the fine view of the Thames. The woman was dangerous. The sexual attraction between them could not be denied. He rarely allowed himself to remember the old days when their lust had been so all-consuming they had not managed to move from the space behind the front door before ripping the clothes off each other. Making love on the hall floor had become so frequent Caitlin had confessed she rarely wore panties when they were due to meet up. They would make love anywhere. They were reckless. Once she had sat on his lap in a taxi . . . With a great effort of will he managed to stifle the memory and shifted uncomfortably from one foot to the other.

But he was more determined than ever not to allow memories of their passionate affair to make him weaken. He would not succumb, having learned a bitter lesson about what misery an adulterous affair could cause to so many people. Besides, he did not want to be disloyal to a wife who was blameless and whose life was devoted to making him happy.

Ben returned to his desk, still unable to concentrate on anything other than Caitlin. He was still surprised she had written such a contrite letter. It was she who had come on to him, not the other way round. How could he blame himself? It was not his fault, particularly when he was tanked up. And let's face it, he was feeling randy, not surprising since Carol was away. What man could have withstood that onslaught when it looked like Caitlin?

He'd long given up wondering about her motives. When she'd first contacted him on her return from America he'd been wary but she had never given any indication that she regarded him as more than a useful political conduit for her clients. And she had some of the most influential people in Europe as clients. They'd discussed how few people of influence there were in the entire world, only about five hundred, and she boasted that with her American associates she had access to at least fifteen of them.

When Caitlin had come back into his life he had tried to fob her off with his deputy but she had been adamant that she must deal with the top dog. If he were to fob her off she would simply decamp to a rival, she had told him testily. He could understand her need to negotiate with the decision-maker but why had she chosen his paper out of all of them? He wasn't stupid but until the night of the press ball he had been able to keep her at arm's length.

Some of the best stories in his newspaper, including those which had helped win the award, had come from her sources.

Apart from a brief question about his family when he had praised Carol effusively, they had studiously avoided talking about their personal lives. He had gathered she'd gone through a divorce in Washington, the main reason she had returned to Britain, but had no idea whether there was a new man in her life. He folded the letter decisively and put it in his pocket. It would have taken Caitlin a great deal of courage to write a letter like that and she deserved a response. He clicked on her address in his email file and typed, 'Thanks for all the help you've given this newspaper in the past few months, which helped us win the award, and thank you for this morning's letter. I agree with all that you say and hope we can continue to do valuable business together. Regards.'

A few days later Caitlin phoned to alert him to a story about to hit the American press. They talked as if nothing untoward had happened and Ben satisfied himself that their business relationship could work. He would make damn sure never to put himself in that situation again, then surely they could carry on as before.

Carol retreated to her hut to have a much-needed shower and was vaguely irritated to find Zoe still in the room. Usually the nurse disappeared as soon as Carol made an appearance but this morning she was sitting on her bunk and appeared in no hurry to go so Carol showered, changed and made a start of removing varnish from her toes. She had noticed she was the only female in camp to wear nail polish and although no one had mentioned it, Carol assumed it was too frivolous for high-minded scientists. As Caro she wanted to be regarded in the same light as the others.

Eventually Zoe produced a clipboard and said in a rather formal manner that as the medical officer in the camp she needed to take some health details; she had been too occupied to do it earlier. For the next few minutes she busied herself with questions on Carol's past illnesses. She listened to her heartbeat and took her blood pressure, both of which she pronounced normal.

Instead of dashing out the door when this was finished she sat back on the bed and remarked in a much more conversational tone, 'You won't have to put up with me for much longer. I've asked for a transfer.'

'Why?' asked Carol, hoping to encourage this seeming display of friendliness.

'In a word, Alex. I can't bear him any more and if you take my advice you'll have as little to do with him as possible.'

Asked what was so bad about the camp's leader Zoe launched into a diatribe about his shortcomings. He was a bully and if you showed weakness he would make life a misery. He had favourites. It was OK if you were one of those but woe betide you if you fell out of favour with the master. You would be frozen out, not told things, excluded from the magic circle.

The man sounded dreadful, but there was something so bitter about Zoe's criticism that Carol was inclined to think she might be exaggerating. The man had a few redeeming features, according to Diana, George and a couple of the other scientists who had certainly been respectful of his qualities. They were united in praising his organisational abilities which enabled them to carry out their work far more efficiently than on many other expeditions. But the leader Zoe was describing appeared to be an overbearing personality who practised favouritism, not qualities which would hone a team, and it seemed to Carol they were a team, there was a camaraderie that would not be out of place at Jolly Good Food. Ben had always told her that if the troops were happy it meant the captain was a benevolent despot, able to assert authority without stifling initiative. As far as Carol could gather, none of the personnel had left since Alex Woollescroft had arrived and that certainly could not be the case if he were the tyrant Zoe described.

As the nurse began to pack her stethoscope into the medical bag, Carol was longing to know what had provoked such enmity but she could not bring herself to ask. This was a prickly woman and Carol needed to be tactful, especially as she would be stuck with her until she left.

'I'll be interested in judging him for myself,' said Carol finally. 'People seem to have such differing views.'

Zoe snorted. 'You'll have no trouble with him. Alex loves attractive women, that's why poor Diana never had a look in.'

Zoe sounded like the proverbial woman scorned and Carol was certain something had gone on between them. She would have loved to have drawn her out further but the sound of a gong signalled it was time to return to the kitchen to prepare lunch.

Each time Carol rushed down the wooden ramp towards the dining hut, hanging on to the rails, she blessed the fact that she had not been in the camp before the walkway was established and everyone had to make their way across the forest floor, dodging the creatures that lurked in the undergrowth.

She arrived in the kitchen to find Anak and her helpers unpacking boxes of porridge oats and baked beans. That meant the supply boats from Bandar had arrived. And with exclamations of delight they unwrapped the crates of vegetables and dozens of huge pineapples.

'Everyone very happy tonight,' said Anak. 'Meat and things arrive in boat.' She took from her pocket a large stamped envelope, bearing a British postmark. Carol's heart leapt when she recognised the handwriting and swiftly she tore open the envelope to find inside five separate letters, one from each of the children, Lisa and, best of all, Ben. She wanted to savour each word so reluctantly stored them away in her pigeonhole to await a tea break.

It was just before the evening shift began that a commotion at the jetty caused Anak to peer out of the doorway. Immediately she clapped her hands for attention and called out to Carol, 'Mr Alex and the others back. We make everything good.'

The announcement heralded a frenzy of activity in the kitchen as Anak ordered the peeling of more potatoes. 'They will not have eaten much. Quick, quick. They hungry and tired.'

Carol watched fascinated as the staff scuttled around the kitchen, their gait far removed from the usual careful pace adopted to cope with the intense heat. The arrival of Alex and his party back from Fish Eye Falls had galvanised them. And for Carol the news provoked a tremor of apprehension coupled with, she had to admit, some curiosity.

George's head appeared around the door, much to Anak's disapproval. Anyone other than kitchen staff was strictly forbidden to enter her territory.

'Sorry,' said George, meeting her eye. 'Caro, can I have a word?' She moved towards the doorway and he whispered, 'Just saw Alex. Frightfully sorry, think I landed you in it.'

Carol looked at him nervously.

'He asked why I was lounging around instead of working. I stupidly told him there was nothing for me to do because the crystals had been lost en route.'

Inwardly Carol groaned but George's distress was so evident that she found herself comforting him, saying Alex would have soon found out anyway when he read Francesca's message.

'Can I give you a word of advice? If he asks to see you now, make some excuse that you can't leave your post. Wait till he's eaten and rested. Apparently the journey was hell.' George added stoutly, 'Don't worry too much. Remember, whatever bullshit he gives you, cooks are as important to this camp as scientists, more so I reckon. They need you far more than you need them.'

She attempted a laugh. 'They haven't eaten much of my cooking yet.'

'They'll love it,' George smiled and ambled off.

As she stirred one of the saucepans simmering on the hob Carol caught sight of the pigeonhole where her precious mail lay waiting. She would not allow this man to intimidate her, not when there were people back home who longed for her return. If she aspired to toughen up, then this was her first challenge.

She'd had plenty of time to think about her old life. While Ben was never less than courteous towards her, after what had happened in the past few weeks, she'd come to realise he'd taken her good nature for granted. It was true they'd hardly ever quarrelled but she was beginning to think this was because there wasn't enough passion in their relationship. Perhaps she had tried too hard to please him, mindful of how grateful she'd been he had chosen her. After seven years of organising his children and his home, she had never, not once, thought how lucky he was to have married her.

A slight darkening of the doorway alerted Carol to the presence of a tall, well-built figure. Because of the light shining behind him she could not make out his features. Involuntarily she peeled off her bright yellow gloves and gave an uncertain smile.

'Anything I can do for you?' she asked.

'Yes.' The voice was curt. 'I'll see you in my office in ten minutes.' And after a barely imperceptible pause, 'Please.'

Her stomach did an about turn. So this was the mighty leader. Angus Roberts had criticised him for having a chip on his shoulder and she could see that with his peremptory manner, not bothering to introduce himself, Angus might be right. She'd been warned that she would have to assert herself from the beginning or risk being submerged. There was no mistaking that air of authority, but althought he was boss of the camp he was not going to order her around like a naughty schoolgirl.

Even in the few days she had been working here she had grown in confidence. Anak was partly responsible because she was amiable enough not to worry about status. She'd made it clear she was happy to share responsibilities with the newcomer and Carol thought it generous of her in the circumstances. Anak had been impressed when she had instituted a system of preserving samples of cooked meat and fish in Freddie's Pots, so beloved by Jolly Good Food, to help medical diagnosis, if it were needed.

'Whenever people ill, always blame food,' she complained.

The highly-educated women of Brunei eschewed menial work, as they saw this, which was why Malays were hired. Unfortunately, many were unskilled when they arrived and did not adhere to the rather stricter British regulations. Hygiene standards had been one of the reasons, she'd been told, for sending cooks out from London, although Carol could find no fault with Anak's routine, she was meticulous. But persuading staff not to overload the fridge was an ongoing job. Anak, while paying lip service to the need to keep it working at maximum efficiency, had not been rigorous in carrying it out and welcomed Carol's back-up.

Carol had warmed towards the ever-cheerful quartermaster after she had made the grave mistake of allowing one of the scientists space in the fridge for one of his experiments. That had been on her first day. Anak had gently pointed out that the scientist was taking advantage of a newcomer. 'He knows he not allowed.' But this had been said later. Anak had not embarrassed her in front of the staff. That would mean a loss of face, something she was already aware was anathema to the people of Asia.

After she had finished finely chopping the chillis and galangal, the local ginger, Carol slowly washed her hands and smoothed her hair which was beginning to come out from its coil. Then she made her way to Alex's office. It was nearly half an hour since they had spoken and despite the lecture to herself her heart was beating uncomfortably fast. She wiped the sweat off her brow with a cotton handkerchief. Today the four o'clock downpour had hardly cooled the atmosphere and, George was right, the air was exactly like treacle.

She was surprised to see the leader's door tightly shut, as it was the custom in the camp to leave doors open to catch any available breeze. Then she spotted the air-conditioning unit cut into the wooden wall. As she knocked firmly on the door she couldn't help being reminded of her schooldays waiting for the dreaded voice of her headmistress to give her permission to enter.

There was no response. Maybe he was out. She was about to knock again when the door opened abruptly. Disconcerted, she found her face a few inches from his chest and stepped back.

'I said ten minutes.'

'I'm sorry,' she stuttered, then cursed herself for immediately falling into the role of the supplicant. This was not how she wanted to begin.

He turned on his heel and lowered himself down onto a chair behind a trestle table covered with neat piles of paper.

As her eyes adjusted to the cool gloom of the interior he barked, 'Shut that door, can't you?'

She had been told he was thirty-five, but he looked younger. There was an alertness about his face which sprang, she assumed, from ordering people around. His hair was black, cropped short, emphasising the squareness of his jaw, and she could see why some women would find him attractive. He looked competent, with an air of authority about him, and from everything she'd heard he wouldn't be easily fazed by problems.

She closed the door with a fair amount of force. 'You might want to think about improving your people skills.'

Incredibly this provoked the glimmer of a smile. 'Depends on the people I have to deal with. It seems London's sending me amateurs these days.'

'I expected to be a cook, not a courier,' she retorted, stung.

His eyes washed over her, as cold as yesterday's bath water, and she willed herself not to blink, something she'd had to learn when dealing with Becky. He was first to look away.

Ostentatiously she dragged a chair from the side of the room in front of his desk and sat down.

He was leaning back in his chair, toying with a pencil, and she couldn't help noticing his fingers were long and slender, not the kind she had seen among the scientists, which were mostly covered in cuts and calluses.

'You're lucky,' he said. 'Francesca Stone has sorted out the problem you landed us in.' His tone was milder and she responded in kind.

'Good. I'd hate a misfortune like that to hold up George's work.'

The truce did not last long. 'We can do without that kind of misfortune.'

To her annoyance Carol began to blush and started to defend herself but he cut her off.

'This isn't Kensington, you know. We can't take chances. Our work in all areas of the camp must be meticulous. Mistakes like that at best slow us down, at worst cost lives.'

At the back of her mind Carol was thinking if it had been vital medical supplies then maybe she would deserve a dressing down but crystals for preserving butterflies was in a different category, for God's sake. However, her experience of dealing with three children taught her to recognise when it was to her advantage to pursue a more conciliatory line. 'I'm sorry it happened but George has been very understanding.'

'I, on the other hand, am not,' he said sternly. 'The reason this field expedition has had no serious problems is because we follow the proper procedures. You did not.'

She was here as a volunteer, for God's sake, not a serf. He might know how to order around a platoon of squaddies but certainly didn't know how to get the best out of women. She had tried Carol's approach and it hadn't worked. Now it was time to unleash Caro.

'I don't need lectures,' she snapped. 'You've made your point.'

'Right, right. Now we've cleared that up, how are you settling in?' He gave a grin and it was almost as if a circuit had been switched in his head. First the stick, now the carrot.

'I was OK until now.'

She was treated to another display of dazzling white teeth before he proceeded to tell her about the impending visit of a professor from Brunei University who would be accompanied by his wife and son. 'He's responsible for supervising our funding, seeing that it comes through on time from the Sultan's office, so he's important to us.' He levered himself out of the chair and towered above her. 'He's very Westernised, went to my old college in Cambridge, so I'd like to give him some good old British food. He won't be here for a few weeks but it'll take you a while to get acclimatised and sort out a menu. If you draw up a list of supplies we can order it from Bandar. Think you can handle that?'

It was the heavy emphasis on the last word that riled her. She got to her feet. 'You'll find I can handle that and most things.' She fought back the urge to add, 'Including you.'

Chapter Sixteen

While Carol did battle with her new boss, back home Lisa was tackling the complexities of trying to persuade finicky young palates of the nutritional value of homemade fish fingers over packaged varieties. She had made a bet with Carol that she would win them over, but it was a bet she was losing. She had not yet given in although she had resorted to bribery with chocolate mousse left over from an executive lunch.

The children were spooning the mousse with relish and Lisa found she enjoyed pleasing them. This was a world away from catering for strangers where her pleasure came from the size of the cheque.

Lisa was unaccountably nervous in her new role. This was her first experience of being exposed to children on her own. Previously when she had been here for lunches or teas their stepmother was around, acting as a buffer. She had an inkling of what Carol must have gone through at the beginning, putting in more effort than was required. Like Carol, she had gone overboard. She became the best pusher of swings, the most prolific buyer of ice cream, the most enthusiastic player of board games. But at cooking, which she thought would be the easy part, she came a cropper because her food 'did not taste like Mum's'. They pronounced the chicken casserole to be 'different' and apparently the reason was that Carol usually diced the chicken whereas she had left hers in portions and, horror of horrors, she had flavoured the dish with braised onions. At this early stage, Lisa had no confidence to lay down the law and order them to eat up. She accepted they liked things done exactly the way their mother did them and did her best to adapt her style of cooking. However illogically, she was disappointed by their reaction since she was used to her efforts being praised by grateful clients.

She appreciated the openness of the children, especially from the younger ones. They had not yet learned to dissemble, unlike some of the adults she came across. Lisa was frank enough to admit she enjoyed the power that flowed from their requests to settle some minor argument, happy that they accepted her decisions without too much rancour. And she had decided on a different tack with Becky. Treating her as more of an adult, she would tell Carol, seemed to be paying dividends.

The idea of getting a kitten had been a brainwave. The children had persuaded Ben that Muffin Two would be a wonderful addition to the family and would help them cope with their mother's absence. It was when they were at the animal rescue place and had to make the decision between a coal-black moggie or a half-Persian that Lisa had the first inkling this idea might have been a mistake. 'I wish Mummy was here to help choose it,' said Katie, stroking one of the kittens, 'because it will belong to her as well, won't it?' It was far too late to talk them out of it and she hoped her impulsive suggestion would not backfire. She hadn't thought that Carol might be upset at being excluded from this important event. But Ben hadn't seemed to worry about this so once they arrived back home Lisa put it out of her mind.

At first the eldest child had been in charge of supervising Katie's bathtime but once or twice, when Becky had other plans, Lisa had taken over. It was at these moments, when pink-cheeked and pink-pyjamaed the little girl would climb onto her lap and demand a cuddle, that Lisa would feel a warm glow. Of all of them, Katie was missing her mother the most and Lisa tried hard to give the child reassurance that Mum would be home soon. As she hugged the chubby figure, Lisa wondered how Carol was coping without her family.

At the end of an exhausting first week she'd confided to Andrea that she had never worked so hard in her life. However, when the Australian volunteered to take over some of the duties, Lisa promptly brushed the offer aside. To her surprise she did not want anyone else encroaching on her territory. She wanted to explain to Andrea how the children had suffered enough disruption and the introduction of yet another person into their lives would not be helpful. But in truth this was not the real reason. At the moment she was the centre of their universe and Lisa revelled in it. She loved the novelty of being among the mothers at the school gates, of seeing the children seated around the table waiting for their tea, and being able to answer the questions they had stored up during the day made her feel that this was a status she might enjoy.

The first crisis came with the arrival of the Thursday ballet classes for Emmy. The ballet mistress was Russian, a martinet, an obvious admirer of the Stalinist regime, judging by her teaching methods. She had a strict code of dress, insisting on girls with long hair having it tightly plaited and then coiled into a bun covered by a net. Carol apparently was brilliant at making plaits but after several abortive attempts Lisa had to make a mad dash to the local chemist's shop to buy the entire stock of Kirby grips. Katie was late for the lesson because it took so long to achieve the right effect. But when she reported that Madame had approved of the hair, Lisa felt as great a sense of achievement as if she had received a couple of Michelin stars. She told herself it was a good omen for the day when she would meet the right man. She would find it no hardship to give up her so-called freedom for the delights of being a wife and mother.

The next hurdle was dealing with their homework. Emmy was having a problem with her maths. 'I hate it and I hate the teacher,' she said, pushing the textbook across the table. When Lisa remonstrated mildly, she said, 'I don't care. It's no use, I don't understand it. Miss Whiteley thinks I'm stupid and she's right.'

Although Lisa thought this was probably exaggerated she stressed to Emmy how hopeless she had once been with figures, until she started her own business. The child looked at her uncomprehendingly. This would be a challenge. How could she make figures mean something to a twelve-year-old with no talent for mathematics? The next day she spent an hour browsing through the bookstores looking for inspiration. But it was while she was passing the local supermarket that she had a brainwave. The following day she and Emmy went on a shopping expedition. Every time they took a product off the shelf she would ask Emmy how much was left of the twenty pounds. Her reward came when Emmy pointed out that the last jar of jam had busted the budget.

When they were discussing it later, Emmy admitted she had found it easy-peasy. 'Mum always helps me with my maths, but it's different when you're spending money. Can we do it again?'

Lisa smiled and enjoyed a moment of triumph when Emmy presented her with a bar of chocolate bought out of her pocket money. Her maths marks showed such improvement that she was awarded her first silver star and a disloyal thought, immediately suppressed, entered Lisa's mind. Shouldn't the child's mother have been the one to crack the problem? This incident forced her to consider what she wanted out of life. She enjoyed being a surrogate mother. But of course it would end soon.

Bored with pubbing, tired of clubbing, Lisa had often paid lip service to the idea of settling down and becoming a wife and mother, without any idea of what it entailed until now. At an admitted forty-two, but really forty-four, she was leaving it very late. In any case, though she wanted a child of her own, she had no wish to be a single parent. She had seen at first hand what having sole responsibility for a family had done to friends. Though she admired their courage in taking on the role of both mother and father, such sacrifice was not for her. She did not think she could cope with the responsibility on her own.

The singles agency had not produced a candidate remotely suitable. It was after a particularly grisly session with a solicitor she had met through the dating agency that she swore not to humiliate herself again. He had spent the entire evening telling her every dot and comma of his recent divorce, asking not one question about her. He had been the third disaster in a row and the next morning she asked the agency to delete her name from their books. She wasn't looking for Sir Galahad or Einstein. She wanted someone pleasant to look at, sociable and warm-hearted, who liked kids. It was a pity Ben didn't have a brother.

Normally Lisa would leave when Ben arrived home at around eight o'clock. But one evening he had phoned, very agitated, asking if she could possibly stay over as the Prime Minister had summoned him to Downing Street. Apparently the PM wanted to refute a malicious rumour circulating in rival newspapers that his election campaign had been funded by someone close to a drug baron. Emmy had at once suggested that Katie move into her bed to make room for Lisa.

It must have been nearly midnight when Lisa woke with a start, realising it was the sound of Ben downstairs which had disturbed her. She found it difficult to go back to sleep and climbed out of bed, put on a dressing gown, and went to see if he needed anything more to eat.

The kitchen was half lit and Ben was at the kitchen table, jacket off, tie askew, tucking into the snack she had left out for him. 'This is just what the doctor ordered,' he said, waving the crabmeat baguette at her. 'Politicians with a mission to explain never think of offering you anything to eat.'

She poured them both a cup of coffee from the flask she had left on the tray then sat opposite, pleased she had made an effort to produce something other than cheese and pickle.

Still high on adrenaline, Ben was crowing at being the only political journalist to be selected by Downing Street, and regaled her with descriptions of Number Ten, what the Prime Minister had said, what the premier was like as a person. He seemed in no hurry to end his discourse, transporting her into an unfamiliar and intriguing world, so different from her workplace, where the conversation usually revolved around domestic concerns. She took care not to interrupt his flow, fearful that he would say he needed some sleep. Eventually the talk switched to the children and as he sounded her out about their day, it was obvious how much he cared for them.

As she watched him, toying with the coffee cup, his eyes full of warmth and enthusiasm, Lisa realised with a start that this was the first time in her adult life she'd had a late-night conversation with a man that didn't involve sex. The list of unsuitable lovers was longer than she cared to recall, mostly she had been intent on getting them to leave as speedily as possible, rather than stay to chat. But if Ben wanted to stay up all night, that was fine with her. He was treating her with respect, and what they were talking about mattered – children, the home, his job. What he did not talk about was Carol and she wondered why.

It was when they were sharing a rather fine brandy that she began to view Ben in a different light. He had briefly squeezed her shoulder when thanking her for stepping into the breach. There were no sexual undertones and she had no doubt the gesture was inspired by gratitude but it was as if a switch had been clicked on. Ben was no longer the good mate, her best friend's husband, but a man she fancied. She had always seen him as an attractive man but why had she never noticed how his blue eyes blazed when he was deep into some anecdote and what beautiful hands he had? She began to daydream about how they would feel stroking her naked body.

She jumped to her feet, horrified that she should be indulging in these traitorous thoughts and quickly said goodnight. Ben was out of bounds and she had to remember that. Still, she couldn't help thinking wistfully, Carol was a lucky woman.

Carol wasn't sure whether it was the encounter with her patronising boss but she found herself looking more critically at her appearance. Maybe she had to change her image, look more in control, like Francesca and Zoe.

One day during the customary afternoon downpour, instead of running for cover she allowed the cool water to cascade on to her burning skin. How the kids would have loved the excuse to play in this warm rain, a far cry from a soaking in a wet winter drizzle in London.

Squelching her way into her hut, she saw her image reflected in the small mirror. With her hair flattened by the rain she looked less like a surburban housewife out on a rescue mission and more like the professionals around the camp. Short hair would be far more practical in this weather and she had become increasingly irritated with the heavy mane clinging to the back of her neck.

Emerging from her hut to dry off in the sun, she came across Anak resting beneath a canopy near the kitchen. Carol had noticed that the Malaysians in the camp, when they finished work, would simply sit outside their hut, quite still. Not reading or listening to music or playing cards, just looking out towards the forest. Their tranquillity was enviable. When she knew her better she planned to ask Anak how to achieve this calm state.

As the camp's unofficial barber, Anak had the reputation of being nifty with the scissors and on impulse Carol made a chopping motion with her fingers and asked, 'Can you cut my hair?'

The cook nodded vigorously and ran inside, returning seconds later with two pairs of neat scissors and a stool, which she plonked down in the clearing.

'OK,' said Anak. 'You show me to where I cut.'

In a fit of bravado Carol said, 'The lot.'

'Like a boy?'

Carol nodded and Anak's normally imperturbable features broke into a grin and she giggled. 'Like Mr Alex.' She held the scissors aloft, asking if Carol was sure about the length. 'People shout when I cut too much.'

Relieved to see the camp was relatively deserted, only a couple of porters visible down at the landing stage, Carol gave the go-ahead then nearly changed her mind as a six-inch strand dropped to the sandy ground, but it was too late for second thoughts. Then from out of nowhere the two women were surrounded by a circle of curious onlookers staring at the increasing pile of wet hair falling to the ground.

'They not understand woman who take her hair off,' smiled Anak.

And when she was handed a small mirror, nor did Carol. At first she was shocked by the vision that confronted her. The change was startling. Gone was the conventional shoulder-length bob favoured by the women who did the school run. Staring out at her was a tanned, spiky gamine, who for a second reminded her of the film star Meg Ryan. She should be so lucky but she had a momentary vision of how Ben would react. Unhappily. When they made love he said he enjoyed the feel of her hair on his bare skin.

These days she noticed her shorts were flapping around the waist. She had lost some weight and her body had become firmer. Rising early, being on duty for most of the day and then interspersing her rare leisure time with walks she had definitely developed muscle tone. But the trade-off was that she had more energy and all in all she was pleased with her leaner shape. The back of her neck felt cool and she tossed her head in pleasure. It felt so light with that weight of hair gone. It was ages since she had cut her hair short.

'Better than I thought.' Anak was approving. 'Your eyes bigger.' Maybe she was right. Carol was twisting her neck this way and that to get a better view when she caught sight of a figure in khaki chinos towering over the porters. Hurriedly she handed back the mirror and began brushing off her shirt, irritated that she had become the centre of such interest. Alex caught her eye but his expression was difficult to fathom. He inclined his head towards her but directed his words at Anak.

'The longboat goes to Bandar in an hour.'

'Today?' Anak's surprise was evident.

'We have to pick up a special package from London.' He gave Carol a swift glance. 'If you want any extra supplies, have the list on my desk.' He was about to stride off but paused to add, almost over his shoulder, 'Same for you, Caro.'

Every time this man spoke to her, he made her hackles rise. How could anyone think he was making a good job of commanding people?

Chapter Seventeen

The head teacher at Becky's school had been soft-spoken yet she imbued her words with such authority that Ben cancelled his appearance at the afternoon's editorial conference. He pulled on his jacket and was driving out of the office car park almost before he realised it. No, the head had said, the matter could not wait, she needed to see a parent immediately. If he was busy could Mrs Mitchell . . . ? Ah, well then, what time could he be there? And when he'd asked what Becky had done for him to be summoned, the woman merely repeated she did not wish to discuss this on the phone; a personal visit was necessary.

He snapped off the car radio and turned into the cul-de-sac where the school buildings, set within small but pretty grounds, dwarfed the surrounding houses. For a minute he sat silently, thinking about his eldest daughter.

She was the child most affected by her mother's death. Ben did not have a favourite but he supposed he tended to treat Becky more gently than her siblings. The family's tragedy affected her in a strange way. She threw out her pretty dresses and turned into a tomboy. A psychotherapist friend of Ben's analysed this as the 'rejection of the female role model'. Becky was in a state, he said, not to trust any female on the basis of 'why love someone? She'll go away and die.' He predicted she would rebel, become difficult, tempestuous, and pick on her two sisters. Privately Ben thought this diagnosis was over-gloomy and he had been right. Becky soon reverted to her sweet-tempered self though she hated being away from him. He was aware that in the early days Becky would have preferred Carol not to be around and even now she and her stepmother still had an edgy relationship though Carol had tried hard to become friends. About a year ago, as if to prove his friend's prediction right, Becky had metamorphosed into the female equivalent of Kevin the terrible teenager on television. She could try the patience of a saint and Carol sometimes despaired but until now there had never been any trouble with her at school.

Ben climbed out of the car, locked it and trudged towards the substantial front entrance. Whatever the hell she'd done had to be cataclysmic for the head to insist on dragging him from the office, and mentally he prepared himself for bad news.

A few minutes later he sat staring at this woman across the desk. *Smoking?* This teacher who was used to being obeyed, she with her pursed lips and holier-than-thou mien, had hauled him from work to complain about Becky smoking?

'I know it's serious and I'll certainly talk to her.' He gave a self-deprecating smile, adding, 'I'm afraid I used to have a quick puff behind the bike shed when I was her age, it's just kids experimenting, isn't it?'

'Is that what you call it, Mr Mitchell?'

Didn't the woman know anything about young people? 'Forgive me, I'm not trying to minimise it but you'd be pretty busy if you brought parents to school every time their kid was caught smoking.'

She snapped shut a small box of paper clips. 'Not cigarettes, Mr Mitchell. Rebecca was smoking an illegal substance, a Class B drug. Cannabis.'

Ben lost his composure. 'I can't believe it. We've always warned her against . . . this type of thing. Are you sure?' His voice died away because the head's eyes flashed angrily though her voice remained measured.

'I know this is a shock, Mr Mitchell, but she was caught in the act by my deputy and you can ask Rebecca herself, she is waiting down the corridor.'

'What happens now?' he found himself asking meekly.

'As it's a criminal offence,' she paused, 'I will have to report it to the police.'

'Good God, why? Can't we handle it? I mean, it's not good for Becky and it can't be great publicity for the school.'

'Precisely. Which is why I intend to expel her.'

Ben was appalled. 'But this is the first time she's been in any serious trouble. Can't you give her another chance?' he pleaded.

She fiddled with the paperclip box again. 'I'm not sure we can. Rebecca has not been the easiest of pupils recently. She seems to be waging her own private war against anyone who stands in her way.'

He'd heard nothing of this from Carol. Surely she must have noticed if there'd been a change in Becky's behaviour? Why hadn't she told him about it? He found his anger building towards his wife rather than his daughter. If his eldest daughter was having problems, what kind of mother was it who went off at a time like this? She ought to be at home providing support and advice instead of gallivanting thousands of miles away.

Silently saying a prayer, Ben used his formidable powers of persuasion to evoke memories of the trauma Becky suffered with the sudden loss of her mother and the head finally weakened and agreed to think again. She would suspend the girl for two weeks, after which she would have to be convinced that there would be no repetition of her behaviour.

If he expected Becky to be contrite, Ben was mistaken; indeed she said she didn't know what the fuss was about. Smoking a joint was no big deal, 'everyone' did it and wasn't it better than the drugs he used, coffee and alcohol?

Try as he might during the journey home, Ben was unable to convince her of the seriousness of the situation. Every negative aspect he raised about cannabis, the memory loss, the mood swings, the search for the higher kick which often led to hard drugs, she scoffed at. That was propaganda. 'Everyone' knew it was just a matter of time before they legalised it. Didn't he know cigarette companies had even registered the brand names they would use when it happened?

'So you want to throw everything away, do you?' he shouted, unhappy at losing his temper but unable to stop himself. 'Keep this up and you'll get chucked out of school permanently and I won't be able to do anything about it. Then what will you do?'

Becky cocked her head to one side and looked innocently up at him. 'But Dad, you've always told me I should think for myself and that's what I'm doing.'

'You're not thinking for yourself, you're just going with the flow. Well, it stops right now. I want your promise that you'll never use drugs, any drugs, ever again.'

She faced him coolly. 'It's my life. I don't have to promise anything.'

'I'm afraid you do,' he said firmly, gripping the steering wheel so tightly his knuckles were white. 'You are still under-age and while you live under my roof I am responsible for you.'

'You're such a hypocrite,' she said hotly. 'Don't tell me you didn't use dope when you were young.'

Bloody hell, he did want her to be independent. He did want her to think for herself and not accept anything slavishly without clearly working it out for herself but how could he answer that question? Of course he had tried the stuff, but that was different.

'We know a lot more about the damage cannabis can do now,' he said and realised she would take this weak reply as the confession it was. 'Well, there's no pop concert for your birthday and you're grounded.'

'For how long?'

'For as long as it takes.' She unnerved him by beginning to cry and he was stymied. Unused to facing problems alone, he once again cursed Carol's absence. He had tried to be unselfish, encouraging her to go, but it had turned out to be a terrible mistake. She was needed here at home. He'd have to email her and see if it was possible for her to come back.

When they reached Tollbridge Road, Lisa was in the kitchen, having fetched the other two back from school. Becky went upstairs to her bedroom and the other two disappeared into the sitting room to watch television. Ben found himself confiding the events of the past hour. Lisa was a good listener and seemed to take Becky's transgression calmly, for which he was grateful.

'I think I'm going to ask Carol to come back.'

Lisa considered this for a while. Privately she thought this was an over-reaction, especially as Becky had been given a reprieve. She asked him what was the point of getting Carol worked up and wrecking her little adventure.

Ben was doubtful. 'I'm not happy with that. Carol ought to know.'

Lisa suggested he might allow her to talk first to Becky before making a decision. Because she was not a parent she could probably talk to Becky on a different level.

'Becky thinks we're all making a fuss about nothing,' he warned, 'but all right, go ahead if you think it'll do any good. And then I'll make up my mind about what to tell Carol.'

Lisa disappeared into Becky's room and Ben made himself a cup of tea, wondering how soon he would be able to dash back to the office. He was about to call his secretary when he thought better of it. This had been the pattern of his life. Work always came first and luckily the woman he had married had never complained, nor come to think about it had she made him feel guilty. The year after Fay's death had taught him how hard parenting could be but since then he had leaned more and more heavily on Carol. But she wasn't around so he couldn't just turn his back on his daughter until he had extracted some kind of promise about her future conduct. As the girls grew older he had to take on board that they would need him more, not less. What sacrifices was he prepared to make? His job was all-encompassing and he wasn't the kind of guy to do things in half measure.

When Lisa and Becky emerged after about ten minutes they were all smiles and his daughter appeared to have undergone a Pauline conversion. 'Lisa and I have talked it over, Dad, and I promise you I'll never smoke dope at school again.'

Ever suspicious, Ben questioned her closely. Did she really mean it or was this just to make him feel better?

'Lisa says after all we've been through I shouldn't make you unhappy and I don't want that. I'm sorry, Dad, and I'll phone the head tomorrow to tell her as well.'

Ben hugged his wayward child and, despite his cynicism, was touched by her penitent air. As a gesture of faith he offered to reinstate the visit to the pop concert. It was a treat for her fifteenth birthday, after all. But the grounding stayed and to his relief Becky seemed satisfied with this.

Once she had joined her sisters, Ben put an arm round Lisa's shoulders and gave her a squeeze.

'I don't know how you did it,' he said, 'but you're a star, gold-plated.'

'It was easy. She doesn't want you upset so I played on that.' She smiled. 'I did promise she could help at the kitchen for the next two weeks, if that's all right with you.'

Terrific solution; he'd been wondering how to occupy Becky while she was on suspension.

'I don't think we need to tell Carol, do you?' said Lisa. 'At least not until she gets home.'

Ben agreed promptly. Why worry her? It looked as though things were going to work out.

That night Ben arrived home a little earlier than usual, bearing two bunches of pink roses, wrapped in the kind of cellophane favoured by garage chains. It was pleasant to be appreciated and Lisa pondered on how rarely she received flowers with no strings attached.

He was in an expansive mood, obviously relieved that the problem with Becky had been solved, however temporarily. When he suggested that she freeze the chicken dish she had prepared for his supper and go out with him to celebrate, she didn't hesitate. Becky was told they wouldn't be more than an hour and she seemed pleased to be trusted to be in charge of her younger sisters.

At the Italian bistro on the corner, Ben insisted on sitting inside one of the cubicles, rigged up for some obscure reason to look like a rowing boat, and when Lisa asked for a glass of wine, he brushed this aside, saying they would certainly be able to finish a bottle between them. After they had chewed over the events with Becky and the headmistress, Ben wondered out loud whether they shouldn't tell Carol what had happened.

Once again Lisa was adamant that it would do no good. The crisis was past and Lisa would be keeping a very close eye on the little madam.

'That's the point,' said Ben. 'It's unfair on you. It's not what we envisaged when we asked you to help out. It's taking too much of your time and too much energy and it's not even your family.' He raised his arm to the waiter and scribbled in the air.

'If I feel it's too much I'll tell you.'

'That's the problem. I'm not sure you will. If Carol knew about what's happened I'm sure she'd come home.'

'Don't spoil my fun,' said Lisa swiftly. 'This is far more interesting than cooking food for executives.'

While he was settling up the bill, briefly Lisa examined her motives. It had started out as a favour to Carol but now the last thing she wanted was for her to come home prematurely. Lately she had found her thoughts dwelling in fantasy land. Carol would say she loved the life over there and would never come home. Ben, bereft, would turn to her and one, two, three she would be the one pouring his morning coffee, waiting for him in his bed at night and mothering his children. He would tell her often that he had never been happier or more fulfilled. The trouble was she couldn't whitewash a woman out of existence and she told herself it was madness to imagine a future with Ben. Carol – her best friend, remember – would be back soon enough.

That was when she woke up. Never by word or deed had Ben ever given the impression that he regarded her as anything more than a good pal, someone who had selflessly stepped into his wife's shoes for a short while. No more, no less, she told herself fiercely.

Ben might not have been so sanguine about his daughter had he been privy to Becky's diary. She had not gone into the television room as they had thought, but back to her bedroom. She unlocked the red leather diary, a present from Carol last Christmas. She had been filling it in faithfully every day, although there was a quote on the front page which had almost put her off. 'Only good girls keep diaries. Bad girls don't have time.' Tallulah Bankhead, whoever that was.

Becky doodled with her Biro for a moment before writing, 'Big trouble today at school. Beany called me into her office, said I was going to be expelled for smoking a joint. Dad came to school, and fixed it for me to be on suspension for two weeks instead. Yippee.'

She began to bite the end of the pen, wondering how frank she dare be. She would have to find a new hiding place. The lock was no protection. Emmy had threatened to snap it open and show the diary to Carol. She was only joking but it had made Becky nervous.

'Had chat with Lisa,' she went on. 'She was cool. Understood it was no big deal. She smokes regularly and there's nothing wrong with her. Says good way to lose weight, GREAT IDEA!!! Secret plan: she and I will share a joint when it's safe on condition I work at her kitchen while on suspension and don't tell ANYONE. Said sorry to Dad. Won't smoke at school – not when I can at home!'

Becky shut the diary, turned the key and, still clutching it to her bosom, rolled over onto her back to stare up at the ceiling. Fourteen and eleven-twelfths was a horrible age, too old for toys, too young for boys, they said. But she felt years older than her age, everybody said it was because Mummy had died and she'd had to look after the little ones. Yet Carol still thought of her as a little girl and so did Dad. Lisa was the only grown-up who spoke to her as an equal. She loved that. Lisa said she would take her to the Face Place to learn to put on make-up. Carol would never have thought of that. Carol was OK for making sure clothes were clean and driving you places but Lisa was FUN.

Chapter Eighteen

The first month at base camp had tested Carol's stamina. The work was unrelenting, unlike looking after children when at least there was a break during school hours. Here, no sooner had she finished serving breakfast than they began the task of filling rucksacks with boxes of sandwiches, fruit and water for scientists off on a three- or four-day trek. Hardly was that ended when it was time to sort out lunch for those remaining in the camp.

Sometimes she managed an hour's respite in the early afternoon before reporting back to the kitchen to help prepare supper. There were usually around thirty to feed and they were always dead on time, reminding her of a weekend at a health farm with Lisa, where the inmates, on an 800 calorie-a-day regime, were always hanging impatiently around the dining-room door, waiting for it to be unlocked.

One of Carol's first hurdles was to make herself understood by their Chinese supplier on the short-wave radio. Francesca had told her about the Chinese storekeeper who had cornered the market in supplying foreigners with meat and provisions. He had also appointed himself provider of domestic staff to base camp.

'His name's unpronounceable but we call him Mr Chow,' she'd said. 'He tries his best to be obliging but you'll find his English is practically non-existent; you'd better bone up on a few words of Bahasa, the language used by the Malay staff. Alex says he learned a hundred words in three hours but of course that's Alex.'

Mr Chow pretended a familiarity with the English language which seemed tenuous judging by his pronunciation. It took many minutes to make out that 'Ow July den?' was phonetic English for 'How do you like them?' and 'Judo one?' was 'Just the one?' and longer than that to translate 'Tendjewberrymu' into 'Thank you very much'.

Over the weeks Anak had been coaching her in Bahasa. At first Anak had done most of the ordering but she insisted that Carol would lose face if this continued. In her weekly letter Carol tried describing to Ben her first attempt at ordering the week's supplies via the radio in Bahasa. The Chinese storekeeper spoke the language but with a Chinese accent and he certainly didn't seem to understand her pronunciation, inflected as it was with her English accent. The radio persisted in crackling through the entire tortuous conversation and at her request Anak took over. Even then the order was mangled, which is why tonight they had beef (*dagan sapi*) on the menu, rather than the lamb (*dagan domba*) they had requested.

Carol's nerves had been more severely tested when one of the kitchen staff arrived excitedly one morning bearing a dead snake, which he'd found drowned in a water tank. The staff crowded round him and began patting him on the back. Carol did not need to understand their language to gather this was considered a great delicacy. Then, to her horror, he shyly proffered his prize to her.

At first she could not bring herself to touch the creature but surrounded by a staff with shining eyes and rapt expressions, Carol was in no doubt this was a watershed. She made an attempt to arrange her features in such a way as to hide her distaste. Could she get away without actually handling the creature? The thought of touching the slimy snake almost made her heave. Miraculously she must have managed a smile for the faces encircling her showed no change. Nerving herself to take the creature by the tail, gingerly she laid it on the chopping board. She confessed in a letter later, to Becky, that this provoked another outburst of chattering. 'I would've died if they'd expected me to dissect the thing but luckily Anak came to my rescue and volunteered to skin it and cut it into steak-sized pieces. Thank goodness they didn't expect me to eat any of it! Actually, on the barbecue it didn't look all that different from small pieces of chicken. It took no time to cook and they quickly ate it all in a flash, smacking their lips afterwards. But I can't see Snake Flambé making it onto the Jolly Good Food menu!'

Carol greatly appreciated the unceasing good nature of the kitchen staff, their capacity to cope cheerfully with the long hours and to work uncomplainingly at any task they were set. They were a mixture of Iban, the indigenous forest people, Malays, Chinese and a couple of women from neighbouring Borneo and Sarawak lured to the country by the prospect of regular wages which they mostly sent back to their families.

'We have to do the menial jobs in this country,' one of them commented ruefully, failing to spot the irony of saying this to an English person who had travelled halfway around the world to do exactly that.

Everything in nature astounded Carol. Ferns were the size of trees back home and trees were taller than the BT tower. She had tried to give Ben and the girls some idea of the enormous scale of things by writing what George had told her, that it took six men to encircle the average tree trunk. She would be able to see for herself if she ever went on one of the camp walkabouts arranged now and then as a relaxation from work. The only problem for Carol was that the most spectacular scenery was on the far side of a swaying rope bridge, many hundreds of feet above the water. She had already watched nervously as one of the scientists had made his way across this perilous-looking structure, spanning the river like a giant spider's web. She waited breathlessly as he held on to the rope trellis, carefully placing one foot in front of the other on a narrow plank not much wider than a trapeze wire. He didn't appear to be bothered that the entire bridge was rocking under his weight. Carol was sure she would never be able to tackle it. But because Diana had assured her that the crossing was a lot easier than it looked, one afternoon when no one was around Carol nerved herself to try. She nearly froze with terror when she looked down at the fast-flowing river far below, and determined to keep her eyes on the horizon, as Diana had advised. But after two faltering steps, when the entire bridge see-sawed alarmingly, she was certain she was about to somersault into the fast flowing river. Overcome by nausea she stepped carefully backwards until she reached the safety of the bank. It was several moments before her heart stopped thudding and she wondered if she would ever have the courage to try again.

During the first weeks Carol found the pace so unremitting she would return to the hut merely to have a quick shower then fall into a deep sleep. This cut out any necessity for conversation with her roommate. Zoe appeared to be less truculent though she maintained her distance and Carol did not have the energy to care. But by the second month Carol had begun to pace herself and when one night after supper Zoe unexpectedly suggested they share a beer on the verandah, she found herself agreeing.

Contentedly sipping her lager, Carol gazed upwards at the velvety sky carpeted with a dazzling array of shimmering stars, shining more clearly than she had ever seen them in Britain. Would she and Ben ever be able to bring the kids over here? It was a lovely thought and she was pleased Zoe was not spoiling the tranquillity by grumbling. The only sounds were the clicks and grunts of the sonorous cicadas.

'They'll stop soon,' commented Zoe, 'and then the frogs will start up. The sounds of the forest are one of the things I'll miss most about this place.'

'How long do you have left?'

'Don't know. Depends on Alex.' After a while Zoe asked, 'How are you getting on with him?'

'We had a bad start but he seems to be leaving me alone,' said Carol carefully.

'I'm surprised. You're his type. Attractive. A woman.' Zoe's voice was steely. Carol thought it wiser not to respond. This could be a minefield and she made an attempt to change the subject by remarking on how unpolluted the atmosphere seemed to be.

Zoe ignored this. 'Basically I don't think the guy likes women. He's more interested in the chase, being the hunter. Soon as he's got what he wants, it's over.' She rubbed a hand over her forehead. 'Bastard.'

Carol was embarrassed. She hardly knew the woman and she appeared to want to spill out her secrets but she didn't know how to get away. It was too dark to wander and she was forced to sit and listen to a stream of invective about Alex and his shortcomings. When eventually Carol tried to mutter something about him running an efficient camp, Zoe scoffed, 'That's because they all kowtow to him. He's a control freak. Haven't you noticed that?' She went into the hut and came out with another bottle of beer, which Carol refused. Zoe refilled her glass.

'The trouble with Alex is that he prefers women who don't give him any trouble. He's used to spending his time with silly debs, the kind that get jobs as secretaries in Buckingham Palace. They like to be seen with someone like him, very politically correct, you know, yah.' Zoe grew silent and then to Carol's amazement this seemingly tough woman began to whimper. 'I didn't plan to become involved with him. In fact I held off for quite a long time but then he asked me to come with him to watch the sunset and that's how it started. We spent every spare moment together, planning what we'd do when we left here. He said I was different from the usual types he met and that he wanted us to travel the world. He was going to show me a waterfall in Rangoon and a wonderful beach in Argentina that only he knew about. He made it sound as though there was some kind of future for us. All those dreams and then without any warning, phutt, it was over.'

'What happened?'

'That's the trouble. I just don't know. One minute we were talking about the type of dog we'd have. It had to be a black Labrador and we would call it Belalong, Bel for short, and the next, his eyes iced up when they saw me.'

'Didn't you ask him?'

'All the time. But he blanked me. He's such a coward, he hadn't the guts to tell me why. I still don't know. That's what upsets me most. If only I knew what I'd done wrong.'

'It wasn't you, it was him,' said Carol. 'Maybe you got too close and he's afraid of commitment.' She had been unfair to judge this woman so harshly. Like one of the children, she had lashed out at Carol when she was feeling devastated.

Zoe shook her head miserably. 'He wanted commitment, he told me. That's what first made me take an interest. I tried everything to get him back, played hard to get by making myself scarce. Then I bombarded him with notes. I don't know what else to try.'

'I don't think it's worth playing games.' Thank goodness Ben had never been like that. A wonderful change from the painful lesson she had learned with a lover in the past who had blown hot and cold. She remembered the anxieties, the wondering whether or not the phone would ring. It had been a humiliating experience realising she had become like a puppet, played with when it suited him and back in the box when it didn't. She hadn't been the one to finish it, which still caused her a pang of annoyance when she thought about it.

'Before I leave I'm going to tell that shit exactly what I think of him.' Zoe downed the last of the beer. 'He's one of the cleverest men I've met but I should've known not to trust a man who's managed to stay single until the age of thirty-five. He's probably a closet homo.' She peered through the darkness at Carol. 'But just in case, don't accept an invitation to look at the sunset. That's the first sign he's ready to pounce. And I'm still too raw to watch you getting involved with him.'

Carol assured her there was no danger of that and Zoe said that was good to hear. She stretched her long, thin arms above her head and said she was ready for bed. Carol waited out in the warm, dark night until her roommate had settled down before making her way inside.

As Zoe had predicted the frogs were making their presence known and while Carol was cleaning her teeth she heard other familiar sounds of the forest, which she described at length in letters home. The swish of the trees as they bent in the wind, the sigh of bats' wings as they flew low over the hut on their sorties and the rustle in the undergrowth from other creatures intent on foraging for food. One day she would bring Ben and the children here so they, too, could experience this enchanting place for themselves.

With this comforting thought, Carol gazed fondly at the pictures of her family on the bedside table then switched off the small light and fell instantly asleep.

Chapter Nineteen

Humidity of nearly a hundred per cent had slowed the camp right down and everyone moved as if they were under water. At night Carol's hut was as hot as a sauna. She had been tempted to sleep outside like some of the others but decided against it when Anak merrily told her about the large, black rat which had run across her bare feet. 'He not bother me, I not bother him; go back to sleep.'

The generator, working overtime, was carefully rationed and she'd noticed that Alex's office door was open. He had switched off the small air-conditioning unit to conserve power for the refrigeration units in the cooking quarters and for scientific experiments.

Bathing in the river offered some relief from the heat but the effect lasted for only seconds. After she had finished serving lunch Carol went down to the river bank, intending to walk into the water, clothes and all. On the wooden jetty, she saw Alex who, when he spotted her, made a beckoning motion.

As she drew near he told her he had an appointment in Bandar and asked if she could go with him. He would be leaving shortly. 'It's only an overnight but I think it would be a good idea if you made use of this trip to see Mr Chow.'

Did his eyes hold hers for a fraction longer than necessary before glancing away?

'I've overheard some of your conversations with him. I think you'd understand his version of English and, come to think of it, his Bahasa, far better when you're face to face.' She would also find it helpful to wander around the store and see the range of goods. 'Don't forget,' he added, 'Professor Woddaulah and his wife and son will be paying the camp a visit in a couple of weeks and I want you to pull out the stops for him.'

Carol's hesitation lasted only a second. It would be a welcome break from routine and she said she would be ready in ten minutes.

It was mid-afternoon when the longboat pulled into the jetty at Bandar, well in time for Alex's appointment. Francesca was waiting at the quayside coffee shop and as soon as the camp leader hove into view she became what Carol could only describe as skittish. After the most cursory of greetings, Francesca then ignored her, concentrating on her boss.

Slightly irritated, Carol wondered at the change in her. During her first day in Bandar, Francesca had given every impression of being a pleasant, intelligent companion, far removed from this excellent imitation of a silly schoolgirl. She asked Alex's opinion of the most trivial of things, insisted on pouring his coffee and listened in apparent rapture whenever he spoke, her eyes hardly leaving his face. Worse was the effect her coquettishness had on Alex. He appeared to bask in her fulsome admiration and Carol wondered why she found this disappointing.

While Francesca fluttered her lashes, Carol amused herself by watching the water taxis zipping backwards and forwards like angry wasps, leaving a boiling wake behind. The speed and proximity of so many boats would never be allowed in Britain and she marvelled at the way they raced towards each other, avoiding accidents at the last breathtaking minute. Pity she didn't own a video camera to film the scene for the children.

Francesca made great play of the tremendous amount of work she'd been doing, listing the officials she'd seen, the emails she'd sent, and Carol thought this amount of detail must surely bore Alex but he appeared to be listening intently. After some minutes of being ignored, Carol interrupted.

'I need to send an email. Could you show me the way to the office, please?'

Carol noticed an amused expression flicker across Alex's face as Francesca halted abruptly. Perhaps he was pleased with the respite from her Niagara of words. Francesca darted a furious glance in Carol's direction.

'Come on then. Be right back, Alex.' With a toss of her hair she hurriedly gathered up her papers and led the way to the office, one high-ceilinged, air-conditioned room within a large building occupied by their benevolent landlords, a British oil company. It was well-furnished though its functional mahogany desk was as cluttered with piles of papers as was the cramped expedition office back in London. Francesca hastily turned on the computer before excusing herself to rush back to Alex's side. Carol clicked on the email programme. As her fingers raced over the keys, Carol used her journalistic experience to the full to describe the memorable sunset, the spectacular waterfalls, the superb colouring of the butterflies and best of all how she had won the race amongst the newcomers to erect a bivouac. She would have to show them when she came home and they would never again need to quarrel over those tent pegs.

Carol pressed the 'Send' button that speeded the email on its way and was about to heave herself out of the leather chair when her eye caught sight of a telephone. Guiltily she picked up the receiver and dialled her home number. Becky answered at once, telling her Dad was still at the office. How good it was to hear her voice and, after a few moments, Emmy and Katie on the bedroom extension. The main topic of conversation was Muffin Two. The cute way the pitch-black kitten stared at them through his paws, his blue, blue eyes, his playfulness, his funny ways.

Katie interrupted to say that Lisa had bought the kitten a smart red collar. The others joined in. It was Lisa said this, Lisa said that, Lisa was taking them here and there. They thought her food was yummy. It was at this point that Carol said abruptly that she had just sent an email and had better ring off. All three children chorused that they missed her and wished she was back home already. But when Carol replaced the receiver she was by no means sure they meant it. For the first time in her life she experienced a slight frisson of jealousy towards her friend, which she tried to squash at once. She was being unreasonable, behaving like a child herself. The kitten was a novelty, so was Lisa come to that, a pleasant interlude. It was good – no, it was excellent that the children were happy and involved. She was glad they had settled into this different routine. Maybe Ben had too. But when she went to find the others, her spirits were low.

Alex had disappeared to keep his appointment at the university and Carol was taken by Francesca to meet Mr Chow. List-making had assumed even greater importance in her life since there was no corner shop to run to if anything was forgotten. Francesca left her to browse and Carol spent an interesting hour looking around Mr Chow's emporium which was stocked with every known spice, several unfamiliar to her. Face to face she was able to understand a little more of his English than was possible over the air waves. When she discussed her ideas for a memorable meal she would cook for the VIP visit, it took some effort but she finally made him understand that the visiting professor was used to Western food. This was the reason for the unfamiliar ingredients she needed, different from those base camp usually ordered. It was then that the Chinese supplier entered into the spirit of the occasion. With a great grin and with disarming enthusiasm, he assured her that she would get the 'besevting', which she interpreted as being the 'best of everything'.

Retracing her steps to the office, she wondered which Francesca she would be stuck with, the posturing schoolgirl or the twenty-first-century professional. Neither, it seemed. Evading her eyes, Francesca asked if she would mind if they could skip supper as she was bushed and needed an early night. This was obviously a cover story and Carol assumed she and Alex had plans for an assignation. Why did that make her feel slightly disgruntled? They were both single and, besides, she would appreciate some time on her own. She supposed it was because they were leaving her completely alone in a strange city. However, she was a big girl and it was the first time in a long while that she had been left to her own devices. Francesca had booked her into the hotel right next door to the office, frequented by visiting staff. It had only two stars but boasted an efficient plumbing system. She entered the hotel determined to spoil herself with some delicious food followed by a slow bubble bath, something attainable at base camp only in her dreams. She ordered a superb meal of giant prawns with a tangy sauce and scented rice that seemed better than anything she had tasted for years. After eating, she idly switched on the television, hoping to be diverted. There seemed to be only one channel available and that showed a robed mullah, eyes fixed on the holy book, solemnly intoning from the Koran. A few seconds of this monotonous voice was enough and she attempted to get engrossed in a book lent by Diana who had mistaken polite interest in her work as a desire to be better informed. The book's major excitement was to describe the lifestyle of ants and in a few minutes Carol gave up and went through to the bathroom.

Luxuriating in the lather and having made full use of the lotions and potions in the hotel, Carol's thoughts began to wander. It was facile to say that life out here was uncomplicated. She was sure there were the same strains in jobs and similar family problems as there were in the West. The Brunei way of saving face, for example, was ingrained and it created stresses. Yet there was a tranquillity about the people she'd come into contact with, a graciousness that was disarming. They smiled a great deal and appeared to be genuinely happy and although she had not spotted any poverty around the capital, she did not think this seeming contentment was all to do with material possessions.

In the West people were ever-reaching, ever-rushing. Ben's life, for example, was wired towards work. When he wasn't hurrying around the House of Commons, he was on the phone at the office or batting hell out of the computer trying to meet a deadline. At home, though he tried to switch off, he made sure he watched the news on every TV channel and however tired, would never dream of missing an edition of the current affairs programme *Newsnight* which began at 10.30 p.m. Sometimes he was invited to appear on it as a pundit. And what did all that effort, that enthusiasm amount to? Pages in a newspaper, which admittedly were read by opinion formers but, after the weekend, these were out of date, as much use as a fur coat in Bandar.

There was a great deal to be said for simplifying life. The way the camp had celebrated George's birthday stood out in her mind. Very little money was spent and yet they'd all had a good time planning the event. First, what to serve as a special birthday meal. They all agreed George was a meat and potatoes fan, that he liked stodgy food. His all-time favourite, shepherd's pie, was far too heavy for the climate, but nevertheless they decided that was what would please him. Though she had experienced the usual difficulties explaining to Mr Chow via the crackly radio that she needed the meat to be minced, it had been worth the effort to see the delight on George's face when she brought in the dish. He was exactly the type to enjoy nursery food though the recipe had only a vague connection to its British counterpart as powdered potatoes were not nearly as tasty as the real thing.

She suspected he might have imbibed a little too much beer for afterwards he confessed that he had a secret love. She hazarded an educated guess. 'The lovely Francesca?'

'Picked that up, did you?' George beamed. 'Spent a few days with her in Bandar after I arrived. Worship her but sadly she doesn't know I'm alive. When I leave here, that'll be that. Story of my life.'

For a moment Carol was tempted to let this pass, especially since she believed Francesca's affections were engaged elsewhere. But working with women at Jolly Good Food who liked to analyse every dot and comma of their private lives tempted her to say, 'She can't know how you feel if you don't tell her.'

George looked gloomy. 'Too scared, dear girl. I'll do my usual thing. Keep my mouth shut and just move on.' He drained his coffee. 'No sense in talking about me. Lost cause.'

Carol had a vision of this ageing scientist, locked away in his laboratory, letting the outside world pass him by. And yet she'd found him an interesting, charming companion. Someone, somewhere would be grateful for his loyalty and love which would be steadfast, she had no doubt. She could not help comparing him with Alex who seemed to be irresistible to females in spite of his treatment of them while poor George stood on the sidelines, longing for a woman he could not bring himself to approach. The difference between the two? Only genetics, an arrangement of facial features, a scattering of hormones, but the unfair result was a man who effortlessly attracted the opposite sex and another who did not.

Carol thought she was settling into the routine of base camp rather well. Being away from home had been a positive experience. Apart from being forced to made decisions for herself, she had learned to make her wants known, without being aggressive. The old Carol of Battersea would have crumpled in the face of George's disappointment when his precious crystals had been lost. Alex would have walked all over her. She hadn't won that many battles with him but she was certain he didn't regard her as a doormat. Within the kitchen, her authority was respected and she no longer felt like a novice but a useful member of an important expedition. The only problem still to be solved was that damned rope bridge. She could picture it now, swinging lightly in the breeze, a symbol of her fear. The unassailable Caro seemed to disappear when faced with its challenge. The week before, Carol had girded her loins and made another attempt to cross to the other side of the bank, persuaded by Diana who seemed to think it was her mission in life to get Carol over this hurdle. Diana had skipped to the other end where she stood calling out encouragement. How difficult could it be if the ant lady managed it so effortlessly?

This time Carol managed three whole steps before the swaying movement made her freeze to the spot. She stayed motionless so long, Diana was forced to retrace her steps and with her hands under Carol's elbows she guided the petrified woman back to the safety of the bank.

Afterwards Carol promised herself that she would cross the bridge before she left, she definitely would. But not yet.

The noise of the hotel's air conditioning did not disturb Carol though her dreams did, punctuated by visions of Ben making love to a succession of women. She was standing in the doorway of their bedroom watching his energetic performance in the marital bed. Of all the female forms, bizarrely it was only Andrea's that she recognised. This dream was followed by a series of flashes in which the children were staring at her from a swimming pool. She could see Katie's hand stretching towards her but try as she might she couldn't hear what the child was saying and nor could she make herself heard. As she was puzzling what to do, a black kitten jumped on her chest with a thump and started clawing at her. That woke her and she sat up, startled, conscious that the telephone was ringing.

It was Alex asking where the hell she was. They should have left fifteen minutes ago.

Mortified, she shot out of bed, visited the bathroom cursorily before pulling on jeans and searching for her hairbrush. In under ten minutes she was out of the door and she hoped he would not guess she had been fast asleep when he phoned.

The ferry was already loaded, with its engine running, but there was no sign of Francesca. Carol wondered if there had been a lover's tiff or whether she was too exhausted by the night's exertions to rouse herself. Alex, immaculate as ever, showed no signs of having had anything other than a good night's sleep. Carol stifled a yawn and he disconcerted her by giving a wide grin.

'Appears you've had a more interesting night than I did.'

Did that mean that he had not been with Francesca?

He seemed in the mood to talk and was in the middle of explaining what had happened at the university when the engines began to roar. He shrugged his shoulders and mouthed that it would have to wait until later.

But later never came. As soon as they got back to base camp he was too engrossed in unloading the supplies to pay her much attention and the next morning his bonhomie appeared to have vanished, replaced by a glowering expression when he sought her out after breakfast.

'I've just been told you used the office phone.'

Francesca. The sneak.

'Yes, I did.' She forced herself to look him squarely in the eyes. 'Is there a problem?'

'Personal calls are not allowed, especially one of that length,' he said. 'The call monitor timed your connection at six minutes twenty seconds. Everything here is costed and we keep to a tight budget. You do know that, don't you?'

At his sarcastic tone she allowed herself a cool incline of her head.

'What would happen if everyone started to use the phone?' he asked curtly.

'Few people here go to Bandar, certainly not regularly,' she said, 'so I doubt there would be a problem. However in my case, as a volunteer, for whom you pay only a subsistence wage, I'd say you're getting cheap labour. One call to my family seems not unreasonable. Don't you agree?'

To her delight he appeared discomfited and a note of wariness crept into his voice. 'Naturally we're very grateful, er, that is to say . . .' Suddenly he seemed anxious to leave. 'I'd prefer it if you didn't do it again. Or rather, if you'd mention it beforehand. All right?'

Gravely she nodded and turned on her heel, mentally rubbing her hands. Game, set and match.

The undergraduates at camp had from the start adopted Carol as one of their own. Though she was older, there was an empathy between them, brought about, though they did not realise this, through her experience of dealing with children. The students had chosen to go on the expedition for two reasons: either because they wanted their CVs to impress future employers or to do something before going to university. One young man, Errol Fitzpatrick, said to come from the eighth richest family in the UK, bragged that his father was always complaining that 'Errol is taking a gap year between doing nothing and doing nothing'.

It was this young man who shyly told her one day that she was a 'good sport' because in his opinion she was attractive but wasn't flirtatious. 'In a small place like this, it's not wise to have favourites,' he told her earnestly, 'and you seem to like us all equally.'

Her heart went out to this boy of eighteen who had all the money in the world but no sense of his own worth and she spent time trying to convince him to find something in which he was interested so he could make his own way in the world. Unfortunately, though he had a great capacity for partying, Errol showed little aptitude for anything else.

She would not easily forget the laughter-filled midnight barbecue, with Alex safely away on a field trip, when she was persuaded by the undergraduate contingent to try the distilled rice wine. It was called arak and was made by the forest people. Carol had sampled only a quarter of a glass before her head felt about to explode. She could not feel her lips move and the students proudly boasted the stuff was as powerful as methylated spirits. Unfortunately, they said, they were unable to get the recipe as the Iban guarded it fiercely. After that night, whenever there were drinks available Carol stuck to the much gentler homemade frothy beer-like substance called tooak.

She continued to develop muscles where none had been apparent before. That was not only due to the sheer physical work she did, handling heavy saucepans or serving dishes, but also to the yomping trips organised regularly by the staff. On the rare occasions she had a day off she would ask to accompany the small group of scientists with their undergraduate helpers who went into the surrounding hills to look for new varieties of plants or insects. It was the lads who taught her how to erect a bivouac, as well as how to make a fire (although she cheated by always taking firelighters with her) and Errol in particular would point out the galaxies of stars which in that clear atmosphere looked within touching distance. She was living in a fascinating and beautiful world utterly unlike anything else and she relished this new, sometimes uncomfortable environment. It was Diana who put it into context: 'The jungle is not threatening if you can put up with a few stings and bites; it is up to you to decide how to approach it.'

George's project was coming to an end and as he was due to leave shortly Diana suggested it would be the most convenient time for a leaving party. She thought they ought to have a picnic at Sungai which could be reached easily in daylight, leaving plenty of time for eating and splashing around in the spectacular fall of water before the return journey. Carol and any of the kitchen staff who wanted to come were included in the party but the Malay staff laughed at the idea of walking for pleasure. Anak and her colleagues were quite happy spending any leisure time sitting in the shade and said they had never been able to understand the Western passion for exercise under a hot sun.

Carol accepted the invitation with pleasure until she learned the whereabouts of the Sungai Falls. The trek meant crossing the dreaded rope bridge.

'I don't think I'll go,' she said to Diana. 'There's masses of work I can do in the kitchen, especially with everyone out of the way.'

Diana saw through this flimsy excuse. 'Everyone's scared of that bridge when they arrive. You have to force yourself to get across it once, then you don't think about it. It becomes second nature.' The answer, she said, was to grit your teeth and just get on with it. 'I'll stand behind you every step of the way,' she promised. 'And we'll have a lot of fun on the picnic. You need a break from the work, we all do.'

Carol desperately wanted to prove to herself and everyone else that she could conquer her cowardice. Yet even to please this kindly woman she could not bring herself to attempt the bridge.

Diana offered to try and persuade the boatmen to row her across. This was not normal procedure since the swift current made it a perilous journey. Also Carol realised she would be unpopular because, on Sundays, the boatmen usually took their craft upriver to see their families. Unfortunately the others got wind of her refusal to go and after that they would not be deterred, nagging her at every opportunity. Carol still held back. She would do it, she said, when no one was around and at a time of her own choosing.

Diana pointed out that the rope bridge would be the last hurdle to overcome. In the short time she had been with the expedition Carol had learned to control her fear of insects, bats, rodents and even snakes – she had cooked one, for heaven's sake. She ran a creative and cost-conscious kitchen, earning admiration from her staff. Now she had to make one more effort.

Much against her better judgement, Carol allowed herself to be persuaded. Nevertheless, until the day of the picnic she had nightmares about the rope snapping, leaving her to dangle hopelessly from one perpendicular strand of rope over the river. She usually woke up as her wrists gave way and she was falling through the air to certain death.

As she prepared the food baskets, Carol hoped for some miracle that would mean she could stay behind but fate proved unwilling to intervene and all too soon she found herself trudging up the incline towards the bridge. While she waited in line for the crossing she marvelled at the ease with which her colleagues half ran across to the other side. Then Diana stepped onto the board. She turned round to face Carol and ordered her to take a deep breath. Then she grasped hold of her hands, pulling her onto the bridge and slowly began to walk backwards, urging her to follow in her footsteps.

The weight of the two bodies caused the bridge to sway violently and in a panic Carol wrenched herself free from Diana's hands to snatch wildly at the supporting side rope. This upset Diana's balance and she fell heavily onto her bottom. For a frightening second Carol had visions of the bridge overturning and of the two of them being flung into the river.

'Caro. Keep still. You too, Diana.' Alex's voice came from the bank behind them.

Carol was almost whimpering and she had trouble controlling her limbs.

'Diana, leave her to me. Make your own way across.' To Carol, Alex said, 'Stay absolutely still until she reaches the other side.'

His note of calm authority seemed to have an effect and Carol drew in great gasps of breath in an effort to control her terror. Her body was half crouched trying to balance itself and she still clutched the side rope when from behind she felt firm hands grasping her waist and gently begin to pull her upright.

'You are not going to fall. I won't let you.' Alex's mouth was close to her ear and with a great effort of will, Carol straightened, her clenched knuckles holding tightly onto the rope, her body as taut as one of the wire strands holding the bridge in place.

'Start with your left foot,' he instructed. 'That's it. Now your right.'

Instinctively, for she seemed to have no conscious control over her limbs, she reacted to his instructions. Slowly, painstakingly, he holding her upright and guiding her faltering steps, they made their way in tandem towards the opposite bank.

'Keep it up, you're doing fine.'

Diana and the rest of the party had long disappeared and Carol blessed their discretion. It was humiliating enough to have to deal with Alex without having an audience as well. When they reached the bank, her trembling legs forced her to sit down.

Alex stood waiting until she gained some control. Then he held out a hand and lifted her to her feet. Avoiding his gaze, she started to make her way along the trail.

'Stop right there.'

Startled she turned round to find him staring at her sternly.

'You'll go back right now and cross that bridge. On your own.'

To her chagrin Carol felt tears welling. Where was the strong, assertive person she had brought with her to Brunei?

'I'm sorry, I can't.'

'Yes, you can. You must.'

She gazed across the river, thinking that it would be impossible. Alex placed his hands on her shoulders and waited until she was looking him in the eye.

'Believe me, Caro, you will do this.'

Maybe it was the use of her new name, maybe it was his expectations, but she found herself, as if in a trance, making her way back on to the bridge. She heard an ominous creak from the wood as she placed her foot on the walkway and bit her lip so hard she could taste blood. The feeling of his eyes boring into her back forced her on and she took another step. And then another. On and on she went, keeping her gaze ahead, never daring to drop her eyes. Suddenly, with surprise and delight she spotted the bank only a few yards away and felt a surge of euphoria. When she finally stepped onto solid ground she let out a whoop of triumph and waved delightedly across at Alex.

He cupped his hand around his mouth. 'Good effort. Now don't think about it. Come straight back.'

Without giving herself time to panic Carol stepped back onto the walkway, and keeping her gaze firmly on his face, made her way steadily back over the swaying bridge. Because she was taking slightly longer strides, it seemed to take no time at all and she was grateful to Alex for making her do it. Without him she would still be clinging to the side ropes, too terrified to move, but he had transmitted such unqualified confidence that she had been able to move her almost-paralysed limbs. She realised now what George and the others had meant when they praised his leadership abilities.

This had been a supreme test of her nerve and she had survived. Better, she appeared to have gone up a notch in his estimation, something, she realised to her surprise, that also gave her pleasure.

Alex was wearing a broad grin and she began to laugh with excitement. It seemed the most natural thing for them to hug each other in sheer exuberance.

'Well done. I think we'll try you on monkey ropes next,' he said, still holding her close. 'I knew you had the guts to do it.'

Carol was first to draw away and immediately he walked off to follow the others. As she watched his muscled back disappearing along the narrow track, occasionally dodging the overhanging vegetation, she remembered the feel of his rock-like arms when he hugged her and the firmness of his grip when he held her waist. Those strong, narrow fingers had been like bands of supportive steel and without warning a thought slid into her mind. What would it be like having those same hands stroking her body?

Aghast at where her thoughts were leading, she halted. Then she began to smile. Sex starved. That was it. Perfectly normal when her husband was thousands of miles away and most of the scientists looked like George. It was only natural she should be momentarily attracted to such a virile specimen as Alex. Perfectly natural. She was not meant to live a celibate life, that was for sure. She missed the feel of Ben's warm lips as his mouth trailed across her neck to find her breasts . . . Her reverie was broken when Alex called out and she hurried to catch up with him. Soon she would be back in Ben's arms. Till then she would have to stifle any fantasies about Alex.

Becky tiptoed past the living room hoping to get upstairs before anyone noticed her. It was an hour past her curfew but the party had been worth the trouble she was bound to face. Usually she was allowed a little leeway at weekends but since that bother at school Dad seemed to be taking far too much notice of her movements, asking Lisa to record the time she came in.

From the living room came the sound of people talking and she couldn't resist seeing who it was Lisa was entertaining. She had stepped in when Dad hadn't been able to get a babysitter so perhaps it was a boyfriend.

The door was ajar and she looked through the narrow crack. The lights were low and she saw Lisa, glass of wine in hand, smiling at someone just outside her range of vision. Intense curiosity overcame Becky. To hell with the lecture she would get about her late hours, she had to see who it was.

She pushed open the door and was surprised to see her father. He was in shirtsleeves, tie askew and sitting there very relaxed, quite close to Lisa on the sofa, thighs almost but not quite touching. Becky had always thought her dad was the most attractive of all her friends' fathers and sitting in that light, rumpled, hair flopping onto his forehead, he looked a hunk. Lisa was staring at him all cow-eyed. Music was playing softly in the background and to all intents and purposes they looked a couple.

For as long as Becky could remember, Dad had never come home on a Saturday until the early hours. What was going on here?

'Hello, late bird. Come in and explain yourself,' he said cheerily. Did she imagine the slight shadow in Lisa's expression? 'I suppose you didn't realise the time.'

'Come on, Ben, she's been working hard at school,' said Lisa, 'give her a break.'

Becky glowered. She didn't need Lisa to stick up for her. 'Dad, why are you home this early?'

'To catch you out, my girl,' grinned Ben. 'Actually,' he went on, 'your clever father finished his section and had special dispensation to come home.'

Home to Lisa?

'Pop up to bed, darling,' Lisa added. 'I'll soft-soap your dad.'

How dare she say that? But her father seemed happy to allow Lisa to treat her like an unfortunate interruption. It was obvious what Lisa was trying to do: get off with Dad behind Carol's back. 'I'll go if Lisa comes up with me,' she said, addressing her remarks to him before turning to Lisa. 'Would you, please?'

Lisa gave an amused nod and smiled at Dad as if to say, 'See how the child adores me?'

Becky turned away to hide her annoyance and as she climbed the stairs to her bedroom she heard Lisa say, 'Ben, there's another bottle of Chardonnay in the fridge, I won't be long.'

Lisa appeared surprised to see Becky sitting on her bed, arms folded, waiting for her.

'What are you doing with my father?' Becky made no attempt to disguise her hostility.

'Don't be so silly,' said Lisa, crossing over to the dressing table and straightening up the array of cosmetics scattered on the top. Perversely this infuriated Becky. God, Lisa was acting like her mother.

'You're trying to break up his marriage.'

'Don't be melodramatic. Your father and I are having a drink. That's all. Carol's my best friend, why on earth should you be thinking these ridiculous things?'

'Because I've seen the way you look at him. Whenever he's around, you're staring at him all the time. I've just realised it. You want him for yourself.'

'You're being absurd. I won't dignify it with an answer.'

'Because you know I'm right.'

Lisa was impassive. 'Your father and I are friends, just friends. That's all. Can't friends have a drink together without your going off the deep end?'

Becky was momentarily unsure.

'Becky, what's got into you?' Lisa sat down next to her on the bed. 'All I've ever wanted was to be your friend. Look,' she went on, 'you're over-excited. Why don't I get you a nice, fat spliff?'

Becky felt a surge of outrage. A grown-up offering her a joint. That was when she began to see Lisa's game plan. Coolly she faced up to the older woman.

'That's how I know you're a double-crosser. You say one thing to Dad, that you've sorted things out, but behind his back you're offering me the stuff. You're wrong to do that. Carol would never do anything like that.' Becky's eyes were cold as marble. 'Everything you do is to suck up to my father. And if I see you coming on to Dad again I'll tell him what you're up to.'

She had struck home. Lisa's lips tightened. 'I was on your side, trying to help you. But if you say anything of this rubbish to your father I'll deny everything. And who do you think he'll believe?'

For a moment Becky was at a loss, but as Lisa left the room she rallied. 'Remember, I'll be watching from now on.'

She heard the footsteps receding and after five minutes Becky could hear noises in the hallway. She peeped down to see Ben walking Lisa to the front door. He kissed her – impersonally on both cheeks, Becky noted – and waited while she climbed into the car and drove off.

Becky went back into her room, opened up her small desk and took out an airmail letter that Dad had brought for her. Sitting on the floor, her back against her bed, pen in hand, she started to write. 'Dearest Carol, how are you? Everything is fine, couldn't be better though we miss you. A lot. Went to a party at Patti's house and you won't guess what happened . . .'

Chapter Twenty

Two weeks later, on the morning of the VIP visit, Carol assisted by Anak dragged a black plastic sack along the river bank in search of decoration for the dining hut, to the incredulity of the kitchen staff. Used to the indifference of scientists to their surroundings, they had never felt the need to embellish their eating quarters. But not for nothing had Carol been dubbed the presentation queen of Jolly Good Food and she was certain that once the table arrangements were set out, the staff would appreciate the difference they made to the rather stark surroundings. Carol would take pleasure in doing it and she was determined to make the place look festive for the special supper in honour of Professor Waddaulah, his wife and teenaged son.

Anak in particular saw little merit in tramping through the undergrowth to look for the brightly-coloured jarum-jarum flowers and variegated leaves of the riverside trees but she always tried to be co-operative, a trait much appreciated by Carol. The enjoyment of the task was marred only by the constant fear that she was about to step on something nasty, although Anak assured her that the noise of their footsteps would send snakes or other creatures scuttling for cover. Carol was not entirely convinced because one night, after working late in the kitchen, she had been dive-bombed by a colony of bats. They had brushed so close she'd felt the draught from their wings. The scientists scoffed at her, saying bats had amazing radar and have never been known to bump into humans. But that didn't allay her fears.

The mist-shrouded trees and valley slowly cleared to unveil the sights and sounds of honking hornbills, and other birds which made splashes of metallic blue, fluorescent yellow and neon scarlet among the trees. Though it was a protected forest George had told her nobody minded common specimens being cut for firewood and the like and there wouldn't be a fuss about a few palm leaves being used to brighten up the place.

If florists went to heaven this would be the place, thought Carol, gathering clumps of bamboo, ferns and palm leaves and almost salivating at the amazing diversity of plants in every variety of green. The foliage would look spectacular against the wooden walls of the dining hut and they would have enough to decorate the VIP hut to be used by their guests.

After a pleasant half hour they returned in triumph to the kitchen. Anak joined in enthusiastically as they stripped, cut and layered plants across the walls and into rinsed-out baked bean cans, their sides carefully camouflaged by trailing creepers, the jarum-jarum providing a vivid orange centrepiece for the main table.

As far as Carol could discover British food had rarely before been prepared here – apart from her attempt at shepherd's pie for George – so Alex's request provided a stern challenge. She had decided on a bold approach: a typical Sunday lunch of roast beef and all the trimmings, including Yorkshire puddings. Despite her bravado Carol had misgivings about preparing this in the middle of a rainforest and in that kitchen, having experienced the inconsistency of the oven. Timing was more crucial than usual since fresh meat and potatoes had to be consumed on the day of arrival. If the longboats were late, the main part of the menu would not be ready. But these problems had the effect of galvanising her. By providing a beautifully served feast for the important visitors she intended to show Alex she was no amateur. Indeed, he was lucky to have her working at the camp.

There were difficulties from the beginning. Despite her detailed talk with Mr Chow when she'd visited his emporium, he had had problems coping with the order. Over the short-wave radio, Mr Chow seemed to have forgotten their conversation about the special meal. She dispensed with English and used the now-increasing number of words she knew in Bahasa but it still took ages for him to understand that Missy wanted a different cut of *daging sapi*. In the end he said he would try and send what she needed.

Other problems arose. Carol couldn't help noticing that the smiles she took for granted when working in the kitchen were absent. Anak, usually very co-operative, murmured that the special dish would place an extra burden on the staff. Since the Malays had almost no experience of Western cooking, Carol said she would prepare the meat and Yorkshire puddings while the rest of the staff cooked the usual meal for the scientists.

When the longboat arrived with the supplies, more or less on time, Carol was relieved to find that Mr Chow had come up trumps, not only with the cut of beef she wanted but also the rest of her order. So far, so good, she thought, as she prepared the batter for the puddings and scraped and chopped vegetables to be put in the fridge, ready for use later.

That afternoon Alex invited Carol to join the party walking to Sungai Ridge, the best vantage point to view the magnificent sunset. She could not easily forget Zoe's words that an invitation to see the sunset meant he was 'ready to pounce' and she wondered after the contact between them on the bridge whether he assumed she might be interested in something more. If watching the sunset was tantamount to becoming involved with him, that was definitely not on her agenda. Unfortunately, she told him, she could not spare the time.

'Nonsense,' said Alex crisply and it quickly became apparent that the invitation was more an order than a request. The trip to Sungai was for the benefit of their VIP guests and her task would be to stick to the wife and son while Alex devoted his energies to the professor. This was a great opportunity, he said, for her to talk to the wife about the work involved in producing meals in the camp and for him to impress upon the professor how important was the next tranche of funding. When Carol learned the reason for the invitation she accepted with relief, saying she would be delighted to assist and was looking forward to seeing the view.

Alex proved to be a knowledgeable guide, drawing on his studies of environmental sciences at Cambridge, she supposed. He drew their attention to a flock of pieridae, a species of butterfly whose bright yellow wings made a brilliant splash amongst the green foliage. The scientists, he told them, had counted three hundred and twenty-four different butterflies within one kilometre of the camp and with luck the party might see scores of different specimens on the trail to the vantage point. She could see the visitors were charmed by him and Carol found herself having to acknowledge that, in one sphere at least, he could be an agreeable companion, a different person from the disciplinarian of the camp.

He led the way, climbing rapidly but from time to time leaning downwards to extend a helping hand to the professor's wife whenever the terrain was difficult. Though it had rained recently the temperature was still high enough to make them perspire and they were all relieved when, after a fifteen-minute brisk climb, they reached the summit. It was worth the effort. The view across the canopy of trees was towards a range of mountains bathed in a deepening shade of purple. Alex warned that the sunset would be over in a matter of minutes so counselled them not to allow their attention to wander from the horizon.

As the sun began to sink the sky was layered with ribbons of grey, lavender and scarlet, casting long, pink shadows which had the effect of giving their skin a warm glow. As Alex had predicted, the fiery display did not last long. Without warning the sun began to disappear into the landscape almost as if it were on a piece of giant string which someone was tugging from the bottom. Within seconds their eyes were blinking, trying to adjust to the darkness which enveloped the mountain.

Out of the inky blackness came Alex's voice. 'Professor, this is the best place to see your beautiful country and all its marvels. No matter how often I see that sunset, it never fails to impress me.'

Unpacking a torch for each of them, Alex led the way back to camp. From time to time strange rustling sounds came from the undergrowth and Carol felt her heart racing. But however scared she was, she would make no sound; she did not want to give Alex the satisfaction of thinking she was a wimp. Nor would she want to let him down in front of their guests.

She returned to her hut hoping she would have time for a quick shower but on opening the door she found Zoe hurriedly cramming clothes into suitcases. She had been weeping and Carol stepped towards her with some concern. The look of hostility from the nurse was such that Carol retreated. 'I won't stay another night in the same hut as you, not after this.'

'What have I done?'

Zoe continued to hurl clothes into the suitcases. 'You're such a hypocrite pretending to be sympathetic and then behind my back you're scheming how to get him for yourself.'

Carol held her ground and said as quietly as she could, 'I have no idea what you're talking about.'

'There you go, Miss Innocent. Pretending she doesn't know what's going on,' sneered Zoe. 'Didn't I tell you what it meant going off to see the sunset with Alex?'

'This was different. We weren't alone, there were others—'

'That's how it starts, don't you see? First he asks you when there are lots of people around. The next time, you go with him alone.'

'I couldn't say no, Zoe.'

'Yes, you could.' Armfuls of clothes were being stuffed willy-nilly into the cases. 'Do you think I can stay in the same room as you and watch you come back from assignments with him, knowing where you've been and what you've been doing? I told you, I'm still too raw but you don't care, do you?'

In vain Carol told her she had no designs on Alex, that she was happily married, that she would soon be back home. Zoe would not be diverted. By this time the suitcases had been snapped shut and she was hauling them through the door.

'I trusted you,' she said bitterly. 'I opened myself to you, told you things I've kept secret from everyone else. And this is how you repay me.' As she manoeuvred the cases down the ramp towards a nearby hut she aimed her parting shot. 'From now on whatever happens remember, you brought it on yourself.'

Carol recalled the expedition's organiser telling her people went stir-crazy after being away from home for a long time and Zoe, clearly unhinged by jealousy, obviously suffered from this syndrome. Zoe was waiting for a replacement before leaving base camp and would be gone soon. Carol decided not to give the nurse any more thought. This was a problem which would solve itself. Carol hurried across to the dining block and was soon immersed in her duties in the steamy-hot kitchen. She had crossed her fingers when putting the Yorkshire puddings into the oven, hoping it would not switch off suddenly as happened when there was a small surge in the power supply.

Her efforts were rewarded by the broad smile creasing the professor's face when she brought in the beautifully presented food set out on a platter before them. She noticed Alex's expression; like the professor he was impressed, which pleased her more than she would have dared show. While the professor concentrated on the food, his wife was struck by the beauty of the floral decorations and said she would copy it in her own home on the university campus.

The roast beef was a trifle overdone but Carol consoled herself that was probably a good thing in this climate. However, the Yorkshire puddings, served with baby sweet corn, green beans, white cabbage and gravy, were perfection and made up for any shortcomings, like having to serve fruit salad instead of a more showy confection like Apple Snow or possibly Baked Alaska.

Later Carol was called from the kitchen to be congratulated by the guests. 'This is such a treat for me and I am glad for my wife and son to sample the food I was served during my three years at Cambridge.' Judging by the amount she and the son had eaten, his family was less enthusiastic but nothing could spoil the professor's pleasure. 'If I'd known there was a five-star restaurant around here I'd have visited sooner,' he said, smiling.

Alex cut in quickly, 'Produced on a very small budget.'

The professor laughed. 'As always, funding is never far from your mind.'

Alex, sitting back, replete and relaxed, winked at Carol. She was momentarily disconcerted. 'Caro, I'll be along in a moment to thank the rest of the people in the kitchen,' he said. 'You've all done a fine job.'

For a moment she read in his expression approval, yes, appreciation and what else? She turned swiftly away, embarrassed and irritated with herself for becoming too aware of his presence. She had felt a charge between them since the incident at the bridge and something else, a softening of his features when he talked to her. He did not seem to have the brittle or sarcastic note in his voice which had been present when she arrived. And she could not help noticing that, when they relaxed after their work was done, Alex was more often to be found joining in the conversations. She was aware of catching his eye more frequently than before. But nothing else in his demeanour suggested he viewed her as anything other than a member of the team. Once again she attributed any unsettling thoughts to being starved of Ben's attention. She reread his letters regularly. Being a writer they were full of evocative language, light-hearted references as well as interesting snippets about the children and his work. He always ended with assurances that she was much loved and much missed. But she noticed that he always included himself with the children in these endearments. It did not seem to occur to him that there was a need for him to send her greetings which were more personal.

She had never thought she could be attracted to any other man and she had to admit that Alex held some kind of fascination for her. She had never met anyone like him, an antediluvian, dominant male but capable of showing, as at the sunset, a more sensitive soul.

Carol excused the attraction she felt because she was living in limbo land, a place without borders, without boundaries. She told herself there was no danger of losing the very essence of what she was: faithful, loyal, grounded. She wasn't a dizzy teenager and she didn't doubt her ability to douse these subversive imaginings.

Chapter Twenty-One

After her affair with Ben, Caitlin had been a patient of New York's most famed cosmetic surgeon, noted for his skill and discretion, and he'd done a perfect job increasing her meagre breasts to a satisfying 34C. She wished she'd done it years ago because of the impact they had on men. Including, she was sure, Ben. Although he had never made any personal remarks since she had returned to London, she'd seen his eyes flicker over her cleavage when they were dining alone and felt certain she still held some sexual power over him.

As she flicked through the rails trying to decide what to wear for her meeting with him this evening, she reflected on how much the operation had really cost her. Out had gone all the buttoned up shirts and enveloping jackets in favour of skimpy jersey or silk tops that clung to every curve and fitted jackets that buttoned tightly against the waist. It had been a pleasure to throw away all those padded bras and replace them with wired, lace cups which did a wonderful job of uplifting her bosom to produce a gentle swell.

Caitlin slipped off a soft grey two-piece that she'd picked up from Chloe on her last trip to Paris. She'd winced at the bill but already it had paid its way in the form of a new contract with a major London advertising agency. As she surveyed her reflection in the cheval mirror she nodded in satisfaction at the image of understated sexiness. Just the effect she was trying to create for this crucial encounter.

She'd already filled the flat with pale yellow roses bought at great expense from the nearby flower stall, and the South African Nederberg white wine was being chilled in the fridge, together with the crystal glasses, a tip she'd picked up in America. Caitlin had planned the meeting to take place in the small sitting room of the flat rather than her office. As it was early evening he would hardly think this was threatening. She looked with approval at the sand-coloured twin sofas softly lit by two uplighters and adjusted the switch to throw a stronger beam. No point in being too obvious. But her plan was working. She knew it. Why else would his wife have left him for such a long time? It was obviously a trial separation. She hadn't liked making the phone call to his wife, but my God it had been effective. And she wouldn't have had the idea at all if she had thought they were happy.

Caitlin found herself pacing around the flat, adjusting the stem of one of the roses, tweaking one of the already immaculate cushions, the suspense building up as it always did before a major presentation to clients, when everything depended on how she choreographed the meeting. It didn't help that the damned man was late. He'd been reluctant, asking why she'd chosen the flat rather than a restaurant to entertain clients but had succumbed once she'd told him the information was highly confidential. She'd given him enough good stories for him to take the bait and he would have phoned if he wasn't able to come.

As the minutes ticked by Caitlin Thomas was beginning to feel more like a newly-appointed office junior than the boss of a million-dollar international business.

Ben's taxi was snarled up in traffic around Westminster and miserably he assumed he was coming down with a cold. His head felt heavy and he'd been snuffling all day. If Carol were here she'd dose him up with Vitamin C and he wondered if there was any left in the bathroom cabinet. He didn't feel he could ask Lisa to buy personal stuff for him, she already had her hands full looking after the kids. God, she'd been magnificent these past weeks. She'd make some guy a great wife. He must suggest to Carol that she find out what Lisa really wanted so they could buy her a superb present.

He leaned his head on his hand, closed his eyes and felt very sorry for himself. He was sure he was running a temperature. Carol would fuss over him, insisting that he go to bed and bring him a steaming bowl of homemade soup. Ben reached in his pocket and retrieved the email he'd received from her that morning. It had been forwarded by someone called Francesca Stone and that was why he supposed the language was somewhat formal. He preferred her letters, which were always full of warmth and colour and entertaining stories, though they took longer to arrive of course. She ended her email with individual messages to each of the children, with special love to him.

Ben sighed and was about to put the message back into his pocket when he noticed a misprint. Someone had left off the last letter in Carol's name. It reminded him this was not the best way to stay in touch, with strangers typing personal messages. They would both find it inhibiting.

Not, he reflected, that they were an overly demonstrative couple. But he had grown used to Carol's quiet presence around the house, her equable temperament and her obvious pleasure when he returned from work. Even after all these years he was flattered at the way her face would light up when he walked through the door. He enjoyed being the focus of her attention, and it made him feel protective. When he compared their marriage to others, especially those in his office, he was pretty satisfied. Carol always wished that he worked more family-orientated hours but they hardly ever rowed and he looked forward to their evenings together. He would be forever in her debt because she was such a great mother to his kids; indeed, except for Becky, who was at a prickly stage, they looked on her as their mother. Apart from actually giving birth to them, in every other way she was their mother, coping with their triumphs and tantrums with equanimity, good humour and, yes, love.

If he were pushed against the wall he'd have to admit that his proposal to Carol had been propelled by the threats Julia was making about his unsatisfactory child-minding arrangements. But it was a decision he had not once regretted. What he did regret sometimes was that as a new bride she had not had any time alone with him, being catapulted into the role of instant motherhood. And with one a baby and two traumatised infants, that had been emotionally draining. He had tried to share the tasks as much as possible but he had to earn a living for all of them. Still, he was glad she was having this chance to do something for herself. Spending three months away from all of them would give her the chance to put her own wishes first, something she had never been able to manage with three demanding children, a home to run and a part-time job. He had been hasty wanting her to be around for Becky. Lisa had been right, it would've been a shame to bring her back, though from all accounts the trip to Brunei was no picnic but at least it was something she wanted to do. It was hard on those left behind but he was lucky that his work totally absorbed his attention and when he returned home Lisa was adept at keeping him company while he ate his meal, listening attentively to the day's dramas. And if the kids were still around she was sensitive enough to melt away, leaving them alone. She was a good egg.

He blew his nose and wished once again that he could order the taxi to turn round and head for home. But Caitlin had been persistent and he had found himself agreeing to a 'quick drink' with clients at her flat, a venue she often used to entertain overseas visitors, believing, quite rightly, that people relaxed more in informal surroundings than in a hotel conference centre.

He had met her a couple of times since that embarrassing incident at the press ball but never by a flicker of an eye or a gesture had she inferred that there had been anything physical between them and he was beginning to feel more comfortable with her. He'd rationalised his behaviour that night as being due to too much champagne. This evening he would use his cold as an excuse to stick to soft drinks.

Ben spotted the danger signs as soon as he entered the room: no clients, Caitlin in a dress that showed plenty of cleavage, lights too low for business and gentle music playing in the background.

'I can't be the first to arrive, can I?' He made no attempt to remove the sarcasm from his voice.

'I'm sorry, Ben. I knew you wouldn't come if I said you were the only guest.'

He headed for the door. 'Caitlin, I thought we'd gone past all that.'

The seriousness of her expression made him pause. 'Sit down. I'm not playing games. I've got something you have to hear.'

Against his better judgement he retraced his steps and sank down into one of the sofas, his apprehension increasing. Oh God, she was going to make something of the press ball incident. He had assumed that she would be adult. It was unlike her to put him on the spot. He thought he had made it clear he had absolutely no intention of resuming their affair and though she might be planning to change his mind while Carol was away, there was no chance of that. He would soon put her straight. God, he was feeling dreadful. He fished out a handkerchief and blew his nose. What the hell could she tell him that needed to be said here? It was obviously a ploy to get him alone. He felt let down and irritated with himself that he had believed her.

'Look, I have to get back to the kids,' he said briskly, and refusing the white wine said he would stick to water as he had a cold coming on.

She disregarded this and poured them both a glass of wine. 'I think you might need this later,' she said, sitting down on the opposite sofa.

She made some attempt at small talk but impatiently he brushed this aside. 'Look, Caitlin, do you mind if we get on with it?' He took out a notebook. 'What have you got for me this time?'

'Put that away.' She looked at him steadily. 'This is personal.'

Later he found it difficult to remember his exact emotions. It was as if he was having an out-of-body experience, looking down on himself, watching himself react.

'Ben, did you know I had a child?'

He shook his head, wondering where this was leading. He had heard about her divorce but there had been no mention of a child.

'William's just had his seventh birthday.' She paused. 'Exactly twenty-two months younger than your Katie.'

That was when Fay died and their affair ended. What was she trying to imply?

'Naturally everyone assumed it was my ex-husband's child. And that's what the birth certificate says. But you've guessed, haven't you? He's our child, yours and mine.'

He stared at her, his mind filled with questions. How could she be sure? Where was the proof? How could it have happened when they always took precautions? Why, if it was true, had she not told him before? But he sensed at once it was useless to go down this road. Whatever he knew about Caitlin, she was not the type to play games. She would not say this if it were not true. There was DNA testing and she was shrewd enough not to try and fool him.

'Why are you telling me now?'

'Because our son needs a father.'

Chapter Twenty-Two

The morning after the VIP supper Alex did not appear at breakfast, nor did the guests. Carol assumed he had taken them for a dawn trek up in the hills. At first she was too preoccupied with the preparation of the lunch baskets to notice the unaccustomed silence in the kitchen and it was Anak who broke the news. The camp leader and his guests had succumbed to what appeared to be a violent reaction to the meal last night and were being treated for food poisoning. Apparently they had fallen ill an hour or so after dinner.

Carol stared at Anak, aghast. Had anyone else who'd dined that night been struck with the same bug? Anak shook her head. Not one.

Despite the heat Carol felt a chill run through her body. She remembered how emphatic she had been about preparing everything herself. In attempting to win Alex's approval for her cooking prowess she had decided to take sole charge, from cleaning and peeling vegetables, to marinating the meat, to peeling onions for the gravy. Indeed she had turned away offers of help.

Four people had eaten her special meal; four people had been laid low. The implication was obvious.

'Don't worry,' said Anak, ever the optimist. 'I give them boiled water. They be all right soon.'

Carol ran over the meal preparations in her mind. She had been extra careful with the ingredients, washing everything carefully and thoroughly. Thank God she had taken small samples of the ingredients and put them into several Freddie's Pots. She checked they were still there before going to find George.

He sympathised with her predicament. Bugs were often brought into the camp from outside and she shouldn't necessarily blame herself. But Carol could not be consoled. She must have done something wrong. In her first weeks she had been scrupulous about using purified water for everything. Had familiarity with the kitchen made her careless? She didn't think so but what other explanation could there be?

It was disastrous for the expedition that it was the professor and his family who had been stricken by food poisoning. His goodwill was essential for future funding and Alex might find it difficult to rescue the expedition's reputation in the circles which mattered in Bandar.

She asked George if it was possible for him to analyse the samples she had kept. The scientist was impressed with her efficiency and said it would take at least twenty-four hours before the results became known and in the meantime he had to ask whether anyone else could have touched the ingredients before or after cooking. No one, she replied and her heart sank as she noted his solemn face.

'Perhaps I should try and see Alex and apologise.'

This was not a good tactic, said George. Though he was over the worst, he was not in the mood for company. 'He's somewhat grumpy and tired and I think it might be better if you wait a while.' He hesitated. 'I'm sure he'll calm down when he feels more like himself.' Carol's heart sank.

During the day Carol spotted Zoe, for once wearing her uniform, walking briskly between the VIP huts to the leader's quarters. But when she tried to find out how the patients were faring, Zoe offered no comfort.

'As well as can be expected when they've just been poisoned,' she said, an air of self-importance very evident. 'These things are bound to happen when people with no experience of tropical hygiene are put in charge.'

Carol flushed. Stupid vanity had made her too ambitious in her efforts to impress. She wished fervently she had stuck to the tried and tested menus instead of experimenting. Maybe it was a mistake to let George test the food samples. So far there was suspicion but no real proof that she was the culprit. Perhaps she should have left it like that.

Her confidence at rock bottom, Carol made her way back to the kitchen to begin preparations for the midday meal. She scrubbed her hands so hard her skin started to tingle and wondered how many people would risk eating her food after this scare. She needn't have worried, the diners tucked into the food as enthusiastically as if they were unaware that four stricken people were under the care of the camp's nurse.

She passed a fitful night and hoped she could apologise personally the following morning to the professor and his family. But they did not appear for breakfast and she discovered from Anak that they had left for Bandar earlier, without saying goodbye. According to Anak, the professor and his son seemed to have recovered but his wife still looked unwell. She wanted to get home without delay to consult her own doctor.

That was bad enough but it was Alex's opinion she was even more worried about and of him there was no sign.

When lunch had been cleared away and she was about to return to her hut, one of the admin. assistants brought a message from Alex. He wanted to see her. Though apprehensive about their interview, she comforted herself with the thought that at least he'd been able to rise from his sickbed.

Alex's posture was ramrod straight and he gave no impression that he had been ill but there was no mistaking the expression. He had reverted to being a cold-eyed stranger. There were no courtesies, not even an invitation to sit down. But without being asked Carol sank into a chair, partly to assert her independence and partly because she felt immensely tired.

'I hope you're feeling better.'

He nodded curtly. 'Thank you, I am. But I'm seriously worried about what this has done for the reputation of this camp. The professor is going to have to make a report about what happened.'

'I'm sorry. I can't think it was my fault, at least. I know I took every precaution possible.'

'No one else was ill, only those of us who ate the food you prepared.' She could see his knuckles tighten on the arm of the chair. 'I just hope that the professor and his family are gracious enough to forgive.'

Carol mentioned that George was doing tests to try and rule out infection from the food, though privately she was virtually certain it would confirm her worst fears that it must have been a bug in the meat. He made no comment, frowning while playing with a couple of pens in front of him.

'I've gone over everything and I don't know what I could have done differently . . .'

For a moment she thought he might try and cheer her up, say that it might be a virus, that these things sometimes happened. Anything to take away this terrible feeling of blame. But when he spoke his tone was flat.

'That's the trouble, Caro. You might be a professional cook but you don't have experience of these conditions. There hasn't been a problem like this for months. We've been scrupulous about hygiene. That's why I insisted on a cook from London, I wanted to keep standards high, to trust the people in the kitchen. It seems I can't.' His dark brown eyes bored into hers. Damn him. For weeks she had been at pains to work hard to produce interesting and varied menus in primitive conditions. All who ate in the dining hut apparently appreciated her efforts but the moment something went wrong, she was put on the rack.

'I'm sure it wasn't anything to do with the hygiene in the kitchen . . .'

'I've made my investigations,' he interrupted. 'You prepared the meal from start to finish and it was contaminated.'

Carol stood up. 'Before I'm found guilty, don't you think you ought to wait for the tests? Or do you propose to continue being judge and jury?'

'You were very willing to take the compliments last night . . .'

'And you were very happy to rest on my laurels,' she said tartly.

She expected him to bring the interview to a close by asking her to be even more scrupulous in future. Instead he said gravely, 'I know it's a tough break, but you were warned about this. I remember telling you when you arrived that there were no circumstances when I could afford to take risks with the health of the people in my charge.' A pause. 'No circumstances.'

She sat down again. 'What are you saying? That you want me to leave?'

He gazed down at the desk. 'I don't think I have any other option.'

She allowed the silence to continue while she tried to control her emotions.

'Very well,' she replied at last, grateful her voice didn't tremble.

At once he turned practical. 'It'll take a couple of days to bring somebody out from Bandar temporarily, to fill in until Andrea Wilmot arrives. I'd be grateful if you could wait till then.'

Carol would have given anything to be able to march out of the camp, leaving everything and everybody behind. Much as she would have loved to cause Alex more disruption, she could not bring herself to leave Anak and the rest in the lurch. Somehow she found herself agreeing to stay until a new temporary could join.

Within minutes it seemed everyone in the camp had heard the news of her impending departure. They were sympathetic and appeared to be genuinely upset that she was leaving weeks ahead of schedule. She wouldn't have wanted them to go out on a limb but it would have boosted her morale had they suggested asking Alex to give her another chance. She supposed George, being emotionally constipated, was totally unable to battle on someone else's behalf. And Diana, who had enough guts to tackle Alex, indicated this was an administrative matter, not something that involved the scientific team and she couldn't interfere.

George did, however, promise to speed up his tests and rushed back to his laboratory to see how the analysis was going. Diana, trying to show some solidarity, arranged for her to make an emergency call on the satellite phone. It took several attempts before the connection was made to Ben's office but his excitement at hearing she was coming home three weeks earlier than anticipated made up for the circumstances in which she was leaving. She did not spell them out, and he did not ask questions. They agreed not to tell anyone, especially the children, until her flight was confirmed. 'They'll give me no peace,' he laughed. Carol fought back the tears. It was wonderful to make contact with him. Until that moment she had not realised just how much she had missed them all and she vowed this would be the last time they would be apart.

She was smiling when she put down the phone, which seemed to disconcert George who came panting into the communications hut. He had been trawling the camp looking for her, he said, waving a computer printout.

'I've tested for every known strain of salmonella common to the Far East.' He straightened his shoulders. 'My conclusion is that it's unlikely to be from impurities in the kitchen.'

At first she could barely take it in. 'Nothing to do with the kitchen? You're wonderful. Thank you.' She patted his arm delightedly and he coloured.

'Glad to help.'

'But if nothing in the kitchen was responsible, what on earth was it?'

'That's what I asked myself,' said George promptly. 'Apart from the known causes of food poisoning, what would make people violently ill in such a short space of time? I had a hunch and when I tested for it, bingo.' He paused theatrically. 'Ipecacuanha.'

In the face of her obvious bafflement, he explained it was a drug used as an emetic. 'Every camp has some on hand in case any of us swallows a poisonous berry or suchlike, but how it got into the Yorkshire pudding batter I haven't a clue.'

Who on camp would have such a drug? Only the nurse, she thought angrily. Carol remembered leaving the batter to cool in the fridge. Zoe could have entered the kitchen without being challenged. Anak and the others would assume she was storing one of her medicines.

As soon as she could disengage herself, she went to find Zoe. But the hut she had been using had been cleared out. Sheets were folded on top of the mattress and the shelves and cupboards had been emptied.

Despite the heat, Carol ran the short distance to the jetty where she saw a longboat loaded with suitcases and Zoe standing quite relaxed among a small group of people saying goodbye. Making her way to Zoe's side, Carol asked if she could have a quiet word. Graciously Zoe excused herself from the others and walked, unhurriedly, to the shade of a tree. She carried the orange-coloured life jacket and slipped her arms into it.

'Got the chance of leaving this place today because they're picking up a medical officer in Bandar on the return journey,' she said conversationally, as if chatting to a next-door neighbour, while tieing the life jacket around her waist.

'It wouldn't be guilty conscience causing you to leave, would it?'

'I don't feel at all guilty,' retorted Zoe, carelessly tossing back her hair. 'I arranged for a replacement.'

'You know that's not what I meant.'

Zoe waved gaily at a group of people standing on the verandah. When she turned back to Carol, a smile was playing on her lips. 'What are you talking about?'

'You put an emetic into the pudding batter.'

Zoe smiled. 'It was poisoning from your food. Why are you accusing me?'

'Because we both know you did it. You have access to ipecacuanha.'

'So do several others around here.'

'But they don't want to have me sacked. They aren't insanely jealous.'

At this a slight crease appeared on Zoe's forehead and Carol thought she was not going to answer but then the nurse said fiercely, 'I've seen the way he looks at you.'

The tension of the last two days caused Carol to erupt, but she kept her voice low. 'You stupid woman. How could you make innocent people suffer?'

Zoe looked at her stonily. 'I deny I had anything to do with it and you can't prove otherwise.' She turned on her heel and made her way back to the landing stage. Carol watched her climb into the longboat, helped by a short, stocky figure. He appeared to be comforting her, patting her on the shoulders. To her surprise she saw it was Angus Roberts.

What was he doing here? He must have arrived with the boat and now he was going back with Zoe. Why would he bother? Perhaps, she thought, he had delivered something to the camp. As the paddles began dipping in and out of the current, taking the boat towards the bend of the river and out of sight, Zoe sat staring at the people who were calling out messages of good luck, searching, Carol was sure, for one particular face.

An hour later Carol was sitting on the verandah outside her hut drying her hair. The colour had bleached in the sunshine and had turned it from a somewhat ordinary-looking brown to rich honey. It had grown a little since Anak's effort but it was still wonderfully easy to manage and in that climate took minutes to dry. She folded the towel and rose to go inside when she spotted Alex advancing purposefully in her direction. She watched him approach, her face immobile.

'George has told me about the analysis and what he found in the samples,' he began. 'It seems I owe you an apology.'

Ah, he was coming to eat humble pie.

'Yes,' she said coolly. 'You do.'

'I think you'll agree there was every reason for me to reach the conclusion I did. But that drug could not have got into the food unless it was put there deliberately and I have a shrewd idea of who was responsible. I suspect you do, too. Could we go inside?'

Silently she followed him into the interior of the cool hut. She saw his gaze take in the half-packed suitcase and the scattered belongings.

'Look, there's no proof but of course Zoe was the only person who had the opportunity and the motive. She and I . . .well, let's say things were exaggerated in her mind. But I'm not prepared to overlook something as serious as this.'

Carol described Zoe's reaction to her accusation, that nobody could prove a thing.

True, said Alex, but he had nonetheless forwarded a report to

London about the nurse's actions. Without hard evidence it was not something they could follow up legally but as he was certain of his facts, he had asked the BGA to try and keep it out of the public domain but make sure her professional body was aware of what had happened and why.

Carol asked him why Angus Roberts was being so solicitous to Zoe.

'Angus was here? Why wasn't I told about that?' Carol shrugged, and he thought for a moment. 'That fits. Angus has been trying to make trouble for me ever since I was appointed. He was turned down for the job and Zoe would have been fertile ground for him to work on.'

'What can you do about it?'

He narrowed his eyes. 'I think Angus will find out that I always win, however long it takes.'

She gave a mock shiver. 'Just as well I'm leaving.'

'I wish you'd reconsider.'

When she shook her head decisively he began to pace up and down. 'It's difficult being a leader on this kind of expedition. Sometimes you need to take harsh decisions because you think it will be for the good of everyone here. In your case I had no other option open to me.'

She said nothing, determined not to make things easy for him.

'If I'd said, oh well, learn from your mistake, that would have sent the wrong signals to the others. That's the reason I made the decision I did. Believe me, I didn't want you to leave.' He ceased pacing then looked out through the doorway. 'And I don't want you to go now.'

Carol experienced a flash of pleasure but replied, 'I'm sorry. I think it best we leave things as they are.'

He smiled ruefully. 'I'm prepared to beg, you know. And it's not something I do often.'

This caused her to laugh and seemingly encouraged he sat down on the bed. 'There aren't many things I regret but this is one of them. Is there anything I can say to make you change your mind?'

She did not trust herself to speak, only shook her head. He gave a decisive nod and got to his feet. So did she.

'I'm sorry it has to end like this,' he said.

To her surprise he did not leave immediately. Instead, he took hold of her hand. She looked down at his brown hand enfolding her own. For a moment his grip tightened and he stared down into her eyes. She closed them, wondering whether he, too, was experiencing the surge of electricity she was feeling. But he broke away and rushed out to stride down the walkway.

Yes, she thought, it was a good thing she was leaving. More time here with Alex might create a problem and there would be no hiding the shift that had come about in her personality. Ben had married a somewhat accommodating woman, who invariably gave way in arguments and who rarely had the courage to express what she was feeling. She couldn't see how she could revert to being a Carol but how would Ben react to Caro? How would he manage with a partner who was independent, assertive and, most importantly, who would expect rather more from him?

She would soon find out.

Chapter Twenty-Three

When faced with a predicament, Ben became ice calm. Outsiders might think that this denoted a person who was impassive, unable to give vent to feelings. In reality it was because he simply put emotions on hold, to analyse later. He was able to take on board what Caitlin had told him. It was quiet in the flat and a part of his mind noticed that a clock on the mantelpiece was twenty minutes slow. He began to experience a curious sensation that time had slowed down, that everything was happening at a deliberate pace.

From a distance he heard himself telling her he needed time to think, that he would be in touch soon. He must have used the right words for he saw that she was not alarmed. Indeed, she said she was agreeably surprised at how well he was taking the news. She thanked him for not questioning whether the child was really his, told him that she'd already had one DNA test done to prove to her ex-husband that William could not be his. But she was quite willing to have another one done should he wish it.

She would try and be patient and wait until he was ready to discuss plans for the future. In the meantime did he want to see a photograph of his son?

His son.

He could not quite bring himself to visualise a human being with his and Caitlin's genes, not at that moment. Somehow he found himself outside her flat, hailing a taxi to take him home. Caitlin wanted the child to be integrated into his life. How would that affect Carol? And what of his children? How would he explain to them that they had a half-brother only about eighteen months younger than Katie? Even Emmy, poor as she was at maths, would work out that the child must have been conceived while their mother was still alive. Ben cradled his face in his hands and allowed his emotions to erupt. The groan, like that of a cornered animal, was fierce enough to cause the taxi driver to turn his head and inquire if he was all right. Ben ignored this and asked if there was any way to avoid this jam, which produced a litany of complaints about London's badly managed traffic and what the taxi driver would do if only they had the sense to put someone like him in charge.

When Ben got home he excused himself and went straight up to bed, telling Lisa he was coming down with a cold. She thought it had to be more serious than that. Since she'd been around he had never missed spending time with the children when he came home from work, however tired he was. When she took him up a tray of hot food and a bottle of paracetamol half an hour later he was still fully dressed, sitting in a bedroom chair, looking miserable. Lisa put down the tray on the bedside cabinet but he said he wasn't hungry.

'I don't want to pry,' she said tentatively, 'but you look as though you could do with a friend. Anything I can do?'

He shook his head. 'Thanks, it's kind of you but . . .'

'Is it work?'

Another shake of the head.

Lisa sat down on the edge of the bed and regarded him with some sympathy. She had never seen Ben as downcast as this in all the years she had known him.

'Are you missing Carol?' she asked eventually.

'Of course.' A beat. 'But that's not it.'

She was reluctant to leave him alone in this state and filled the silence with talk of the day's activities. Emmy had been given a silver star for maths, Katie wanted to learn the piano and there had been a quarrel over who the cat loved the most. Even this didn't elicit a smile.

Finally, he looked up and said, 'You're a good pal, Lisa. I'm glad you're here.'

'And there's no way I can help?'

'You're Carol's friend and I'd rather not implicate you.'

Implicate her? Lisa was uneasy. It seemed to her this was tantamount to a confession and she wondered how far she should push him. She had heard often enough from Carol that Ben found it difficult to unburden himself when it came to personal problems but usually responded if she persevered. Later he would comment how much better he felt for having shared his worries. Lisa asked him again what was wrong.

This time he hesitated and she was sure he was about to unburden something but at the last minute seemed to check himself. 'It's complicated. You wouldn't understand.'

Emboldened by the fact he hadn't asked to be alone, Lisa decided it had to be about the anonymous phone call. Perhaps he had found out who was behind it.

'Is is anything to do with that person who phoned Carol?'

'Not directly.' He breathed deeply and appeared to make a decision. Almost to himself, he added, 'But that was when she found out about the woman I was having an affair with when Fay was still alive.'

'And your problem concerns this woman?'

A curt bow of the head.

Lisa risked another question. 'Is it serious?'

Ben rubbed a hand over his face. 'Yes. Very.'

The affair must still be going on. And the woman was putting on the pressure. Lisa waited but Ben seemed reluctant to say much more except that he'd have to sort it out himself and because Carol would be coming home soon he wouldn't have much time. Lisa was startled.

'You're not going to tell her, are you?'

'I don't want to but she'll have to know.'

'Oh my God. How do you think she'll take it?'

'I'll have to take my chances and hope she'll understand,' Ben said wryly.

Lisa was appalled. Was he serious? No wife would 'understand' there was another woman in her husband's life. Not for the first time Lisa marvelled that however intelligent a man was he had a great ability to fool himself.

She put the bottle of painkillers on the bedside table and said slowly, 'If you change your mind and want to talk, I'll be around for a while.'

As she walked out with the tray, Lisa remembered clearly how fiercely she had defended Ben when Carol had been distraught about the anonymous phone call. Then she had tried to calm her down when Julia's revelations about the custody battle had really upset her. It was Lisa who had portrayed Ben as a loyal husband who could be trusted and who valued his family life. Had she been wrong? How much could this man value his marriage when he was still involved with Caitlin? Why would he risk all that he had built up with Carol and the children for a woman who had already destroyed one marriage? She must have quite a hold on him. Poor Carol.

Lisa's observations might have stayed private had it not been for a call from Ben a few days later. He had meant to take his dark grey suit to the cleaners but had rushed out and forgotten it. He hated to bother Lisa but would she take it out of his wardrobe and drop it in on her way to collect Katie? The dry cleaners was a few blocks from the school.

It was when Lisa went to find the suit that she noticed the one-page letter on the small table next to the wardrobe. She might have ignored it except her eye caught sight of the bold signature at the bottom of the page. Even while telling herself she had no right, none whatsoever, to pry, her hand had picked it up. It was a short letter but each word proved to Lisa that Ben was continuing his affair with Caitlin. Lisa remembered she had scoffed when Carol said her instinct told her these two were still involved. But she had been right.

Ben was one of the most attractive men Lisa had come across and she could understand why a woman wouldn't give him up easily. God knows there had been times in the past few weeks when she had allowed herself to fantasise about him. Becky's accusations that she was 'after him' had been uncomfortably close to the truth. Indeed she had chastised herself for her disloyalty but living this life had focused her mind on what she truly wanted out of life: to be part of a family unit. Her own family unit.

The questions Lisa had to ask herself were simple. What was she going to do about the letter? Keep her mouth shut? Or tell Carol?

Chapter Twenty-Four

They were waiting for the longboat to arrive with supplies and mail when Alex announced he intended to accompany Carol to the capital. This was not to extend the goodbyes, he told her, but to see the Sultan's representative. Despite the mishap to the professor and his family, the man had hinted there might be funding for another expedition the BGA were planning in another region of the rainforest and London were keen for him to follow this up speedily.

Carol waited, chafing, while Alex sifted through the mail bag, wondering if the children had written and whether Ben had had a chance to send her an email since she had told him of her plans to return. Finally, Alex passed her a letter and two computer printouts. One was from Ben but there was no hearts and flowers message, simply a brief note to ask for details of her flight. He would pick her up and still hadn't mentioned her arrival to anyone. Carol folded the paper feeling deflated. Her emails, Ben knew, could be read by anyone at the office in Bandar and at the camp but still it would have been reassuring if he'd at least mentioned how impatiently he was waiting and how much he was looking forward to seeing her. They were husband and wife, for God's sake. But the letter from the children was satisfyingly thick. They had each penned their own diary, as they said they would. She would read it later when she was alone.

The other email was also terse and Carol read the message through twice before becoming uneasy. It was from Lisa and, like Ben, she had kept her message short and impersonal. No gossip, no fond regards. 'Need to speak to you privately. Nothing wrong with the kids. Please call me at my office immediately you get this. But don't tell Ben you're phoning. This is important.'

Don't tell Ben? She glanced at her watch. There was a good chance Lisa would be at home and awake. She squashed the email onto her lap and hung back until she was alone with Alex.

'I need to make a call on the satellite phone. It's an emergency.'

He leaned forward with a concerned expression. 'Of course. Give me the number. I'll get it for you.' Despite telling herself to keep calm, Carol's voice betrayed her extreme nervousness. Lisa did not easily panic. Something must have happened, something too bad to break in an email.

Alex was successful on the third attempt and handed her the receiver. Vaguely, in the background, she heard him say he would wait outside and to call if he was needed.

Lisa assured her there was nothing wrong with Ben's health. Nor with the children. Carol started to relax. Perhaps Lisa was being melodramatic. She waited for her to get to the point. It seemed to take a long time. Lisa described Ben's distressed state when he had come home recently. 'I wouldn't have told you anything but then I found something relevant. I wasn't prying,' she said hastily, and explained how Ben had asked if she would be kind enough to take a suit to the cleaner's.

Carol, listening intently, said nothing.

'The suit was slung on a chair in the bedroom and on the table next to it I saw it. A letter. The signature was visible. It was from Caitlin.' She paused. 'Carol? Are you there?'

'Yes. Go on.'

'I'm sorry and I'm not sure whether you want to know but I think they are still having an affair.'

Carol's throat constricted.

'What did the letter say?'

'That she should never have allowed it to happen.'

'That sounds as if it was Ben who started things up again.'

'Then she wrote that she didn't want him to feel guilty and to spoil what they had together.'

After all her husband's fine words, his promises, his entreaties to trust him. Carol's pulse was racing. 'Oh God, I feel such a fool. I believed everything he told me.'

The line went silent for a second before a stream of words from Lisa made clear the decision to contact Carol had been difficult. She had spent a sleepless night worrying about it. Finally she had come to the conclusion that Carol could not be allowed to return home without being warned what she would face. And if Carol thought she had no right to interfere, her only defence was that, in Carol's place, she'd want prior warning. Had she done the right thing?

Carol swallowed hard. 'Yes, you have. I'm glad you told me. I do need to know.'

It was obvious that Ben had not told Lisa of the change of departure date for she suggested that Carol cut short her trip and come home immediately to sort things out. Then the line began to break up and the connection was cut abruptly.

For a short while Carol sat in silence before realising she was still in Alex's office. He must be outside waiting for her to finish and she jumped up.

He stared at her keenly. 'Everything all right?'

'The line went dead before we finished.'

'Want me to get it back for you?'

'No,' she said dully. 'There's no need.'

He took her arm and gently guided her back into the office.

'Is there anything I can do?'

There was a gentleness about his face that seemed completely out of character. Where was the tough leader who'd roasted her such a short time ago?

'If it would help to talk then I'm here.'

Carol could have dealt with aggression and hostility but this compassion made her crumple and however hard she tried she was unable to halt the wave of misery overwhelming her.

'Had somebody died?' he asked quietly and she became aware of the squeeze of his hand on her shoulder.

'In a way, yes.'

Miles away from home, missing her children, remembering the look on her husband's face when dining with Caitlin, Carol felt a great desire to confide in someone sympathetic.

'It's my marriage,' she said, suddenly engulfed by a fresh bout of weeping. 'It was wobbly before I came out here but I didn't think that behind my back he'd . . .'

She couldn't carry on speaking and Alex handed her a tissue. 'Perhaps you shouldn't have come here.'

She sniffed into the tissue. 'What kind of relationship would that be? It was happening while I was there and I thought . . .I thought . . .if I left he might realise what he was missing. I was wrong.'

'Maybe you ought to go home right away and straighten things out.'

Go home? The idea was suddenly repellent. She couldn't face Ben now. She needed time to work out what to do about their marriage. If it wasn't for the children, that decision would be made for her. She had no doubt that Ben was grateful for what she had done for them and loved her in his way. The difference was he was *in love* with Caitlin and the bonds between them were so powerful it was obvious they couldn't live without each other. They had both tried hard. Caitlin had removed herself to America. He had remarried but it hadn't worked. Carol was quite sure that when she returned Ben would be truly sorry and would not want to hurt her but the reality was that their marriage had been based on a lie. It had been a sham from the beginning. Only she, poor blind fool, hadn't realised it. Well, she didn't plan to spend the rest of her life as a substitute, a second-best. Whatever this experience in the rainforest had taught her it was that she did not want to lead a life as a cipher. Caro had proved she could stand up for herself. Carol had to do the same.

But what about the children? That needed some hard thinking.

She blinked the tears away. 'No, I've thought for some time that there was something wrong but I don't want to go back, not yet. You asked me to stay. Is that offer still open?'

Chapter Twenty-Five

For the next twenty-four hours every time the phone went Lisa jumped but there was no word from Ben. She didn't think Carol would betray her confidence but, however much she criticised Ben's actions, she still agonised about whether she had done the right thing interfering in her friend's marriage. It was frustrating that she couldn't get through to the camp after the line went dead. She would have liked to know what excuse Carol was using to come home early. Andrea also tried and failed to reach Carol. She managed to get hold of someone in the office in the capital called Francesca but she had said a succession of storms had resulted in the lines being brought down and though she would try she'd probably have to wait for the next supply boat to get a message through.

After Lisa found out about Ben's adultery she wasn't able to behave normally towards him. He didn't seem to notice that she didn't look him in the eye and though she continued to try and sound friendly, it was an effort. Lisa couldn't help worrying about the distress ahead for Carol and the kids. If she'd kept quiet maybe Ben might have managed to keep the affair secret.

So why had she done it? It was a question she asked herself many times in the days that followed. She had been impulsive, acting solely on instinct. The conscious reason was to forewarn her friend so she could take control of the situation rather than have it thrust upon her as had happened several times in her own life.

This was solid reasoning, pious even. But if she were honest she would have to own up to a darker motive. Until lately Lisa had regarded herself as Carol's superior as a professional caterer with a thriving business and the active partner in their friendship, organising all the treats and pushing Carol into doing things she wouldn't attempt on her own. But in the weeks Lisa had been in charge of the Mitchell household, she'd come to appreciate the richness of Carol's life. She would never worry whether she was important to the family, she took it for granted. Even though Ben was involved with another woman, he was still at pains to keep his transgression from Carol. He did not want to lose her. Despite everything, Carol would never have to come home to a dark empty house.

More than once Lisa had found herself listening for the sound of Ben's key in the lock. She realised this was simply because she was used to living alone but she also enjoyed seeing his grin break out as he burst through the door. She appreciated his humour, and his sharp mind provoked her into more serious thinking than was required by menus and food orders.

What these past weeks had taught her was that she valued simple pleasures. Unqualified affection from the children (until the problem with Becky). A late-night drink with Ben. Planning a special treat for the kids. With them she was free to be herself. Unlike all her previous relationships there was no subterfuge involved. It gave her great satisfaction to see their eager faces around the kitchen table and more than once she couldn't help thinking that if she had been their mother she would never have left them for so long. She had instantly doused the disloyal thought but it was painful to admit the reason she had told Carol about her husband's adultery was that she was jealous. That underneath the veneer of friendship and in other circumstances she would have liked Ben and his family for herself.

But when she'd found out about his continuing affair with Caitlin, whatever her fantasies she'd been forced to realise there was no hope. It was time to check into the real world, to take a brutally frank look at her life.

Until now Lisa had been scared to reveal any vulnerability to the men she met, she supposed for fear of rejection. There had been one or two who had been eligible but she had frightened them off. And she could see why. As a single career woman she had been sending out the wrong signals, making it clear she was more interested in the transitory things of life, his job, the type of car he drove, where he would take her to dinner, rather than the man himself. Instead of wondering whether her friends would approve – to be frank, whether they would be envious of her – she ought to have taken trouble to get to know the man, not the package he could provide.

Maybe she would try again with the dating agency. Only this time she would have a different idea of who she wanted.

* * *

Carol could not push aside thoughts of Ben's betrayal and was plagued by sudden visions of him thrashing about in bed with Caitlin.

Intelligent, sophisticated, successful Caitlin.

Carol would bet that her talents included skill in the art of lovemaking. Caitlin would never allow herself to be seen not looking her best. Carol remembered her mother telling her with approval that the Queen and Prince Philip had different bedrooms. 'Always a good idea for your husband never to see you when you first wake up.' It was such old-fashioned thinking Carol had laughed at the time. But damn it, remembering all the times Ben had come home to find her not having combed her hair since morning, make-up non-existent and wearing his cast-off tracksuit, maybe there was a germ of truth in it.

And Caitlin was a top businesswoman, involved in his world. Carol had seen for herself in the restaurant that she was a stimulating companion. Whereas his wife hadn't even had time to read the newspaper by the time he arrived home.

Why was she having such retrograde thoughts? That was the thinking of her old self. She had to watch it. However tough the going, she had to encourage Caro to take the upper hand.

After the nightmares about Caitlin came the worry about how she would face up to Ben when she arrived home. Carol had toyed briefly with the idea of pretending she knew nothing, that Lisa had not phoned, allowing things to stay as they were, mostly because of what a break-up would do to the children. Part of her still wished she could believe Ben loved her. Until the anonymous phone call there had been no reason to doubt him. Still he had managed to smooth-talk his way out of that, even encouraging her to come on the trip to Brunei. Now she could see his game plan. What a naïve idiot she had been, leaving the field clear for him to conduct his sordid little affair. To think that only a short while before she had been desperate for him to be the father of her child. It was a bitter thought and she felt despair at what the future held, not only for her but for the children.

The afternoon downpour had started and sounded like a lorry-load of hammers being dropped onto the roof. It was by now such a familiar sound she hardly noticed. She caught sight of herself in the small mirror. How different from the pale, tired-looking individual who had turned up in Bandar, unsure of herself and her abilities. The sun-lightened hair framed a face the colour of pale mahogany, the eyes were bright and the cheekbones more pronounced. Sadly she came to the conclusion that improved looks did not compensate for a wretchedly unhappy state of mind.

She had to let Ben know of her change of plans. He might be puzzled but she would just say she had promised to stay until Andrea's arrival. When she asked if she could send an email message Alex actually delayed the longboat to Bandar, an almost unheard of occurrence, while she finished writing it.

In her hut, Carol's fingers toyed with a pencil. What do you say to a cheating, adulterous liar when you don't want him to know he's been found out? She started the message several times, 'darling, dearest, dear' . . .then changed her mind. She couldn't be hypocritical; on the other hand she didn't want to alert him. In the end she dispensed with endearments and simply wrote his name. He could make of that what he wanted.

'Ben: Sorry, plans have changed. Impossible to leave before Andrea arrives so am staying till the end of the contract. Glad you didn't tell the children. I'm missing them. Will advise you of date of homeward journey and flight arrival time.' She gritted her teeth and added, 'Miss you too.' It wasn't a complete lie. She missed the touch of the Ben she had once known. Not the Ben he had become.

The crisis in her marriage seemed to bring out the best in Alex. He appeared genuinely anxious about her and said she was to come and see him any time she needed to talk. She pretended that this was to be expected from a conscientious boss, concerned about the welfare of one of his staff. But she was not a fool. In the following days, she sensed there was something more than concern in Alex's attentions and she couldn't help but be aware of a growing physical attraction between them.

She remembered the rope bridge, the gut-wrenching fear, the blinding sunlight and then those magnetic eyes urging her across on her own. But the hug had been spontaneous, pleasure at his part in her triumph and not by word or deed until lately had he given any hint that he saw her as more than simply a member of the team.

She could not help smiling at the irony of the situation. Far from home, with an attractive man taking some interest in her, she was being as virginal as a medieval wife with a chastity belt. Why was she being noble when her dear husband was cavorting with his mistress?

She allowed herself to think about the feel of Alex's powerful arms around her on the other side of the bridge. If she had not broken away, what might have happened? More disturbingly, what did she want to happen now?

She told Diana a little of what was happening at home and to take her mind off her problems the older woman tried to include her in treks into the forest whenever possible. The last trip with the students had worn Carol out, so when Diana told her about a yomping field trip Alex was planning, Carol shook her head. Half-running the whole way, with a full backpack, never stopping until the destination was reached was too much for her, she said. Nonsense, said Alex, when told of her refusal. Perhaps that might have been true when she first arrived but not any longer. Much against her better judgement she eventually fell in with the plan and found herself jogging alongside the fitter undergraduates and other expedition members. They were making for the Fish Eye Falls to look for new species of ferns and it took nearly a day to get there. They did have rest stops every two hours, she was sure for her benefit, and she took full advantage of the pauses to try and quell the pounding of her heart. But at the journey's end, standing in front of a sweeping wall of water, completely drenched in sweat, she experienced a sense of achievement that obliterated her tiredness.

Alex suggested they eschew the bivouacs and sleep that night under the stars. 'Caro, you can't really say you know the rainforest until you do.' She was determined not to protest or show fear though she was first to settle herself near the camp fire, knowing that it would deter the animals which roamed the forests. Away from the protocol of the camp she noticed Alex became less hierarchical. Although he was regarded with respect out here in the forest the scientists also treated him with a certain amount of relaxed humour. Throughout the journey she had been aware that he was close by her side and each time she had felt her lungs would explode, he had called for a rest stop. She worried that the others might notice he was paying her more than customary attention and tried not to show any reaction when Alex placed his sleeping bag next to hers. It was a strange situation. If she moved a fraction to the left, their bodies would touch, albeit through the sleeping bags. She could hear his breathing and when she risked a glance she saw, in the firelight, that he was staring at her. She hadn't slept this close to a man since she had met Ben and she felt discomfited. But there was little time to mull on this fact for, exhausted, it wasn't long before she fell into a deep sleep.

By the time they returned to camp later the next day Carol had all but lost her fear of rustles in the undergrowth, and like all the others paid little regard to the stings and bites of the clouds of insects which followed their steaming bodies along the trail. She had been shown how to walk on the outside of her feet to lessen the risk of noise from snapping debris and rapidly learned how to freeze when one of the scientists raised his arm to indicate a find. Working with the scientists at close quarters she saw how painstaking they were, how excited they became at the prospect of discovering a species they hadn't seen before or something rare. They seemed to be pleased she was interested and were generous with their information.

Immersed in their world for hours at a stretch she forgot completely about her marital problems and when finally they did surface she reminded herself that with each week that passed she was becoming stronger, physically and mentally.

Chapter Twenty-Six

Ben was walking through the central lobby of the House of Commons after interviewing the Home Secretary. Having hinted he was in favour of the idea of co-operating with an American firm pitching to run Britain's jails, the Home Secretary had turned evasive. When he refused to confirm or deny that talks had already started, Ben decided the tip might be worth pursuing. He had a day to firm up the story if he wanted to make that Sunday's paper.

He'd missed lunch and decided to call in to the Commons cafeteria for a sandwich when he saw in the distance the one woman in London he did not want to meet. Caitlin was deep in conversation with a man he recognised as MP for one of the areas in which the jails were situated. Before he could back out of the door she caught sight of him and waved. He returned the greeting but strode rapidly to the self-service canteen and picked up an egg and tomato sandwich. To avoid any possibility of having to talk to her he would eat it in the car on the way back to the office. But as he reached the cashier, Caitlin was at his side.

'Buy you a cup of coffee, sir?' she inquired brightly. She was wearing some sort of browny-red suede jacket which he thought made her look tired though he noticed she was the object of some attention from the mixed crew of off-duty policemen and researchers who found time to be in the cafeteria in the afternoon.

'Sorry, not this time, have to rush.'

'Pity because I know who you've been talking to. If you want the gen on those prisons I'm the one to give it to you.'

Ben hesitated. He had told his secretary not to put through her phone calls but he had promised himself he would talk to her about the child once he had broken the news to Carol. Perhaps it would be a good idea to tell her that now. And he did need the story.

She had not lied, she was familiar with all the details. Apparently an

American client had a financial interest in privatising prisons and he would prove a valuable lead. But Ben did not have to wait long before the subject was changed.

Caitlin fixed her gaze on his face. 'Why are you being such a coward, running away from my phone calls?'

He was about to tell her he was aware of his responsibilities when they were interrupted by a cheery voice.

'Well, he-llo, if it isn't my favourite lobbyist.' The portly figure of the honourable member for Broadgate sat down heavily beside them, gave a nod of recognition in Ben's direction before regaling them with a triumph he had just enjoyed in the chamber, baiting his opposite number on the government benches. 'I told him he had the sort of brains of which cabinets were made. Our side of the House appreciated that,' he chortled. 'Anyway, Caitlin my dear, what are you handling these days or should I say "who"?'

Ben got to his feet. 'Forgive me, but I've got a story to write.'

'Can I have a lift, please?' asked Caitlin swiftly. 'I'm going in your direction.'

'Can't you stay?' asked the member. 'I was about to suggest we pop over to the Pugin Room for a glass of champagne.'

Caitlin managed to look regretful. 'Another time.'

They strode in silence to the House of Commons car park and Ben drove, faster than usual, up the Mall and round Buckingham Palace. It was only when they reached Hyde Park that Caitlin broke the silence and pointed out a layby several yards ahead, saying they needed to talk. 'You've been running away from me but you can't hide from this. You have to face it sometime. I've told you our boy needs a father.'

His mouth tightened and he said stiffly, 'I've no intention of shirking my responsibilities. William shouldn't suffer for our mistakes. I'm quite prepared to share all the costs of his upkeep.'

Caitlin was clearly irritated. 'You know what I want and it isn't money,' she snapped. 'William needs to spend time with you, to get to know you.'

But Ben was determined not to be railroaded nor would he give promises he could not keep. 'I have to tell the family in my own time. I thought Carol was coming home this weekend but I've just received an email to say she's sticking to her schedule. I can't tell her about William by mail, can I? It needs to be done face to face.' He dreaded having to square things with Carol. God knows how she would react. But most of all he feared telling the girls. It would be a terrible shock and what would they think of their father then?

'I don't want William to wait too long. Your wife gets back in three weeks so what are we talking about, a month, six weeks?'

Ben was alarmed to think she wanted to integrate William into his life in quite such a direct way. If he'd thought about it he would have said a visit perhaps once or twice a month might be something he could schedule but the way Caitlin was talking it appeared to be more, far more, than that.

He evaded the question. 'Carol and I haven't had an easy time lately. She had an anonymous call saying . . .well, it doesn't matter about that but she found out about our affair.'

'Didn't she know before?'

'I didn't think it was relevant; it was over long before I met her. Could your ex-husband have made the call? After all, he makes a habit of these things, doesn't he?'

Caitlin shook her head. 'There's no reason why he would. Besides, he's still in Washington and has a very nice life, on the alimony I pay, I might add.'

'I presume he knows I'm William's father.'

Caitlin began to toy with her pearls. 'Suspects. When I found out I was pregnant I had to get away from London. You'd made it clear there was no future for us and I didn't want to beg. It was just easier to let him come with me and in the beginning he did think he was the father.' She shrugged. 'It seemed the lesser of all evils, and he made himself useful in my company, acted more or less as my wife, really. Only it was impossible to go on living with him, I couldn't bear it. William was only a few weeks old when I asked him to move out although we were still connected through business. I had the DNA test soon after and then we were divorced.'

Ben pondered for a moment. 'So he never got to know William?'

'No, it was his choice. He wanted to have very little to do with my boy once he knew the truth and of course there's been no contact with him since we've been here. William began asking questions about his father when he was about four.'

Ben was startled. 'Does William know my name?'

Caitlin hesitated then gave him the answer he dreaded. 'Indeed he does. I've even shown him your photograph.' She gave a sad smile. 'Every Sunday he tries to read your articles, I suspect he's making a scrap book of them. That's how much he wants to get to know you.'

'Caitlin, I really wish you hadn't . . .'

'It's all very well for you to say that,' she said tensely. 'You weren't being pestered with questions. At first I simply tried to avoid answering but it became too difficult. In the end when I said we would be going to live in London, which was where you were, I had to promise that I would do all I could to make sure we might become a family.'

'Did you have the right to promise that?'

She became defensive. 'I felt the child needed something to cling on to. Some hope for the future.'

Their talk was drowned momentarily by the clanking swords of soldiers from the Household Cavalry, parading by on a column of gleaming black horses. When the soldiers had passed, Caitlin leaned towards Ben. 'In his whole life William's never called anyone Daddy. What he wants more than anything in the world is for you two to spend time together, to become friends.'

With every word, he thought despairingly, Caitlin was drawing him ever deeper into her web. How could he turn his back on the poor kid?

'He's a lovely boy, intelligent, sweet, not unlike you.' She began fishing in her handbag. 'Take a look.'

She held out a photograph and for a moment Ben did not respond. After a while he slowly held out a hand to take the print.

'This is your son,' she said, before letting go of the photograph.

The picture showed a young boy in a field. By his side was a large kite and he was grinning directly into the camera.

There was no doubt in Ben's mind that he was looking at a replica of himself at about that age. The curls, the eyes, even the tilt of the head had been passed on to this child.

As if she could read his mind she said, 'He's great, isn't he? It's not much fun for him only having me. That's why I sent him to boarding school but he doesn't like it much. I'd like him to have some kind of family life with his three half-sisters. I know they'd love him. He doesn't have much dealings with girls in that damn school so it'd be good all round.'

This wasn't a side of Caitlin that Ben had seen before and despite his anxieties he had a rush of compassion. Bringing up the child in these circumstances must have been difficult for her. But then he remembered how great she was at railroading people. He could not allow her impatience to cloud his judgement.

'Caitlin, I can't make any promises. Why are you trying so hard to graft him onto strangers? You might marry again, anything could happen.'

Her lips set. 'I shall never marry again.' She paused. 'Unless it's to you.'

Chapter Twenty-Seven

Now she was actually leaving base camp Carol felt a rush of affection for the small community who had become her friends. Would she see them again? Good intentions invariably withered once submerged in real life. George had promised he would contact her in London – he was leaving himself in a couple of weeks – but she was not sure his shyness would allow that. Diana had another few months in the field studies centre but said when she was on leave she would phone. Perhaps she would. A few of the others took her address and said they would write but she would not hold her breath.

Carol entered the kitchen to find Anak weeping which set the others off and caused her to blink back tears of her own. They shyly presented her with hand-carved presents of a butterfly and a wonderful miniature tree. Attached was a beautifully coloured card, which they had all signed with loving messages. She promised to try her best to return for a visit, this time with her family.

She had said her goodbyes to the rest of the scientists after the last breakfast she would supervise and the camp had emptied almost immediately afterwards. Some of the scientists had left on a two-week major exploration of the interior, assisted by six Gurkhas.

In a small way, and for a short time, Carol had felt part of an important expedition pushing back scientific frontiers. She had even had a butterfly named after her, in fun it was true but still 'Anthene Caro' would make a great story for the children.

She would never forget the day it happened. George had thought it would be fun for her to join one of his short expeditions and as most people were away from the camp Anak said she could manage for a day on her own. Carol was pleased to find that as soon as they had walked away from base camp George underwent a startling transformation. Gone was the bumbling manner, replaced by a keen-eyed professional, teaching her how to move quietly through the foliage in order not to frighten away the insects. He boasted proudly that he had discovered hundreds of different species of butterflies and moths within a radius of only one kilometre of the camp and only about fifty of those could be considered common. He couldn't wait to get home and publish his results. He had some remarkable specimens to show that would, he was sure, impress even his hard-boiled colleagues.

They were walking through a stretch of lowland forest when Carol spotted it, resting for a moment on the branch. The butterfly seemed to be larger than the varieties she had noticed fluttering around the camp area but it was the colour that attracted her attention. The wings were a shade of vivid violet-blue but when it fluttered and flew to a nearby branch she could see the reverse side which was bright yellow. The combination was startling. She grabbed George's arm and pointed. Silently he crouched towards it and with a deft flick of his wrist caught the creature in his net with a soft cry of triumph. It was a glorious example of the Lycacnid species, he told her, but he had never seen such colouring.

She implored him to let it go but he shook his head. 'It'll be dead by tonight anyway.' When she still looked upset he patted her hand. 'I'll name it after you. Your little bit of fame. Will that make you feel better?'

'It's a nice gesture but I still think you should have left it. You have so many anyway.'

'Ah, but there's always the one you can't have. And that's the one you want.'

She laughed. 'Like Francesca.'

He looked at her over his spectacles. 'I think I've moved on from her,' he said before busying himself with the preserving crystals. Carol was touched but George gave no hint that he expected her to react and the outing continued amiably enough. His attitude never changed from one of undemanding, almost avuncular friendship. He seemed to realise that they would have little in common apart from a few months of shared experiences at base camp and she did not expect to see him in London.

Having said her goodbyes to everyone, she watched from the shade of the river bank as Alex supervised the loading of the luggage onto the longboat. He needed to visit Bandar anyway and it would be pleasanter to make the journey in tandem. He motioned her to take the seat in front of him and tie on the life jacket before signalling to the boatmen to begin the journey.

The boat began to move slowly away and Carol swivelled her body to watch the collection of huts recede into the distance. Working here had been a valuable experience and, mostly, a positive one. She had learned to accept herself, foibles and all. She had a sick feeling about what she was to face at home but her time at the camp had given her confidence that whatever happened she would be able to cope.

The experience of dealing with the vagaries of nature as well as a demanding collection of people on her own had toughened her mentally. She felt she had changed from being someone who needed to live her life through someone else to being a grown-up who could fend for herself. It was a pity she had not had this belief in herself when she first met Ben. She would have been more of an equal for him and maybe he would not have felt the necessity to have an affair. But would he have married the kind of woman she had become? Perhaps it was as well the marriage had floundered before she could put this to the test.

The longboat rounded a bend in the river and now the field studies centre was obscured from view. She would never tire of the quiet of the river, the only sounds being the swish of the paddles and the occasional cry from a swooping bird. It was a hush unknown in the developed world and Carol made a conscious effort to imprint the wondrous colours and stillness on her memory, hoping she could conjure it up when she returned home.

Alex leaned forward and she felt his breath on her ear. 'I'm going to miss this place,' he said.

She half turned. 'But you still have a while to go, don't you?'

He looked serious. 'I've kept it quiet but I've told London I want out early and they've found an excellent man at the university to replace me. He's Brunei-born which is even better.'

No hint of his departure had surfaced around base camp and seeing her surprise he said that at thirty-five, it was time to get back to the real world. 'I've gained enough experience to start my own show.'

Apparently he had been thinking about establishing an expedition logistics company probably based in the UK for the last couple of years. He had an army colleague who wanted to inject some capital into the business. He was describing this man's superb contact list when one of the Iban boatmen called over, muttering something Carol did not understand.

Alex looked up at the dazzling blue sky. 'He says there's a storm on the way and he thinks we ought to stay near the bank.'

The boatman was right. As always in that part of the world, weather changes were swift and dramatic. Seemingly out of nowhere towers of dense clouds darkened the sky. Forks of lightning crackled above the trees, illuminating the landscape as if by a giant searchlight. The ear-splitting claps of thunder reverberating through the tunnel of trees was so deafening it was almost like sitting on the barrel of a cannon. Carol started in fear and clutched at Alex's arm as the storm erupted and a heavy curtain of water obliterated the sight of the bank. This was nothing like the afternoon downpour she had come to enjoy. This deluge began to lash down relentlessly, stinging cheeks, drenching clothes and then filling up the boat.

Alex grabbed the spare oar and strenuously paddled in tandem with the boatmen but their efforts made little headway against the suddenly swirling water. Within seconds, the river had risen to twice its height and was spilling over the bank in angry breakers.

Alex was shouting something but Carol could not make it out over the howl of the wind, which was driving the rain in horizontal sheets. On the bank, the trees were bending so low it seemed they would snap. But the water was still a churning cauldron, which made the boat rock violently and Carol squeezed her arms tightly around her body, willing the three men to gain control of the vessel which appeared alarmingly frail-looking against these conditions.

At that moment there was a yell and the lead boatman turned round in dismay as his paddle flew into the air and swiftly disappeared into the boiling current. Swiftly Alex handed over his paddle and the two Ibans, arms flailing, tried to manoeuvre their way through the fast-moving water littered with torn-off branches wrenched from the forest.

The sky was beginning to clear. Was it her imagination or was the bank getting nearer? Carol couldn't be sure but the boatmen had so far skilfully managed to avoid the debris whirling past the boat. She assured herself they could be trusted to get them out of danger, they must have experienced these conditions many times and she would have heard if there had been serious accidents, wouldn't she?

Alex gave her a tap on the shoulder, an exhilarated grin on his face, followed by a thumbs-up sign. He shouted, 'We call this river surfing.'

'Next time, don't invite me!' she yelled though she didn't think he could hear above the roar of the water. He began to point furiously to the prow of the boat. She turned to see an enormous tree trunk hurtling towards them.

'Jump, jump!' he cried and as they and the boatmen threw themselves sideways, the tree smashed into the side of the boat, splintering the prow with a mighty blow. Carol sank momentarily under the torrent, her eyes, nostrils and throat filling with the murky water. Coughing and spluttering she gulped for air as her life jacket pitched her to the surface. To her relief Alex was only yards away and he paddled fiercely towards her, putting his arms under her shoulders to lift her upwards until she could regain her breath. Out of the corner of her eye she saw the two oarsmen but when she turned her head they were gone.

She found herself being whirled around and was grateful Alex was holding on to the back strap of her life jacket, which was keeping her buoyant as the current swept them downriver at frightening speed. It was difficult not to swallow the churning water, which every now and then engulfed them. Alex shouted at her to try and control her breathing. 'Keep blowing out, not too fast.'

For what seemed an age they were at the mercy of the angry water, unable to do more than try to avoid choking. Carol had a sense of disbelief that all this was happening to her and incredibly found herself thinking that she had to survive because Katie would never forgive her if she missed her birthday. That was when the doubts began to surface. If Alex lost his grip on her she would be finished. But despite being bobbed hither and thither, not once did he slacken his hold, keeping one arm through the back of her straps. She could not get out of her mind that even with his strength they could not bowl along in the current for much longer without being either hit by debris or overwhelmed by a freak wave. At this point the river began to curve and they were propelled round the bend at alarming speed. Alex reached to grab at an overhanging branch, holding on to her with the other arm. For a few seconds they dangled just above the water and Carol's heart leapt, they were saved. Then the slender sapling snapped under their combined weight and they were flung back into the river. Fortunately the current was beginning to ease and, following Alex's example, she began to use her free arm as a paddle, scooping sideways to try and reach the overhanging branches. Eventually he was able to grasp at the overhead foliage and this time it held firm.

'Quick, work your way to the bank,' he said, gasping for breath. 'I'll hold the branch steady. Go on.'

Hand over hand, muscles straining, Carol made agonisingly slow progress along the branch until at last her feet brushed against the squelching mud of the river bed. She let go of the branch and bent double to crawl on all fours towards the bank. Panting for breath she lay there and watched as, with seemingly little effort, Alex followed her.

'Thank God, thank God,' she repeated, wiping the mud from her face. 'I thought we'd had it.'

'It was a bit hairy.'

At this understatement she let out a weak laugh. He untied her life jacket and she flopped back, overcome by exhaustion.

'Come on, we can't stay here.' Alex pulled her to her feet. 'We must keep going and find the boys before dark.'

Every muscle ached as wearily she trudged behind him, dodging underneath the giant foliage he held back for her, trainers squelching, every step an effort. They continued in this way for an hour, stopping now and then to call out but they were met only by the sounds of a distant honking of excited hornbills. She was on the point of collapse when Alex came to a halt and listened intently. She could see no sign of life but when he called out a greeting, the bushes parted a few yards ahead and the two boatmen appeared.

They smiled shyly at Carol and directed excited chatter at Alex.

'They say that's the worst storm for many years. They're almost proud of it.'

'I'm so glad I'll be in the history books.'

Alex turned back to confer with the men. This involved much gesturing on their part but finally they appeared to be listening to his instructions before they gave her a jaunty wave and began heading in the direction of the capital.

'They said the boat smashed up in seconds and all the luggage vanished.'

She gave a quick thought to her clothes and passport which had also disappeared but it seemed irrelevant, not worthy of comment.

'You and I had better go back to the camp. It's nearer than the jetty. I've asked those two to make their way to Angus Roberts. He'll contact Francesca to cancel your flight and he'll get a replacement longboat sorted out.' Alex appeared to have thought of everything. He estimated it would take over three hours to reach the camp and as he set off at a smart pace, Carol feared that her trembling limbs wouldn't last that long. But she would damn well try.

To add to their misery it started to rain again, not as ferociously as before but it had the effect of slowing down their progress. One foot plodding in front of the other, Carol tried to focus not on her bone-aching exhaustion but on thoughts of a cool shower and a strong gin. Alex was some way ahead when he turned back and asked her to halt a moment while he scouted the terrain from a ridge above.

'Take as long as you like,' she said gratefully and made her way down to a tree trunk which had fallen obligingly under the umbrella of a neighbouring fern, providing a modicum of shelter. After a few steps she felt the ground soften under her feet and when she tried to turn back she found she couldn't move. Impatiently she tugged with all her strength at her right foot, only for it to sink deeper. She cast about to find a stem thick enough to hold on to. There was one to her right, but it was out of reach. Her first thought was to take off her trainers to release her feet but she quickly found that the mud was tightening around her ankles as if held by a giant fist, sucking her downwards.

'Alex, Alex.' Carol's voice began to croak in terror. She looked around wildly before spotting him running towards her. 'I can't move. I'm sinking.'

Swiftly he took in the situation. Almost without halting his stride he had gathered up several dead branches and flung them in front of her, criss-crossing them like a trellis. Then he picked up a long bough and stepped with some care onto the makeshift platform. He held the bough towards her.

'Hang on with both hands but don't move. Let me do the work,' he instructed and she rallied at the note of command in his voice. Dry-mouthed she grabbed the branch and her body jerked forward as he gave a tremendous heave but her calves remained stuck fast. He moved closer and she could see his neck muscles straining as he gave another hefty pull. This time her feet moved slightly, and with a third mighty effort her feet were freed and she was able to crawl across the makeshift platform to safety.

He held her up as she sagged in his arms and he half carried her up the ridge where she lay panting, wishing she might never have to move again

'You haven't the strength to go on,' he said.

'I'll be all right, just give me a minute.' She almost didn't recognise the reedy voice. She sat up hugging her knees and felt tears spring to her eyes. As they spilled over they made runnels through the mud on her face. Alex tore the edge of his shirt and began awkwardly wiping the mud off her skin. She sat still, did not say a word, allowing him to clean her up.

He patted her gently on her shoulder.

'I spotted a pondok not far off. You'll be able to rest there.'

She had heard Diana talk about pondoks. They were made with tarpaulins and guy ropes and were set up throughout the forest by the Gurkhas for the benefit of scientists on their field trips, who had enough equipment to carry without being burdened by heavy bivouacs.

Carol took his arm and he guided her a few hundred yards to where she could see a crude type of tent in the clearing. Alex opened the flap of the pondok and dragged out a small plastic trunk. After much tugging, he managed to prise open the lid and began examining the contents.

'Great. Blanket, food,' he waved a tin of corned beef, 'biscuits and some water. We'll soon have you sorted out.'

He shook out the thin grey blanket and draped it round her shoulders. Although it was warm and humid, Carol felt surprisingly chilly, a mixture of nerves and wet clothes, she supposed.

'I'd better make a fire, there's bound to be some matches and a knife in here somewhere.'

He began to rummage amongst the contents. 'Ah, here they are,' he said triumphantly, unwrapping a box from its foil container.

He poured the water into a plastic cup and held it to her trembling lips. It was warm and tasted brackish but obediently she swallowed a few mouthfuls.

'And try and eat this,' he said, handing her a biscuit.

'What about you?'

'I'll be all right,' he said. 'Go on. You'll feel better when you've had something to eat.'

Carol forced herself to nibble at the dry oatmeal slab which was foul but she realised she was extremely hungry and after a minute or two it did have the effect of calming her knotted stomach. She sat on the dirt floor hugging the thin blanket around her shoulders. Her wet shirt was beginning to make the blanket damp.

'I think you should take off those wet things and we'll dry them off in front of the fire.'

It was growing dark and Alex said he would need to forage for dry foliage in the undergrowth before the light faded completely. She must have looked apprehensive for he added, 'I won't be far away and it won't take long.'

While he was away gathering wood, Carol decided to follow his advice. Rapidly she stripped to her bra and pants and prised off her mud-caked trainers. She hung the wet shorts and T-shirt over a guy rope and began to rub her limbs through the blanket.

She'd been lucky to survive and if it hadn't been for Alex she would probably not have made it. She was not a strong swimmer and even with a life jacket could not have held out for long against that fierce current. Alex hadn't shown any fear even when she was being sucked into the mud. He had been calm but firm, telling her exactly what to do. If it hadn't been for his presence of mind on both occasions, Carol was convinced she would have died.

Alex reappeared holding a plastic bag filled with water in one hand and a sheaf of twigs in the other. 'This is rainwater, those palm leaves act like a bowl. Remember that if you ever find yourself in a situation like this again.'

She smiled weakly at his attempt to lighten the situation and gratefully accepted a plastic mug of the rainwater which tasted fresh and sweet.

'Use the rest to clean yourself up,' he said.

She attempted a rudimentary sluice of her filthy limbs, taking care to keep within the shadow of the pondok. Alex disregarded her activities, busying himself making the fire a few yards away. After splashing her face with the cool water, Carol began to feel more human. It only took a few seconds for the fire to crackle into life and she emerged from the tent.

'You've done this before,' she said, smiling.

'Just a few hundred times.' He added a few decayed fern leaves to the fire. 'Bring me your things and I'll prop them up over these stakes.'

The clothes quickly started to steam and Carol pulled at the scratchy blanket, suddenly feeling awkward. She was alone in a remote forest and totally under his control. But he had given no hint of treating her other than a mother would a dependent child. He had a reputation for breaking hearts and she was in a highly vulnerable state. Her marriage was over but though she owed her life to this man she did not want him to misunderstand her gratitude.

Alex began unbuttoning his shirt and instinctively Carol moved away. He cast an amused glance in her direction. 'Don't worry, the strip show stops right now.'

He draped the garment near hers and she saw his muscled upper torso rippling in the half-light. Hurriedly she looked away and heard him say, 'We'll have to stay until daybreak. I suggest you try and get some sleep.'

Oh God, sleeping next to him? She gazed at him uncertainly and he said, 'You take the tent. I'll kip out here, beside the fire.'

She thought she was exhausted enough to drop off to sleep immediately but she lay awake listening to the sounds of the forest, marvelling that she had come through the experience. She wasn't sure if she would tell the children exactly how much danger she had been in, but she was sure the events of the day would continue to alter her attitude to life.

Some time later the rain started again and she decided it was stupid for Alex to remain outside. She crept towards the flap and peered around. Alex had made another fire, much smaller, a few yards away from the first one which was beginning to splutter. She could see him crouching under a tree and she called out for him to come into the tent.

'Better not,' he said. 'I'm fine here. Get some sleep.'

Guiltily she crept back into the pondok and lay down, feeling that her turbulent thoughts would never allow her to sleep. But to her amazement it seemed only a few minutes later when his voice penetrated her deep slumber. 'Caro, wake up, the sun's about to come up.'

She raised herself on an elbow groggily and yawned. She had missed her flight home, she had no luggage and no passport but she found she didn't care. It was good just to have come through that terrifying storm and the quicksand and to know she was alive and well.

The rays of the sun were already shining through the foliage, making the drops of dew on the broad leaves around the pondok glisten like miniature diamonds. She threw the blanket back then let out a terrified scream. A giant leech, its black skin shiny with slime, had attached itself to her arm. Alex appeared in an instant and she held out her arm oblivious to the fact that she was naked. Swiftly he plucked the creature off her flesh and threw it through the tent flap.

The tension of the last few hours erupted in a torrent of tears and with almost a groan he folded her in his arms and held her tightly against his bare chest. He lifted one hand and tilted her face towards him, kissing her lips gently, then fiercely, almost savagely. As if a match had ignited cordite, she found herself responding in the same way. One of Alex's hands was locked in her hair, holding her head back. The other arm gripped her body tightly. The thought flitted across her mind that she must stop this madness now. But intense, irresistible desire surged through her body and she clutched him as if she were once more drowning. Alex lowered her onto the ground, his mouth never leaving hers for an instant.

Carol felt that her life must have been saved just so she could experience this moment. Over the next hours, as dawn turned into morning and the sun rose high in the sky, she would learn what lovemaking could really be like. And should be like. Not the routine, rather predictable sex she had grown accustomed to in her marriage. But the wild, abandoned feeling of two people giving each other so much pleasure that at times it felt almost unbearable in its intensity.

After kissing her until their mouths began to hurt, Alex disentangled himself from Caro's embrace and then gently arranged her body so that her arms were thrown back in abandonment behind her head, and her legs were spread wide apart. Slowly, he began kissing her tingling skin as he moved, inch by inch, towards her thighs. For a moment she moved to stop him. It was too personal, too soon. But then with an involuntary groan she gave in. It seemed that he knew without any words being exchanged how her body was reacting. As he gently kissed her she yearned for him to be rougher and as soon as the thought formed in her mind, he obeyed instinctively, taking her right into his mouth.

Then his hands were under her buttocks, pushing her upwards. Slowly, tantalisingly, he moved his hand in a slow, hypnotic rhythm, until she was crying out for this yearning void to be filled.

'Come into me, oh God, please, I beg you,' she cried, surprising herself. This was shy, inexperienced Carol, who couldn't tell her husband what she wanted in bed, even when he thought to ask. But Alex wasn't ready for that yet. With a swift, athletic move, he flipped her over, so that he was lying on the ground with Carol on top of him, on her knees. He lifted her a few inches, then slid down underneath her so that she was directly above his mouth. Oh, his mouth – that sweet instrument of pleasure. 'Alex, please, I can't,' she heard herself saying. But her body was telling her something else.

Now Carol thought she would explode. A groan rose out of her, as she gasped and shuddered with pleasure. It was too much; dear God, would he never stop. But on it went, as waves of ecstasy swept through her groin and throughout her body, leaving her thighs shaking so much she thought she would collapse.

Just as she thought she could stand it no more, she began to quiver uncontrollably and then she was rocked by another orgasm, this one so strong, so all-encompassing that she could hardly believe it was happening. She closed her eyes and gave in to the shudders that were sweeping through her body. She threw her head back and gasped, then realised she was shouting, screaming out her pleasure in that forest where no one could hear. She felt abandoned, other worldly, freed of all inhibitions, and she knew in that moment that whatever happened in the future the old Carol had gone and a new woman had been born in her place. As she slowly came to her senses, Alex once again changed their positions, carefully lowering her onto her back. Then he propped himself up on his elbows and slowly eased himself inside her.

Now again they were kissing wildly, biting, thrusting with their tongues. Carol felt a new wave of desire sweep through her body, despite the magnitude of the orgasm that had engulfed her just moments before. This was sex as she had imagined, and more. She could feel every fibre of him inside her, thrusting until she thought she could take no more, then withdrawing until she begged for him to return. And all the time his supple hands were stroking her body, and his mouth was all over her, on the nape of her neck, on her nipples, teasing, biting, driving her up and up to the crescendo of a third orgasm. This time they shouted together, their words echoing through the forest as the sun beat down through the dappled leaves. It took them a long time to catch their breath. Silently they lay in each other's arms. Alex was the first to break the silence.

'I wanted you from the first moment I saw you. Didn't you realise that?'

'You made a very good job of disguising it.' She prodded his naked chest with a forefinger.

Alex confessed that when he'd first seen her working in the kitchen he'd watched her for several minutes before she had spotted him. 'I can remember your exact words. You said, "Anything I can do for you?" It was all I could do to say "Yes, come with me" and rush you to my hut.' She smiled up at him and he bent to kiss her gently. 'When we were watching the sunset, Caro, I wished I could get rid of the others so that we could be alone. And why did you think I invited you to Bandar that time? I said it was so you could see Mr Chow but I just wanted you near me.'

'Then why did you sack me?'

'Mainly because you were taking up too much of my thinking time. Then when you decided to stay I reckoned I'd leave it to fate. But I wouldn't have touched you except . . . I'm only human.'

Alex seemed in no hurry to get back to base camp and suggested they have a swim. When they inspected the river it was as if yesterday's storm had never happened. He took her hand and pulled her towards him, and their bodies melted together as they slipped into the cool water. Splashing like children they whooped and hollered in the bright sunlight. Afterwards they lay like lizards basking on the bank, waiting to be dried by the soft wind.

Under her lashes Carol admired his lithe body next to hers. She now knew that his skin was smooth and perfect except for a long crescent-shaped scar just below the collar bone. Idly she traced the outline with her finger. Without opening his eyes he told her it had happened when he was at school. He had fallen on a spike on the playing field. The wound had been deep and had needed several stitches. His adoptive parents had been stationed in Borneo and by the time they were able to visit him the scar was nearly healed.

'It must have been awful for you, on your own in hospital.'

'I didn't think about it,' he said without a trace of self-pity.

He had been born in a village a few miles north of Cape Town, and his family had worked for their relative, Leon de Vries, a farmer. Alex had been orphaned when he was still a baby. He would probably still be living in South Africa if it hadn't been for an accident of fate. A British couple, touring the country, had car trouble a few miles away and Mr de Vries who was coming home from the market gave them a lift to his home to wait for the local garage to fix the car. But the part required had to be sent from the city and although the couple wanted to move to the hotel, Mr de Vries insisted on putting them up. The car was fixed after three days but the Woollescrofts stayed for an extra week because they were enchanted by five-year-old Alex.

Brigadier Anthony Woollescroft, a professional soldier, and his wife Danielle had no children of their own and after a few weeks they wrote from the UK asking permission for him to have a holiday with them with a view to adoption. Alex had never returned to Africa. The farmer had died and though Alex's adoptive parents had taken him back to the land of his birth many times, he regarded himself as a nomad, British by upbringing but with no sense of belonging. He did not feel any connection with his native land either. His education had, he told her, moulded him into someone who could rely only on himself; insecurity, he said, made him too eager to make an impression on strangers. Boarding school, university and then the army had cut him off from female companionship.

Alex opened his eyes and stared at the sky. 'I suppose that's why I find it difficult to be on equal terms with a woman. I've never really understood them, so I go for young ones who don't give me trouble.' A mischievous glint came into his eyes. 'Unlike you.' He leaned over and his mouth encircled her nipple. 'You're totally irresistible.'

She leaned back, stretching luxuriously as Alex's tongue began to work its magic. 'Tell me what you want,' he murmured. Both of his hands were beginning to caress her breasts while his mouth moved downwards, downwards . . . She closed her eyes giving herself up to the sensuousness of the moment. 'Do you like this?' she heard in the distance. She didn't answer. There was no need.

Afterwards, they lay clinging together, unable to speak. Alex raised himself on an elbow. In the cleft between her breasts there was a bead of perspiration and gently he ran his hands over it and then over her breasts. 'You're beautiful,' he said, kissing them, kissing her. Lazily he rolled over. Then he sat up and squinted at the position of the sun. 'Damn. We've a long walk ahead. I'm afraid we'd better start making tracks.' He stood up and held out his hand to help her.

But she was not ready to face reality yet and she broke away and ran back to the water. He sprinted to try and catch her but she swerved, avoiding his outstretched arms to rush back into the cool river. He followed, swimming towards her. Holding her in his arms they kissed, bodies pressed so tightly together she could hardly breathe. For a few minutes longer they floated like this, lazily enjoying the peace of the moment.

Carol felt desired, desirable and glad to be alive. And grateful to Alex for showing her how lovemaking could be.

She had been wildly, deeply unfaithful to Ben but incredibly she did not feel one iota of guilt.

News of their adventure had reached the camp by the time they arrived a couple of hours later, sweaty, hungry but exhilarated. Anak was in her element, delighted to see her dear friend again and within half an hour had conjured up a tasty omelette filled with vegetables.

Francesca had been at her most efficient. She had been on the short-wave radio to say she had booked a seat to London for that evening. She had bought a change of clothes and toiletries for Caro and had arranged for the High Commissioner's office to stay open so they could issue a temporary passport. A longboat could leave within the hour for Bandar. Alex reluctantly informed her he could not go with her this time. There had been extensive storm damage to the camp and he was needed to supervise repairs.

On the trek back, Carol's body had tingled each time she remembered their lovemaking but by the time they reached base she had almost succeeded in convincing herself that sex with a stranger, however mind-shattering, must inevitably be transitory. A dream, not reality. She could never recreate the dramatic circumstances of the escape from drowning, the primitive conditions and the terror of the situation which had made her cling to him. Whatever happened in the future she would be forever grateful to Alex for showing her how to abandon herself to the pleasure of making love, not to think but just to follow the dictates of her desires. It had been wonderful but she would not expect anything from him. It was an exotic fling, she told herself sternly, in no way connected to real life.

Alex had asked if she could come and say goodbye privately and after showering and dressed in clothes she had borrowed from Diana she made her way to his hut. She was about to knock on his door when a noise from the direction of the jetty alerted her to the arrival of the longboat which was to take her downriver – this time, she hoped, with less dramatic consequences.

Alex's face lit up when she came into his office and he drew her into his arms. Despite all the strictures to herself, she clung to him and they kissed with mounting fervour. She made no attempt to disengage herself and he said softly, 'There's something about you that's got under my armour.' He gave her mouth a soft kiss. 'I think it's because you're older.'

'Thanks a lot.'

'No, don't misunderstand. You're more mature than the women I've been with in the past and I like it. You don't let me get away with a thing and there aren't many women who can do that.'

'You can't have met many grown-ups.'

'Maybe you're right. So far the types who seem to be attracted to me are either those who think it's cool to date a black man or the ones who want to have a good time, with no thought for the future.'

'I've never been aware of your colour. It's made you what you are, a pugnacious shit.'

He laughed. 'I don't know what'll happen to us, Caro, but I know I want something to. I suppose what I'm trying to say to you is that I'm looking for something more now.'

Carol tried to disguise her apprehension. She had to accept her marriage was over but she was a long way from looking for a replacement. She flung her hands dramatically into the air and said, 'Oh God, you're not talking the C word, commitment, are you?'

If she expected him to rear back in alarm she was wrong. His serious expression did not alter. 'Maybe that's what I am saying.'

Outside, footsteps along the verandah were followed by a soft tap at the door. 'Boat must go soon,' said Anak. 'Waiting for you, Caro.'

Alex ran a finger around her cheekbone, as if to memorise her features. 'Remember, I'll be arriving in London soon. And then, darling Caro, I'm coming to get you.'

Chapter Twenty-Eight

As Carol heaved the wayward luggage trolley through the customs hall exit she caught sight of the helium balloons before she spotted the eager faces underneath. Katie, holding Ben's hand, was bouncing up and down pointing at her. Emmy ran forward waving frantically, closely followed by Becky. Ben brought up the rear, his face split into the broadest of smiles. Carol had spent much of the long flight worrying about how she could meet Ben's eyes without alerting him that she was aware of his infidelity but it proved relatively easy because the children formed a laughing, screaming barrier between them. It was several minutes before he was able to disentangle her from them and the balloons to whirl her around in his arms. My God, what an actor. If she didn't know better she would have believed he was ecstatic at her arrival. In the babble of excitement, she had only this brief moment with him before the children claimed her attention again, shouting in delight at her 'cool' new hairstyle and her 'brilliant' tan.

Jet lag forgotten, Carol spent the entire journey home with her head swivelled towards the back seat where the three children asked a hundred questions about the trip, had she seen snakes, what about spiders, were they gi-normous, before the car approached Battersea. The two younger ones began bouncing on their seats and Becky tried in vain to shush them for they seemed intent on revealing a surprise waiting at home. It was when Becky shyly told her they had tidied all their drawers in preparation for her homecoming that Carol felt an overwhelming sense of love for this prickly, difficult child. Sometimes in the past the others had taken their cue from her behaviour and if Carol's absence had changed her attitude, the trip would have been more than worthwhile.

As the car nosed its way into their drive the three begged her to close her eyes and not to open them until told. Ben switched off the engine and she heard them giggle as her door was opened and a small hand took hers and pulled her out. Carefully they steered her towards the house and Becky commanded, 'You can look now.' The banner stretched across the front door reached almost halfway along the house. In bright red paint the words proclaimed, 'Welcome home Mum'. There was a chorus of claims for the idea before Ben said, 'Give credit where it's due, who put it up?'

Inside, balloons decorated every doorway, the kitchen was festooned with streamers and the table was set with party food. 'Lisa helped but we did most of the cooking,' said Emmy proudly. The centrepiece was a large iced cake with 'Happy Homecoming' in wobbly blue letters.

For a moment Carol could not speak. The poignancy of the situation was almost more than she could bear. However carefully she handled the break-up, it would be the end of the children's happy, secure world. For the second time in their short lives they would experience loss if she were to leave. For the umpteenth time since she had heard about Ben's adultery she wondered how she could even consider walking out on them. But how could she stay? How could she live under the same roof as a man who loved another woman?

The antics of Muffin Two, young and playful, momentarily diverted her and the children took such delight in introducing their pet, showing off its acrobatic prowess in leaping for a feather toy, that all resentment at its arrival vanished.

Several times during the celebratory party Ben caught her eye and looked at her with such love she wondered how he could be so hypocritical. But then he'd had years of practice, she told herself quickly. She wanted the party to go on for ever, postponing the moment when she would have to talk to him alone, but inevitably, when the cakes were eaten, presents admired and champagne drunk, the activities and emotion of the day caught up with the children. The younger two insisted Carol should take them to bed and before Becky shut her door she said, 'It's good to have you back.'

Carol ruffled the teenager's hair. 'I thought you'd prefer Lisa. I bet she wasn't as strict as me, was she?'

Becky frowned. 'I prefer you here,' was all she said. Carol was amazed, and deeply moved.

Before she went downstairs Carol phoned Lisa. She was profuse in her thanks for the superb way Lisa had looked after the family. The children had adored her food and she would be hard pressed to get back in their good books with her cooking. Lisa had been right, the kitten was a wonderful addition to the household. They chatted in this vein for several minutes and it was Lisa who was the first to raise the subject uppermost in Carol's mind.

'I've been having nightmares about telling you about that letter. I hope it was right to interfere.'

Carol assured her she had done the right thing. In her shoes she would not have hesitated.

'Have you talked to Ben about it?'

'Just about to.'

'Maybe the affair's already over?'

'Maybe, maybe not, but there's a good chance our marriage is.'

By the time Carol went downstairs, the kitchen clutter had been tidied away and Ben was relaxing on the sofa in the sitting room, sipping a coffee. A cup for her stood on the side table and as soon as she entered the room, he pressed the cafetiere into service. Then he patted the seat beside him. For a moment she hesitated before walking towards the easy chair opposite. On the plane Carol had counselled herself to act like Caro. To remain calm, to say what she had to in a straightforward manner and, above all, not to crumple before she had made her point.

He raised his eyebrows. 'Tired from the trip?'

'Tired of play-acting.'

Ben placed his coffee on the table in front of him. The relaxed expression on his face disappeared and he sat quite still, waiting for her to continue.

'I've found out you're having an affair with Caitlin.'

He sighed. 'Why on earth are you bringing that up again? We've gone over it before. It wasn't true then, it's not true now.'

'Ben, I'm not the trusting fool I was when I left. If there's nothing to find out, what was her letter all about?'

He looked bewildered and she felt a flash of intense irritation. Why was he keeping up the charade? Even now he evaded the central issue, asking instead, 'How did you know about that?' She did not answer and his expression altered. 'Lisa. I suppose she thought she was being a good friend.'

'It's not important how I found out. What's important is that I can't live with your lies any longer.'

'Carol, I'm not lying. We did have an affair eight years ago. I told you that. But whatever you've heard now, you're wrong. My relationship now with Caitlin is exactly what I told you, purely business, nothing more.'

Not bothering to hide the sarcasm in her voice, she said, 'So what did she mean when she said you shouldn't allow guilt to spoil what you have?'

Ben put his fingertips to his temples and gave a weary laugh. 'It was the night of the press awards. I'd had a lot to drink.'

'Oh please.' She turned her head away.

He rose from the sofa and grabbed her by the shoulders. 'Listen. We'd won the Newspaper of the Year award and the political scoops were probably the reason. I was grateful to Caitlin and the alcohol combined with all the congratulations . . . we kissed. Once. I'm sorry it happened but that's as far as it went.'

The urge to hit him across the face with her fist was overpowering but Carol fought to keep her temper.

He gave an exasperated sigh. 'Judge for yourself. I'll go and get the bloody letter.'

While he was out of the room, Carol had her first moment of doubt. Could Lisa have misunderstood the situation? Ben was back within minutes, pushing the letter into her lap.

'This is Caitlin's attempt to patch things up. She thought I wouldn't have anything to do with her again after that night and she was right. She wrote this because she was afraid to lose one of her best press contacts. Read it in that context.'

Somehow the words did not seem so sinister. '*I never should've allowed it to happen.*' She had assumed this referred to lovemaking but, equally, if Ben was telling the truth, it could allude to a kiss.

Ben leaned over her shoulder. 'See where she says, "Don't allow guilt to spoil what we have together. We're too good a team." Can't you see she's talking about the way we work together, nothing more?'

For a moment Carol was uncertain. What if Lisa was wrong and Ben was right? Her thoughts flew back to the river bank and her passionate lovemaking with Alex. One kiss. What was that compared with what she had done? But the difference was she had thought her marriage was over.

Ben was studying her. 'Carol, listen to me. I've never made love to another woman since we met. You have to believe that, otherwise what have we got left?' He took her hands in his and his eyes did not waver. She wanted to believe him. It was the easy way out, she realised that, but the alternative for the family was too frightening.

Ben was still gazing at her intently. 'Let me try and show you how much I've missed you.'

In the half-light Carol's face was only an impression. Ben reached towards her and moved a strand of damp hair from her forehead. For a moment they lay quite still. 'Welcome back. It was almost worth losing you for all those weeks.'

And it was true. Their lovemaking had been amazing, there was no other word for it. At first he had been overcome by a sudden sense of shyness but whether it was because of the row or because he had not made love for months, this time it was different. She was different. Carol had always been a willing partner but he had been aware from the beginning there was a holding back, that she wouldn't welcome anything too adventurous and he had never tried to force her.

Incredibly, her inhibitions seemed to have vanished. If it had been anyone else, he might have been suspicious that she had been unfaithful but with Carol that was unthinkable. And he would certainly never ask her. But whereas before she had usually waited for him, tonight she had taken the initiative. My God, she had even told him what she wanted him to do. She had never spoken during sex before and it was wonderful. They had made love twice, something that hadn't happened since their honeymoon. And she had climaxed each time. He hoped it would continue.

Her body had been transformed. It had become leaner, more muscled, he supposed from intense physical work and a nutritious diet, which Carol had described as being a bit like a health farm's, no fat, no butter, no processed foods.

From the minute she had stepped into the arrivals hall Ben had recognised the difference in her. At first he had attributed it to her appearance, that golden glow on her skin and the shorter, sophisticated hairstyle, of which he thoroughly approved. But it wasn't just that. She had an air of assurance, a certainty about her that had been missing before.

Carol had become an exciting, vibrant woman, not the preoccupied wife and mother he was accustomed to, worrying whether the children would hear them in bed, and she seemed to have adjusted her attitude towards the kids. Before she went away, one of the few criticisms he had never voiced was that she would allow the children to bicker sometimes to the point of tedium. From the beginning he had vowed not to intervene, thinking that she would lose confidence, or, worse, that the children might think he was someone to whom they could appeal.

But today he observed how speedily she had been able to take charge before an altercation between Katie and Emmy threatened to erupt. She was less tentative, more authoritative and he supposed the command structure at the camp might have been responsible for teaching her how to manage. Only Becky seemed to hold back, yet Carol did not remark on it. Before, she would have puzzled about it, worried about it, but now she appeared to be taking it in her stride. Ben thought this was exactly the right way to handle Becky. His daughter had tried to make him promise not to mention the cannabis incident but he had told her there could be no secrets from Carol. More pragmatically, he pointed out that her headmistress might well raise the matter with her stepmother. That had caused a pouting fit but he had held firm.

Ben gazed across at his wife lying next to him, rosy and warm from their lovemaking. She looked adorable. Becky's problem could wait. And, he decided, so could the revelation of a much bigger complication. William. Carol gave a small sigh of contentment and lay back in his arms, kissing him on the cheek. He would wait until after the conference in Moscow. Wouldn't it be counter-productive to drop that bombshell and then leave her alone, festering? Yes, far better to have the discussion once he returned. Ben acknowledged he was being cowardly but why spoil the moment?

He ruffled her hair. 'How do you do? I'm Ben Mitchell.'

She giggled. 'What are you talking about?'

'As you've come back a new woman, I just thought I'd introduce myself.'

'And what do you think of her?'

When they came up for air she said, 'A weird thing happened when I left here. They misspelled my name on all the papers. They left out the "l" in my name and everyone called me Caro.'

'Yes, I saw that on your email.'

'Well, it had an enormous effect on me. I believe it helped change my personality. Do you think a different name could do that?'

Ben considered this. 'Isn't it more likely that you were meeting a new bunch of people who had no preconceived ideas? You had the chance to choose the kind of person you wanted to be.'

'Reinvent myself, you mean.' She raised the pillow and propped herself against the bedhead. 'But I like myself better. I don't intend to change back.'

'I don't want you to,' he said earnestly. 'You won't go off and leave us again, will you?'

She shook her head then sat up, arms around her knees, and began to recount her near brush with death during a flash flood. He was horrified and began to castigate her for not telling him about it before.

'What good would it have done? No one anticipated the force of the storm and no one could tell that the boat would overturn.'

Thank God that the expedition leader had been with her, he thought, or he might have lost her. But, she explained, that had contributed to her change of attitude. When death came so close, a person had to reassess what they needed and what they had. 'I've learned that what I want is right here. But I want things to be different, Ben. I want us to have a child.'

He chose his words carefully. 'I think you deserve to have what you want. I'm sorry I wasn't enthusiastic before and if I'm honest, and I want to be, I don't particularly relish the idea of nappies again. But it's a selfish attitude.' He kissed her soundly. 'I'm willing to try for a baby. Try very hard.'

She grinned. 'But I'm not going to hang around waiting to get pregnant. I want to find myself something to do, something more of a challenge than Jolly Good Food.'

She told him she'd been thinking of trying for a job with the British Geographical Association, who had asked to see her for a debriefing session. It was a long shot but if they couldn't help she would try other organisations working in a similar area. Three months' experience in the field didn't sound much but it had been intensive training and she felt it could be regarded as the equivalent of a year's work in London.

'I'm fine with that. Not,' he added hastily, 'that you need permission.'

He grinned. 'Old habits. Now come here, woman, let me ravish you again.' He didn't think he could manage a third time but it would be fun trying.

During the days that followed, the children began to tease them. Parents weren't supposed to be lovey-dovey. Why were they always kissing? Carol made a joke about it but was secretly pleased that they'd noticed how different things were since she returned.

The atmosphere in the house was lighter, worries about Caitlin and the anonymous caller faded into the background and Ben was making great efforts to be home earlier. Mondays took on a whole new dimension. Whereas before they had been in the habit of going for a late lunch after he had finished his paperwork, now they had breakfast in bed together, everything forgotten but making love. Their sex life had never been better and for much of that she had to thank Alex. The thought almost brought a smile. She would never confess to Ben about her brief fling. It had happened when she had been convinced their marriage was irrevocably broken. The experience had also taught her it was possible to be attracted to men other than Ben, something she had not thought possible since she had met him. But exciting sex with a strange man was not a patch on intimacy between husband and wife, which because of shared history had far more meaning.

Once Emmy, who had been dropped off early after a school trip, had almost caught them in bed and they had jumped into their clothes in seconds, feeling like naughty teenagers. It was more like a second honeymoon, said Ben. Quite right too, said Carol, thinking back to their one romantic night away before having to get back to the family.

The only sour note struck during this time was when she learned about Becky's transgression. Her first reaction was one of anger at being kept in ignorance. 'If I had been told about it, don't you think I would've come home?' she had stormed at Ben.

Ben said his first instinct had been to tell her but that Lisa had put things into context. She pointed out that Becky was at an experimental stage of her life, trying to push back boundaries, but as soon as she found out where the limits were she would curtail her activities. And he was sure that she had learned her lesson.

'Oh, really?' Carol took him up to Becky's bedroom to show him a flyer from a nightclub. It said, 'Less is more, tight is just right and more often than not if you wear a bra top you can get into the club for free.' He had been horrified and confessed that he was beginning to realise how little he knew about what was going on in his daughter's life. Carol had agreed and that night they had sat Becky down on the sofa, switched off the television, and told her firmly where the limits were. Again Ben was impressed by the way Carol handled the situation. She started by telling Becky that there were two directions in which she could go, the right way and the path she was tentatively treading at present, which was certain to lead away from the people she valued. She was a much-loved member of the family and they would always stick by her whatever she did but her life was her own responsibility. From now on there would be no checking up on her. If she was expelled from school they would not try to reverse the decision. She would always have shelter and food but she would be given no money, none whatsoever. She would have to support herself. Instead of going to university, which she wanted to do, she would have to find a job. Those available to an unskilled girl of her age would be pretty limiting but it was her life. She had to live it her way.

Becky's reaction proved that she appreciated being treated like an adult, something she had been arguing for since her last birthday. She apologised again for taking the cannabis and confessed that, yes, after the school incident, she had tried it again. Just once – twice, tops. In a rush she said she didn't really like the taste and as she'd told Lisa, it had no effect on her anyway. Carol picked up the reference but did not remark on it. Lisa had a different attitude towards soft drugs but she was quite sure her friend would not have encouraged Becky.

This time, Becky said, she really did promise not to touch any drug again. She wanted to make something of her life and realised that without education she would end up in a dead-end job without too many prospects. The session ended on a mood of optimism, with Ben privately thinking that if he could have as much success when he told her about William he would be a much-relieved man.

Carol had not been looking forward to her first day back at Jolly Good Food, especially as she was about to give in her notice, but the clamour when she arrived was gratifying. They crowded around her, peppering her with questions and were very complimentary about her appearance, especially her new hairstyle. She had a great time telling them about her adventures, carefully avoiding too many mentions of Alex, and exaggerated slightly her battles with the jungle stove.

Andrea had already left to take her place and sadly, apart from a hurried phone call, Carol had little time to tell of her adventures though she had found time to send a couple of lengthy emails describing working conditions, the kitchen staff and recipes that had gone down well. These were gratefully received though Andrea, having been on an expedition before, was more confident of her abilities to cope than Carol had been.

As soon as she could Lisa spirited her friend away to her little office to apologise once again for jumping to conclusions about Ben and Caitlin before Carol could break the news of her departure. When Carol told her friend of Ben's explanation of what Caitlin had written, Lisa castigated herself, swearing she would never interfere again in anyone's business. She was sorely tempted to excuse herself by saying that it wasn't only the letter that had made her suspicious. Her late-night conversation with Ben had led her to imagine that Caitlin was becoming a problem, but caution prevailed. If Ben had squared things with Carol, she would leave well alone.

It was as well Lisa was in full sackcloth and ashes mode or she might have asked more questions about Carol's activities at base camp. As a poor liar Carol might not have been able to avoid the subject of Alex. However she was saved from this by Lisa's abject apologies and also by the fact that it would never enter Lisa's mind that her friend would ever stray.

Carol accepted that Lisa had acted out of concern not malice. Yet she couldn't help thinking that her action could have led to a permanent split between her and Ben. Say he had mislaid the letter? Or thrown it away? How would he have persuaded her of the true nature of his relationship with Caitlin then?

At the first opportunity Carol told her friend she wanted to leave when Lisa could find a replacement. Lisa was anxious to keep her and offered to create a new post of marketing manager but Carol insisted her interests now lay in another direction.

In the event, Lisa had persuaded the ever-obliging Connie to work full-time, so Carol would be able to leave as soon as she clinched a new job, though she was aware that Lisa was hoping she might change her mind and stay.

'You're unsettled, bound to be. When everything gets back to normal . . .' Her voice died away when she saw Carol's expression. 'Ah, I see you don't want them to. OK, work here as long as it takes to sort yourself out.' She was rewarded by a grateful smile.

At the debriefing with Phoebe, as soon as Carol had mentioned she was looking for a new direction in life, the expeditions leader had promised she would tell her if a job were to turn up at the BGA. She could not guarantee a position, of course, but she rated Carol's chances highly, especially in view of her practical experience and organisational skills.

Carol had been back just over three weeks when Ben had to leave for Moscow to cover the G12 summit of European leaders. He would only be away for a few days and Carol decided to use the time to redecorate their bedroom. She had tired of the little-girl gingham curtains and matching duvet cover she had chosen a couple of years ago and wanted to surprise him with something more sophisticated to match her more outgoing personality and reflect their invigorated love life. They were not taking precautions and Carol hoped that in her relaxed state she would become pregnant.

Why did the doorbell always ring at the most inopportune moments? Up a ladder, her hair in a scarf and wearing her oldest jeans, she was tackling her least favourite job, stripping a cornice of its many layers of paint. At this time on a Monday afternoon, the younger girls were involved in drama lessons and Becky was visiting a school friend so it couldn't be any of them. Irritated, she dashed down the stairs at the second ring.

Standing in the doorway was an impeccably-groomed woman – grey wool trouser suit that looked as though it had come off a Paris catwalk, make-up perfect, every strand of hair in place.

Heart thudding and pulling off her scarf, it was a second or two before Carol found her voice.

'Yes? Can I help you?'

'I'd like to see Ben Mitchell.' The voice had a faint American twang.

'He's not here. He's abroad.'

Caitlin eyed her for an instant. 'To be honest I knew that. I really came to see you. I'm Caitlin Thomas.'

Carol's heart skipped a beat. She'd almost managed to convince herself over these past weeks that Caitlin was what Ben said she was, old news.

'I know. What do you want to see me about?'

'It's difficult to talk on the doorstep. May I come in?'

Instinctively Carol closed the door a fraction. 'I have nothing to say to you. Ben's told me everything.'

'I don't think so.'

It was hard to read her expression, which remained impassive; only her eyes hinted at trouble. There was a glint in them that made Carol apprehensive. For a moment she hesitated. Ben had asked her to trust him. By inviting this woman in, was she being disloyal?

'I can come back tomorrow if it's not convenient, or the day after,' said Caitlin, casting a sideways glance at Carol's paint-streaked jeans.

Slowly Carol opened the door and led the way to the kitchen. She was damned if she would allow this woman to upset her. From the letter she had gained the impression Caitlin had dismissed the incident at the press ball as easily as had Ben but maybe she was trying to fool him. Perhaps she still harboured hopes that he would break up his marriage to be with her. Well, thought Carol, she would have to disabuse her of that.

She did not offer coffee, nor did she ask Caitlin to sit down. She was determined to take charge, to get rid of her as speedily as possible.

'Ben showed me the letter you wrote him.' Caitlin frowned as if she was finding it difficult to remember.

'The one you wrote after that stupid incident in the car park.' There, that would show her that Ben hadn't kept his wife in the dark.

'Oh that.'

'Isn't that why you're here?'

'No.' Caitlin removed her jacket, draping it carefully over the wooden chair before sitting down. She leaned back, legs crossed, seemingly at ease. Carol remained standing but hoped she was disguising her lack of composure.

'You think everything's over between Ben and me, do you?' Caitlin asked with what Carol thought was irritating casualness. When she nodded firmly, Caitlin smiled. 'He's told you that and you believe him?'

'Yes. I do.'

Caitlin went on smoothly, 'What you don't seem to understand, my dear, is that he and I have a bond you'll never be able to break.'

Carol wouldn't allow doubts to creep in, not when she and Ben had discussed it thoroughly, not when they had just enjoyed the best period of their marriage.

'I'd like you to leave now,' she said. 'I can't see any reason to continue this conversation.' She moved in the direction of the door but Caitlin stayed where she was. It seemed as if Carol had not spoken.

'Whatever Ben has said about our relationship he's told you some of the truth. But not the whole truth.'

Razor blades began to whirl around Carol's stomach. Fighting a desire to escape, she turned back towards the table where Caitlin was watching her intently.

'Did Ben mention, for instance, that he and I have a child? A son?'

Carol's face must have paled for Caitlin leaned forward with a show of concern. 'I think you'd better sit down.'

A son. Their son.

Carol sank on a chair next to her.

'I'd hoped he would tell you himself but I can see that he didn't. What a naughty boy he is.'

It must be true. No one would make up such a lie.

Caitlin did not wait for a response but continued brightly, almost as if at a coffee morning with friends, 'Yes, his name is William and he's seven, nearly eight. That's a few months younger than Katie, isn't it? He's the spitting image of his father and Ben says he wants to be a proper father to him, get involved in his life. I really came here to make some arrangements with you. I'd hoped . . . but then men are such cowards, aren't they?' Caitlin began to rummage in her handbag. 'Would you like to see a photograph?'

Carol's 'No' came out more fiercely than she intended and she bit her lip, annoyed that she had allowed this woman to witness how rattled she was. Why hadn't Ben told her about this? He had shown her the letter, he had appeared to be completely open about Caitlin, reiterating there was nothing between them; why hadn't he been brave enough to tell her the entire story? At the same time as keeping her sweet, could he have been planning with Caitlin how he could play a part in their child's life? Probably. This whole episode illustrated the pattern of their life together. She would find out one fact and he would explain it away but not volunteer anything extra.

How could he expect to be a 'proper father' to this child without her finding out? His son. Caitlin had given him a son. No wonder he had not been enthusiastic about the prospect of her becoming pregnant. Having fathered four children, why would he be?

Dimly she heard Caitlin say, 'We were always meant to be together.

You should realise Fay's death unhinged us all. I was a fool to go off and leave Ben at the very time he needed me. I'm afraid, my dear, you've always been second best as far as Ben's concerned. But he's a very kind person, as you know. In all the time we've spent together he's never said a word against you, I'd like you to know that. He always says you're a very nice woman. And a wonderful mother.' She giggled. 'You're quite an act to follow.' Caitlin stood up and slowly began to put on her jacket. 'I suppose you know he's been unfaithful many times since your marriage.'

Carol felt as if she had been slapped but made no reply.

'But he's promised me he's stopped all that. And I've learned my lesson.' Caitlin paused and said with emphasis, 'I don't intend to leave him again.'

Carol had no ammunition to fight and watched dumbly as her nemesis walked out of the room. Somewhere in the distance she heard the front door close.

She caught sight of herself in the pine-framed mirror. Her eyes seemed to have sunk into their sockets, her pallor under the tan made her appear years older. Dispassionately she studied her features, the features of a fool. Time and time again Ben had talked his way out of tricky situations and each time she had allowed herself to believe she was hearing the truth. It was as if she was in a giant maze. Ben showed her the way forward. She followed him, only to be led deeper into the maze instead of towards the exit.

Before he came back from Moscow she would have to make decisions. She needed a plan, if only for the short term. Whatever excuses he came up with she could not go on with him this time. She began to think of the practicalities. She had no job, no money of her own, and what would she do about the children?

In a daze she made her way back to the bedroom. Only an hour ago she had been planning a new career, a new bedroom, a new life. Angrily she threw a paintbrush into the wastepaper basket and was about to stow away the stepladder when the phone rang.

'I've stood up Vladimir Putin to make this call,' said Ben's cheery voice. 'I hope you're properly impressed that the Russian president is having to wait.' She made no answer and he asked, 'Carol? Are you there?'

Eventually she cleared her throat. 'I've just had a visit from Caitlin. I know about your child.'

This time it was his turn for silence. She heard him say something about how he could explain everything before he said, 'I'm getting the first plane back.'

'Don't. It's too late.' And she slammed down the phone.

Chapter Twenty-Nine

True to his word Ben cut short his Moscow trip and returned home but Carol refused to listen to anything he had to say. After trying in vain to persuade her to talk to him about Caitlin, he had to agree to her suggestion that he should stay in the office flat until she calmed down.

He stared at the dingy light bulb and wondered why, with all their profits, management didn't splash out on a higher wattage. The bedsitter itself was reasonable enough, if without any frills, and he had used it very occasionally on election nights. But he hated staying there. He found it difficult to sleep away from home these days and hoped he could persuade Carol to let him come back soon. He had never known her so intransigent. All right, he accepted he'd been a coward in not telling her about the child. He tried to explain again and again his reason for keeping quiet, that the trip had come at a bad time, that he would have told her immediately he had returned, but she wouldn't listen. And she had a point. In the aftermath of his shock at finding out about William he had not thought straight. If he had he would have confided in Carol immediately. He could see that clearly now, especially since she was desperate to have a baby of their own. But was his foolishness sufficient reason to end a marriage?

The trouble was Carol refused to talk it through, said they had done too much of that in the past and what was the use? This was a Carol he had not seen before, stronger, in no mood to compromise and apparently determined to shape a future without him.

He had tried everything. When words didn't seem to work he had sent a letter, even a tape recording in which he had poured out an abject apology for hurting her again. All useless. These days Carol would only talk about the children and their needs and headed him off each time he tried to broach the subject of their marriage.

They had told the children their father was working on an important story, which was why he was coming home in the mornings and back again for a couple of hours at their bedtime. He didn't know how long they would get away with this charade, especially with Becky, but so far the children, wrapped up in their own hectic schedules, were not outwardly suspicious.

Carol was putting up a good show in front of the kids, friendly and to all intents and purposes interested in what he was doing. But when would they notice that she never touched him? If he made the smallest gesture towards her she would manage to brush him aside without making it obvious. He had thought about sending her flowers every day but dismissed it as corny.

Sitting alone most nights in the company flat Ben had done a great deal of thinking and had come to the painful conclusion that he was part of Carol's problem. Because she had shown such great interest in everything he said and did, he had taken it for granted that was all she needed. He had accepted that she lived her life through him and had taken advantage of it, happy that she had been the type of woman defined as being a wife and mother. But now she was her own person.

The paradox was that he had undergone a genuine conversion. What had started as a grateful friendship had transmuted into a love affair on his part. Incredibly enough, and he could hardly believe it himself, he had fallen in love with the woman who had returned from Brunei. She was Carol writ large. More feisty, more sure of herself and excitingly sexy. But how to convince her of that? When he asked her to be specific about what Caitlin had said so he could refute her allegations, she had cut him short and flew at him. 'What's the point?' she'd shouted. 'I never know with you what's true and what isn't. Who else is going to come out of the woodwork with affairs you forgot to mention?'

What was he going to do if Carol refused to give him a second chance? He began pacing the narrow bedroom. What did he have to do to convince her that his love was genuine?

Well, they said actions spoke louder than words. Now he would have to act.

The sky was oppressive, a dark, metallic grey, aptly mirroring her mood. She hated the idea of meeting Ben in a solicitor's office but supposed it was inevitable. Obviously Ben wanted his freedom so he and Caitlin could be together but their divorce would be more complicated because, as he very well knew, she would never easily give up the children even though as their father he would undoubtedly win custody. But she would listen to his proposals for them before making her own.

He had not waited for her to start divorce proceedings, nor had he bothered to discuss it with her but had taken the initiative and arranged tonight's meeting after work. They weren't communicating much.

Carol chose her clothes carefully. She might feel as though she was going to a funeral but she was damned if she'd let anyone see it. The green linen suit would be a good choice, not too formal, not too casual, a halfway house between a smart lunch and a school play. She had lost weight and the jacket fitted better than when she had bought it. Her hair, now an inch longer than when Anak had cut it, had been expertly shaped by a hairdresser so expensive she had blanched at the bill.

The children were definitely getting suspicious about the reasons Ben wasn't at home. How could she blame them? Last night Becky had hung back until the two younger children had disappeared upstairs, and began to ask such pointed questions. Carol became uncomfortable yet she was still reluctant to admit anything until she and Ben had come to a decision about arrangements.

'Something's changed between you and Dad. Don't deny it. When I told Ally about it she said that just before her parents divorced her dad also left. What's going on?'

'It's difficult to explain. Sometimes when two people have problems...' she faltered, not knowing how to continue. However carefully they handled the split she was bound to feel insecure, and possibly rejected. Carol longed to give her a hug, but feared she might break down herself.

Becky was making efforts to control her trembling lips. 'When you came back everything was great but I can see it isn't any more and I know something's wrong.'

Carol wished she could be frank but she had promised herself she would hear what Ben was proposing before involving the children. Yet she could not leave Becky in this state.

'Yes, something is wrong but Dad and I are having a big meeting tomorrow evening and we'll be talking things through. And then I'll tell you everything. I promise.'

She fully expected Becky to argue that she didn't want to be fobbed off but to her surprise she put an arm around her shoulders and gave her a quick kiss on the cheek.

'I'm sorry you're unhappy,' she said. 'I know I've been a pig sometimes but I didn't mean it. I love you very much and when you were away I missed you loads.'

Carol's eyes glinted with tears. 'I love you too, darling.'

Becky had gone upstairs to finish off her homework, and Carol had dabbed at her cheeks and poured herself a glass of wine. The children were part of the fabric of her life, as she was to theirs. She was the only mother Katie had ever known. But over the years the others had also come to accept her as their mother.

There was so much to remember about all three. Katie's warm body wrapped in a towel snuggling against her after a bath, shopping with Becky to buy the girl's first lipstick and compromising on Pretty Pink rather than the Rich Ruby Red for which she had pleaded. The tooth fairy episode with Emmy had turned into a family legend. Carol had sprinkled gold glitter from Emmy's bed onto the windowsill, supposedly marking the fairy's trail. The excited child had carefully collected each fragment of glitter, holding them in cupped hands to show Carol, only to give a mighty sneeze and scatter the lot.

Whatever happened in the solicitor's office this evening, one thing was certain. She would not allow Ben and Caitlin to take the children away from her completely. She pulled a brush through her hair and it sprang back into an obedient bob – she thought the cost of the hairdresser had been worthwhile. Satisfied that she gave the impression of a woman in charge of her life, she phoned for a taxi, wanting to arrive without having the hassle of public transport.

During the journey she psyched herself up, reminding herself she was no victim. She couldn't any longer be dominated or be forced into a situation that was not to her liking or advantage. She did not intend to rely on memory or notes and would insist on using the miniature tape recorder she had bought yesterday.

When the taxi stopped outside a small block of flats in a cobbled street off the main thoroughfare, she could see no name plate and queried whether it was the correct address. The driver gave her a jaundiced look and assured her he had been a cabbie for twenty-five years. Did she think he could make a living by bringing passengers to the wrong place? She paid the fare and for punishment gave him such a negligible tip he crashed the gears before moving off. The incident had done just enough to stir her aggression and she pushed the button for flat number five rather too fiercely. The door release buzzed at once and she found herself inside a small vestibule. A vase of fresh flowers sat on a mahogany half-moon table. She caught sight of her strained face in the rather ornate gilt mirror and tried to relax her features as she cast about for the list of occupants. There was none. Did the firm own the entire building? If so, the solicitor must be very expensive to be able to afford elegant premises like these.

The lift had a row of brass numbers and Carol pressed the one marked 5-7. Ben was waiting for her when it reached the second floor.

'Sorry to have sprung it on you at such short notice but I want to sort things out as soon as possible,' he said.

What the hell was the hurry? she thought dully and allowed herself to be ushered through the doorway. Puzzled, she looked around the hall. It had a formal air but gave no impression of being a commercial office. Ben took her elbow and steered her into what seemed to be a living room. Perhaps this was how lawyers conducted business these days.

A pair of sand-coloured calico sofas dominated the room and Ben suggested she sat down. He remained standing, hovering near the door, and seemed rather on edge. Somebody was talking in the next room; Carol assumed it was the lawyer. Female by the sound. The silence deepened and Carol became self-conscious, avoiding his eye by pretending to be busy setting up the tape recorder. The silence was becoming oppressive when Ben cleared his throat.

'I talked to the kids this morning.'

'I know.'

'They seemed all right.'

'Well, they're not. Becky's asking lots of questions.'

'What did you say?'

'That I would tell her something after this meeting. I think we should both do it.'

'Perhaps there won't be much to say.'

Before Carol could respond, an interior door opened and Caitlin Thomas walked into the room.

Ben had expected both women to be astounded to see the other for neither knew the other would be there and just for a moment he was panicked. Would his plan work? He had doubts about pulling it off and watching Carol's angry face he wasn't sure if she would stay. Asking Caitlin if they could meet in her flat to discuss their child had been the easy part. She had been surprised at the request but had willingly agreed. Said it was time they discussed how to introduce Ben to his son. But now he had to concentrate on keeping Carol here long enough to hear what he had to say. That would be more difficult.

Caitlin recovered the quickest. Without taking her eyes off Carol she asked, 'What are you up to, Ben?'

Before he could attempt an answer Carol sprang to her feet and made for the door but Ben had anticipated her reaction and had stationed himself there to bar her exit.

She stood mutely in front of him and when he didn't move said fiercely, 'Get out of my way.'

He held his ground. 'I want you to hear me out.'

'No. I won't discuss anything in front of that woman.'

'The feeling is entirely mutual,' Caitlin drawled.

Carol kept her voice low. 'Ben, stand aside.'

His eyes locked into Carol's. He could see she was struggling to keep her emotions under control and he tried to take her hand, show he was sympathetic, but she moved aside. He heard Caitlin say, 'For goodness sake, let her go.'

How to persuade his wife to stay? That was the weakness in his plan. In her present state Carol would not give him time to say much and he had thought of little else these past few days but of how to phrase the few words he would be allowed.

'Listen to me,' he said urgently, desperately trying to hold her attention. 'Caitlin's been lying to you and to me. She wants to break up our marriage. Go now and she'll have succeeded.'

Carol stared at him stonily.

First objective achieved. She appeared to be listening. His rate of breathing slowed. Across Carol's shoulder he saw Caitlin's eyes widen.

Ben said gently, 'Please sit down. What have you got to lose? And what I have to say may change your mind.'

He had tried many times since Caitlin's visit to explain what her agenda was but Carol had closed her ears. He figured the only way she might accept his version of events was to confront Caitlin, with Carol by his side. Only then might she give him credence.

'You see, Carol, the person who made the anonymous call to you was not Caitlin's husband. It was Caitlin herself.'

She was in the middle of a bloody theatrical event, thought Carol, but it all made sense now. This woman who had borne Ben a child had returned to claim her lover. That was the reason for the phone call, an inspired touch of spite because it had achieved its aim.

Caitlin had maintained there was a bond between the two of them and Carol had to admit she was right. In the restaurant she had recognised it from across the room and she could not easily forget Ben's face alight with interest and amusement as he watched, laughed and chatted with the woman.

If Caitlin was obsessed by Ben, had he encouraged her? The letter she had written, he'd explained, was the aftermath of one kiss. What if he were lying? What if Lisa's assumption of their affair, so easily dismissed by Carol, was the true version? That would give Caitlin reason enough to make the call, to visit Carol at home and cause all this trouble.

Ben must have been crazy to think this meeting was going to change her mind. Carol hated being in this woman's flat and was furious with Ben for putting her in that humiliating position. Yet part of her was curious to find out why he had done it.

'All right,' she said, after a long pause. 'I'll listen . . . for a moment.' She made for the furthest point of the room, folded her arms, and as if Caitlin didn't exist stood leaning against the wall, waiting.

Ben positioned himself in the middle of the room facing Caitlin square on. 'I want you to admit it was you who made that call.'

'I don't know what you're talking about.' She shrugged impatiently. 'Do you really think I'm capable of something like that?'

He did not answer but opened his briefcase and took out a manila envelope. 'This is a computer print-out of every call made to our house that day.' He walked across to her and pushed one of the sheets into her hand. 'One of the items is highlighted. That's the anonymous call. It's timed a few minutes before Carol phoned me to tell me about it.' He'd had to pay an enormous bribe to his contact at the phone company but it had been worth it. 'Recognise the number, Caitlin?' He turned to Carol. 'It's her mobile.'

Caitlin made a pretence of studying the paper.

'I thought at first it was someone after my job, trying to destabilise my home life. But when you turned up at home and told Carol those stupid lies about us destined to be together, I didn't really need the phone records to know who the caller was.'

Caitlin tossed the telephone records to the floor. 'I did it to help you.'

'Help?' Ben snorted in derision.

'Your marriage was unhappy. You only stayed with Carol because of the children.'

'How dare you say that? Carol, don't believe her. It's another of her lies.'

'Really? Let me ask you this. Would a devoted husband come on to somebody else the way you did with me?'

'You have a great capacity for self-delusion.'

Ben's tone was withering but Carol thought he looked discomfited. Was it likely Caitlin would have continued her campaign without any encouragement?

'I have never been unfaithful to Carol since the day we married.'

'Knowing your sex drive I'd dispute that.' Caitlin gave a slow smile. 'Can you deny that if I had offered we wouldn't have ended up in bed? That night at the press dinner—'

'You did offer and I was the one who broke away.'

'Ran away, you mean.'

Carol could hardly bear to listen. However much Ben protested, she had seen for herself the effect Caitlin had on him.

Caitlin turned her attention to Carol. 'You might've been rubbing along quite nicely but why do you think Ben put so much energy into his job lately? Because I was connected with it, he could use it as an excuse to see me.'

'Why are you doing this?' Ben sat down heavily on the sofa.

'Because we belong together and I want to be your wife. Just as we were planning before Fay died.'

Carol had heard enough. She was about to take flight when a noise made her pause. The bedroom doorknob had begun to rotate. She hadn't realised someone else was in the flat. She turned round and watched as the door was pushed ajar, then a fraction wider.

Framed in the passageway stood the small figure of a young boy, his shape silhouetted against the light coming from the bedroom. Bizarrely, the first thing Carol noticed was his pyjamas, covered in drawings of

First World War aeroplanes. Everything about him reminded her of a picture from Ben's childhood, the floppy hair, the gangling limbs, even the set of his jaw. Hesitantly, he stepped forward, gazing at the adults in turn before making his way over to Ben.

'Are you my daddy?'

Carol saw Ben swallowing hard. 'Yes, William. I am.'

Ben stood up and held out his hand, his face showing a mixture of surprise and concern. 'I'm glad to meet you. I didn't know I was going to see you today.

Hesitantly the young boy shook his hand and stood looking up at his father, a shy smile beginning to curve on his lips. 'I did. Mummy told me and I've been looking forward to it all week.'

Ben guided William towards the sofa where they both sat down and Carol saw her husband give an anguished look towards her. She blinked furiously to prevent the tears that were threatening to spill over. But she was determined not to let that woman see her cry. Caitlin had successfully changed the agenda. They were not discussing lies or anonymous phone calls any longer.

Her instinct was to get the hell out of there and let Ben sort out the mess himself, she need not be involved. But if the past few months had taught her nothing else, it was that she should face problems head on. She had been inclined to allow others to dictate her actions rather than to take control of events.

She moved purposefully towards William and at that moment the child smiled at her politely. She took a small hand in both of hers, gripping it firmly.

'I'm very happy to meet you, William,' she said, sitting down on the other side of him.

'This is Carol, my wife,' she heard Ben say.

Poor child, he was the victim in all this, an innocent pawn in the game Caitlin was playing. Well, as far as she was concerned the marriage was over though she doubted, from everything he had said today, that Ben would end up with Caitlin. But William's existence put a different complexion on things. Ben would have to organise a truce with the woman.

'I think the three girls will be happy to know about you,' said Carol.

'I know the names of all my sisters,' he said proudly, 'Katie, Emmy and Becky. When can I meet them?'

Carol gave her husband a steely gaze. 'Soon. Your father will probably tell them all about you today and then we can fix up something.'

The child beamed and Carol patted his shoulder, saying she had to leave right away but looked forward to being there when he met the girls.

'Couldn't you stay for a while?' asked Ben, looking anguished.

She shook her head. The last image Carol carried with her as she swept through the door was Ben sitting beside a younger version of himself, Caitlin in the background watching proudly.

Her eyes misted over and she was barely able to read the buttons on the lift as it carried her downwards.

Ben watched his wife walk out of the flat with a feeling of immense gloom. When he had fixed up the meeting with Caitlin it was on the basis that they would discuss the practicalities of fitting William into his life. Meeting the boy would then be engineered at a time of his own choosing, after he had talked it over with the girls. Carol, too, if she was still around, though after today that prospect seemed remote. She would never believe he had not been a party to Caitlin's scheme. He wished he could rush out after her and try to smooth things over.

As always Caitlin had wanted to push things along, 'make things happen' as she would put it, without thinking of the consequences. But the person he had to protect from her scheming was William.

Caitlin brought a glass of orange juice and biscuits for William and offered Ben a glass of wine but he refused. The youngster sat munching happily, his knees touching his father's. His hair was flattened at the sides, looking as if an attempt had been made to smarten it up but a lock had escaped and was sticking up from his crown. As if the boy had read his mind he said suddenly, 'These are my best pyjamas.'

'Very smart,' agreed Ben, overcome by the child's obvious pleasure at seeing him.

William was a delight. Unspoiled, pleasant, talking about how he wanted to be a pilot when he grew up. Despite his sadness at the way Caitlin had turned the tables and manipulated him into seeing his son, Ben had to admit the child was a credit to her.

Caitlin was watching from the shadows, wisely not interfering. This was a woman who had wrecked his last chance with his wife. She had wanted to drive Carol away and had succeeded. She had wanted him to bond with her son and this was what was happening now. His carefully thought out plan had only one winner.

Like Ben had been at his age, William was taller than average. His eyes had a greenish tinge, like Emmy's, and Ben wondered what the girls would make of him. They would be kind but how would he explain the existence of a half-brother conceived while he was still married to their mother? This wasn't the most auspicious time for him and William to have been introduced but Ben was touched by the boy's ready acceptance of him as his father.

William was losing his shyness, and answering Ben's questions about his school friends, what were his favourite games and whether he liked London better than Washington, which he apparently did, although the weather here was 'lousy'.

At this point Caitlin intervened, her demeanour reflecting maternal pride. 'I'm glad you two are getting along so well but I'm afraid it's bedtime, young man.'

With half an ear on the boy's familiar argument about why he shouldn't go to bed just yet, Ben reflected that it couldn't have been easy growing up without a father and with a mother who was a workaholic. He had probably been left to his own devices more than most children, which might account for his air of self-possession.

Caitlin appeared to have won the bed argument. William sighed heavily then his face brightened as he asked Ben, 'Will you be able to come and watch me play football?'

He looked so vulnerable that Ben scooped him up in a bear-like hug which was enthusiastically reciprocated. 'Of course I will,' he said.

Over the child's shoulder he observed Caitlin abruptly turning away to dab at her eyes and with sinking heart Ben was forced to acknowledge how clever she had been.

It was a pity Ben had found out she had made the call, but all in all Caitlin felt pleased with herself. Getting William out of school for the night had been a good idea. As she expected, William seemed to like his father very much and for his part Ben appeared to show great interest in the boy. And Carol had stormed out. It was a far better result than she could have anticipated. The icing on the cake would be if she could entice Ben into bed. Carol had been quite antagonistic towards him and

Caitlin couldn't imagine they were on lovemaking terms, which might bode well for her.

Ben looked rather serious as he put the wretched list of itemised calls into his briefcase. On the other hand he seemed in no rush to leave. She wondered if wine might delay his departure and went to the cabinet where she had installed a bottle of Merlot, already opened, in anticipation of a successful outcome. She poured out two glasses and walked slowly towards him, her eyes fixed on the top of his head, willing him to notice her.

'I thought you and William looked wonderful together,' she said, placing the glass on the table in front of him. 'I know I'm prejudiced but isn't he the dearest thing?'

She was glad to see Ben's expression soften and at least he met her gaze.

'Yes he is.'

'Will you see him regularly?'

'I think I owe it to him,' he replied and Caitlin fought to hide her feeling of triumph. Meetings with William would ensure she had every excuse to see Ben in a more personal environment. Although Ben was ostensibly trying to save his marriage, Caitlin could see the signs of an irrevocable breakdown. And with Carol out of the way, she was certain she could re-create the passion and yes, the love they had shared before.

She sat down next to him on the sofa and pushed the glass nearer to him.

'Ben, you've no idea how lonely it's been, bringing up William on my own.' He appeared to be lost in thought and she moved slightly, closing in on him so their thighs were almost touching. 'When I had to sit up with him all night when he was ill once, I had some inkling of how it had been for you as a single parent. It's hard coping on your own. I understand exactly why you needed a mother for the children.' She put down her glass and turned to face him. 'Hold me, Ben. I've been so unhappy.'

She closed her eyes. Ben, darling Ben was about to take her into his arms. She caught the faint aroma of the aftershave he had used for years. It triggered memories of great moments of anticipation before their bodies locked together.

Her mood was rudely shattered. 'Caitlin, stop this nonsense. You've been wrong about every aspect of this whole business. I'm sick of it. I'm going back to my house, back to my wife. I much prefer her company.'

Caitlin was scornful. 'I don't believe you. I've seen it in your eyes. You want to run away because you don't dare touch me. If you did you'd never go back to her. And you know it.'

Ben clicked his tongue in annoyance. 'Those days are long over.'

She dismissed his protestations. 'They're not over,' she said, tears coming into her eyes. 'You couldn't wait to be with me. You used to scheme to get me alone.'

'Yes, I did. Caitlin, I hate to be blunt but you don't seem to be getting the message. It was for sex.'

'It wasn't. You loved me. I know you did. You didn't have to say it. You showed it every time you touched me.'

'You're deluding yourself. We never discussed the future. We only had a life within hotel bedrooms. What makes you think it was anything other than sex?'

She dismissed his protestations. He was trying to be loyal. He always did sacrifice his happiness for those children.

'It was much more.'

'Caitlin, I thought we understood each other pretty well. We were both married and we never discussed the future. Why are you making it something it never was?'

'Don't say that. I remember how it was.'

'You're remembering a fantasy past because of William.'

She had to find a way to make him sit down again. If she could just make him kiss her, press her body against his just once, she'd win. She knew it. Caitlin held out her arms to him. 'But all I want is for us to be together.'

He gave a harsh laugh. 'Forget that. I give you my word that I'll see William regularly, the boy deserves that. And I'll make arrangements for that through you. We will have contact but only to do with when and where I can see William. That's all.'

'But in time . . .'

He gave a frustrated sigh. 'That's not going to happen, Caitlin.' Ben clicked the briefcase closed. 'If you carry on like this I won't find it easy to see William. Let me make myself so clear you can't possibly misunderstand. You've tried to spoil my marriage and you've probably succeeded. But whatever happens between Carol and me, I'll never be with you. Never.' Ben stood up and went to the door. 'Is that unambiguous enough for you?'

After he had banged the door shut behind him, Caitlin sat quite still staring at the wall. She had failed. Ben was off her agenda. All these months of planning, scheming . . . all for nothing. Slowly she leaned over and began plumping up the cushions and straightening out the room before taking the glasses to the small kitchen. While she rinsed them, her mind was going full tilt. Had she fantasised the past? Could she have imagined Ben's face lighting up when she came into the hotel bedroom? After their lovemaking – love, not sex please note, Mr Mitchell – he did not leap from the bed to hurry away. Most of the moments she remembered best were afterwards, languidly lying close together talking. If their relationship had been purely physical, would he have lingered?

Caitlin began stacking the glasses and opened a drawer to take out the almost new drying up cloth. Ben blamed her for the break-down in his marriage when anyone could see it was foundering. Why else would his wife have retreated to the other side of the world?

He had said some hurtful things but even now, she was sure, the words came out like that because he dared not trust himself to be close to her. He was afraid of where it might lead. She recalled his car hurtling out of the underground car park after that passionate kiss, the only one they'd exchanged since her return to London. Whatever his lips said, his body language could not lie. He wanted her. Perhaps he couldn't acknowledge this even to himself.

That night as she lay in bed she replayed the events of the evening through her head as if it were on video. Suddenly she could see things from his perspective. Understandably, he was loath to commit himself. Until he and Carol were actually divorced, he would not allow himself to think about the future. She'd be far better for him in every way than his wife but if he could not realise it, she would have to find ways to make him understand. But how? In her mind, she fast-forwarded images of his cruel outburst, rewinding the imaginary film to study Ben's face while he was talking to William, focusing on his soft expression as he hugged his son.

His only son.

Caitlin was suddenly imbued with a sense of uncertainty. If she could inveigle him into her bed all things became possible. But Ben was giving her no encouragement, seemingly stuck on that milk-water wife of his. Though William was a powerful magnet Caitlin could see it would need a great deal of scheming to bring her plan to fruition. Yet she needed Ben as a father to her son and must do nothing to frighten him away. Not now when William had bonded with his father.

She would be restrained when he came to pick up William, make herself scarce if Ben wanted to visit him at home, do nothing to make him nervous. She would discipline herself to hide her feelings, and wait to see what would happen.

If Ben proved to be off the agenda it was time to cast about for someone new.

Chapter Thirty

Ben drove straight home. He had to talk to Carol, try and begin to win back her trust.

Before he had a chance to put the key in the lock, he heard the thudding of three pairs of feet running to the door which was flung open. Katie shouted, 'We saw your car through the window,' before the three of them pulled him inside. Laughing and shouting, they half dragged him through the hall, down the corridor and into the kitchen where a figure was emptying the dishwasher. It was his neighbour, Brenda Porter.

'Where's Carol?'

'She phoned to say she was going to the supermarket,' replied Mrs Porter.

Ben couldn't work this out. Someone who had been through the emotional wringer Carol had just been through would hardly decide to do something as mundane as shopping, would she? No, she must be using it as an excuse to be by herself to think things over.

He thanked his obliging neighbour for her help and Katie and Emmy saw her to the door. Becky hung back.

'Is everything OK between you and Carol?' she asked.

'I hope it will be,' he said carefully.

'I don't know what that means,' said Becky.

'I want to talk to you three,' he told her, 'about something else.' At that moment the other two came racing back into the kitchen and he asked them to sit down and listen to him for a few minutes.

How to tell three loving daughters that their father, their hero, had feet of clay? Confronted by those trusting faces Ben, for all his facility with words, found himself searching desperately for the right way to start.

'I think you're grown-up enough to know that sometimes parents do things they regret. But however sorry they are they can't change what's happened.'

They waited expectantly. He wanted to tell them as much of the truth as possible without whitewashing his actions. But neither did he want to leave them with the impression he was an out and out shit. How to start?

'When your mother and I married we were very happy and we both worked hard to stay that way.'

'You used to shout at each other,' said Becky. 'I remember that.'

'Yes, though we did try not to let it affect you and Emmy. Katie wasn't born then.' He looked across at the little girl and said, 'Both of us wanted to try and be happy together and then you came along, Katie.' God, this was difficult. They didn't make any comment but he felt the tension and sprang to his feet to pace around the kitchen. 'Do you understand so far?'

Three heads nodded simultaneously though Katie appeared bemused.

'But nothing worked and we still weren't very happy together. Then I did a very silly thing. I met another woman and she became my girlfriend.'

Katie's mouth formed into an ooohh. 'How can you have a wife *and* a girlfriend?'

Emmy looked at her pityingly. 'You'll understand when you're older.'

Ben pressed on. 'Then your mother had the terrible accident and so I said goodbye to this lady because I wanted to look after you.'

'Why didn't she come and help you?' asked Katie.

'It wouldn't have been fair to ask her because, you see, I didn't love her. And it all turned out well in the end because after that I met Carol.' He let them absorb this for a moment.

'Why are you telling us this now?' Becky's eyes were bright.

'Because today something happened.'

'What?'

'I found out the lady I was talking about had a baby boy.'

'Is he your baby, Dad?' asked Emmy.

'Yes, darling, he is my son and he's your half-brother.'

To his amazement, the two younger girls squealed in delight, maintaining this was wonderful news because they had always wanted a brother. They rained questions down on him. What was the little boy's name? How old was he, where did he live, and when could they meet him? Heartened by their reaction, Ben promised he would organise something soon. He explained that the reason he had found out about

William only recently was because the boy had been living with his mother in Washington. Now they had both come to England to live and there would be many chances for the girls to get to know him.

Throughout all this Becky had remained silent. Ben cast an apprehensive glance in her direction and suggested that perhaps Em and Katie would have time for a computer game before bed if they hurried.

As soon as her sisters were safely out of earshot, Becky turned accusing eyes on him.

'Is this why Carol's upset?'

'Not really. She knows about William and we both met him today.'

'What does she think about it?'

'She accepts it happened before I met her.'

'Then why is she unhappy?'

Ben didn't know how to give a frank answer. When he and Carol had a chance to discuss their separation he might be better equipped but he didn't want to tackle this discussion alone.

'We didn't get a chance to talk because William was there.'

Becky wouldn't be easily diverted. 'Has Carol found out you have a girlfriend?'

'I haven't.'

'You did before.'

'I wouldn't do that to Carol.'

'You did it to my mother.'

Oh God.

'I told you, I made mistakes. Your mother wasn't all saint and I wasn't all sinner. Now when you're a bit older I think you'll understand people fall out of love for many reasons, and we did. Both of us.'

Becky jumped to her feet and began to shout, her face reddening.

'You made my mother unhappy, you're making Carol unhappy. I hate you.' She stood frozen in the doorway for a moment, staring at him aggressively. 'If you bring your precious William here, I'll walk out. I never want to see him.'

The lights of Battersea Bridge had never appeared more welcoming. It had taken Carol more than an hour to walk from Covent Garden, passing first through Leicester Square, then Trafalgar Square and down Whitehall, past the Houses of Parliament and along the river bank, her mood of desolation increasing with each step.

When she'd emerged from the building, her first reaction had been to blame Ben for putting her through that horrendous experience. If she had harboured one iota of hope before, it had been dashed by the encounter with that awful woman. She had hated listening to them dissecting their relationship as if she wasn't there, as if she didn't count. Undoubtedly Caitlin's trump card was William and by bringing him to that meeting she had made clear she was there for the long haul.

Carol hoped Ben would take up Caitlin's hint that the girls should be told about his son as soon as possible. After their initial shock Carol was sure they would enjoy the idea of a new brother. It had been Katie's theme song for ages, especially when she had a fight with Emmy. But they would take their cue from her and would be hesitant about welcoming him if she showed any signs of resentment. Carol found to her dismay that the idea of embracing yet another of Ben's progeny would give her problems. She was jealous. When would it be her turn to have a baby? She could date her yearning back to the time Katie had first started school. She had found herself looking into prams, longing to pick up the chubby bundles, wondering whether she and Ben would have a boy or a girl. And since he already had three daughters she had always hoped they would have a boy. That, too, had been taken from her.

Despite all this she had to admit Ben still had a strong hold over her and she despised her weakness. How could she deny that for seven years he had made her very happy? Their shared history could not easily be forgotten and, more, their incredible lovemaking when she had come back from Brunei had brought them much closer. But finding out from Caitlin that she and Ben had planned to marry, something he had not contradicted, meant she had been second-best from the start. All his evasions had destroyed her trust and she would have to disentangle herself somehow. Perhaps the key was Alex.

She was curious to find out whether the electricity between them would survive the more mundane surroundings of an autumnal Britain. Perhaps the key was within herself rather than Alex. She had become her own person while in Brunei and this newly discovered independence was a joy and would not lightly be thrown aside. Yet, she could not deny that in the back of her mind were questions about Alex. He had said he was ready for a deeper relationship but was that because he was still enjoying the afterglow of their magnificent experience on the river bank when both their emotions had been heightened by having just faced death?

She could not possibly expect such wild sex to continue in a domestic setting but it would be fun to find out. Carol half smiled at the prosaic thought of Alex hunting through a sock drawer or popping down to the supermarket for milk. She supposed he must have performed these trivial tasks sometime but she couldn't imagine it. Yet if he wanted to settle down and they could establish an enduring relationship based on something more than sex then perhaps he was worth considering as her future partner, and father of her child. Mentally she chided herself for an over-active imagination. She and Alex had spent very little time together and that was her old self thinking. Besides, she was going to concentrate on a career, and was excited about the possibility of a new job. Phoebe had phoned to say there was a post in the office with flexible hours. She would have to be prepared to handle phone queries, soothe expedition members as well as tackle the archaic filing systems. And they hoped, in time, she could also write press releases.

When she reached Chelsea Bridge, Carol paused to rest her aching feet. The colour of the street lamps flickering on the water went unnoticed, as did the passing traffic down Cheyne Walk and the dog walkers and joggers making their way to the winding road along the bank. Slowly her steps were taking her home to Tollbridge Road when she spotted a phone kiosk on the corner.

Carol had hoped that she and Ben would have come up with some solution that would cause least harm to the children. She had been thinking that they could sell the house and maybe buy two adjoining properties where they could live separately but close enough for the children to see both of them every day. She had been determined they would present a united front on whatever decision they made, but that hadn't happened and if he were waiting at home it would be difficult to talk privately. They would need to organise some kind of working relationship but in the meantime she wanted him to stay at the office flat.

Ben picked up the receiver after two rings and immediately asked where she was. Walking by the river, she told him.

There was a pause and he said, 'I'm sorry about what happened.'

'So am I. Why did you humiliate me like that, tricking me into going to her flat?'

'I couldn't think of another way to get you there. I wanted you to hear for yourself what a liar she is.'

'I hated being part of it, using a little boy in that way.'

'It wasn't supposed to be like that. I didn't even know William would be there. It's yet another example of Caitlin's utter lack of scruples, and I despise her for it.'

'Well, she's forced the issue now. Have you told the children about him?'

'Yes.'

'How'd they take it?'

'They were surprised, of course, but the younger ones seem OK.'

'And Becky?'

'Not so good. She's also worried about how you're taking it.' He sounded anxious.

'What did you say about that?'

'Nothing much. Just that you knew the situation.'

Carol gripped the receiver and said quietly, 'Today's given me a great deal to think about and I need time on my own to do it. I'd appreciate it if you'd go back to the company flat.'

'I'd rather not. Don't you think we need to talk things over?'

'Not until I've seen my solicitor.'

'Please, Carol. Don't rush anything.'

If, she thought later, Ben had left it there perhaps things might have turned out differently but he added, 'Remember your decision's going to affect more lives than yours or mine. Think of what these kids have gone through.'

Always the children. No mention of her.

'You should have thought of them before,' she snapped.

Ben had no choice but to capitulate. To make things easier, he said, he would engineer a trip to Washington for a few days which would provide a genuine cause for him not being around. 'I need to go over anyway, I'll just bring it forward.' He promised he would be gone by the time she arrived home.

He kept his word. When she neared the house she saw with relief his car was not there. She felt a moment's compassion for him. However bad all this was for her, it couldn't be easy for him living this kind of nomadic life.

The younger girls were fast asleep but Becky, who had been asked by her father to baby-sit, was a huddled heap in her bed, her head under a pillow. Gently Carol touched her shoulder and a tear-stained face emerged from the bedclothes. Carol took her into her arms and for a while cradled her body against hers, rocking her gently. Poor Becky, she thought, trying to be grown-up but sobbing like a child.

'Sshh, darling,' she said. 'I know about William. He's a lovely little boy and you'll like him.'

'I won't,' said Becky through her tears.

Carol cupped her chin in her hands and wiped the tears away with a finger. 'Dad's not going to love you less because of William.'

'It's not just that,' Becky managed eventually. 'That's why you've been unhappy, that's why you and Dad aren't together, because you found out about this boy. Did Dad love this boy's mother more than Mummy?'

Carol found herself defending Ben, saying he couldn't possibly love Caitlin as much as he did her mother.

'I hate him.'

'No you don't. You're just angry. He loves you very much.'

Carol rocked her and talked to her and Becky went to sleep hearing how much he cared for her and her sisters, that he was and always would be her loving father.

Chapter Thirty-One

Waiting for the interview at the BGA to begin, Carol tried to exude a self-confidence she did not feel. She had read enough advice in the bestseller she'd bought, *How To Get The Job You Want*, to realise that body language was one of the first aspects the interviewers noted. As she sat in the hard wooden chair, she hoped the relaxed posture, hands lightly folded on her lap, face composed, gave the impression of someone who would be calm in the face of crisis and competent enough to be an asset to the expedition organiser's office.

Phoebe Tugendhaat gave Carol an encouraging smile as she tried to answer the interviewing panel's questions with honesty and self-confidence. She candidly admitted that her three months' experience made her no expert. But it had taught her how to use her initiative and how to improvise and she felt it would enable her to give pertinent advice to others setting out on expeditions. Of course her training as a journalist, she told them, might be useful, enabling her to glean and impart information and also, if asked, to write press releases for national and local papers.

She was asked to wait with the other applicants in the common room while the panel talked in private. As she was the last applicant they told her she would not have to wait too long for their decision. Like most of the interior at the association's headquarters, the common room was a fine example of Georgian architecture, with high, moulded ceilings and elegant wood panelling, used by Fellows for morning coffee and snack lunches.

Anxious not to be caught up in conversation with the other applicants, Carol kept her eyes firmly fixed on her cup of coffee, her main concern whether or not to have a piece of shortbread. Growing tired of studying a piece of porcelain, she allowed her eyes to roam and speculated which among the others were her rivals. She was wondering how long they would have to wait when the door opened and attention focused on the tall, ebony-skinned figure striding towards her.

'Caro,' said Alex, breaking into a delighted smile, 'they told me you were here.'

Why the hell hadn't he phoned to say when he was arriving? Then she would've been able to prepare herself instead of trying to cope with him here, in front of all these gawping strangers.

'I didn't know you were in the country,' she said, conscious of a critical note in her voice. 'How long have you been back?'

'Only a few hours.'

'Why didn't you let me know?' She had to stop sounding aggrieved.

'Because I wanted to surprise you and then I saw your name written in the visitors' book in reception so here I am. Pleased to see me?'

Before she could answer he bent over, pulled her out of the chair, and seemingly oblivious to the attention they were attracting hugged her ardently to his chest. The feel of his arms encircling her was comforting. Right then it was exactly what she needed.

Without letting her go, she heard him say, 'I have to know right away, Caro, have you gone back to your husband?'

'No.'

'Good,' he whispered in her ear. She smiled back at him nervously, thinking that the last time she saw him he said he would be coming to get her. Assuming he had not had a change of heart, was she ready to make the kind of promise about the future that he might want?

'I've borrowed a flat just up the road. When are you finished here? I've so much to tell you.'

She was saved from answering by the sight of Phoebe Tugendhaat racing down the stairs.

'Caro, a word.'

'Hello, Phoebe,' smiled Alex.

'How are you?' said Phoebe. 'I heard you weren't feeling well.'

'Bit of a cold coming. It's the change of climate. I'll be all right.'

'I'd be happier if you'd let our medical people check you out.' But he shook his head and she began to guide Carol into the ante-chamber.

He shrugged and said to Carol, 'I'll wait for you.'

Phoebe motioned her to a chair. 'I must say, of all the candidates you were by far the least qualified.' Phoebe gave what for her passed as an impish chortle. 'But we liked your enthusiasm and your honesty and the journalistic background will come in handy. The most important thing is we think you'll fit into our team. Congratulations, I have pleasure in offering you the job.'

Carol lost her breath for a second. 'Thank you,' she said. My God, she had done it. She had a job with flexible hours. OK, the salary wasn't marvellous but it was a start and she was looking forward to working with people who would treat her as an independent woman, not as someone's wife or someone's mother.

Was she able to start in a couple of weeks? Definitely. Ben would be back by then. Phoebe stood up. In that case she would write to her with details of her contract, just details, nothing to worry about.

Carol almost ran out of the room in her eagerness to share the news with Alex and he immediately suggested they celebrate with champagne which is how she found herself in his Kensington flat at noon with a glass of Bollinger in her hand.

She had been half expecting him to whisk her straight into his bedroom and on the taxi drive to the flat wrestled with her conflicting emotions. The encounter on the river bank now seemed like a dream. But this was real life, and she needed to be sure of her own desires before she gave Alex further encouragement. Already she was regretting her impulse to come back to his flat and was wondering how she could gracefully explain she had been over-excited by the success of the interview. But she needn't have worried. Alex busied himself finding glasses and opening the bottle and seemed more inclined to talk about her triumph.

'I don't understand why you're so surprised. You can do anything, Caro. You've proved that after what you went through in Brunei. Nearly drowning, conquering the rope bridge, sleeping out in the jungle. You'll find this new job a piece of cake.'

He appeared genuinely happy at her success and in her euphoric state they slipped back easily into the camaraderie forged by surviving a perilous experience. They spent some time discussing the new job and where it might lead. She was in the middle of a sentence when Alex took out a handkerchief and began to mop his brow.

'Is it hot in here?'

Carol put down her glass. 'I don't think so.' Alex began to shiver. 'What's the matter?'

'I've suddenly got a blinding headache. Could you see if you could find some aspirin?'

Carol dashed to the bathroom cabinet but could find no painkillers. She would have to go out to buy some. She put her head round the door to tell him she wouldn't be long but Alex had disappeared. It was a second or two before she found him, sprawled unconscious on the floor. She raced to his side and felt his pulse. Thank God, she could feel it. She loosened his tie and rolled him on to his side to ensure his airways were not blocked. What the hell was wrong with him? He'd always appeared so fit and healthy.

Wildly she looked around the room. God, she didn't even know where the phone was. She tried to quell the familiar surge of panic when facing a potentially disastrous situation. Through her mind flashed an image of herself flagging down a strange motorist in an effort to get Katie to hospital. She had coped then and she would cope now.

Carol rushed from the room, found a telephone in the hallway and hurriedly dialled the emergency services. The ambulance arrived within minutes. She told them Alex had recently returned from Brunei and they decided to take him directly to a hospital specialising in tropical diseases. The crew clamped an oxygen mask across his face and wrapped his shivering body in a sheet of foil. She held Alex's hand throughout the journey but he remained unconscious, seemingly unaware of her presence.

The ambulance siren blared all the way to the hospital and though she tried to gain reassurance from the medics they fended off her questions by saying a doctor would have to examine him. Their evasions increased her anxiety.

At the hospital she explained to the duty doctor who his patient was and what kind of job he did and he immediately telephoned the BGA for more information. The conversation with Phoebe seemed to go on for some time. Alex was whisked to an isolation ward and Carol was asked to give a sample of her own blood so they could rule out any infection. When the grey-haired doctor finally came off the phone he told her that he suspected Alex was suffering from the early stages of Weil's disease, transmitted in water contaminated by rats' urine. 'We have to do tests before we can be sure but it looks that way.' He made a note on a chart and then asked, 'Are you his wife?'

Carol shook her head. 'Just a friend.'

His pen hovered. 'Then who should I put down as next of kin?'

'I'm not sure, probably the BGA, but take my number as well,' replied Carol, alarmed. 'How ill is he?'

'We won't know for a few days. We're rushing through your blood test and I suggest you go for a cup of tea while you wait.'

After an hour Carol was given the all-clear and it was suggested she should return home as there was nothing she could do. The euphoria of the day had been completely obliterated and Carol decided to go back to BGA headquarters to see if she could track down contact numbers for Alex's family. She realised how little she knew of his background, apart from the fact of his adoption.

The BGA staff informed her that according to their records Alex's father had died several years earlier. As for his mother, all they knew was that Alex had a standing order made out to a nursing home in Weybridge. Apparently she was suffering from an advanced stage of Alzheimer's. It seemed he had no other close relatives.

Carol went home and before she went to bed she rang the hospital. She was told that Alex had regained consciousness and was sleeping peacefully. The next morning she phoned again to be given the good news that he had been moved out of the isolation ward and that she could visit him in the afternoon. It would be after school hours and Becky would baby-sit for the younger two.

As she was leaving for the hospital, Ben phoned from America. There was the shortest of pauses when Carol told him she'd accepted a job from the BGA. He seemed pleased, saying he realised it was the kind of career she was seeking. Then he spoiled the moment by asking what arrangements she'd made to get the children looked after.

'I've asked for flexible hours,' she said tartly, 'so they won't suffer.'

Before he could react to the annoyance in her voice she said she would go and look for Becky. But his daughter refused to talk to him. Unlike her sisters, the existence of William still made her angry. Carol had explained how unhappy Ben had been with her mother, how much they had both tried to make the marriage work but Becky still held back. While Ben hung on, Carol pleaded with her at least to listen to what her father had to say. Nothing could be resolved without contact, she heard herself saying, conscious of the irony of her own situation. Finally Becky relented and went to the phone and although Carol was not privy to their conversation having tactfully withdrawn, Becky seemed happier afterwards. Carol left for the hospital saying she would be out for only a short while. Thankfully Becky did not ask where she was going.

As Carol entered Alex's private room she was startled to see he was not in bed but sitting in a chair, a sheaf of papers on his lap, wearing navy blue pyjamas and a dressing gown, obviously borrowed from the hospital's store. They were faded with washing and were at least a size too small. He appeared a little tired but his face lit up as he spotted her coming through the door. She thought again what a striking-looking man he was.

'Ah, my very own Florence Nightingale. Come in. I have a lot to thank you for. If I hadn't been brought in straightaway, things could have been much worse.'

She smiled at him. 'Well, you could say we're even now.'

A nurse appeared with an electronic thermometer which she placed at his ear. 'Coming down nicely,' she announced before fussing around him, totally ignoring his visitor. The nurse complained that he ought to get back into bed, he had to stay warm or he might have a relapse. Did he want her to reserve a ham omelette for supper, he had to keep up his strength and how would he do that if he didn't eat?

Carol found herself becoming irritated. Now the nurse was making great play of smoothing the bedclothes. Carol wondered if all her patients merited the same treatment or did she reserve this special attention for good-looking men? She wished the woman would disappear.

Alex gave Carol a wink and at last the nurse acknowledged her presence.

'He knows more about his illness than we do,' she said, glancing at Carol. Then she smiled admiringly at him. 'If you're sure there's nothing you want?' He shook his head and finally she left them alone.

Carol couldn't resist the temptation to tease him about the effect he had on women, even when he was at death's door.

'I'll tell you my secret,' he said. 'It's these stylish pyjamas. Come here.'

'I see you're getting better,' she said, remaining seated. 'What do the doctors say?'

He pushed the papers onto the bed. 'I should be out of here in a few days. I'm annoyed that I didn't spot the symptoms myself instead of thinking it was flu. It was a stupid mistake to make.'

'It's always easier to diagnose other people's problems than your own.'

He pulled a face. 'What about your problems?'

'Coming along. Ben and I don't talk much but he's arranged a meeting to sort out a few legal things. I think this is the first step towards divorce.'

'Good,' said Alex. 'Then you can concentrate on me. You'll find the more you get to know me, the more irresistible I become.'

'And the more modest.'

His expression altered. 'I still feel the same as I did in Brunei, Caro. What about you?'

She twisted her wedding ring. 'I can't make those kinds of decision at the moment, Alex.'

'Darling, of course you can't. We've all the time in the world.' He reached over and took her hand. 'Now what were we saying before we were rudely interrupted by my falling to the floor?'

Carol was pleased he was not trying to railroad her and liked his sensitivity in changing the subject. They spent the next few minutes discussing ideas on how she could develop her new job and with his experience of the inner workings of the BGA he was able to offer practical advice. But he felt rather sour about the organisation.

'They're an unforgiving lot,' he said. 'Which is why I'm getting out earlier than my contract. Angus Roberts was jealous of me and was making life tedious making allegations about my leadership. It made me realise it was time to move on.'

'I disliked that man from the moment I met him.'

'You have good instincts, Caro. But don't worry, he won't get away with this.' His face turned stony. 'I'll win in the end, I always do.'

Carol asked why he had not tried to defend himself and he told her that the BGA had offered to set up an inquiry but he had blocked it. 'It would've harmed not only that project but future ones.' He indicated the papers on the bed. He had been working on a business plan for his new company, how it was going to be financed . . . and then he stopped abruptly.

'Whatever happens, Caro, I want us to be together.' He dropped his voice to a stage whisper. 'But what I want most of all is to make love to you. Right now.'

She played along with him. 'Then what a shame it is, Mr Woollescroft, that you don't have a lock on your door.'

A few days later the phone by her bed tinkled and sleepily she picked it up.

'Good morning, Alex,' she said, knowing it could only be him phoning her at that early hour. She had given up complaining. Apparently getting up early was a requisite for an expedition leader and he could not break the habit.

'I can't start the day without hearing your voice.'

She gave a mock groan. 'You're such a smooth-talking bastard.'

He laughed. 'You'll be happy to hear the doctor's given me a clean bill of health and you know what that means.'

Carol wriggled back into the pillows.

'I thought of a nice bottle of wine, some good food and then we'd take the phone off the hook. On second thoughts, not in that order.'

Now that the day was here she was apprehensive but the memory of his lovemaking sent shivers of anticipation through her body. If celibacy did not suit her, what must it be doing to him?

They arranged to meet at seven and suddenly galvanised Carol leapt out of bed to check on the whereabouts of her diaphragm. She located it, tucked into the back of the drawer where it had lain unneeded since the morning of her departure to Brunei.

It was tempting to speculate about how life would be with Alex. Exciting? Definitely. Unpredictable too. Maybe his plans to start his company had made him want to settle down. But it was early days to consider the chance of a fresh start with a man who was at heart an adventurer. Would it be wrong to snatch happiness where she could? Even if Alex did not prove the solution to her problem, would he make it so much worse? She was sure he could win the children round. When he set his mind to it she doubted whether anybody could be impervious to his charm. But as always she was running ahead of herself.

Carol took a deep breath and went into what the family called Cattle Round-Up Time. Emmy was always first in the bathroom, Katie took a little longer to spring to life but it would take something like a nuclear explosion to eject Becky from her bed.

Two hours later she was back home having supervised the washing, dressing, breakfasting and ferrying of three children to three different destinations. Thank God next year Katie would join Emmy in the middle school.

The post usually arrived before she left the house but today it was late and as she opened the door she found a mound of bills, mail order leaflets and other junk mail. Hastily she sorted through it and was about to bin the unwanted stuff when she caught sight of a postcard sticking into the back flap of a brown envelope.

She recognised the face of the Sultan of Brunei on the colourful stamp. It was from Andrea and dated four weeks earlier. What was going on with the post office? Carol took the card into the kitchen and half-filled the kettle. While the water was heating, she picked it up, thinking she would show it to Lisa later.

She read the card twice. Andrea was loving life at base camp, she liked the people, 'especially the camp leader. You're a spoilsport not to have mentioned what a hunk Alex is,' she wrote. 'We've already seen the sunset together and the stars (not that I saw much of them!!). Tonight there's a BBQ just for two. Great stuff!'

Now keep calm, Carol counselled herself. Andrea was an enthusiast and could have misinterpreted Alex's actions. But from a distance she heard Zoe's querulous voice, 'It always starts with the sunset.'

Hurriedly she picked up the phone.

'Darling,' said Alex, when he heard her voice, 'don't say you can't make tonight.'

She ignored this, instead telling him she had received a postcard from her successor at the camp. He seemed bemused that she should take the trouble to phone up just to announce the arrival of a card. But the banter ceased when she read it out, adding, 'It didn't take you long to get over my departure. I can see now you repeat the same performance for every new girl.'

'I fear she's exaggerating.'

'Why should she lie about it?'

'OK, some of it's true. I did take a party up to see the sunset. Andrea was one of them.'

'She said she didn't see much of the stars.'

'Nothing to do with me. Maybe she had her eyes shut.' Alex's laugh infuriated her.

'Stop that.'

'You're jealous. That's good.'

'What about the barbecue for two?'

'The barbecue for twenty-two.'

There was a pause. Andrea was prone to exaggeration. 'Alex, maybe I did jump to conclusions but you can see why.'

'That's OK. Shows you care. Don't be late.'

But romance took on a different hue when experienced in the middle of real life. The bedroom light fused in the middle of making up her face and it took her a while to track down a torch and find the safety switch in the hall cupboard. Then just as she was leaving someone rang to try and sell her double glazing. And as she was looking for the car keys, Becky started her questioning. Which friend was she seeing? Carol made her voice sound casual. 'Just someone I met in Brunei. He's been ill. I've left a contact number on the hall table.'

'"He?"' A pause. 'Will there be other people there too?'

'Don't really know, I expect so. I won't be late.'

She walked to the door conscious of Becky's suspicious expression. All this was hardly conducive to an evening's passion though it was forgotten when she pressed the doorbell of his Kensington flat.

She could hear the strains of Barry White belting out his number one hit when Alex opened the door, singing to the lyrics, 'You're the first, the last, my everything,' before taking her into his arms and dancing her up the corridor and into the bedroom.

Still without speaking he kissed the side of her neck and pushed her gently onto the coverlet of a king-sized bed. They lay close together while his lips held hers, his tongue darting backwards and forwards, his hands caressing her body. Carol began to tremble and impatiently he started to fumble with the buttons of her shirt, eagerness making him clumsy. Eventually she decided to help him and slipped the shirt over her head before unzipping her skirt. She lay on the bed in her bra and pants, watching as he stepped out of his jeans, admiring his lean, muscular body which then stretched itself on top of hers. Skilfully he unhooked her bra and his hands roamed her untrammelled breasts before he rolled down her panties. But to her intense disappointment, within seconds he had entered her and almost immediately reached his climax.

Alex groaned as he withdrew and began apologising profusely. 'Sorry, it's been such a long time and you're so gorgeous. See,' he grinned, kissing her nose, 'it's all your fault.'

Carol reassured him that she didn't mind but it was a lie and she could see he wasn't convinced.

'Just give me a minute. It'll be better then.' He stood up. 'I think we need some wine,' he said, and disappeared into the kitchen.

Carol stared at the ceiling. Although she had not expected their lovemaking to be quite so wonderful as on the river bank she had thought that his sexual prowess would make him a more considerate lover. He had made very little effort to arouse her, or to hold himself back. Alex was proving to be a mere mortal whom she had mistaken for a superman. But then she started making excuses for him. He was just out of hospital. And when they made love again it was bound to be better.

She giggled at the sight of him, naked, carrying a small tray with a bottle of white wine and two half-filled glasses.

'What shall we drink to?' he said, handing her a glass.

'Faithfulness?'

Damn. She didn't know what made her say it. Probably memories of Zoe's bafflement at being dropped, she supposed, and was annoyed with herself at her tactlessness. This affair was at its earliest stage and she needed to get to know him far better before she could trust him with her future. So why was she forcing the issue?

Alex had an easy smile on his face and didn't seem to be fazed.

'Sure,' he said, holding his glass aloft. 'Now that I've got you, I'll drink to that.' His dark eyes stared at hers solemnly over the rim of his glass. 'And I have got you, haven't I, Caro?'

Carefully she put down her glass. She didn't want to squash him but neither did she want to be rushed. She and Ben had still not discussed the future of their marriage or the children. There was no way back for her and Ben, not after all that had happened. But this did not mean she wanted to jump straight into another commitment.

'Alex, let's not talk about the future. Let's just enjoy what we have now.'

'That's fine by me but you know we're good together.' His eyes were full of warmth. 'I can make you happy, Caro.'

Could he? That's what Zoe thought once and probably Francesca as well. She should tread warily.

'Why should you want to take on someone like me, with my baggage?' She was as certain as she could be that Ben would allow her unlimited access to the children.

'What do you do if baggage gets too heavy? You get someone to share the load.'

She stared at him, amazed. My God, the mighty Alex, willing to take on someone else's children.

'Don't look so surprised. You haven't seen me with children, I'm good with them.' He kissed her tenderly. 'When you left Brunei I said I was coming to get you. Well, now I'm here and I want you, Caro.' He put down the glass and took hers to place it on the bedside table.

'Now, for a spot of toe dancing. Ever tried it?' He gave a grin at the sight of her expression. 'Give me your right foot.'

He was guiding her leg to the exact strategic spot when, in the hall, the phone rang. Alex ignored it. 'Just there . . . yes . . . now all you do is wiggle your toes . . .'

The ringing continued. She turned her head in the direction of the sound.

'. . . and while you're doing that . . .'

Ring-ring.

'Ignore it. I have no intention of answering it. Instead I'm going to do something really nice to you . . .'

She pulled her foot away. 'I'm sorry, I can't concentrate . . . I left this number. It could be a problem at home.'

At once he released her and she ran out of the room and snatched up the receiver.

'Mum,' said Emmy, 'can you come home? Only Becky's locked herself in her room and . . .' her voice wobbled, 'I don't know what to do.'

'Is she answering you?' asked Carol, alarmed.

'Yes. She says she won't come out until you come home.'

Carol was irritated but Alex agreed she ought to be at home to sort out the trouble and she was touched by his understanding. In the taxi on the way to Battersea she could not help remembering that on the first occasion she and Ben had been making love Emmy had disturbed them. He had called her a passion killer then and it was a peculiar coincidence that the same thing had happened tonight with the same child.

When she had succeeded in getting Becky to unlock the door she faced a pair of hostile eyes.

'Why are you frightening your sister like that?'

'I didn't mean to. It's just that,' the girl's lip wobbled, 'I got very scared. And I needed you to be here.'

'Well, you have your wish, but what were you scared about?'

'It's happening again. The talking behind closed doors, the whispers around the place . . . it's the same as when Mum died. I couldn't understand why she was gone and I'm frightened you're going away too.'

'Darling Becky, I'm not going away from you. Ever.'

'Then why do you keep on disappearing?'

'The leader at the camp I stayed at in Brunei is just out of hospital and I wanted to see that he was all right.'

'Where did you go to see him? At his home?'

Carol could not help her eyes sliding away. 'Yes,' she said, fearful of where this questioning would lead.

'You never talk to Dad when he phones. Is that because of this man?'

'No it isn't.'

'Do you know what I think? I think you're sorting out your life because you're going to leave us.'

'You're wrong,' Carol answered firmly. 'I've promised you that whatever happens, you three are going to be with me as often as you want and I am not going to break that promise.'

'What's going to happen with you and Dad? Why have things gone wrong?'

Carol couldn't tell her that she had found out Ben had married her simply for convenience. It would put him in too much of a bad light. Instead she tried to explain that she had changed since she came back from Brunei and that she wanted different things from her marriage. She was taking the risk that Becky would blame her for the break-up but that was preferable to driving a wedge between father and daughter.

'But you two seemed much happier when you first came back.'

'We were at first.' She sighed. 'I don't expect you to understand. I barely understand it myself.' She paused. 'Your father and I have a lot to talk about and I'll tell you as soon as I can what we're going to do. Please wait till then. Will you do that for me?'

Becky flung herself back into Carol's arms. 'Don't leave. Please, Mum, don't leave us.'

It was the first time Becky had called her Mum.

With Ben still in America she told Alex it would be unfair for her to be out in the evenings. She expected arguments, perhaps a sulk. But Alex seemed to understand that for the moment she had to concentrate on being the stable constant at home and remaining a cheerful mother. Especially since she suspected Becky had not wholly accepted her story of being nurse to someone just out of hospital.

On the phone to their father it was comparatively easy for the children to maintain a cheerful front but they had been fooling her as well. It was when Carol opened Emmy's door to find a perfectly-made bed, toys seated in a row and not a book or garment out of place that she recognised her true state of mind. More than their instant obedience whenever she asked them to do anything, this illustrated how upset and worried Emmy was.

When Ben came back from Washington next week, they would have to sit down and acknowledge that their marriage was at an end. It would be a painful discussion but it was one they could no longer postpone. She would try to say that although they were not able to make a success of their relationship, they could at least try to make a success of their divorce, for the sake of the children. He was sure to agree with that, she thought wryly. For the first time his obsession with their welfare might work to her advantage.

The news would be devastating to the three girls and they had to be the priority in what followed. She tried to be logical, to think of a plan which would, to put it mildly, be the least bad solution. There was no doubt what that would be: for Carol to live with the children in the family house and for Ben to have daily visitation rights. As it was, the girls were used to seeing their father mainly in the late evenings and on his days off. This way, they might see more of him because he might make more of an effort to keep regular hours.

Of course she had realised at the start of all this that stepmothers had no legal standing but as her plan would involve less upheaval for the children, Ben might agree, especially when he realised she was firm about splitting up.

Carol supposed that, in the end, they would buy two separate homes and the kids would be presented with a hideous choice, of where to live. But in the short term this was the best compromise she could suggest.

During the days that followed, as soon as the children had been packed off to school, Carol took refuge in a furious bout of cleaning, even scrubbing the skirting boards and going as far as to use a toothbrush to scour the crevices behind the kitchen taps.

Alex phoned regularly, still being sensitive to her needs and patiently waiting until her problems were sorted out. Several times he invited her out but when she refused, he put no pressure on her. And this made her believe his feelings for her must be genuine. Whereas before there was always something holding her back, now she found herself contemplating the idea that he was a man of substance, someone she might do well to consider as being part of her future.

A week before the lecture Carol found herself standing in front of the mirror talking to an imaginary audience. When Lisa phoned to say could she come round for a sandwich lunch, Carol welcomed the chance to try out her technique on her friend.

After listening patiently to a list of her new boyfriend Mervyn's virtues, especially regarding his prowess in bed, Carol asked Lisa to pretend to be an awkward questioner in the lecture hall. Carol answered spiritedly and only hoped she would be as confident when the real challenge came. Lisa demanded to know what she intended to wear, saying she had to look competent, confident, yet sexy and laughingly Carol led her upstairs to choose this all-purpose garment.

As they settled on a navy blue crepe two-piece which Carol rarely wore, but which flattered her leaner figure, Lisa's expression became thoughtful.

'I found Caitlin's letter right there,' she said, pointing to a side table next to the wardrobe. 'I've really agonised over whether I should've told you about it. Mervyn says I shouldn't.'

'I'm glad you did. I would've found out sooner or later.'

'Oh,' said Lisa, sounding relieved, 'because it wasn't only the letter. Ben came home a couple of evenings before that and actually confessed to me that he had a problem, a serious problem, with a woman he had been involved with before he married you. I took that to be Caitlin, of course. So when I saw what she'd written . . .'

Carol slumped onto the bed. 'You've had a lot more experience of men than me. Do you think I'm right to get out of the marriage?'

Lisa's troubled eyes met hers. 'Only you can say if you can trust him still, because without trust it can't last.'

Carol was fighting a desire to cry when she was startled by a ping at the front doorbell. This was followed by sounds of someone entering the hall before Ben's voice called out, 'Carol, are you there?'

Lisa grimaced and intimated that she would leave. Fiercely, Carol shook her head and asked her to stay. Reluctantly, Lisa agreed but said she would remain upstairs out of sight.

The eyes that followed her movements down the staircase were watchful. Ben handed her a small package, bought, he said apologetically, from habit. It was her favourite scent by Calvin Klein but with his admission to Lisa ringing in her ears Carol took it reluctantly, barely able to thank him.

Ben excused his sudden arrival and said he had come over only to pick up his mail. He would like to come back that evening to see the children but for the next day or so he would stay at the company flat.

'I think that's for the best,' said Carol briskly. 'I have an appointment with a solicitor next week' – she saw his face fall – 'and would prefer not to talk about anything until I've taken advice.'

He started to protest but she put up a hand to interrupt. 'Ben, I need to find out my options then, I promise you, we can talk all you like.'

He gave her a penetrating stare before picking up his mail from the hall table. Carol, unable to trust herself to speak, said goodbye and vanished into the kitchen. Ben had hardly closed the door when Lisa came scuttling down the stairs, asking why Ben had left so quickly.

'I think he realises it's over,' said Carol.

Lisa sighed. 'I can't believe you two are breaking up. I need a glass of something,' she said, going to the fridge. 'But I suppose it was kind of inevitable. You've certainly changed since the trip. Maybe you need to get out there and meet someone new. Can I open the Sancerre?'

Carol nodded and watched Lisa expertly pull out the cork and pour two glasses. She was weighing up whether or not to be frank, and decided it would be a relief to talk to somebody about Alex. For the next twenty minutes she unburdened herself, interrupted only by the occasional exclamation of amazement from Lisa, especially when she confessed to what happened after the storm.

'And you say you've seen him since he came back to London?'

'Yes, but not often because he's been ill and while I'm sorting out my life with Ben I don't want to give him too much encouragement. After all, he's nothing to do with our break-up.'

'If the sex was so good, are you sure about that?' asked Lisa, helping herself to another glass.

'Lisa, you can't make decisions about the future because of good sex.'

'Don't see why not,' Lisa grinned, dodging a flick of Carol's hand.

'I'm trying to do the best for the children and everybody. For now Alex has to wait.'

'Well, Mervyn wouldn't stand for that. I hope for your sake Alex doesn't mind.'

Later, as she watched Lisa disappearing around the corner towards the taxi rank, Carol wondered whether she expected too much of Alex. Would he be patient and realise she had to sort things out with Ben before she could think of the next phase in her life? And if he was part of it, he needed to know that she did not want to lose the much-prized independence of spirit she had gained in a far-flung country.

On impulse she decided to call him and waited, hearing the most doleful sound in the world, the incessant ringing which signified that her lover was not in. She tried at intervals throughout the following day without finding him at home and she concluded unhappily that he was avoiding her, having decided she was too much trouble.

Chapter Thirty-Two

A sea of attentive faces was turned towards her. Sitting on the podium of the lecture theatre at BGA headquarters, Carol hoped she presented an image of a competent, confident member of the panel of four.

After years of accompanying Ben to functions where, as soon as people found out her job was looking after three children they would either switch off or use her as an ear for a monologue about their fascinating lives, she had lost confidence. But here she was, employed by a highly regarded organisation, with a name plate in front of her: 'Carol Mitchell, Expeditions Office'.

Once, she remembered, she had confided to Lisa that she longed to be an individual to whom people listened. Well, now they were.

To her surprise the two older girls had insisted on going with her to the seminar. At first she had tried to dissuade them, thinking it would be boring for them and it might be more difficult to perform having people she knew listening to her. But they had persuaded her they wanted to share in her evening and she had relented. There they were, sitting proudly in the front row, having chosen the clothes they normally reserved for lunch with Julia. Carol was inordinately pleased since she'd been worried that Becky might wear her current favourite, jeans cut low enough to show off her navel.

The hall was almost full to capacity and Carol was last to speak after the other three panellists. As she awaited her turn, she developed a nervous flutter. She'd often heard that this tension was an essential ingredient to giving a worthwhile performance but still she longed for the ordeal to be over. In the event, she need not have worried. The audience warmed to the account of the novice who had been thrown into base camp in the middle of the jungle and expected to feed an army of hungry scientists. Though she had been thoroughly briefed, she told the attentive audience, and she had researched the BGA library for possible pitfalls, nothing had prepared her for the reality. As she assumed there was no member of the expedition present, she allowed herself to embroider the cooking of the recently-killed snake, the constant battle to keep the kitchen hygienic and the perils of braving the raging torrents to bring back the only thing the camp could not manage without: baked beans.

Carol was gratified by the warm applause that followed her talk. Phoebe Tugendhaat, in the chair, opened the Q and A session, suggesting that members of the audience put their hands up but remain seated while asking their questions. The lights in the auditorium were switched on and the first questioner, a smartly-dressed woman, asked Carol if the experience 'out there' had changed her.

She took her time to consider the answer. 'Base camp was quite tough at times. I had to conquer all kinds of physical fear but you do when you're up against situations you can't control.' She gave a mischievous glance around the hall. 'I don't just accept things now, and if necessary, I argue my corner and I believe this'll stand me in good stead when I start work in the expeditions office.'

The woman nodded approvingly and Carol began to settle down and enjoy the evening.

Watching from the back of the auditorium Ben thought her performance was terrific. Sitting up there surrounded by experts she had more than held her own. He liked the self-deprecating humour, the skill with which she involved the audience; above all he was amazed at the level of confidence she exuded.

The kids' pleadings had persuaded him to come here straight from a stressful day at the office after an all-night sitting at the House of Commons but tired as he was, Ben was glad to be there. The kids' dearest wish was for the two of them to be together again and he was grateful to be told about the lecture – anything to help break down the barriers between himself and Carol, though he was far from optimistic about the chances of a reconciliation. He had asked them not to let Carol know he was coming. It might put her off her stroke although judging from her performance tonight, he had been underestimating her abilities.

Admiring Carol on the platform, slim, still tanned, by any standards an attractive feisty personality, Ben cursed his stupidity in allowing her to slip away from him. This woman was someone he could respect as an equal but the irony was that she seemed to have moved on. He couldn't blame her. Because of his cowardice in selecting what he had told her of his past, he had created a climate of mistrust and in their current state of polite hostility Carol had made it clear that she did not want to be in his company. Whenever he saw the children she would make herself scarce, confining her conversation to non-contentious subjects. Every attempt he made to justify his past behaviour was impatiently squashed.

Only once during this miserable time had she asked a personal question, which was whether or not he was seeing anything of William. He'd made a vow that from now on he would never dodge telling the truth, however embarrassing or whatever difficulties it created. So he'd told her that he had taken the boy out and had become fond of him, he was an intelligent, affectionate child. Ben was conscious that William referred to him as 'Daddy' rather more frequently than his own children. And in the letter he had written, William had drawn a smiley face in the D of Daddy, which had touched him. Ben hadn't been able to share any of this with Carol but he recognised the boy's deep need for an involved father figure, something he thought William deserved. Ben was quite determined that in the fullness of time he would introduce his son to the girls.

The one conversation Ben had had with Caitlin since that dreadful meeting in her flat had been surprisingly friendly. He supposed this was because she needed him on her side for William's sake and he reflected that when Caitlin was being charming, he could overlook some of her overbearing traits. She made no reference to their previous encounter and never deviated from the subject of the dates and times William would be available from school. It was clear she had, at last, given up her futile attempts at trying to win him back, for which he was heartily grateful.

After thirty minutes there were, inevitably, fewer hands waving to catch the chairman's attention and in that hiatus someone stood up. Carol's eyes widened when she saw it was Alex.

For a few seconds he remained quite still until the murmurings of the audience had died down. Curious faces in the front of the auditorium turned round to look and when he appeared certain that he held the attention of the hall, he smiled directly at Carol. Try as she might she could not prevent her face registering embarrassment. Across the heads of the audience she and Alex stared at each other. A slight smile played on his lips and he seemed in no hurry to speak, standing perfectly relaxed, one hand resting in the pocket of his immaculately pressed blazer. Had she annoyed him? Would he try and humiliate her? The silence was almost theatrical and when she could bear it no more, Phoebe spoke.

'Ladies and gentlemen, can I introduce Alex Woollescroft who was the leader of Carol's expedition. Yes, Alex, your question?'

'Carol,' he said in a voice which reverberated around the hall. 'I do have a question. I love you and I want you to spend the rest of your life with me. Will you?'

There was a collective intake of breath from the audience and Carol winced as if she had been struck. She wanted to try and pass it off as a joke but she couldn't make her mouth move. Her eyes sought out the children. Becky's jaw had dropped and Emmy was shaking her sister's arm, trying to get her attention.

Amid the buzz of astonished mutterings Alex stood impassive, his gaze unflinchingly on her face.

Phoebe jumped to her feet, her notes scattering, and swept her hand towards the door. 'Drinks are waiting, ladies and gentlemen. If you make your way to the room on the left of the hall . . .' her voice faltered as the audience ignored her invitation. They were sitting still, as if in a Wimbledon tennis match, looking from face to face, waiting to see what would happen.

Carol hurried down the steps of the platform to collect Becky and Emmy from the front row. As she was rushing them towards the exit, Emmy asked her, 'What did that man mean?'

'Nothing,' she shouted over the din, 'it was a joke.'

'But it wasn't funny,' said Emmy. Becky, walking alongside her, said nothing.

The crowd was beginning to move now and Carol threaded her way through to the doorway. There was no sign of Alex and to her great relief she spotted the anxious face of Lisa on the other aisle and gestured they should meet outside in the hallway. Once there, Lisa asked, 'I have a car outside. Shall I take you all home?'

'No, I have to sort this out,' replied Carol. 'But could the kids go with you?'

Becky turned an anguished gaze towards Carol, impervious to the curious onlookers. 'Dad's here,' she said loudly. 'I don't want to leave without him.'

Ben? Here? Carol looked around wildly. There were so many people milling about she could not spot him.

It was only when Lisa promised Becky and Emmy that she would take them straight back to their house to wait for him that she managed to lead them away.

'Excuse me, please. Make way.' The imperious commands parted the crowd and heralded the arrival of an agitated Phoebe. 'That was unforgivable of Alex. What was all that about?'

'I'm just going to find out,' said Carol. 'Do you know where he is?'

'Yes. Waiting for you in my office. And find me afterwards, please. I want to know exactly what's going on.'

Promising to do so, Carol climbed the stairs and found Alex leaning against a desk, arms folded.

'What the hell do you think you're doing?' she demanded.

'Don't be cross. I'm serious about what I said.'

'So serious that you haven't phoned for two days.'

'Because, woman, you told me I had to wait for you. Anyway, I've been in Paris, doing deals for my new company. But I've really missed you. Caro, I want you in my life, permanently. And I didn't want to wait any longer to tell you that.'

'But in front of all those people . . .'

'So you can't ignore me.' His expression was solemn. 'I'm asking you to marry me, Caro, as soon as you're able.'

The proposal took her by such surprise that she gawped at him. He had said he was ready for commitment and this proved it. She hadn't had to scheme or play games, here it was, the ultimate proof of his love. But she couldn't find the words to express this and finally managed a weak, 'We don't know each other, not really.'

'I know that you're the only woman I want, and won't it be fun finding out? Come here.'

When she did not move, he went on, 'I could make your life so exciting. My new company is going to be a great success.'

'I don't know why you're so sure. Don't you need the people you've just discomfited downstairs?'

He laughed. 'That's what they think but I don't need this old-fashioned institution any longer. I'm off to a brand new life in America. I've got the finance to make it the best-run expedition business in the world. Plenty of opportunities, plenty of money.' He stretched his arm towards her. 'You keep on putting up other people's reactions. What about yours? Are you going to marry me?'

She stared at him, completely lost for words. In one stride he was across the room to her, but he did not touch her.

'Caro, have you ever had the feeling that your life was at a crossroads? That you had to make a decision? I get that feeling for us. This is the moment.' He took hold of her hands and gripped them tightly. 'In Brunei life was full of risks. Didn't you find that when you faced fear and conquered it you could achieve something worthwhile?

'Come on, Caro,' he urged, 'take a risk.'

He made it sound simple and despite her reservations she was suddenly filled with a surge of optimism, a feeling that life needn't be as bleak as it had been. There could be life after Ben and happiness if only she were brave enough to grasp it. But she was mother to three kids. He sensed her indecision.

'We could sort out all the problems together and we'd have a splendid life. I promise you that.'

All she had to do was say yes.

'Oh, Caro, there are so many things I want us to do together. I want you to be a partner in the business.'

Her face glowed, remembering how he'd said it was difficult for him to be on equal terms with a woman, but here he was offering to give her a share of the business.

Nothing could have illustrated how much he had altered his attitude and she thought perhaps *she* had helped him to change. This was a man willing to make a public spectacle of himself, for her. No one had ever done such a thing and despite her initial mortification, Carol had to accept it showed how much he was committed to her.

She gave him a soft smile and, seemingly encouraged, he said enthusiastically, 'With my new job we can travel the world. There's so much I want to show you. I'll take you to a waterfall in Rangoon that's so crystal clear it's almost transparent and there's a beach in South America no one knows about except me.'

It was like being doused with a bucket of cold water. He hadn't even bothered to change the script he had used on Zoe. The only thing he'd left out was the bloody dog. And who knew how many others had fallen for these honeyed words? Including Andrea. Now that she thought about it, why should the Australian have made up those remarks? She couldn't have known the significance of the sunset.

When he saw her expression change he added quickly, 'But we won't travel all the time. I'm quite prepared to settle down, buy a house for us when the kids come and visit. A large place, somewhere in the country. With a stream maybe. Children like playing in water.'

Carol disengaged her hands and walked towards a chair and sat down. Was she being unduly cynical? Might he just this once be sincere?

'You make it sound wonderful,' she said carefully. 'I like the idea of the house you have in mind and if the garden was big enough . . .'

'It will be.'

'. . . we could have pets. A goat perhaps? I know the kids would love a pony.'

'Wouldn't they prefer a dog? I love Labradors, don't you? Nice, friendly breed.'

'A black one,' she said dully.

His face lit up. 'I knew we were on the same wavelength.'

So many people had warned her and yet she had been vain enough to think she could change him. How could she ever have thought that Alex was speaking the truth? Yes, he had unleashed her sexuality, for which she was grateful, but she had no doubt that once they became used to each other, that side of the relationship would lose importance. Then what would be left? Looking after three children had made her more prosaic. Lust was all very well but it wasn't powerful enough for her to uproot herself completely for a lying adventurer like Alex, someone who obviously had emotional dyslexia.

Tonight proved there was only one person in the world important to Alex. Himself. How could she have been stupid enough to be flattered by his action this evening? He had not been concerned about what his public utterance would do to her standing in the organisation. She was due to start work there and was now facing the prospect of being the subject of endless speculation, that was if she kept the job at all.

Zoe was right. Alex was a hunter, he liked the thrill of the chase. She had no doubt that if she accepted his proposal he would give every indication of happiness. But how could it last? Once she was completely in his thrall as Zoe had been, their relationship would fall apart, as all his others had done. Then, without explanation, he'd be off, unable to resist the challenge of entrapping someone else.

No. Alex would never be her life partner and she would tell him so. But she needed a modicum of revenge. She turned to walk to the window while he waited for an answer to his proposal, no doubt satisfied that he had said all the right things to make her accept.

And then she had a flash of inspiration and had to fight hard to hide her amusement. There was an easy way to find out the depth of his sincerity. What had he said? That he'd buy a house 'for when the kids come and visit'. Well, that was logical. Why would a father give custody of his children to a step-mother? She turned round to face him with an expression of pleasure.

'Any woman would be thrilled to have the chance of a whole new life and I want to say yes.' She paused and he reached out for her.

'Darling, I knew—'

'I think I could make you happy.'

'You're making me very happy right now.'

'There's only one problem.'

'We can solve it,' he said briskly.

'Ben and I have reached an agreement about the children. He's being absolutely wonderful about them. Because he travels so much with his job, he's agreed that they can live with me. But,' she continued earnestly, 'you don't have to worry about them being a problem for us. They're old enough not to be any trouble. I know they'd love you and they would adore to live in America, especially the youngest. It'd be so good for her asthma.'

If only she had a camera to record his reaction for posterity. It was as if a huge volt of electricity had surged through his body and he leapt almost to attention. His face gave a pained spasm and an image of Edvard Munch's painting of 'The Scream' sprang to her mind.

'Take on three kids?' he yelled. 'Are you crazy?'

Carol was damned if she would lose this job because of Alex. As she walked into the common room the conversation virtually halted. Phoebe looked up to discover why and immediately left her companion, asking Carol if she would accompany her to the adjoining room.

The omens were not good. But Carol was determined that Alex's behaviour was not going to blight her future so she decided on her strategy: she would be economical with the truth.

'I've sorted it all out,' she told Phoebe. 'Basically Alex exaggerated my interest in him.'

The older woman looked keenly at her and then nodded. 'That fits in with everything I know about Alex. He's a great leader but for some reason he tries to make every woman who crosses his path fall for him.'

Carol nodded. 'At base camp I relied on him a great deal and he misunderstood, thought it was something romantic when it wasn't. The problem is I couldn't get him to realise he meant nothing to me and tonight he attempted to force my hand.'

'Good,' said Phoebe. 'I'm glad it didn't work and I'll spread the story around. Shall we go back to the party?'

Phoebe went to the mirror to tidy her hair and Carol politely waited for her.

'Alex is his own worst enemy,' said the older woman. 'He thinks his downfall here is because of Angus Roberts putting the knife into him but that was only an extra factor.' She gave a smirk. 'Of course it didn't help that he tried to seduce Angus's young wife.'

Carol did not show her chagrin. What a close shave she'd had. He was obviously one of those control freaks to whom the challenge was all. Once he'd netted the butterfly it was the beginning of the end. The pity of it was he probably didn't recognise this in himself and he would go on and on through his life searching for the ideal specimen.

Thank God she had escaped. And double thanks that she had taken precautions to stop herself from becoming pregnant.

Chapter Thirty-Three

Lisa's car was not parked in the driveway, as Carol had expected. Instead she saw with dismay that Ben was in the house and she hesitated at the doorway, bracing herself. How could she explain Alex's extraordinary outburst? And how would she cope with Becky and Emmy? They had blamed their father for the problems in the household and suddenly they had found out she had another man in her life. She certainly owed them an explanation.

Ben was sitting in the kitchen, obviously waiting for her. Behind him, the brightly coloured painting pinned to the noticeboard seemed to mock her: 'To Mummy, who is speshul, love Katie.'

He scrutinised her face and Carol had a sudden vision of how their roles had changed. Once she would search his expression for signs of his mood. Now he appeared to be doing the same thing to her.

'Were you going to tell me about him?'

Ben's icy calm was more unnerving than the outburst she had been expecting. His body was taut, his eyes hard. He had never stared at her with such disdain and for a moment she could not speak.

'I think you owe me that much.'

Stung by his contemptuous tone she retorted, 'That's rich from somebody who's kept secrets all our married life.'

He thumped his fist on the kitchen table so hard she backed away from him.

'I have never been unfaithful,' he said with emphasis, then his voice rose and he shouted, 'Can you say the same? Can you?'

'Ssshush,' she said. 'I don't want the children more upset than they already are.'

'And whose fault is that?'

Becky's anxious face appeared round the door. 'What's going on? I heard shouting.'

'I'm sorry, darling,' said Ben, 'it's my fault.'

'Are you two going to split up?'

Carol hesitated. 'Dad and I need to talk. I think it'd be better if we go out for a little while, just to the bridge. Is that OK?'

Becky began to cry. 'You're going to break up and it's all my fault. If I hadn't been so horrible, you wouldn't have gone off and then you wouldn't have met that man.'

Carol was appalled. The poor child. It had never occurred to her that Becky would take the blame for this upheaval.

'Your behaviour has nothing to do with this,' she said, her voice breaking, 'it's nothing to do with any of you children. It's between your father and me.'

Becky's eyes were frightened. 'Are you going away with that man?'

'Certainly not,' said Carol, aware of Ben's rapt attention.

'But he said—'

'It doesn't matter what he said. He was just trying to make trouble. Remember, Becky, whatever happens, nothing will make me stop loving you.' She put her hand under the girl's chin. 'Do you believe that?'

Becky began to dry her eyes and nodded.

'Good,' said Carol. 'Keep an ear open for the other two. We promise not to go further than the bridge.'

Becky watched as she and Ben walked in the direction of Battersea Bridge, Carol careful to keep her distance.

At that time of night the river was quiet, only the lapping of the water as it slapped against the fortified bank broke the silence. The Thames was like a moving carpet of giant fireflies, caused by the reflection from the dazzling orange and yellow overhead street lamps, far removed from the inky blackness of the Belalong. For a moment she stood looking at the shifting patterns in the water before she noticed Ben was gripping the railing, the skin stretched across his knuckles.

'I can't bear the idea of you making love to another man. Did you come straight from him to me?'

The question hung in the air. It took her a few moments to gather her wits. On each occasion she had made love to Alex she had genuinely thought her relationship with Ben had ended. But how would she answer him? He had dark circles under his eyes and for the first time Carol thought he looked his age. There was no doubt he was suffering and she was genuinely sorry. She took no pleasure in causing him further pain, particularly since Alex was going to be no part of her life. If she told him the truth they would spend hours discussing her infidelity when their real problem lay in their own relationship. Better to convince him that Alex was unimportant.

'He means nothing to me,' she said, hoping Ben would be satisfied with this.

'There must've been something between you otherwise why would he ask you to marry him?'

'Phoebe could tell you that he goes after the newest woman at the camp whether they encourage him or not.'

'Didn't he know I existed?'

'Yes, but he got the impression that our marriage was over. So did I. It was only when you explained about Caitlin's letter that I realised I had been wrong.'

'And you swear there's nothing between you and that man?'

She shook her head vehemently.

'I'm glad.' He looked into the middle distance. 'If I hadn't been such a coward, not telling you about William . . .' His voice grew stronger. 'Carol, is there any hope we could get back together again? I want that more than anything and so do the children.'

Even at this stage he was still bracketing himself with the children.

She passed a hand over her forehead. 'You still don't understand what this is all about, do you? You think it's about what happened in the past but it's not. You don't want me to leave you, not because you can't bear it but because of the effect it'll have on the children.'

He lifted his eyes from studying the river and she saw a shadow of apprehension pass over his features.

'You've pretended from the beginning to be the loving husband,' she went on, 'but it was clear to everyone but me, blind fool that I was, that you only needed someone to look after the children. What hurts is that you married me out of gratitude, not love, and whatever you say that's what you feel now.'

'If you think that still, then I've failed and I deserve to lose you.' His eyes clouded over. 'If we have to go our separate ways, let's at least do it for the right reasons. You want me to be completely honest? All right, I will.'

Carol braced herself but she had been waiting for this. However hurtful the truth it was better to have no illusions.

'You say all this has nothing to do with the past but I want you to understand what happened then so you can appreciate where I am now,' he said slowly. 'You and I met less than a year after Fay's death and at the beginning I think I was emotionally stunted. I hadn't got over her death. I was wracked with guilt about the way she died. I don't think I knew what real love was. Certainly I didn't love Caitlin. When I asked you to marry me, I wasn't capable of giving any more than I did. In retrospect I think we married too soon.'

He gave a deep sigh. 'You were right. I hate to say it but yes, I was grateful you married me and it was convenient. I needed you for the children's sake rather than mine.'

At last he had admitted it. The loneliness and despair of the last days were summed up in those miserable words. She had not expected him to be so blunt but presumed that now they both accepted their marriage was over he could allow himself to be completely honest. Yet to hear him reduce their marriage to such basic needs, a man casting around for child care, was almost more than Carol could bear.

'I had a succession of nannies, as you know. Some were more efficient than others but I could see the children were sinking. I did consider writing from home and giving up my staff job but that would have meant a drop in income and selling the house. After all they had gone through I couldn't do that to them. And then you came along.'

He lifted his hand momentarily and she thought in the lamplight that he looked close to tears. 'When I saw you sitting looking miserable in the office canteen you brought out some sort of protective instinct. I wanted to help you. You weren't tough enough for the job and I liked you the better for that. Once I got to know you it didn't take me long to discover there was a sweetness about you that I had rarely encountered in women around the office. You didn't have any guile and I suppose I was flattered when you didn't try to hide your love for me.'

His hair had fallen over his forehead and Carol had to fight her habit of smoothing it back. She thought back to those days when she had been grateful for any attention from him, when she would time her visits to the office, hoping to bump into him 'accidentally' in the lift. She thought she had been subtle.

He rested his arms on the rail, staring into the middle distance. 'But the difference between you and the other women I'd brought home was that you were good with the kids. Em and Katie, particularly, formed a bond with you right from the moment they clapped eyes on you. Even Becky said you were less revolting than the others. From her that was high praise.'

This made Carol smile and she caught him looking at her.

'Sure you want me to go on?'

She nodded swiftly.

'I know I'm taking a risk telling you this. But you wanted the truth. Here it is, unvarnished. When yet another nanny didn't work out, I had to think about alternatives. By that stage I had come to see what a special person you were. OK, I admit I wasn't in love with you but I did love your warmth, your loyalty, your support. And you appeared to love the children as well. As I told you before, that was the clincher.' He exhaled heavily. 'I drew up a list of the pros and cons of marriage to you versus the advantages of hiring another child-minder.'

Carol flinched. It was hard to listen to how calculating he had been. She was conscious of him watching her, waiting for some comment but she was unable to speak, unable to meet his eyes.

Now that he was holding nothing back, being brutally honest, she didn't like it. But she had pilloried him enough in the past for not being completely candid so how could she complain? In the past few awful months, Carol had come to the same conclusion as to why Ben had married her but it was still hurtful to hear him say it. Yet if she were being honest, hadn't she used him too? The timing of his proposal couldn't have been better for her. It had allowed her to escape from having to make a decision about her future. She had welcomed the chance of an entirely new life after her disillusionment with journalism.

Ben startled her. 'Carol, look at me. You think it's cold-hearted to have been so scheming? Let me tell you, when there are three young children dependent on you, what seems cold-hearted to you was absolutely vital for me. I've been quite frank and I apologise if I've hurt you. But I've been honest so you'll believe what I have to say now.'

She held up a hand. 'Please, Ben, I don't think I can take any more.'

'I'm sorry, but it's important that I finish this. I was grateful, but you can't stay married for seven years just because of gratitude.' He reached over and tried to take her hand but she drew it away. 'When you went off to Brunei I missed you. No,' he corrected himself. 'It was far more than that. For the first time in my life I pined.'

Carol's throat constricted. She wanted to believe him but after all the lies and evasions of the past she wondered if it would ever be possible to trust him. But 'pined' was such a strong word.

'When we married I was fond of you, extremely fond, but I wasn't in love with you in the sense of that crazy, head over heels thing. But while I never analysed it, I reckoned our marriage gave each of us what we wanted. Me a stable home life, you a sense of purpose. But when you went away I found I longed for you. I said to myself that this was because it was inconvenient your being away. But a strange thing happened. I looked for you when I got home, I didn't like waking up without you beside me. It took that to make me realise I loved you. And when you came back from Brunei everything changed. As soon as you walked through the door at the airport I could sense the difference. You'd become your own person, Carol, and I love you even more for it. Seeing you on that platform tonight, it all came together. Without knowing it, I had loved you for a long time, way before you left on that trip. I just didn't realise it before. And at that very moment, when I decided that whatever happened I had to tell you, that bloody man stood up.' His voice became choked. 'I couldn't stand it, I had to leave because I thought I had lost you but' – he gave her an anxious look – 'you did say he means nothing to you.'

There was a query in his voice and she nodded tersely.

Ben looked relieved, and gazed at her intently as if he wanted to ask more questions. He made no attempt to touch her.

'That's it, Carol. Here I am, laid bare, no secrets left, fighting to save our marriage although I don't deserve you. I didn't treasure you when I had the chance but darling, I want to make it up to you because you're the woman I love. Will you give me another chance to show you how much I care?'

Carol turned her head away from his strained face. At last he was saying what she wanted to hear, that he loved her, that he wanted her. She had to admit to herself that despite everything he was the man she loved, the person she had loved almost from the moment she had set eyes on him. She wanted to believe him, wanted to trust him. But could she? Something still made her hang back.

Carol was silent for so long Ben was apprehensive. The next few minutes were the longest in his life. He had bared his soul, been more honest with her than he had ever been with anyone, but had he convinced her? If not, he had to accept defeat. There was nothing else in his armoury.

He loved this woman and hoped she would give him the chance to prove it. He had been blind, he deserved to lose her. All through the years of their marriage he had been blanketed by clouds of guilt. It was as if those clouds had parted and the sun was coming up.

She was still staring out over the river. 'You've given me a lot to think about,' she said at last, 'but I've been so hurt it's difficult to know what to do.'

Oh God, he had failed.

'I don't want to make the children unhappy but I have to think of my own future,' Carol went on. 'I'm reasonably sure I can make a living. In fact I've been offered a job at the BGA.'

'Congratulations.' She had already fixed up a life away from him. It didn't look good.

'I'm sure you mean everything you say now but what about in a month, two months, a year? It'll all go back to how it was, with Caitlin waiting in the wings.'

He shook his head. 'You're wrong. She's finally accepted that nothing is going to happen between her and me. I'm told she's set her sights on the MP from Broadgate. I don't think we'll have any more trouble from that quarter. But more importantly I've seen to it that things won't go back to how they were. I'm not going to do the parliamentary stint any more.' From then on, he told her, he intended to do political think pieces, which could be written mainly at home. This would mean a drop in salary but he had spent the time in the company flat completing the often talked-about synopsis of a thriller. His agent had been more complimentary than he expected and was convinced he could sell it. He had also dangled the possibility, a long shot it was true, that this could be the first in a series using the same investigative reporter character. If the advance matched the agent's expectations, eventually he might be able to give up journalism altogether and concentrate on fiction.

'I'm getting pretty tired of writing for tomorrow's fish and chip paper. But that's not the issue,' he went on. 'I want to prove I can be the kind of husband you want – that we can have a far more interesting life together. And Carol, I want you to stay not for the children but for me.' It was the first time he had declared himself in this way but she did not respond and Ben felt as if his guts were being seized in a crushing grip. She was not going to give him another chance. He allowed the silence to hang between them until he could bear it no longer. Placing his hands on her shoulders he turned her roughly towards him.

'Look at me, damn it. I've told you how it was. I haven't held anything back. I admit I took you for granted, I admit I didn't love you the way you wanted me to.' Carol turned her head away but he cupped his hand under her chin until she faced him. 'But I'm telling you things have changed. I love you. Can't you see that?'

Her voice was low and he had to strain to hear. 'I want to trust you but . . .'

Ben's skill in life was putting sentences together in a coherent narrative but perhaps words were not what were needed now. Oblivious of the passing traffic he bent his head and before she could pull away he silenced her with his lips. For a frightening moment he felt her resist but he persisted, gathering her closer, and after what seemed an agonisingly long wait he was rewarded by a slight relaxation of her body. They broke away and he looked anxiously down at her upturned face.

'Carol,' he said urgently, 'only a few weeks ago we were happier than we'd ever been. It can be like that again.'

Before she could answer they both pulled apart, startled by the noise of running feet. Clump, clump, clump. Someone was running across the bridge towards them. Becky, red-eyed from weeping, brushed past him and stood squarely in front of them.

'I couldn't wait any longer. What have you decided?'

Carol gathered her in her arms and began to stroke the back of her head.

Becky hugged her tightly. 'Don't leave us. Please.'

'Ssh, darling,' said Carol. 'It's going to be all right.'

'Is it?' asked Becky.

Carol looked straight at Ben, the man with whom she wanted to spend the rest of her life, the man she wanted to be the father of her children. 'It'll take time but yes, I think it will be all right.'